Praise for *Krampus*

"The creator of *The Child Thief* is back—and this time he's taking on the Christmas Devil. Are you ready for a studly, Nordic Santa Claus, and his scary/sexy wife?"

—Charlie Jane Anders, ios9.com

"Brom is that rare breed: a person who is skilled in more than one area of artistic expression. Here's hoping that he will continue to share his dark and often beautiful dreams with us for many years to come."

—Christopher Paolini, bestselling author of *Eragon*

"This illustrated horror novel by acclaimed gothic fantasy artist, illustrator, and novelist Brom (*The Child Thief*) is perfect for anyone who disdains a cozy, sentimental holiday story."

—*Library Journal*

"Terrific. A wild ride—the idea sounded like a stretch and I'm not sure how many guys could have really pulled it off, but Brom sure has. I loved it. It hooked me and I couldn't put it down. Plus, the illustrations were amazing."

—Mike Mignola, creator of Hellboy

"This fast-paced gory holiday horror yarn puts and entertaining, at times jocular, spin to the story of St. Nick. . . . Filled with action, fans will wonder whether Jesse joined the wrong side as increasingly it appears to him that Santa is evil. Fans will relish the Yule Lord 'is coming to town.'"

—SFRevu

"[A] rollicking, non-stop, action-filled, violent and yet touching story."

—Examiner.com

KRAMPUS

BROM

KRAMPUS

the

YULE LORD

HARPER Voyager
An Imprint of HarperCollins Publishers

Harper Voyager and design is a trademark of HCP LLC.

HarperCollins books may be purchased for educational, business, or sales promotional use. For information please e-mail the Special Markets Department at SPsales@harpercollins.com.

A hardcover edition of this book was published in 2012 by Harper Voyager, an imprint of HarperCollins Publishers.

FIRST HARPER VOYAGER PAPERBACK EDITION PUBLISHED 2015.

Designed by Paula Russell Szafranski

Library of Congress Cataloging-in-Publication Data has been applied for.

ISBN 978-0-06-209566-4

24 25 26 27 28 LBC 16 15 14 13 12

This one is for my wife

and favorite Yuletide pixie,

Laurielee

Santa Claus . . .

How vile your name upon my tongue. Like acid, hard to utter without spitting. Yet I find myself capable of speaking little else. It has become my malediction, my profane mantra.

Santa Claus . . . Santa Claus . . . Santa Claus.

That name, like you, like your Christmas and all its perversions, is a lie. But then you have always lived in a house of lies, and now that house has become a castle, a fortress. So many lies that you have forgotten the truth, forgotten who you are . . . forgotten your true name.

I have not forgotten.

I will always be here to remind you that it is not Santa Claus, nor is it Kris Kringle, or Father Christmas, or Sinterklaas, and it certainly is not Saint Nicholas. Santa Claus is but one more of your masquerades, one more brick in your fortress.

I will not speak your true name. No, not here. Not so long as I sit rotting in this black pit. To hear your name echo off the dead walls of this prison, why that . . . that would be a sound to drive one into true madness. That name must wait until I again see the wolves chase Sol and Mani across the heavens. A day that draws near; a fortnight perhaps, and your sorcery will at long last be broken, your chains will fall away and the winds of freedom will lead me to you.

I did not eat my own flesh as you had so merrily suggested. Madness did not take me, not even after sitting in this tomb for half a millennium. I did not perish, did not become food for the worms as you foretold. You should have known me better than that. You should have known I would never let that happen, not so long as I could remember your name, not so long as I had vengeance for company.

Santa Claus, my dear old friend, you are a thief, a traitor, a slanderer, a murderer, a liar, but worst of all you are a mockery of everything for which I stood.

You have sung your last ho, ho, ho, for I am coming for your head. For Odin, Loki, and all the fallen gods, for your treachery, for chaining me in this pit for five hundred years. But most of all I am coming to take back what is mine, to take back Yuletide. And with my foot upon your throat, I shall speak your name, your true name, and with death staring back at you, you will no longer be able to hide from your dark deeds, from the faces of all those you betrayed.

I, Krampus, Lord of Yule, son of Hel, bloodline of the great Loki, swear to cut your lying tongue from your mouth, your thieving hands from your wrists, and your jolly head from your neck.

PART I

jesse

Chapter One

SANTA MAN

BOONE COUNTY, WEST VIRGINIA
CHRISTMAS MORNING, 2 A.M.

Jesse Burwell Walker prayed that his goddamn truck would make it through at least one more winter before rusting completely in two. The truck, a '78 primer gray Ford F150, had been left to him by his father after the old man lost his long battle with the black lung. A guitar now hung in the gun rack and the new bumper sticker pasted across the rear window of the camper shell read WHAT WOULD HANK DO.

Snow-covered gravel crunched beneath Jesse's tires as he pulled off Route 3 into the King's Kastle mobile-home court. Jesse had turned twenty-six about a month ago, a little tall and a little lean, with dark hair and sideburns badly in need of a trim. He drummed his long fingers—good guitar-picking fingers—on the bottle of Wild Turkey cinched between his legs as he rolled by the mobile homes. He drove past a few faded blow-mold Santas and snowmen, then past Ned Burnett's Styrofoam deer, the one Ned used for target practice. It hung upside down from his kid's swing set, as though about to be gutted and dressed. Ned had attached a glowing red bulb to its nose. Jesse found that funny the first few times he'd seen it, but since Rudolf had been hanging there since Thanksgiving, the joke was wearing a mite thin. Jesse caught sight of a few sad tinsel trees illuminating a few sad living rooms, but mostly the trailers around King's Kastle were dark—folks

5

either off to cheerier locations, or simply not bothering. Jesse knew as well as anyone that times were tough all around Boone County, that not everyone had something to celebrate.

Old Millie Boggs's double-wide, with its white picket fence and plastic potted plants, came into view as he crested the hill. Millie owned the King's Kastle and once again she'd set up her plastic nativity scene between her drive and the garbage bin. Joseph had fallen over and Mary's bulb was out, but the little baby Jesus glowed from within with what Jesse guessed to be a two-hundred-watt bulb, making the infant seem radioactive. Jesse drove by the little manger, down the hill, and pulled up next to a small trailer situated within a clump of pines.

Upon leasing the trailer to Jesse, Millie had described it as "the temporary rental," because, she'd stressed, no one should be living in a cramped-up thing like that for too long. He'd assured her it would only be for a couple of weeks while he sorted things out with his wife, Linda.

That was nearly two years ago.

He switched off the engine and stared at the trailer. "Merry Christmas." He unscrewed the whiskey's cap and took a long swig. He wiped his mouth on the back of his jacket sleeve and raised the bottle toward the trailer. "On my way to not giving a shit."

A single strand of Christmas lights ran along the roof line. Since he'd never bothered to take them down from the previous year, he'd only had to plug them in to join the season's festivities. Only all the bulbs were burned out, with the exception of a lone red one just above the door. It blinked on, then off, on, and then off—beckoning him in. Jesse didn't want to go in. Didn't want to sit on his lumpy, blue-tick mattress and stare at the cheap wood paneling. He had a way of finding faces in the knots and grain of the veneer—sad faces, tortured ones. Inside, he couldn't pretend, couldn't hide from the fact that he was spending another Christmas by himself, and a man who spends Christmas by himself was indeed a man alone in the world.

Your wife sure as shit ain't alone though. Is she?

"Stop it."

Where's she at, Jess? Where's Linda?

"Stop it."

She's at his *house. A nice house. With a nice tall Christmas tree. Bet there's plenty of gifts under that tree with her name on them. Gifts with little Abigail's name on them, too.*

"Stop it," he whispered. "Please, just leave it be."

The light kept right on blinking, mocking him along with his thoughts.

I don't have to go in there, he thought. *Can just sleep in the truck bed. Wouldn't be the first time.* He kept a bedroll in the camper for just that purpose, mostly for his out-of-town gigs, because honky-tonks didn't pay a two-bit picker enough to cover both a motel and the gas home. He looked at the snow on the ground. "Too damn cold." He glanced at his watch; it was early, at least for him. When he played the Rooster, he usually didn't get home till after four in the morning. He just wasn't tired or stoned enough to fall asleep yet and knew if he went in now he'd stare and stare at all those faces in the wood.

Sid had closed the Rooster early—not because it was Christmas; Christmas Eve was usually a decent money-maker for Sid. Plenty of lost souls out there who, just like Jesse, didn't want to face empty living rooms or empty bedrooms—not on Christmas.

Like to shoot the son of a whore that came up with this goddamn holiday, Jesse thought. *Might be a joyous occasion for folks fortunate enough to have kin to share it with, but for the rest of us sorry souls it's just one more reminder of how much shit life can make you eat.*

Only five or six sad sacks had found their way into the Rooster this night, and most of them only for the free Christmas round that Sid always doled out. Jesse set aside his amp and went acoustic, playing all the usual Christmas classics, but no one cared, or even seemed to be listening, not tonight. Seemed the Ghost of Christmas Past was in the room and they were all staring at their drinks with faraway looks on their faces, like they were wishing they were somewhere and sometime else. And since no one was buying, Sid had called it quits a bit after one in the morning.

Sid told Jesse he'd taken a hit tonight, asked if Jesse would take an open bottle of sour mash instead of his usual twenty-spot. Jesse had been counting on the cash to buy his five-year-old daughter, Abigail, a present. But he took the booze. Jesse told himself he did it for Sid, but knew darn well that wasn't the case.

Jesse gave the bottle a baleful look. "She asked you for one thing. A doll. One of them new Teen Tiger dolls. Wasn't a real complicated request. No, sir . . . it wasn't." He heard his wife's voice in his head. "Why do you always got to be such a screw-up?" He had no answer. *Why do I have to be such a screw-up?*

It ain't too late. I can go by the Dicker and Pawn on Monday. Only he knew he didn't have a damn thing left to pawn. He'd already sold his TV and stereo, his good set of tires, and even the ring his father had left him. He rubbed his hand across the stubble on his face. What'd he have left? He plucked his guitar off the gun rack, sat it in his lap. *No, I just can't.* He strummed it once. *Why not?* Damn thing brought him nothing but grief anyhow. Besides, it was all he had left of any value. He glanced at the wedding band on his finger. Well, almost. He sat the guitar down on the floorboard and held his ring finger up so the gold band caught the streetlight. Why was he keeping it? Lord knew Linda wasn't wearing hers anymore. Yet he couldn't bring himself to sell it. As though holding on to that ring might somehow get them back together. His brow furrowed. "I'll think of something. Something." Only he knew he wouldn't. "Abigail, baby doll," he said. "I'm sorry." The words sounded hollow in the truck's cab. Was he really going to say that again? How many times can you say that to a little girl before it doesn't count anymore?

He took another swig, but the alcohol suddenly tasted bitter. He screwed the cap back on and dropped it onto the floorboard. He watched the bulb flick on and off, on and off. *Can't go in there. Can't spend another night in that hole thinking about Linda with* him. *Thinking about Abigail, my own daughter, living in another man's house. Thinking about the present I didn't get her . . . that I can't get her.*

"I'm done with feeling bad all the time." The words came out flat, dead, final.

Jesse hit open the glove compartment, dug down beneath the cassette tapes, pizza coupons, vehicle registration, and an old bag of beef jerky until his hand found the cold, hard steel of a snub-nosed .38. He held the gun in his hand and watched the red light flash off the dark metal. He found the weight of the piece to be comforting, solid—one thing he could count on. He checked the cylinder, making sure there was a bullet seated in the chamber, then slowly set the barrel between his teeth, careful to point it upward, into the roof of his mouth. His aunt Patsy had tried to shoot her brains out back in '92, only she'd stuck the barrel straight in, and when she pulled the trigger, she just blew out the back of her neck. She severed her spine at the base of her brain and spent the last three months of her life as a drooling idiot. Jesse had no intention of giving his wife one more thing to accuse him of screwing up.

He thumbed back the hammer. The damn bulb blinked on, off, on, off, as though blaming him for something, for everything. He laid his finger on the trigger. On, off, on, off, on, off, pushing him, egging him on. Jesse's hand began to shake.

"Do it," he snarled around the barrel. "Do it!"

He clenched his eyes shut; tears began to roll down his cheeks. His daughter's face came to him and he heard her voice so clear he thought Abigail was really there in the cab with him. "Daddy? When you coming home, Daddy?"

An ugly sound escaped his throat, not quite a cry, something guttural and full of pain. He slid the pistol from his mouth, carefully setting the hammer, and dropped it on the seat next to him. He caught sight of the bottle, glared at it for a long minute, then cranked down the window and chucked it at the nearest pine tree. He missed, and the bottle tumbled across the shallow snow. He left the window down, the cold air feeling good on his face. He leaned his forehead against the steering wheel, closed his eyes, and began to weep.

"Can't keep doing this."

JESSE HEARD A jingle, then a snort. He blinked, sat up. Had he fallen asleep? He rubbed his forehead and glanced around. There, at the end of the cul-de-sac, stood eight reindeer, right in front of the Tuckers' driveway. They were harnessed to a sleigh and even in the weak glow of the glittering holiday lights Jesse could see it was a real sleigh, not some Christmas prop. It stood nearly as tall as a man, the wood planks lacquered a deep crimson and trimmed in delicate, swirling gold. The whole rig sat upon a pair of stout runners that spun into elegant loops.

Jesse blinked repeatedly. *I'm not seeing things and I'm not drunk. Shit, don't even have a buzz.* One of the deer pawed the snow and snorted, blasting a cloud of condensation into the chilly air.

He looked back up the road. The only tracks he saw in the fresh snow were those of his truck. *Where the hell had they come from?*

The reindeer all lifted their heads and looked up the hill. Jesse followed their eyes but saw nothing. Then he heard tromping—someone in heavy boots coming fast.

What now?

A man with a white beard, wearing knee-high boots, a crimson Santa suit trimmed in fur, and clutching a large red sack, sprinted down the gravel lane, running full-out—the way you'd run if something was chasing you.

Something *was* chasing him.

Four men burst out upon the road at the hilltop right next to Millie's glowing manger. Black men, cloaked in dark, ragged hoodies, carrying sticks and clubs. Their heads bobbed about, looking every which way until one of them spotted the man in the Santa suit. He let out a howl, jabbed his club in the direction of the fleeing white-bearded man, and the whole pack gave chase.

"What the hell!"

The Santa man raced past Jesse, dashing toward the sleigh, huffing and puffing, his eyes wild, his jolly cheeks flush, and a fierce grimace taut across his face. He was stout, not the traditional fat Santa Jesse was used to seeing, but solid through the chest and arms.

The pack rushed down the lane in pursuit, brandishing their weapons. Jesse realized their hoodies were actually cloaks of fur, hide, and feathers, billowing and flapping out behind them as their long, loping gait quickly narrowed the gap. Jesse caught the glint of steel, noted nails protruding from the clubs and deadly blades atop the sticks. He felt his flesh prickle—their orange eyes glowed, their skin shone a blotchy, bluish black, and *horns* sprouted out from the sides of their heads, like devils. "What the f—"

Two more appeared, darting out from behind the Tuckers' trailer, intent on intercepting the Santa. These two wore jeans, boots, and black jackets with hoods. Santa didn't even slow; he put his head down and rammed his shoulder into the first man, slamming him into the second assailant, knocking both attackers off their feet.

A gunshot thundered. One of the pack had pulled a pistol, was trying to shoot the Santa man. He—it—fired again. A chunk of wood splintered off the sleigh.

"Away!" the Santa screamed. *"Away!"*

A head popped up in the front seat of the sleigh—looked like a boy, a boy with large, pointy ears. The boy looked past the Santa man and his eyes grew wide. He snatched up the reins and gave them a snap. The deer pranced forward and the sleigh—the sleigh actually rose off the ground.

"What . . . in . . . the . . . hell?"

The Santa man slung the red sack into the back of the sleigh and sprung aboard. Jesse was struck by just how nimble and spry the stout old guy was. The sleigh continued to rise—a good fifteen feet off the ground now. Jesse figured they just might escape when the foremost devil man leapt—launching himself a distance Jesse would've thought impossible—and caught hold of one of the runners. His weight pulled the sleigh down sharply, almost toppling it.

The remaining five devil men leapt after the first, four of them clambering into the back of the sleigh while the last one landed upon the back of the lead deer. The reindeer—rolling their eyes and snorting fretfully—pawed at the air and the whole circus began to spin upward.

The pistol went off three more times. Jesse was sure the Santa man was hit, but if he was, he didn't seem to know it. He let loose a tremendous kick, catching one of the men square in the chest, knocking him into another and nearly sending both of them off the back of the sleigh. The pistol flew from the creature's hand and landed in the snow. Another devil man grabbed the sack and tried to leap away. The white-bearded man let out a crazed howl and lunged for him, grabbed him, swinging and clawing. He landed a mighty fist into the devil man's face; Jesse heard the bone-smiting blow all the way from his truck. The man crumpled and the Santa yanked back the sack just as the remaining creatures fell upon him.

The sleigh shot upward, spinning even faster, and Jesse could no longer see what was happening, could only hear screams and yowls as the sleigh spun up, and up, and up. He stepped out from the truck, craning his neck, tracking the diminishing silhouette. The clouds had moved in and it was snowing again. The sleigh quickly disappeared into the night sky.

Silence.

Jesse let out a long exhale. "Fuck." He clawed out a pack of cigarettes from the breast pocket of his jean jacket. About the time he located his lighter, he caught a sound and glanced back up—someone was screaming. The screaming grew in volume and he caught sight of a black speck tumbling earthward.

THE DEVIL MAN landed on the front windshield of the Tucker boy's Camaro, smashing into the hood and setting off the horn. The horn blared up and down the snowy lane.

Jesse took a step toward the car when something crashed down through the trees and slammed through the roof of his mobile home. He turned in time to see the back window shatter and his Christmas lights fall off—that one damnable red bulb finally going dark. Jesse looked back and forth, unsure which way to go, then continued toward the man on the car hood.

Lights came on and a few heads poked out from windows and doors.

As Jesse approached, the horn made a final sputtering bleat like a dying goat and cut off. He stared at the black devil man, only the man wasn't really black or really a devil. He wore a crude hand-stitched cloak made from what must be bear hide, and his hair and ragged clothing were smeared in what appeared to be soot and tar. His skin reminded Jesse of the miners heading home at the end of their shifts, their faces and hands streaked and crusted in layers of coal dust. The horns were just cow horns stitched into the sides of the hood, but his eyes, his eyes flared, glowing a deep, burning orange with tiny, pulsing black pupils. They followed Jesse as he walked around the vehicle. Jesse hesitated, unsure if he should come any closer. The strange man raised a hand, reached for Jesse with long, jagged fingernails. He opened his mouth, tried to speak, and a mouthful of blood bubbled from his lips. The man's hand fell and his eyes froze, staring, unblinking, at Jesse. Slowly, those vexing eyes lost their glow, changed from orange to brown, into normal, unremarkable brown eyes.

"Now that was weird," a woman said.

Jesse started, realizing that Phyllis Tucker stood right next to him in her nightgown, house slippers, and husband's hunting jacket. Phyllis was in her seventies, a small lady, and the hunting jacket all but swallowed her up.

"Huh?"

"I said, that was really weird."

He nodded absently.

"See the way his eyes changed?"

"Uh-huh."

"That was really weird."

"Yes, ma'am, it sure was."

Several other people were venturing out, coming over to see what was going on.

"Think he's dead?" she asked.

"I believe he might be."

"He looks dead."

"Does look that way."

"Hey, Wade," Phyllis cried. "Call an ambulance! Wade, you hear me?"

"I hear you," Wade called back. "Be hard not to. They're already on their way. Fiddle-fuck, it's cold out here. You seen my jacket?"

From three trailers over, the Powells' two teenage daughters, Tina and Tracy, came walking up, followed by Tom and his wife, Pam. Pam was trying to light a cigarette and hold on to a beer, all while talking on her cell phone.

"Why's he all black like that?" Tina asked, and without giving anyone a chance to answer she added, "Where'd he come from?"

"He ain't from around here," Phyllis said. "I can sure tell you that."

"Looks to me like he must've fell off something," Tom said. "Something really high up."

Everyone looked up except Jesse.

"Like maybe out of a plane?" Tina asked.

"Or Santa's sleigh," Jesse put in.

Phyllis gave him a sour look. "Don't believe the Good Lord approves of folks disrespecting the dead."

Jesse pulled the unlit cigarette from his mouth and gave Phyllis a grin. "The Good Lord don't seem to approve of most things I do, Mrs. Tucker. Or hadn't you noticed?"

Billy Tucker arrived, hitching up his jeans. "Shit! My car! Would you just look at what he done to my car!"

Jesse heard a distant siren. *Too soon for an EMT. Must be a patrol car.* His jaw tightened. He sure didn't need any more trouble, not tonight. And if Chief Dillard was on duty, that could be a bad scene indeed. Jesse ducked away and headed back toward his trailer.

About halfway back he remembered that something else had fallen from the sky, had crashed through his roof, as a matter of fact, and the odds were pretty good that that something might well still be in there—waiting. *Another one of them?* He couldn't stop thinking about the thing's eyes, those creepy orange eyes. He knew one thing for certain: he didn't want to be in a room with one of those whatever-the-fucks if it was still kicking around. He reached through his truck window and plucked the revolver up off the seat. It didn't feel so solid or dependable all of a sudden, it felt small. He let out a mean laugh. *Scared? Really? Afraid something's gonna kill you? Weren't you the one that was about to blow your own damn head off?* Yes, he was, but somehow that was different. He knew what that bullet would do to him, but this thing in his trailer? There was just no telling.

He gently inserted and twisted the key, trying to throw the deadbolt as quietly as possible. The deadbolt flipped with a loud clack. *Might as well have rung the goddang doorbell.* Holding the gun out before him, he tugged the door open; the hinges protested loudly. Darkness greeted him. He started to reach in and turn on the lights—stopped. *Fuck, don't really want to do that.* He bit his lip and stepped up onto the cinder-block step, then, holding the gun in his right hand, he reached across into the darkness with his left. He ran his hand up and down the wall, pawing for the switch, sure at any moment something would bite off his fingers. He hit the switch and the overhead fluorescent flickered on.

His trailer was basically three small rooms: a kitchen-dinette, a bathroom, and a bedroom. He peered in from the step. There was nothing in the kitchen other than a week's worth of dirty utensils, soiled paper plates, and a couple of Styrofoam cups. The bathroom was open and unoccupied, but his bedroom door was shut and he couldn't remember if he had left it that way or not. *You're gonna have to go take a look*. But his feet decided they were just fine where they were, so he continued standing there staring stupidly at that shut door.

Red and blue flashing lights caught his eye; a patrol car was coming down the hill. He thought what a pretty picture he painted, standing there pointing a gun into a trailer. *Okay,* Jesse told himself, *this is the part where you don't be a screw-up.* He stepped up into the trailer, pulling the door to but not shutting it.

It took another full minute of staring at his bedroom door before he said, "Fuck it," and walked over and turned the knob. The door opened halfway in and stopped. Something blocked it. Jesse realized he'd bitten his cigarette in two and spat it out. *Don't like this . . . not one bit.* Holding the gun at eye level, he nudged the door inward with the toe of his boot. He could just make out a hunched dark shape on the far side of his bed. "Don't you fucking move," he said, trying to sound stern, but he couldn't hide the shake in his voice. Keeping the gun trained on the shape, he batted at the wall switch. The lamp lay on the floor, the shade smashed, but the bulb still lit, casting eerie shadows up the wall.

Jesse let out a long breath. "Well, I'll be damned."

There was no orange-eyed demon waiting to devour him, only a sack—a large red sack, tied shut with a gold cord. It had smashed through the roof and ended up on his bed.

Jesse held the sack at gunpoint as he plucked out a fresh cigarette, lighting it with his free hand. He inhaled deeply and watched the snow accumulate in his bedroom. A few deep drags, and his nerves began to settle. He set a foot on his bed, leaned forward, and poked the sack with the gun barrel as though it might be full of snakes.

Nothing happened.

Jesse jigged the gold cord loose, pulled the sack open, and took a peek.

"I'll be damned."

Chapter Two

THE SANTA SACK

"Where are my Belsnickels?"

Krampus strained against his chains, the ancient collar biting into his throat. He craned his neck upward, and there, far up the shaft, he caught a faint glow reflecting off the cavern roof. *Moonlight, or the first traces of dawn?*

He scratched at the lice plaguing his filthy hide, studied the bits of crusty flesh and scabby hair clinging to the tips of his broken fingernails. *I am rotting away. While he indulges in life's pleasures, I die a little more each day.* He noticed the tremor in his fingers. *Am I shaking? Do I stand here and quiver like a child?* He clutched his hands together.

And what if they should never return? What then? What chance do I have without my children? There would be no hope, no chance to once again spread my name across the land, and without hope, even I, the great Yule Lord, would eventually succumb to madness. Would wither and fade and he *would win after all.*

"No!" he snarled. "Never! I shall never let him win. If I lie here nothing but a shriveled carcass then so be it, for my spirit shall never rest. I will become a plague upon his house. I will vex him. I will . . . I will . . ." His voice drifted off. He shut his eyes and leaned his forehead against the cold cavern wall. He pressed his palms against the moist stone and listened, hoping to sense the vibrations of their running feet through the layers of earth.

"The Belsnickels will return," he said. "They must return. Must bring Loki's sack home to me."

The light above flickered and his heart sped up. He waited, watched, but knew it was his wishful fancy and nothing more. A draft of cool air drifted down the shaft. Krampus inhaled deeply, catching the faintest hint of pine needles and damp rotting leaves. He closed his eyes, tried to remember what winter dawn in the forest looked like, what it felt like to run and dance among the trees with the crisp cold air biting at his throat.

"Soon," he whispered. "I shall walk sweet Mother Earth once more and they will celebrate my return. There will be festivals and celebrations, like before, *and so much more.*"

Memories unfolded, a kaleidoscope of images piling atop one another, a thousand Yuletides past: the drums calling him from the forest; the horns heralding his arrival; the boys and girls, their eyes full of fear and fascination as they adorned him with circlets of feathers and mistletoe and crowned him with holly leaves; twirling maidens that strew his path with fresh pine needles, perfumed him with crushed spruce, and led him through the maze of huts, the parade of boisterous men clanging sword and shield and yodeling women following in his wake. The doors of the lord's house opening to him, the smell of roasting boar inviting him in. They would seat him upon a giant wicker throne at the head of the long table and there lavish him with feast and drink—all the honey mead one could hold. Then they would parade their plumpest young women before him, and to the cheers and laughter of all he would mount them, one after another, rutting with them like the beasts in the woods, blessing them with fertile, healthy wombs.

And with the people's devotion and fervor pulsing in his heart, he would herald in Yuletide, usher in the rebirth of the land, and chase away the spirits of famine and pestilence. And the cycle of life would continue ever onward.

And soon, he thought, *I will be blessing mankind again. But this time it will be these lost peoples of the Virginias. For this new land of America has dire need of me, need for me to be great and terrible, to chase away their dark spirits, to beat the wicked amongst them. And I shall, for the Yule Lord knows how to be terrible, and I shall be terrible, and they will come to worship me, lavish me with celebration and feast and . . . and again line up their young women for me to glorify.* He nodded and smiled, his eyes focused on something far away. *They will love me. They will all come to love me.*

"WELL, I'LL BE damned," Jesse said again, then once more for good measure.

He could see the corner of a box just inside the Santa sack. He stuck his gun in his jacket pocket and pulled out the box. He grinned. It was a brand-new Teen Tiger doll.

"Yes, Abigail, dear, there is indeed a Santa Claus."

He examined the doll. A seductive pair of blue cat eyes surrounded by heavy eyeliner looked back at him from beneath an explosion of glittery hair. He was contemplating the appropriateness of the doll's pouty, cherry-red lips, tiger-striped miniskirt, and exposed midriff, when it struck him how very odd that the doll should be there in the first place. This being Santa's sack, he'd hoped there'd be toys inside, sure, and he'd also hoped there'd be a Teen Tiger doll, too, hadn't he? And which one had he been thinking of? He looked at the doll again. "Tina Tiger," the one his daughter wanted. And there she was, sitting right on top, as though the sack were handing her to him. *It's like the thing read my mind.* The hair on his arms prickled and he gave the bag a suspicious look. *Okay, settle down. You're already weirded out enough.* He took in a deep breath.

He lifted the sack, surprised at how light it was; he could hold it at arm's length with just one hand. It was about the size of one of those Hefty lawn bags. He shook the snow off and carried it and the doll into his dining room, pulling the bedroom door shut behind him to keep the cold and snow out.

Outside, the EMT had arrived, bathing the room in flashing lights. Jesse tossed the bag on the floor, stared at it until he'd finished his cigarette, then pulled over a kitchen chair and sat down. He hooked a thumb into the lip of the sack and held it open, peering cautiously in, as though expecting something to spring out at him. The inside of the sack was dark, the black velvet lining quickly disappearing into shadows, allowing him to see no farther than three or four inches within. There was something unnatural about those shadows and the more he studied the dimness the more convinced he became that he wasn't seeing shadows at all, but a sort of smoke, a dense, swirling vapor. The smoke ebbed and flowed, yet didn't leave the sack.

He prodded the outside of the bag. It felt substantial, similar to the lumpy beanbag chair he'd had as a kid. He could push it this way and that, but it always regained its form. He really wanted to know what else was in there, but felt in no hurry to go sticking his arm into that smoky goo to find out.

He peered back inside, thought about how delighted Abigail would be if he brought her not one but maybe a couple of those little slutty dolls. He swallowed and eased his hand into the mouth of the bag. His fingers disappeared into the smoke, then his hand, then his forearm. He noticed a change in temperature, the inside of the bag being much warmer, and all at once he had an overwhelming notion that the bag itself was alive, that he had his hand in the thing's mouth, and that the thing might chomp down on his arm like a bear trap. Something bumped his wrist and he cried out, yanking his hand from the bag. He examined his hand and arm like they might be covered in leeches, but they were fine.

"Damn it. Stop being such a pussy."

He thought of another one of the dolls—the Asian one with the dragon tattoo—bit his lip and slid his hand back in, pushed inward until his arm disappeared up to the elbow, praying his fingers would still be attached when he pulled them back out. He fished about until he found the object again. It felt like a box. He pulled it from the sack and wasn't the least surprised to find himself looking into Ting Tiger's exotic purple eyes.

Jesse grunted. *Okay, I get it.* He thought of the Goth one, then the redhead, retrieving both of them. He didn't stop there. Just the week before, Abigail had sat in his lap with the Toys "R" Us circular, naming all six of the Teen Tigers, had explained all their superpowers, had told him which ones she liked best and which accessories were must-haves. She went on to clarify just how hard it was for a girl her age to eat, sleep, or even breathe without having at least one of these awesome dolls in her possession.

A minute later, Jesse had the full gang of Tiger girls lined up across the table, as well as a tiger-striped, red Corvette and two accessory blister packs. And it didn't take any great shakes to see that all those toys couldn't have possibly fit in that bag together. *The sack's making 'em somehow.* Then it struck him. *The bag is making whatever I wish for!* His eyes grew wide and he stopped breathing for a moment. *Really? Had the heavens really just dropped a magic sack into his lap?* He leapt to his feet, jumped over, and bolted the door, then peeked out the front window. The ambulance and patrol car were still out there, but the neighbors had all gone home, well, all except for Phyllis, who was gabbing on a mile a minute to the EMT driver.

Jesse pulled the shades shut and dropped down in front of the sack, his hand hovering over the opening. He closed his eyes, pictured a diamond ring, and slipped in his hand. *There!* He clasped a small velvet case, holding his breath as he slowly withdrew it from the bag. His fingers shook so bad it took three tries to pry it open. "Oh, fuck yeah!" he said, holding the ring up to the light.

His smile fell.

It was a toy—nothing but plastic and painted aluminum. "Dang it!" He shook his head. "Must've done something wrong?" He tossed the ring over his shoulder, closed his eyes again, concentrating this time on a watch. He specifically thought of the gold Rolex he'd recently seen down at the pawn shop. The watch he pulled out did indeed say Rolex on its face, but it was still a toy. "Aw, c'mon! C'mon!" Three tin rings, four plastic watches, and a tall stack of play money later, he got the message: the sack only made toys.

He slid back against the wall. "Well, crap." He leaned his head against the paneling and stared up at the water stains on the ceiling. "Shit never seems to wanna go my way." All at once everything that had happened this long, strange evening caught up with him and he just wanted to crawl in bed and stay there. He glanced toward the bedroom. "Probably build a snowman in there by now." He sighed, plucked the seat cushion from the chair, propped it behind his head, and lay down right there on the floor. He watched the emergency lights flicking through the shades. His eyes wandered over to the dolls. He managed a smile. "I got every one of those little super-tramps . . . every single one." He thought of Abigail's face and his smile turned into a grin. "For once, baby doll, your daddy's not gonna be a loser. For once your daddy's gonna be a hero." He closed his eyes. "Abigail, darling . . . just you hold on to your britches, 'cause Santa Claus is coming to town."

"THERE. AT LAST, my Belsnickels . . . they return!" Krampus lifted his ear from the stone and stared up the shaft, pulling against his chain like a hound awaiting a feeding. The light above now bright enough that he knew it to be dawn. He could see their shadows approaching.

It was nearly fifty feet to the top of the narrow shaft; he wrung his hands together as they clambered down. *Where is it?* He searched their silhouettes for some sign of the sack.

Makwa, the big Shawnee, dropped down first, landing on all fours, his bear fur and buckskin garb torn and soiled, his flesh scraped and bloody. He stood and Krampus clutched his shoulders. "Do you have it?"

Makwa pushed back his hood, shook his head. "No."

Three more Belsnickels slipped down: the brothers, Wipi and Nipi, also of the Shawnee people, and the little man, Vernon, his long, bristly beard full of pine needles. They, too, appeared to have suffered dearly. They'd obviously been in a desperate battle with someone or something. Krampus looked from one to the next; none would meet his eye. "You do not have it? None of you have it?"

"No."

"No?"

They shook their heads, continued to stare at the ground.

No. The word cut through him like a shard of ice. *No.* His knees threatened to buckle. He grabbed the wall to steady himself. "Was it him? Was it Santa Claus?"

"Yes," Vernon answered and the three Shawnee nodded.

"Where is he? Where is the sack?"

"We did our very best," Vernon said. "He was terribly strong and crazed . . . it was unexpected."

KRAMPUS

Krampus slid to the ground, cradling his head in his large hands. "There will never be another chance."

The girl, Isabel, dropped down. She flipped back the hood of her jacket, looked from Krampus to the four men. "You didn't tell him?"

No one answered her.

"Krampus, the sack might still be out there."

Krampus looked at her, confused. "The sack?"

"Yes, the sack. It's out there somewhere."

Krampus found his feet and grasped her arm. "What do you mean, child?"

"We had it. I mean almost. We were in the sleigh, fighting the old man for it, and— Ow! Dammit, Krampus. You're hurting my arm."

Krampus realized he was pinching her in his distress and let loose.

"It was crazy. Santa Claus went berserk. Biting and clawing and . . . and . . ." She trailed off, a look of intense sorrow fell across her face. "He kicked Peskwa out of the sleigh. We were so high . . . I don't know it he made it or—" She hesitated, glancing at the others.

"Oh, he's most certainly a dead little Indian," Vernon put in.

"We don't know that," Isabel shot back.

"Unless he sprouted wings, he's dead. I see no reason—"

"Enough!" Krampus cried. "Isabel. What happened to the sack?"

"Well, when Peskwa fell, he took the sack with him and—"

"So, the sack . . . it is still out there?"

"Yes. Well, maybe? I mean when—"

"Maybe?"

"You see, after the sack fell, the sleigh went spinning out of control. It was all we could do to just hang on. A few seconds later we slammed into some trees. We were all—"

"And Santa Claus? What happened to him?"

"Well, I'm trying to get to that."

"Well, get to it."

"I'm trying. You keep interrupting me."

Krampus threw his hands up in frustration.

"Okay, see . . . hell, where was I? Oh, yeah, when we hit that first clump of trees, we were slung out, but not Santa, he clung on. You should've seen him, completely out of his gourd . . . ranting and raving at us and at them deer. Them reindeer were all tangled and spooked,

23

and off they shot. Up, up and away. Went spinning across the hollow, into the part of the hill where there's nothing but boulders and drops. Slammed into them rocks so damn hard the sound echoed all up and down the valley. None of us seen exactly where old Santa ended up. But I can tell you sure as shit he didn't walk off from that. Ain't no way. He's dead."

"Dead?" Krampus snorted, then laughed. "Santa Claus dead. No. As sweet as such tidings would be, it takes much more than a hard slap to kill such vileness." Krampus tugged the stringy hair sprouting from his chin. "But it is encouraging that his sleigh and the reindeer are lost." He began to pace. "Means there might still be some chance to get to the sack . . . to find it first." Krampus's heart began to race. "Yes, certainly there is! You say the sack fell with Peskwa, did you not?"

Isabel nodded.

"Do you remember where he fell?"

"Yes. No."

"Which is it, child?"

"Hard to say. I mean there's no telling. The sleigh was spinning and—" Isabel glanced at the others. They shrugged.

"The sack will be somewhere near the body." Krampus's voice rose with excitement. "You need to find the body, or where it landed. Should not be that hard to do. Begin your search there. Split up and spread out, and—" He stopped pacing, stared at each of the Belsnickels. "We *must* beat Santa to it. He now knows I live . . . knows about you. He will be sending his monsters. The sack is the prize. It is everything . . . if he should find it first then . . . well, then we are all as good as dead."

He snatched up one of the Shawnees' spears, handed it to Makwa. "You still have your knives? Good. Take the rifle and pistol as well. You will need them should his monsters find you."

"We lost the pistol," Isabel said.

"Wipi shot him," Vernon added. "At least three times at close range. I was right beside him. He hit him every time, right in the chest . . . didn't so much as slow him down."

"No," Krampus said. "No, I wouldn't think it would. Now hurry, make haste. Every second counts."

The Belsnickels snatched up a couple of spears and an old shotgun with a broken stock from a pile of tools. They scrambled away up the shaft, one after another. Krampus shouted up after them, "Keep a sharp eye out for his monsters. You will know them when you see them. You will feel them." Then, under his breath. "As they will feel you."

JESSE PULLED INTO the drive of a small old house with peeling white paint. Linda and Abigail had been staying with Linda's mother since the breakup. He glanced at his watch. He'd overslept and it was going on noon.

He peered into the camper where two garbage bags full of toys sat waiting for Abigail. He grinned, couldn't help himself. Santa's crimson sack sat on the floorboard next to him. He stroked the thick, rich velvet. He had a good feeling about that sack and didn't intend to let it out of his sight. It was magic, and he felt sure that somehow or another it was going to bring him good fortune. He just hadn't quite figured out the somehow yet, but at the very least he figured he could always sell it, had to be someone out there who needed a toy-making sack. He started out of the truck when something in his jacket clunked against the door. He pulled the pistol out of his pocket. "Shouldn't need this," he said, then snorted. "Of course, there's no telling with Linda." He stuck the gun back in the glove compartment.

Jesse knocked on the front door and waited. When no one came, he knocked again, louder.

"Hold your beans," someone yelled. "Be right there."

He heard shuffling feet, then Polly opened the door and stared at him through the screen. She gave him a pitying look.

"Are they here?" Jesse asked.

He thought she wasn't going to answer him at all, when finally she sighed. "Why you wanna go and do this to yourself?"

He tried to peek past her into the living room.

She looked back over her shoulder. "I ain't hiding 'em under my couch. They ain't here, Jesse. Not one of 'em."

"Over at Dillard's," Jesse said. It wasn't a question.

Polly said nothing.

"Damn it!" Jesse stomped his boot on the doormat. "Tell me something, Mrs. Collins. Just what the hell does she see in that son'bitch?"

"I done asked her the same thing about you once."

"The man's pushing sixty. You think that's right? For Linda to be going out with a man near about your age?"

"Linda's never been real good at picking men. At least Dillard's taking care of her. That's more than some folks can claim."

Jesse cut her a hard look.

"Comes home after work like he should. Has a nice truck. Nice house."

Jesse turned his head and spat loudly. "That house was bought with dirty money."

Polly shrugged. "Better than no money."

"I gotta go." Jesse turned and started down the steps.

"If you're wise, you'll steer well clear of that man."

Jesse stopped, turned around, and looked Polly straight in the eye. "Linda's still my wife, y'know. A little fact that everyone seems to have forgot but me."

"I'm just saying don't go stirring him up. You don't need that kind of trouble. No one needs that kind of trouble."

"Well, if he thinks he can just take another man's wife, then it's my job to set him straight."

She laughed, a mocking sound that set Jesse's teeth on edge. "Jesse, you wanna think you're mean, but you just ain't. That much I do know about you. Now Dillard, on the other hand, now there's a man cut from mean stock. His daddy was shot six times in his life and is still here to tell about it, while them men who done went and shot him—every one of them's lying beneath the stone-cold ground. And his granddaddy, well, that man was so mean they had to hang him before he was twenty-two. Dillard's got deep roots in this county, got the law on his side. Can send you away, one way or another. So you need to dial it down a notch while you still can."

Jesse's face flushed. He didn't need Mrs. Collins to lecture him about Dillard Deaton, or Police Chief Dillard Deaton, which sounded much more important than it really was, as there were only two full-time police officers in Goodhope. It wasn't the badge that troubled Jesse but the fact that the man was ear-deep with Sampson Boggs, better known around town as the General. Boggs and his clan ran every sort of racket:

gambling, dog fighting, prostitution, welfare fraud, and could sell you any drug you could name. Chief Deaton's sworn civil duty seemed to include keeping the law off the General's back in return for a cut on the take—been that way as long as Jesse could remember.

Dillard's ties ran deeper still: the Boggs clan and Dillard's kin had a long, crooked history together. Dillard's old man had taken those bullets Mrs. Collins had spoken of running moonshine for the Boggses back in the day. Blood ties meant something in Boone County, and feuds and disputes were more often than not settled outside the law. And a man needed to be careful who he messed with, because blood *always* came first. Jesse, on the other hand, didn't have much kin left to speak of, and the few he had were of no account. Without kin to back you up you didn't matter much; that was just the way things worked around here.

"What's going on between me and Dillard," Jesse said. "Well, that's a different sort of thing. When a man messes around with another man's wife, it's personal. It's understood he's crossing a line and what happens after that is between them and no one else. You won't find anyone gonna argue me on that."

The stubborn left Polly's face, leaving her looking old and sad. "Jess, Linda's finally got something. Don't you go spoiling it for her. Just you leave her be. You hear me?"

"Mrs. Collins, you have yourself a Merry Christmas." Without another look back, Jesse got in his truck and drove away.

JESSE SAW NO sign of Dillard's patrol car and let out a breath. He pulled into the police chief's driveway, parked behind Linda's beat-up Ford Escort, and cut the engine. The house sat on a couple of nicely secluded acres backing up against the river, just on the outskirts of town. Everything had been recently renovated: new bricks and wraparound porch. A late-model white Chevy Suburban sat in front of the three-car garage. "Nice house. Nice car. Amazing what a man can afford on a townie's police salary these days."

Jesse opened his door, started to get out, then hesitated. *What the hell am I doing?* He realized it was easy to talk big in front of Mrs. Collins, but now that he was here he didn't feel so cocky. He glanced up the road keeping an eye out for the patrol car. *Abi's gifts could wait. Always another day.* He shook his head. "I don't think so. She's my daughter and this is Christmas. I'll be goddamned if I'm gonna be cowed by some old limp dick."

He got out and felt naked, exposed. He glanced at the glove compartment, but something in his gut told him bringing the gun would be a bad idea. Instead he walked around, lifted the gate on the camper, pushed his guitar aside, and pulled out the two sacks of toys. He walked up the pathway, stashing the two bags behind the hedge, then mounted the porch. He pushed his hair back out of his face, straightened up his shirt, and pressed the doorbell. Deep chimes echoed from inside.

A minute later, Linda opened the door with a big smile; the second she saw Jesse, her smile fell. She wore a plush lavender robe. Jesse noticed right away the frilly lingerie peeking out from beneath the robe.

"Santa bring you that?"

Linda shot him a cold look and tugged her robe closed. "What're you doing here?"

"Merry Christmas to you, too, honey."

"You shouldn't be here." She glanced behind Jesse, her eyes anxious. "He's gonna be back anytime."

"I'm here to see my daughter."

"Jesse, you can't be making trouble." Linda lowered her voice. "He's just looking for an excuse. He'll take you in this time. You know what that'll mean."

He did. There were times, when the gigs were slow, that Jesse picked up odd jobs to fill in. On more than one occasion he'd run contraband for the General. The Boone County sheriff was an honest man, wasn't on the General's payroll, didn't care much for Chief Dillard Deaton either. One night, the sheriff pulled Jesse over during a run and that contraband turned out to be three kilos of weed. Jesse ended up in jail. Since it was Jesse's first offense, the judge let him off with probation and a stern warning that any more trouble and he'd serve hard time. Chief Deaton liked to remind Jesse about his probation, about what would happen if Jesse were to get out of line.

"Last I checked," Jesse said, "it wasn't against the law for a man to visit his little girl on Christmas."

"Jess, please go. I'm begging you. If he finds you here it'll be bad." And Jesse caught a note of panic, understood that she didn't mean bad just for him.

"Linda, you're twenty-six. What are you doing with that old creep?"

"Don't you do this. Not here. Not now."

"Well, okay, fine. But I'm still Abigail's father and as such I got some say on her welfare, and it don't set well with me one bit that she's living under the roof of a man in cahoots with the General."

Linda looked at him as though he'd lost his mind. "Really? Are you kidding? I can't believe you even said that." She laughed. "Weren't you the one sitting in county jail a couple months back? And for what? What was it, Jesse? Running drugs I believe. Who exactly were you in *cahoots* with?"

Jesse flushed. "That ain't the same and you know it."

She just stared at him.

"Besides, I didn't know it was drugs."

Linda rolled her eyes and let out a snort. "Jesse, I happen to know you aren't that stupid. Well, okay, I tell you what. I could move her into that little trailer of yours. That'd be a wonderful place to raise her. Don't you think?"

"Doesn't the fact that Dillard murdered his wife bother you at all?"

"He did not," she shot back, a noticeable edge in her voice. "That's just talk. Dillard told me what really happened. She emptied his bank account, took his car, and run off. That's all there is to that. He was shattered by what that crazy woman did to him."

"That's one side of it. Too bad Mrs. Deaton ain't around to give her side. Too bad no one ever found hide not hair of her after all these years."

"Jesse, what are you trying to do?"

"Linda, don't move in with this guy. Please don't. Go back to your mama's. Let's give this one more chance. *Please.*"

"Jesse, I'm done waiting for you to grow up. There's gotta be more to my life than watching you pick at that damn guitar of yours. I don't want to be raising a child by myself while you're off playing at some scuzzy honky-tonk. That ain't no kind a life."

"What happened to you, Linda? You used to believe in me . . . believe in my songs."

"How's that demo coming along, Jess?"

"It's coming."

"Have you sent off any of your songs? Did you ever follow up with that DJ from Memphis, that Mr. Rand, or Reed, or whatever his name was? As I recall he was real keen on your sound."

"I'm still working on it."

"Still working on it? Jesse, that was over two years ago. What's the excuse now?"

"Ain't no excuse. Songs just aren't quite ready yet. That's all."

"How many years have I been hearing that? What you mean to say is *you* aren't quite ready yet. Because them songs . . . they're good songs. But nobody's ever gonna know it if you don't let them hear 'em."

Jesse stared at his boots.

"Jesse, we been over this until I'm sick of hearing myself say it. You aren't going nowhere so long as all you do is keep playing to a bunch of drunks in those two-bit bars. You want it, baby, you're gonna have to make it happen. Gonna have to put yourself on the line.

"Look, Jess, some folks is gonna like what you do and some folks aren't, that's just the way it is. You can't go through life worrying about the ones that aren't."

Jesse felt that was easy for Linda to say, she'd never cared a lick for what other folks thought. It was why she was such a good dancer, because she could just lose herself in the beat, just kick up her heels not caring who was watching or what they might be thinking. She'd never been able to understand that it might be different for him, at least while he was performing. He couldn't get past all those eyes on him, watching his every move, couldn't get into the zone, into that magic place where the music and him were one and the same. So yes, perhaps she was right, maybe he was afraid to put himself on the line, but maybe he'd learned that it was better to play good to a bunch of drunks instead of screwing up in front of people who gave a damn.

She let out a long sigh. "You won't send your songs off to no one because you don't ever feel they're quite good enough and you won't play in front of nobody that amounts to a hill of beans because they might look at you funny. Jesse, how can you expect me to believe in you if you won't believe in yourself?"

Jesse just stared at her, tried to come up with a reply, something he hadn't said a hundred times before. "All I know is that I love you, Linda. Love you as hard as I can. Now, you go ahead and look me in the eye and tell me you don't love me. Do it right now. If you can do that then I'll leave you be."

She met his eyes, opened her mouth, then closed it, her lips set tight. Tears began to brim in her eyes. "There's a little girl in there that needs some sort of stability in her life. She don't need a mom pulling double shifts at the Laundromat, don't need a daddy dragging in at four A.M. every morning. Can you understand that? Can you not see that there's more to consider here than just you and me?" A tear fell down her face and she wiped it angrily away. "I gave you every chance. Every . . . damn . . . chance. So don't you come up here telling me you love me and acting like you're all concerned about Abigail's welfare."

"I'll find a job. A *real* job. Just tell me you're willing to give it a shot and I promise . . . promise I'll quit with the music . . . quit it straight away."

She looked at him like he'd stabbed her. "Quit your music? Nobody wants you to quit. You just need to get a plan and a little faith in yourself. Grow some goddamn balls, Jesse, and go after it."

"Okay, I'll get a plan . . . and . . . um . . . grow some goddamn balls. Hell, I'll do whatever it takes to—"

"Stop it, Jesse. Stop it. It's too late. I've heard it all before. We both know nothing's gonna change. Just can't count on you, Jesse. No one can. You can't even count on yourself. Now you need to leave. Right now, before Dillard gets back. Before you screw this up, too. Don't make—"

"Daddy?" a timid voice called from behind Linda. "Mommy, is that Daddy?"

Linda gave Jesse a pained look then opened the door wider. A little girl with long, curly hair, wearing faded flannel PJs, stood peeking into the foyer. The girl saw Jesse and let out a squeal. "Daddy!" she cried and came rushing to him. Jesse scooped her up, spun her around then just hugged her, enjoying the crush of her little arms about his neck. She hugged him like she never wanted to let him go. He pressed his nose into her hair and inhaled deeply. She smelled of soggy Froot Loops and baby shampoo and it was the sweetest thing he'd ever smelled.

"Daddy," she whispered in his ear. "Did you bring me something?"

He opened his eyes and found Linda staring at him. She didn't need to say a word; he knew her "you're gonna let her down again" look too well.

Jesse set Abigail to the floor. "Was there something you wanted? I couldn't remember if there was or not. Last thing I recall you saying was to donate all your presents to charity."

Abigail planted her hands on her hips and screwed up her face like she wanted to sock him. Then her eyes lit up as though just remembering something amazing. "Oh, Daddy, I gotta show you something." She started away then slid to a stop. She held up one tiny finger. "I'll be right back. So don't go nowhere. Okay? Okay?"

"Promise," he said and smiled, but her sincerity pained him. He could see that she was truly afraid he might not be here when she returned. *And why not? It's not like it hadn't happened before?*

Linda looked at his empty hands. "Don't have nothing do you? Put it all toward booze didn't you?"

Jesse tried to look offended. "You'll just have to see. Won't you?"

Abigail came running back, clutching a doll. "Look Daddy! I got one! I got a Teen Tiger doll!"

"Now where'd that come from? Did Santa bring you that?"

"No, Dillard did."

Jesse felt as though he'd been punched. He did his best to smile while he looked the doll over. "Which one's this?"

"It's Teresa Tiger. Ain't she cool?"

"Hmm, I thought you want Tina Tiger?"

"I did, but they was all out down at the drugstore."

"Well, I guess she's pretty a-okay. I mean, if that's the best the old man could do. I can see how it might be that an old fart like Dillard wouldn't want to go driving all over Creation to get the one you really wanted. Elderly men like that . . . it's hard for them to sit for real long on account that they got hemorrhoids." He cupped his hand and whispered loudly. "Itchy buttholes."

Abigail giggled. Linda shot him a sour look and said, "Why don't you ask your daddy what *he* got you?"

Abigail set her big eyes on him.

"Well, Abi, sugar blossom. Did you know that your daddy and Santa Claus just so happen to be real good buddies?"

"Nuh-uh."

"Yup, it's God's honest truth. Why, we go fishing together every now and again. As a matter of fact we're such good buddies that he lent me his magic sack. Told me if I knew any good little girls I could give them whatever toys they wanted. Do you know any good little girls?"

Abigail beamed, and pointed at herself.

"Now, I want you to close your eyes and wish for any toy you want."

Abigail shut her eyes tight.

"No peeking," Jesse called as he stepped back to the bush and retrieved the two garbage bags. Linda eyed the bags suspiciously as he sat them down in front of Abigail.

"Okay."

Abigail opened her eyes, saw the two bags, and gave her parents a questioning look.

"Go on," Jesse said. "Open them."

Abigail laid down her doll and pulled open the top of one of the bags. Her eyes grew wide. *"Daddy?"* she whispered, then opened the bag wider. She just stared, like she was afraid to move or even breathe. She slowly pulled out a Teen Tiger doll, then another, then another, then let out an ear-piercing squeal. She clapped her hands, laughed, jumped up and down, and squealed some more as she emptied all the toys out onto the porch.

"Daddy!" Abigail flung herself around his neck. Jesse hugged her back and stuck his tongue out at Linda. Linda was not smiling, she didn't look happy in the least; she looked like she wanted to jab her finger in his eye.

"Abigail, dear," Linda said, her voice terse. "Could you do me a favor and take all these inside? We don't want 'em to get messed up." Linda knelt down and started putting the dolls back in the sack. "Here, just take 'em in. You can open them inside. That way you won't lose nothing." Abigail, practically dancing with excitement, dragged one of the sacks inside and down the hall. "I'll be there in a sec," Linda called. "Just need to have a *word* with your daddy."

Jesse didn't like the way she said "word."

Linda sat the other bag inside the door and pulled it shut. She glared at him.

"What'd I do now?"

"You know exactly what you did," she snapped. "Where'd all them toys come from? Are they stolen?" She jabbed a finger at him. "Tell me Jess, what kind of a father gives his daughter stolen toys for Christmas?"

Jesse held her eye. "They're *not* stolen."

Linda didn't look convinced.

"They're not stolen," Jesse repeated. "And that's all you need to know. How come you always gotta think the worst of me?"

"Are you telling me you bought these?" This seemed to make her even angrier. "You had cash and this is what you went and spent it on? All the things your daughter needs and you buy her toys? Jesse—" She didn't finish, she looked past him, her face stricken.

Jesse turned and saw Chief Deaton's patrol car coming down the road.

SANTA CLAUS STOOD upon the boulder, staring across the snow-covered wilderness, searching the tall cliffs for the easiest means out. His crimson suit was torn, covered in drying blood, but the blood wasn't his own. A mewling sound came from behind him, from among the pile of mangled beasts. One of the reindeer still lived, its legs broken, its gut busted open, a string of entrails and blood splattered atop the boulders. It began to bleat and bawl, sounding almost human in its suffering. Santa ground his teeth together.

"The house of Loki brings nothing but ruin," Santa Claus hissed. "Krampus, I gave you every chance. Tried to show you charity, show you the path to redemption, but I was a fool to let you live, for once more you have proven there is no grace amongst serpents."

He hopped down from the boulder, walked to the splintered remains of the sleigh. He shoved a few slats aside until he found a bound burlap bundle. He untied the cord, unwrapped the burlap, revealing a sword and a ram's horn.

"For the death of my brother, my wife, the destruction of the house of Odin, for my imprisonment in Hel, for all the thievery and deceit, all the woe your line has wrought, the last of Loki's blood shall be stamped from this earth."

He put the horn to his lips and blew; a single, long, powerful note. The deep bass sound traveled through the earth and air, carried up the valley and out across the world. Santa knew his children would hear, wherever they were, even if they were halfway around the world, they would hear. "Come Huginn and Muninn, come Geri and Freki, come you great beasts of ancient glory. Come help me find this devil. It is time to finish what should have been finished five hundred years ago. It is time to bury Krampus for good."

The dying reindeer kicked and pawed at the rocks with its hooves, trying to sit up. Santa grimaced, picked up the sword, pulled it from its scabbard. It was not a thing of beauty but a stout broadsword, a blade meant for killing. He walked over to the reindeer. It stopped struggling, looked up at him with dark, wet eyes, and let out a long bleat. Santa raised the sword and brought it down hard, chopping the deer's head from its neck with one clean stroke.

Santa Claus wiped the blade clean of blood, replaced it into its sheath. He tied the horn to his belt, strapped the sword across his back, and started away, heading south, toward the little town where he'd been ambushed. He knew the sack had landed somewhere in that trailer park and he intended to find it. "Krampus, my dear old friend, you will pay. Your death is mine and I intend to make it a terrible one."

THE CRUISER PULLED in beside Jesse's truck. Dillard opened the car door and got out. The police chief was a big man, over six feet tall, and while he might've been pushing sixty he still looked like he could knock over a tree. He was in his civilian clothes, a pair of jeans and a tan hunting jacket, and while you could never have made Jesse admit it, he could see how a woman might find Dillard's strong jaw and rug-gedness attractive. *Like a rock,* Jesse thought. *He looks like the kind of man you can count on.*

"Jesse," Linda whispered, her voice urgent. "Please don't make no trouble. Just go. Please." Jesse didn't like it. Linda didn't seem merely put out, she seemed nervous, anxious. He'd never seen her act like this.

Dillard locked steely gray eyes on Jesse, pushed his jacket open just far enough to reveal his service pistol. "Just the man I've been looking for."

"He was just leaving," Linda called, then, softly, to Jesse. "Now go. Please. For me." She pushed him along. Jesse walked down the steps, across the driveway, and over to his truck. Dillard's cold eyes followed him the whole way. "Mind holding up there a sec, Jesse? Need a word with you. Linda, do me a favor would you . . . head on in and give us men a bit of space."

Linda hesitated.

"Go on now, be a good gal."

"Dillard, I was just hoping that maybe—"

"Linda," Dillard said, a strain edging into his voice. "You need to go on inside right now."

Linda bit her lip, gave Jesse one more pleading look, then hurried inside. Jesse wondered what was going on. The Linda he knew would never let a man cow her like that. Was that the same Linda he'd torn up the honky-tonks with? The same woman he'd seen slug a man for grabbing her ass?

Dillard strolled around the cruiser, right up to Jesse, looked him up and down. "Hear there was a spot of trouble out at your place last night."

Jesse said nothing.

"You know anything about that? Maybe hear something? See something?"

"I did. Saw everything. Santa and his reindeer landed and were at-tacked by six devil men. They flew up into the sky and Santa tossed one of 'em overboard." Jesse said all this without breaking a smile. "I think the man you're looking for has a long white beard."

Dillard frowned, rubbed at a spot on his forehead like he was get-ting a headache, then just stared at Jesse for a long moment as though trying to figure out what he was. "Jesse, I knew your mother and father pretty well, and neither one of them was stupid. How come you turn out that way?"

Jesse crossed his arms and spat on Dillard's driveway.

"You just asking me to do this the hard way?" Dillard's tone made it clear he was done dicking around.

"The only thing I'm asking you to do is stay the hell away from my wife and daughter."

Dillard let out a long sigh, like a man dealing with a child. "I think me and you need to have a talk. Y'know, a man-to-man sort of thing, because there ain't no need for this to go down the path it's headed." He pulled out a pack of cigarettes, placed one in his mouth and offered one to Jesse.

Jesse looked at the cigarette as though it were poison.

Dillard lit the cigarette, took a deep drag, and slowly exhaled. "I understand that this ain't easy for you, son. I wouldn't like it if I were in your shoes. Not one bit. So I'm just gonna say it, because someone needs to. It's over between you and Linda. Linda knows it and I think you know it, too. All you're doing now is making things hard on everyone, especially that little girl of yours."

Jesse bristled.

"You two need to get a divorce. Make it official. I'll even help you out with the paperwork if need be. I'm tired of you making her feel bad. You need to man up and cut it off clean so everyone can move on with their lives."

"That ain't gonna happen."

"Yes, it *is* gonna happen. And it's gonna happen soon, because Linda and me is planning on getting married."

Jesse fell back a step. "What?"

"Sorry, son. I didn't want it to go down like this."

"No!" Jesse shook his head. "I don't think so. There ain't no way I'm gonna let that happen. *Ever!*"

"Let me make this plainer. I'm not asking. You understand? We *are* gonna get married. Just as soon as we get you taken care of, that is. Now there's a couple of ways of taking care of you, and it's pretty much up to you to choose."

Jesse held up a shaky finger. "Don't back me into a corner, Dillard. You *don't* wanna do that."

Dillard laughed, shook his head. "Jesse, if you had even a tenth of the balls you think you do, you just might be worth a good goddamn. Son, the only reason I haven't already taken you out of the picture is because you do a little business for the General. You know full well that it won't take much of anything to put you away. Why, I could slap the cuffs on you right now for whatever reason I fancy and you'd be on your way to prison. Is that what you want?"

"You do that and I won't be the only one on my way to prison."

Dillard's eyes squeezed to mere slits. "What did you just say?"

"I think you know just what I said. You take away the only thing that matters to a man and you got a man with nothing left to lose. A man like that just might start talking."

The side of Dillard's face twitched. He took a step toward Jesse. "You need to dig the catshit out of your ears, boy, and listen up. There's more than one way to make you disappear. And no one's gonna even notice one way or another either, because there ain't a soul around gonna miss a piece of trash like you."

Jesse gritted his teeth, forced himself to hold his ground, to hold Dillard's eyes. But he found himself fighting back tears. Had Linda really agreed to marry this old bastard? He glared at Dillard. "I don't believe it. Don't believe she'd ever agree to marry an old fuck like you."

Dillard let out another one of his long sighs, then shook his head and chuckled. "Jesse, Jesse, Jesse. Can't believe I'm letting myself get all worked up over a numbskull like you. I just keep forgetting how thickheaded you are." He took another long drag off his cigarette. "Let me tell you something about yourself, make it as plain and as simple as possible—you're a loser, Jesse. A no-account loser. That's why you live in that tiny rat-trap, that's why you still drive your daddy's old rust heap, and, most of all . . . that's why Linda is *done* with you.

"Now I could tell you this all fucking day, till I'm blue in the face. But it won't mean beans, because nothing's gonna sink into that thick skull of yours unless it's hammered in. So I'm gonna show you. Gonna prove it to you in a way that even you can understand." Dillard walked back to the front of his cruiser and pulled his pistol from its holster. Jesse tensed, sure the man was about to shoot him dead right there in the drive, but he just clicked off the safety and sat the gun on the hood. Dillard then proceeded to walk down the drive, leaving the gun sitting there. He leaned up against the garage door, took a deep drag off his cigarette and looked up at the trees as though he was out enjoying the day and nothing more.

Jesse glanced back and forth between the gun and Dillard—he didn't get it.

"Jesse, you know what I'm about to do? Huh?" Dillard chuckled. "I'll tell you. Right after I finish this smoke. I'm gonna go inside this nice big house of mine, gonna take that pretty wife of yours upstairs and then, and then . . . well, I'm gonna shove my big hard prick right in her sweet little mouth."

"What?" Jesse gasped.

"That's right. Gonna make her slobber all over my knob. Smack her ass and make her bark and whine. Now, if you're inclined to stop me, all you got to do is pick up that gun right there and shoot me. It's that simple."

Jesse squinted at him, his hands clenched into fists. "What? What the fuck is wrong with you? Fuck you!"

"Is that all you got? Son, I'm about to go in there and make your wife choke on my broom handle. Gonna blow my load all over her face. And all you can do is cuss me? If a man done that to my wife . . . said it right to my face like that . . . I'd shoot him dead regardless. Because that's what a real man does."

Jesse looked at the gun.

Dillard grinned. "You won't do it, Jesse. I know this for a fact. If there's one thing I'm good at, it's taking the measure of a man. Thirty years on the force will do that. And I could tell from the very first time I set eyes on you that you were one of the nobodies that don't matter squat. A loser. And now Jesse . . . you know it, too."

Jesse glared at Dillard, then at the gun, back and forth, his heart drumming. He took a step forward, then another, until he stood right beside the gun. All he had to do was pick it up and shoot. There was nothing Dillard could do to stop him.

"C'mon, Jesse. Ain't got all day." And the worst of it was Dillard looked so confident, so completely at ease, this was not a man wagering his life, this was one who was absolutely sure of himself.

Jesse's breath sped up, his hand began to tremble. *Do it. Shoot him.* But he didn't and right there, right then, he saw exactly what Dillard was showing him. *I* am *a loser. Don't have the guts to shoot myself. Don't have the guts to shoot the man screwing my wife. Don't even have the guts to send my music off to some jackass DJ.*

Jesse let out a long breath, fell back a step, and just stood there staring at that gun.

Dillard flicked his cigarette butt into the snow, walked up to the hood of the cruiser, and retrieved his gun. He shoved it back into its holster. "Believe it or not, son, I ain't trying to be a dick. I'm trying to do you a favor, trying to save you years of heartbreak. A man needs to know himself. And now that you can see just the sort of man you truly are, maybe you'll quit trying so hard to be something you ain't. Go home, Jesse. Go home to that piece-of-shit trailer of yours and get drunk . . . then do us all a favor and just *disappear.*"

Jesse barely heard him; he just kept staring at the spot where the gun had been.

"Okay, Jesse. I'm done with you. Done talking, done wasting my time. I'm going in, and when I look out that window in a few, you and that rig of yours best be gone. And just so we're clear, just so there ain't a lick of confusion between us: if you ever set foot on my property again, *ever* . . . I'll break every one of your fingers. I mean that. You won't be playing that guitar of yours ever again."

Dillard turned and walked away, leaving Jesse staring at the car hood.

Chapter Three

THE GENERAL

Jesse pulled up in front of his trailer, killed the engine, and once again found himself confronted by his front door. "My piece-of-shit trailer," he said, his voice laden with scorn. He barely even remembered driving back; the incident with Dillard played out over and over in his head, all the way home. Only each time when he came to the part where Dillard challenged him to pick up that gun, he actually did pick up the gun, actually *did* shoot Dillard, emptied every round right into the son-of-a-bitch's face.

Jesse spied the bottle of whiskey still lying in the snow and heard Dillard's voice in his head, *Go home and get drunk . . . then do us all a favor and just disappear.*

"No. That ain't gonna happen." He glanced at the Santa sack. *Because this loser's got a plan. A damn good plan. A plan that's gonna fix everything.* He tugged the Santa sack up onto the seat next to him, gave it a pat. "Time to get busy."

He got out, walked down the road to the line of mailboxes, checked the newspaper bins until he found one that still had a paper in it and took it. He plucked the sack from the truck on his way back and went inside.

He dropped the sack and newspaper on the floor, walked into the kitchen, opened the fridge searching for something to eat. Found only two dried-up slices of pizza wrapped in foil and rolled them into a pizza burrito. He took a seat on the floor, eating as he dug through the newspaper. He pulled out the Walmart circular and tossed the rest of the paper aside. He flipped to the toy section, found a pen, and began thumbing through the pages, circling pictures here and there as he went.

"Yes. Umm . . . no. Hmm . . . maybe." He tapped his teeth with the pen. "Most certainly. That one would certainly work." He nodded. "Has to work."

He pulled the crimson sack over. "Okay, baby. Do it for me." He clinched his eyes shut, concentrated, wished, and prayed as hard as he could, then stuck his hand into the sack. His hand hit a box. It felt the right size, the right weight. "C'mon." He pulled it out. There, still in the box, was a brand-new PlayStation.

"Yes!" he cried. "Yes! Now we'll see who the real loser is."

AN HOUR LATER, Jesse headed back up Route 3 with four black garbage bags of video game consoles and handhelds piled into the back of his camper. He'd stashed the Santa sack back down into the passenger foot well. It was his golden ticket and he intended to keep it close.

He pulled into a salvage yard on the outskirts of town and tried to avoid the larger potholes as he drove past a few grungy outbuildings and a handful of wrecked semitrailers. He came to a cinder-block wall strung with barbed wire and deer skulls at the very back of the compound, followed it to a metal gate topped with broken glass, and stopped. Jesse honked twice and waved at the security camera mounted above the gate.

A moment later he heard a click and the gate rattled open along its rusty track, revealing a short alley of garage bays. The door of the tall middle bay hung halfway up and Jesse could see five figures leaning over a diesel engine. He pulled up to the bay, cut the ignition, and listened to his engine rattle to a halt. He got out and retrieved one of the garbage bags, then walked under the eave and waited.

The bay was part auto shop and part everything else. Greasy power tools, air tools, and various hand tools lay scattered across every available surface. A dismantled riding lawnmower was shoved into one corner next to an avocado-green refrigerator, the door stained almost black with grimy handprints. Aerosol cans and taxidermy supplies lined several of the back shelves, while above them hung well over a dozen mounts, including a twelve-point buck and a one-eyed black bear rumored to have killed three of the General's hunting dogs.

None of the men bothered to look up, so Jesse ended up just standing there holding the bag, shifting awkwardly from foot to foot. Jesse could see the General fiddling with the camshaft. Finally, one of them—a tall, blond, solid-built man in a pair of faded, grease-stained coveralls—looked up, made a sour face, then put down his wrench. He wiped his hands on an oil rag and headed over to Jesse.

Chet was the General's nephew, had gone to school with Jesse and the two had hung out on occasion. These days Chet was Jesse's contact man—Jesse never actually having talked directly to the General before. That's the way the General handled matters, at least small matters, and it had been made clear that Jesse was a small matter.

Chet scratched at his thick handlebar mustache. "Why, we was just talking about you, Jesse."

Jesse squinted, wondered what that was supposed to mean.

"Nice of you to show up." Chet wore a big smile, what Jesse's grandmother used to call a crocodile smile. "Save me the bother of tracking you down."

"Yeah, well, here I am."

"Hope you don't have any plans for tonight. 'Cause if you did, they just got changed."

Jesse's jaw tightened.

"Got a run for you. Short trip . . . just up to Charleston."

"Can't do it."

Chet raised an eyebrow. "Can't do it?"

"Nope. I'm done with that."

Chet pushed back his cap. "I'm not liking the sound of this, Jesse. Why, you got folks counting on you."

"I'm in a new line of business now."

"Is that so? Just what sort of business would that be?"

Jesse sat the garbage bag down.

"What's that?"

"Something Santa left me."

Chet eyed him. "Ain't got time for your nonsense."

"Got a business proposal for the General."

"Shoot."

"You ain't the General."

Chet squinted at him. "You got something to say, then you best say it to me."

"I'm here to see the General."

Chet grabbed Jesse by his jacket collar, yanked him up onto his toes.

"Chet," a deep voice called out. "Hold on."

"Watch yourself, boy," Chet growled, and gave Jesse a shove.

The General walked over, followed by the other three men, all of them Boggses—nephews and cousins of one sort or another. They gave Jesse the once-over.

The General wore the same getup he had on every time Jesse had ever seen him: a suede cowboy hat over his baldness, a matching fringed jacket like Daniel Boone might wear, and alligator boots. A bristling salt-and-pepper beard sprouted out from his rough, windburned face. Jesse guessed the man must be pushing into his sixties by now. Even so, he still looked like he could hold his own against any comer. His real name was Sampson Ulysses Boggs. His parents had given him a big name in the hopes he'd grow into it, but since the General stood a head shorter than most men, Jesse felt he was trying to compensate in other ways. He'd taken the reputation that the Boggs clan had built running 'shine back in Prohibition, and used it to strong-arm and intimidate his way into every profitable illegal activity in and around Boone County.

"Go on then, son," the General said. "Say what you got to say."

"Well," Jesse said. "I've got a proposal you might be interested in."

"Have you?"

"I do." Jesse tugged the garbage bag open so they could all see the boxes of game consoles.

"I don't play video games," the General said.

"I got a truck full of 'em and can get more."

"Can you now?"

"Yes, sir. And I was thinking you and me should partner up. I got a handle on a steady supply and could sure use a bit of help distributing them." Jesse realized he was talking too fast and made himself slow down. "Be willing to go fifty-fifty the whole way."

The General grinned at that, but Jesse didn't like the look of that grin.

"And just how'd you come by these?" the General asked.

"Well," Jesse hesitated. "Well, sir . . . not really at liberty to say."

"You're not?"

"No, sir. We could just say that Santa brought 'em to me." Jesse made a weak laugh, but no one else even cracked a smile.

The old man stared at him. Nobody moved or spoke. Jesse didn't like the mood, didn't like the way this was playing out, something wasn't right, and all at once he wanted to leave.

The General nodded. Jesse knew the nod meant trouble, but before he could act Chet caught hold of his arm. Jesse tried to twist free, but they were all on him.

They dragged him over to the row of shop tools, forced his right hand onto a drill press, held it over the plate, right where the bit pushed through once it got spinning. Chet snatched up a roll of duct tape and began wrapping the tape around Jesse's hand and arm, round and round, strapping his hand to the press. Jesse struggled to yank his hand free, but it was bound tight. The men pushed him to his knees and held him fast.

The General walked up. "Got a call from Dillard. Any idea what that might've been about?"

Jesse's blood went cold.

"He said you were talking crazy, like maybe you'd turn snitch. Start squealing if you didn't like the way we was treating you."

Jesse shook his head. "No. That's not what—"

The General kicked him in the gut. "Shut up."

Jesse coughed and choked, struggling for breath.

Chet tore off another strip of tape and wrapped it across Jesse's lips. The taste of glue filled Jesse's mouth and his nostrils flared as he fought to get enough air into his lungs.

"Talk like that makes me nervous," the General continued. "I believe you and me, we got a few things to work out. Let's start with what you got to lose. I hear you're pretty sweet on that guitar of yours. Ain't that what you said, Chet?"

"Yup," Chet replied. "Why, I'm willing to bet he'd rather fiddled with that guitar than a hot slice of poontang pie. Told me his dream was to make it big down in Memphis."

"Well, that's gonna be hard to do with big holes in your hand." The General nodded and Chet hit the switch on the drill; a high-pitched whine filled the bay. A half-smirk pushed at Chet's cheek as he slowly lowered the drill, lowered it until the spinning bit just nipped Jesse's skin.

Jesse grit his teeth, struggled not to yell.

Chet let the drill sink near a quarter inch into Jesse's flesh.

"Fuck!" Jesse cried through the tape.

Chet laughed, pulled the drill bit back up, leaving a dot of blood on the top of Jesse's hand.

"Didn't tell you to stop," the General said.

The humor left Chet's face. He looked at the General confused. "But—"

"Do it."

"What? You mean all the way?"

"Hell, yes, I mean all the way."

Chet continued to stare at the General.

"You gone deaf? Press the fucking drill through his hand."

"Thought we was just aiming to scare him."

"He don't look scared enough to me. Now, do it. I want to give him something to remember who he's fucking with."

Chet still didn't move.

The General's face twisted into something resembling a wadded-up dishrag; he stepped over and jabbed a thick finger into Chet's chest. "You need to learn to do as you're told, boy." He shoved Chet aside, nearly knocking him off his feet. The General took hold of the drill and leaned over to Jesse. "Next time your tongue feels like wagging, you'll want to remember this." The General slowly lowered the drill into Jesse's hand, driving it deep into Jesse's flesh.

Searing pain shot up Jesse's arm. His palm felt on fire. He screamed and choked on the tape, tears squeezing out from the corners of his eyes.

Chet and the men winced as the drill punched completely through.

The General didn't so much as blink, just nodded the way you would while enjoying a favorite song, letting the drill spin in place. Specks of tape, flesh, and blood spattered Jesse across the face and the stench of seared flesh filled his nose.

The General raised the drill and shut it off. The men let go of Jesse and he slumped against the drill stand, quivering.

The General removed his handkerchief and wiped a speck of blood off his cheek, then squatted next to Jesse. "You listen up, son, 'cause you're only gonna get this one time. If I ever hear talk about you spilling the beans . . . there won't be no more games. And if you ever cross me . . . in any way, I'll put you and that pretty little girl of yours in a box together and bury the both of you alive. That's a promise, Jesse. You just think about how that would be the next time you get a wild hair up your ass. You get me?"

Jesse nodded.

"We're good then," the General said and stood. He looked at Chet, looked him up and down, looking in no way pleased. "We're all squared up with Jesse now, so let him be." The men nodded and the General headed across the bay and up a set of open stairs draped in flickering Christmas lights. He entered a second-floor office, shutting the door behind him. The moment the General was out of sight, Chet flipped him the bird.

"Better watch that," warned the lean, wiry man standing to Chet's left. Lynyrd Boggs wore a sweat-stained cowboy hat with an eagle's feather stuck in the band. His father was a big Lynyrd Skynyrd fan, so Lynyrd had the good fortune to have his name misspelled in tribute.

"Fuck," Chet said. "That son'bitch needs to chill the fuck out. Just because things is shit, don't mean he's gotta treat us that way."

"Pressure's getting to him, that's all. I remember not too long back when the General was about the only place you could get your fix around here. Now every tweek-head is brewing their own shit right in their own damn basements. General's losing ground and in case you ain't noticed, he ain't taking it real well."

"And I don't care none for this talk of hurting children neither. Ain't the way we do things around here. Not at all."

"Rules is changing. These meth heads, they ain't got no respect for the old ways."

"Goddamn tweekers," Chet spat. "Goddamn meth. Fucking ruining everything."

"Well, that ain't all. I hear we got some competition."

"What are you talking about?"

"Been some Charleston boys down here dealing."

"In Goodhope? You *got* to be kidding?"

"Wish I was. Overheard the General talking to Dillard. Apparently Dillard caught a few of 'em."

"Dillard? No shit. Bet that didn't go so well for 'em."

"You'd be right on that."

"Think they ended up in the deep end of Ned's catfish farm?"

Lynyrd shrugged. "Let's just say you won't find me eating anything caught out of that pond."

"Fuck, that Dillard's a scary son'bitch."

Jesse ripped the duct tape from his mouth and let out a gasp. He tugged and tore at the wad around his arm, working to free his hand.

Chet walked over. "Bit of advice, Jesse. Just you let Dillard be. You might think you got a handle on that motherfucker, but you got no idea what he's capable of."

"Ain't none of your business."

"No, guess not. But I've seen firsthand what he's done to folks that's gone and got in his way. It ain't a game with him. He'll make you disappear."

Jesse ignored him, kept tearing at the tape.

"Don't believe me? Ask yourself this, did anyone ever find a trace of his wife? Some folks believe she ran off. Well, I know different."

"How do you know different?" Lynyrd asked.

"Ain't gonna say."

"You're full of shit."

Chet hesitated, seemed to be weighing something. "Seen a picture of her dead body."

Jesse's blood went cold; he stopped pulling at the tape and looked up at Chet. Chet held Lynyrd's gaze; he looked serious, as serious as a man could.

"A picture?" Lynyrd asked. "You're telling me you seen a picture of Dillard's wife and she was dead?"

"I'd just as soon not have."

"Where'd you see a picture?"

"Dillard showed it to me."

"Bullshit."

"Yeah, he did."

"Now why would he do that?"

"Fuck if I know. I still ain't got that man figured. It was a couple months back when I was helping him move that old freezer into his garage. When we were done he asked if I'd like to have a beer with him. Of course I would. Well, one beer turned into two, then four, then I don't rightly recall after that. I know we pulled down a couple of lawn chairs and got lit right there in his garage. I know after a bit he starts talking about his wife, how much he misses her. He's getting all choked up, but I'm smashed by then so I just roll with it. He pulls a sewing box down off the shelf, a fancy one, painted with pretty red roses. Says it used to belong to Ellen, opens it up and there's a wedding picture of her. Ellen was a right pretty woman in her day I might add. He's staring at the picture like he wishes he could crawl right into it. I'd always heard she'd cleaned him out, so I muttered something about how sorry I was to hear she done him wrong. Then he says, 'Yeah she's sorry, too.' And something in his tone made me pay attention. He pries the back off that frame and pulls out a Polaroid. He stares at it a long while, his face cold as stone, then shows it to me. It was her, his wife. She was dead. No doubt about that, and it looked like she'd died bad. He says to me, 'Never was a woman more sorry about anything.' And the way he said it . . . why, it chilled me right to the bone."

"Damn," Lynyrd said. "Ain't that some creepy shit."

"Yeah, you're sure right about that." Chet looked at Jesse. "And that's why if I were you, Jesse, I'd stay the fuck away from that guy. Ain't nothing good gonna come from messing with him . . . not for nobody."

The blood drummed in Jesse's ears. He'd heard the rumors, but hearing Chet tell about what he'd seen firsthand sent it home. A chill climbed Jesse's spine—his little girl was living with a man capable of cold-blooded murder. What else was he capable of? Jesse yanked the last bit of tape off and pulled his hand free. A dark red hole about the diameter of a pencil sat between the bones of his index and middle finger, welling with blood. He opened and closed his hand. It hurt, but all his fingers moved as they should.

"Looks like you got lucky," Chet said. "Missed your bones. Guess you're gonna have to whack off left-handed for a while, though." He snorted. "But who knows . . . you might still be able to play that old guitar of yours."

For the first time in his life Jesse didn't care if he could play guitar or not, the only thing he could think about was Abigail being alone in that house with Dillard. Jesse pulled himself to his feet and stumbled out of the bay to his truck. He yanked the door open and got in.

"Hey, Jesse." Chet walked up to the truck carrying the bag of game consoles. "You forgot something." Chet pulled a box out. "Mind if I keep one? My nephew's been begging for one of these all year."

Jesse ignored him, trying to dig his keys out of his pocket with his left hand.

"Jesse, just so we're clear. Nobody's let you off the hook for that pickup tonight."

Jesse glared at him.

"At the school . . . round back as usual. Say seven o'clock. Don't leave us hanging. Oh, and do yourself a favor . . . listen up to what the General was saying and don't do nothing stupid."

Jesse sneered.

"Look, dipshit, I ain't telling you for your benefit. I'm telling you 'cause I happen to like Linda and Abigail, and would sure hate for anything bad to happen to either one of 'em. I mean that. Hell, y'know, there was a time I wouldn't have paid half a mind to the General's wild rants neither. But Jesse, after what I've seen lately, I wouldn't push the man. If he threatens to put your little girl in a box, you better take him serious. Face it, he's got your ass coming and going. So just save us all some trouble and play nice. All right?"

Jesse didn't answer him, didn't even nod. He turned the ignition, ignoring the sharp pain in his hand as he put the truck in gear and backed out of the alley, leaving Chet standing there holding the sack of toys.

Chapter Four

DEVIL MEN

Santa Claus glanced back over his shoulder. The two boys on their BMX bicycles were still tailing him. Santa had found a string of power lines late in the morning, had been following the trail west. That had taken him past a double-wide mobile home; the two boys had been out jumping on a trampoline when he'd marched by. They'd stared at him until he was out of sight. Now, a couple miles later, here they were, peeking around a thicket, watching his every move.

They will need a little discouragement. Would not do to have children watch dear old Santa hack Krampus and his abominations to death, after all.

A distant screech came to Santa's ear, a most welcome sound. He searched the sky, found only heavy clouds. He plucked the horn from his belt and gave it one short blast. A second later he was rewarded with another cry and the sight of two dark shapes flying down out of the clouds toward him.

They alighted upon the twisted branch of a fallen oak—the two great ravens, Huginn and Muninn. The magnificent birds were as large as any eagle, their black feathers sleek and shining. They peered at Santa with curious, ageless eyes.

"You remember Krampus? Yes, I know you do. It seems he did not die in darkness as he should have. Somehow he has crawled out from beneath his rock to make mischief, and mischief he has indeed made. Now my Christmas sack is lost—is somewhere out there amongst the near town."

The two great birds cocked their heads, questioning.

"Search for his beasts, his abominations, the Belsnickels. For they will be on the hunt as well. When you find them, stay with them like a dark omen, lead me to them with your cry . . . for my sword thirsts for their blood."

The ravens squawked and nodded, nodded as any person might.

"Go my pets, make haste. Find them and show me the way."

The giant ravens leapt into the air, the wake of their great wings kicking up the frozen leaves as they flew away down the hill.

Santa heard a clink, turned, found that the boys had dared venture closer, much closer than was wise, sitting on their bikes and staring at him. Santa walked up to them. The younger boy looked about to flee; he glanced anxiously over at the older boy. The older boy, a teenager, maybe thirteen or fourteen, looked unsure as well, but held his ground.

"Whatcha wearing that getup for?" the teenager asked.

"Yeah," the younger boy chimed in. "Why you dressed up like Santa Claus for?"

"Because I am Santa Claus."

The older boy snorted. "My ass you are."

The younger boy followed suit with a snort of his own.

Santa remembered why he hated teenagers—they worked so hard not to believe in anything. Did their very best to spoil the magic for everyone else. "Go home."

The teenager blinked. "Hey, this here's a free country. You can't go telling us what to do."

"Is that a new bike?"

"Sure is," the kid said with obvious pride. "Got it for Christmas. Fucking rad."

"Would you please get off of it?"

"What . . . huh? What for?"

"So you will not be upon it when I toss it down the hillside." Santa nodded to the steep incline on one side of the trail that bottomed into a ravine of broken rocks.

"Are you threatening me, mister?"

Santa grabbed the teenager's bike by the handlebars, kicked his boot through the front spokes, and stomped downward, snapping off most of the spokes. The front rim collapsed.

"*Hey!*" the kid screamed. "Hey, you can't do that!" He stood up and when he did, Santa snatched the bicycle out from under him. He lifted the bike over his head and chucked it down the hill. The bike tumbled, spun, bounced into the air, and crashed into the rocks below.

The two boys stood, mouths agape, staring down at the bike.

"I believe it would be a bad idea for the two of you to follow me any farther. What do you think?" Santa didn't wait for an answer—he had urgent business at hand. He turned and headed quickly down the trail.

JESSE SHOT DOWN the highway toward Dillard's house, his brow in a knot, his jaw tight. Without taking his eyes off the road, he leaned over, popped open the glove compartment, and dug out his pistol, laid it on the seat next to him. "Gonna get my daughter," he said, said it loud, like he meant it. "Gonna shoot anyone that gets in my way."

A mile later he pulled into the Gas'n'Go. "Fuck!" He picked up the revolver, glared at it. He heard Dillard again, *You won't do it, Jesse. I know this for a fact. You see, son, if there's one thing I'm good at, it's taking the measure of a man.*

Jesse looked at the hole in his hand. "Gonna shoot the General, too," he snarled. "Shoot every fucking one of 'em!" Only the words rung hollow in the cab, making him feel the worse.

He shut off his truck, got out, headed inside, and found the restroom. He ran warm water over his injured hand, washed the wound out the best he could. He opened and closed his hand. It was becoming stiff, the dark flesh around the wound beginning to swell. He wrapped it in paper towels and wondered if he'd ever be able to play the guitar again. *Maybe the General's done me a favor. Maybe I'm better off if I can't play. If I just give up on my music altogether.*

He climbed back into his truck and decided the best thing for now was to go home and try to figure things out. *What's to figure?* he asked himself, and again couldn't get Dillard out of his head: *I'd shoot him dead regardless. Because that's what a real man does.*

Jesse got back on the highway and a few minutes later pulled into the King's Kastle, splashing through slushy potholes as he drove up the hill, trying his best to clear his head. It was getting late in the day, Chet would be expecting him at the elementary school in a couple of hours, and if he didn't show up, things would get bad right away. *Can't keep making these runs. Gonna end up in prison. Every way I turn is bad. What am I supposed to do? What the fuck am I supposed to do?*

He pulled the pack of cigarettes from his breast pocket and fished for a smoke, but came up empty. He smacked the pack against the dashboard, knocking out a few crumbs of tobacco. "Perfect. Just perfect." He wadded up the pack and chucked it to the floorboard. "Well, shit, look at that." Two enormous birds were circling low over his trailer. At first he thought they might be buzzards, but as he drew closer he could see they looked more like crows or ravens. He glanced at his trailer. "What the fuck's going on now?"

The door to his trailer hung open. He caught movement within; could just make out a hunched figure inside. It was digging through the boxes near the door, its back to him. It wore a dark jacket with the hood pulled up and though Jesse couldn't see its face he knew who his visitor was.

He drove past without even slowing, as though he lived farther up the road, hoping to hell it hadn't seen him. It was a dead end, so Jesse had no choice but to turn around. He pulled into the Tuckers' drive, then backed out as casually as he could, doing his best not to draw any attention to himself. That's when he noticed another hooded figure. It shifted through the underbrush, over among the pine trees behind his trailer, its face low to the ground as though sniffing for something. Jesse glanced at the Santa sack on the floorboard and wondered if these creatures could smell it somehow. He grabbed the sack, intending to toss it out the window and just drive off, when the figure stood up, one clawed hand dangling from an outstretched wrist. It sniffed the air, then jerked its head toward him. It wore sunglasses even though the day was gray and overcast. It lifted up the shades and there was no missing those eyes: burning orange and staring at Jesse, following his truck as it crept up the road.

Jesse shoved the sack back down into the foot well and fought the urge to floor it. "Keep cool," he whispered. "Just keep cool."

The devil man headed toward the road. Jesse avoided looking its way, but could sense its eyes, those piercing orange eyes staring at him as he passed. *Little farther now. Just a little farther.* He kept it in his rearview mirror as it stepped out into the lane. It followed him at a fast clip. Jesse returned his eyes to the road and let out a cry. There, in the middle of the road, stood another one, one of the bigger ones, one with horns, all covered in fur and carrying a spear. "Shit!" Jesse yelled, cutting the wheel left.

It slapped a palm on the passenger window, jogging alongside the truck and peering inside, smiling, revealing dirty teeth.

Jesse gunned it. His wheels spun in the snow and gravel, giving him a second to regret pawning his good tires, then they gained traction and the truck took off, quickly picking up speed as it bounced and bounded up the rough road. Jesse glanced in his rearview—they were gone. A heavy thud hit his camper, followed by tromping on the roof of the cab.

The thing slid down the front windshield, gaining a perch on the hood. Again it gave him that crooked smile. Its eyes alighted on the Santa sack, grew wide, and blazed to life like a stoked fire. It set back its head and let loose a long howl, more of a wail, causing all the hair on Jesse's arms to stand on end. Answering howls came from all around. The creature reared back and drove its fist into the middle of the windshield, punching a hole through the safety glass. Cracks spiderwebbed across the windshield. It yanked its hand free and reared back for another blow when Jesse cut the wheel sharply left, then right, jerking the truck back and forth across the road, throwing the creature from its perch. The creature slid down the hood, catching hold of the wiper.

Up ahead, two more devil men came loping toward the road. "Christ, they're everywhere!"

The one on the hood began pulling itself up. Jesse swerved, purposely driving through a pothole. The jolt sent the devil man airborne, taking the wiper with him. The devil man hit the snow bank and tumbled from view.

The two ahead of him were coming fast, trying to cut him off. Jesse kept the pedal to the floor. The old V8 rattled and roared as the truck shot up the hill. *"C'mon!"* he shouted. *"C'mon!"* He thought he had it, when the forward beast leapt, flying across the snow, and slammed onto the passenger side of the truck. The whole truck rocked. It caught the side mirror, grabbed the handle, and yanked the door open.

Millie's garbage cans and nativity scene were just ahead. Jesse jerked the wheel hard right, toward the cans. The devil man and the passenger door slammed into the cans. There came a few surreal seconds when everything seemed to go by in slow motion. Jesse saw the devil man, Joseph, Mary, and the baby Jesus as they all flew through the air accompanied by Millie's garbage.

The devil man smashed into Millie's picket fence and tumbled across her yard.

Jesse raced away down the hill toward the highway, the potholes and bumps tossing the truck from one side of the narrow lane to the other. He clipped a row of mailboxes near the bottom of the hill, swerved into a ditch and shot up the other side onto the highway. He slammed the brakes and his rear tires ended up in the ditch on the far side of the road. Jesse found himself looking back the way he'd come, saw all five of them running and leaping as fast and agile as deer toward him, and their eyes—those eerie eyes, blazing and locked on him.

"Crap!" He hit the gas, his wheels spinning in the mud; there came a second when he knew he was stuck and it was all over, but the old Ford came through, the tires bit into the asphalt, and he squealed away.

He caught one more glimpse of them far back down the highway. They showed no sign of slowing, or giving up, and at that moment Jesse understood that no matter how far he ran, he'd never escape those burning eyes, that they would be chasing him through his nightmares for the rest of his life.

JESSE WAS DOING near eighty, oblivious to the cold wind and wet snow drizzling into the cabin through the hole in his windshield. The old V8 roared and whined, threatening to blow a rod. Jesse's heart still raced. He was ten miles out of town, heading south, would be coming up on the state line soon, and that suited him fine. He didn't plan on slowing down until he was in Kentucky, or maybe Mexico.

He cut his eyes to the Santa sack, gave it a hard look as though it had betrayed him somehow. Without slowing, he leaned over and rolled down the passenger window. He jerked the sack from the floorboard and shoved it out the window. It bounced along the blacktop and tumbled into the ditch.

He was done with Goodhope, done with West Virginia, done with crazy devil men and their burning orange eyes, done with the General, done with all the bullshit. *And if Linda wants to marry that bastard Dillard so goddamn bad, wants his big house, his big fancy car . . . then she can just have him. Can just have all of it!*

He tried to hold on to that, to not think beyond it, but there was more to all this, something he couldn't turn away from, and deep down he knew it. He focused on the road, on the yellow stripes zipping past, tried his best not to hear her name, her voice . . . *Daddy.* Jesse clenched his jaw, clutched the steering wheel so hard that the hole in his hand began to throb.

You heard the General. You heard him good. He's gonna put Abigail in a box.

"He won't do it. No way."

What if he does? Can you live with that?

Jesse let off the accelerator.

The truck dropped down to forty . . . thirty . . . twenty . . . ten.

No easy way out. Not for you, Jesse. Never is.

He came up on an empty used car lot and pulled in beneath the tattered streamers. Faded letters proclaiming GOING OUT OF BUSINESS SALE were flaking off the showroom window. He got out of the truck and slammed the door. There was a huge dent in the passenger door, the side mirror was gone, he had one wiper left, and, of course, that fist-size hole in the front windshield. He noticed Millie Boggs's little plastic Jesus wedged between the back of his cab and the front of the camper shell. The baby Savior appeared to be looking directly at him and smiling.

"You having yourself a good time?" Jesse shouted up at the doll.

Baby Jesus didn't answer.

"Not exactly sure what it is I ever done to you. Judging by the way things is going must've been something awful." Jesse kicked the door. "Y'know, it's not like I didn't have enough bad shit going on already."

Jesse's eyes dropped back to the hole in his windshield and he let out a long sigh. "That needs fixing." He went around to the back of the camper, dropped the tailgate, and lifted up the camper latch. He shoved aside his guitar, the bags of video consoles, and crawled in. His sleeping bag, a canvas bag full of work clothes, and the few odds and ends left in the truck after his father had died were crammed up against the cab. All the junk being too old and beat up to sell or pawn. He pulled aside a toolbox and a fishing rod, then hefted the old man's hunting rifle. He'd wrapped the rifle in oily rags to keep it from rusting and figured he could use those rags to plug up the hole for now. He unwrapped the gun, piling the rags in his lap, then just held the rifle, a lever-action .22, running his hand along the worn grip and stock. It felt like an old friend and took him back to roaming the woods as a youth, hunting squirrels and rabbits—a time when his only worries seemed to be avoiding the game commission.

A semi roared past and Jesse glanced out. He noticed that it was edging toward dusk and his chest tightened. They'd be expecting him at the school soon and if he didn't show, he'd have more than the devil men after him. "Whatcha gonna do, Jesse?" He patted the rifle. *Just go back and shoot 'em all and be done with it.* He grinned but the grin lacked any humor, because he knew what he really had to do, and knew the doing of it wouldn't be easy. *You're gonna have to go get Abigail then get the hell out of here and that's all there is to it. Head down to Mexico or maybe Peru, somewhere where the General and his crew will never find you.* He had no idea how exactly, especially having only four dollars in his pocket. He shook his head, set the rifle down, and it dawned on him that maybe the General *was* the solution. When Jesse made a run, he also picked up the payment on the other end, usually in the range of two or three thousand dollars. *Just take the cash and run.* He nodded. *Should be enough time to take care of things before the General catches on. Just need to make sure Dillard's out of the house.* He bit his thumb. *That shouldn't be too hard. Set a Dumpster on fire, or better yet smash in a storefront window.* Jesse felt a twinge of hope. A chance, no matter how small, was better than none at all. *Snatch up Abigail while Dillard's out chasing ghosts.*

"And Linda?" His brow furrowed. *Linda's gonna be a problem. A big problem.* He shook his head. *Maybe once I tell her everything she'll see it my way. She'll have to.* Another thought struck him. *Maybe if I can find that photo of Ellen.* He nodded, his heart speeding up. *If she were to see that picture, maybe she'd even come along.*

Except?

"Except what?"

Whatcha gonna do once you get down to Mexico? He looked at the two bags of game consoles. *Wouldn't be too hard to sell those things down in Mexico.* He thought of the sack lying on the side of the road, just lying there where anyone could come along and take it.

"Shit, need to go get that sack."

Jesse scooted out of the camper, slammed it shut, ran around, and jumped into the cab. He stuffed the rags into the window, cranked up the engine, and headed back up the highway.

A minute later, he plucked the Santa sack out of the mud, surprised that none of the mud stuck to it, it wasn't even wet. A screech drew his attention upward; two large birds circled above. It took Jesse a second to realize they were the same type of birds he'd seen circling his trailer, maybe even the *very same* ones. He shoved the sack into the passenger seat and the birds began cawing. The approaching dusk cast the woods in dark shadows. Jesse thought of the devil men, of their eyes. He climbed back in the truck as fast as he could and headed into town.

JESSE PASSED THE NO DRUG ZONE sign, slowed down, and pulled into the Sunny Hills Elementary School parking lot. He cruised around to the back of the cafeteria and parked near the Dumpsters. He noticed his fuel light was on, thumped it twice, watched the light flicker, and made a mental note to inform Chet that if he wanted him to make it to Charleston and back, he'd better spot him some gas money.

Jesse turned off the engine and stared at the monkey bars. He'd spent many a recess hanging about in that playground, back when he attended Sunny Hills, back when he still had dreams of becoming a big-time, guitar-strumming fool.

He glanced up the road. *Where the hell is Chet?* Jesse didn't much care to be sitting in any one place for too long, not with those things out there somewhere. He wanted a cigarette, something to calm his nerves. He scanned the woods for any sign of their orange eyes. It was almost full dark and every shadow and bush looked as though it was creeping up on him. He picked his pistol up off the seat, popped open the chamber, double-checking that the revolver was fully loaded. He wondered if bullets would do any good against something like them, wondered if you needed silver bullets, or holy water, or some such. He slapped it shut and slid it into his front jacket pocket. He noted the Santa sack sticking up and tried to shove it deeper into the foot well.

If I can just pull this off, he thought. *Get Linda and Abigail out of here, then things could be really good. Live someplace where it's warm, near the beach, somewhere nice for a little girl to grow up. Maybe even carve out a little space to play my songs. It wouldn't be Memphis, but it wouldn't be Boone County neither. I'd have my family, and I wouldn't screw things up this time. No, sir, not this time.*

He leaned his head back, closed his eyes, and did something he'd not done since he was a little boy. "Lord, if you got a moment I'd appreciate you giving me a listen. I know I don't deserve your consideration, but if you could maybe ease up on me just a bit, just this once, for Abigail's sake, I'd be mighty grateful. And if you do . . . I swear I'll make it up to you, somehow, someway. I swear."

He heard a caw, snapped his eyes open, and sat up, his heart drumming. He rolled down his window and peered up. The ravens, both of them, were circling above. "Oh, that ain't right. Not at all." He reached for the ignition and noticed two pairs of headlights heading his way.

Dillard's patrol car pulled in and parked at the top entrance of the school parking lot to keep an eye on things, make sure no one interfered. Chet's late-model Chevy Avalanche, black with tinted windows, pulled into the lower entrance and drove over to where Jesse was parked.

Jesse sucked in a deep breath. "Play it cool, Jesse. Don't fuck this up."

KRAMPUS

SANTA'S LONG STRIDE ate up the ground as he cut across the parking lot of the Goodhope Methodist Church. He was grateful for the approaching dusk, keenly aware of the odd looks he'd been getting. As he approached the church, a young woman carrying a cardboard box came rapidly around the corner. The large box blocked her view and she crashed into him, which knocked the box from her hands. Several bags of New Year's Eve's hats and horns spilled onto the walkway.

"Oh, Lord," she said. "I am so sorry, I—" She did a double take and suddenly seemed at a loss for words. She glanced back over her shoulder to the man coming up behind her, an older, wiry man with stern, penetrating eyes. The man also carried a box of party supplies.

Santa Claus, stooped, raked the contents back into the box, handed it to the lady, then set off on his way.

"Hey, mister," the lady called. "Excuse me. You dropped something. Here."

Santa turned. The woman held his horn. He returned and she handed it to him.

"Thank you," he said, and started to leave.

"Merry Christmas," she said.

This brought a slight smile to his face. "Merry Christmas."

The man next to her looked him up and down, frowning at his trappings. He shook his head. "Today is Jesus's birthday. Just pointing that out, brother, on account that some folks get a bit confused this time of year." He laid a light hand on Santa's arm and grinned. "They think it's Santa Claus Day."

Santa met his eye and held it.

"Reverend," the lady said. "Don't you even start." She looked at Santa apologetically. "Just ignore him. He's a bit *impractical* when it comes to Christmas."

"Darn straight I am. Santa Claus and all his little presents tend to get in the way of God's message."

"As can religion," Santa replied.

The reverend squinted. "Well, don't think you can argue that the world needs a whole lot more Jesus and a whole lot less Santa."

"God has many servants."

The pastor addressed the woman. "See, this here's just what I've been going on about. People get confused, especially children. Santa Claus is a fairy tale. Folks tell their children any different, why, they're flat-out lying to 'em."

"What makes you so sure Santa Claus is not real?" Santa asked.

"Ain't ever laid eyes on him, have you?"

"Have you set eyes on Jesus?"

The reverend hesitated. "Jesus is in my heart."

"Is there not room in your heart for both? They both spread peace, charity, and goodwill."

"Only Jesus can save your soul from eternal damnation." A smug smile spread across the reverend's face. "Can Santa Claus do that? Don't think so."

Santa let out a sigh. "We all serve God in our way." Then, almost to himself: "Sometimes whether we wish it or not."

The pastor gave him a puzzled look, continued on, something about salvation, but Santa didn't hear a word, listening instead to the distant cawing. He searched the sky, caught sight of the ravens circling far down the way. *They have found it! They found the sack!*

Santa set off quickly, leaving the pastor and the woman exchanging concerned looks.

ISABEL PUSHED BACK her hood, removed her sunglasses, and searched the sky. She found no sign of the ravens. All five of the Belsnickels stood on the bluff, scanning the valley, the small township of Goodhope sprawled out below them. Darkness was slipping in fast beneath the dense, low-lying clouds. They all hoped the man in the truck hadn't gone far. All too aware that if the man had left the area then there'd be little chance of finding him before Santa or his monsters did.

Makwa gestured north, and they all looked that way.

"You see them?" Vernon asked.

KRAMPUS

Makwa jabbed his finger impatiently. He could speak English, all three of the Shawnee could, but doing so seemed to annoy them. Makwa referred to English as the ugly tongue. Isabel had given up on learning Shawnee, figured if she couldn't pick it up after all these years then she never would. So between the Indians' stubbornness and her lack of language skills, they were all, more often than not, reduced to grunts and pantomime.

"Well, I don't see a thing," Vernon snapped. Isabel couldn't either, but that didn't mean the giant birds weren't out there. Makwa had been with Krampus a long time; Isabel guessed at least four hundred years, and the longer you were around Krampus the more his magic rubbed off. Makwa looked at them as though they were simple-minded, then took off down the trail followed by the two brothers, Wipi and Nipi. Isabel and Vernon shrugged and followed.

All five of them raced through the woods. There was no need to hide their faces in the growing darkness, and Isabel reveled in the winter wind blowing through her hair. Krampus's blood ran through their veins, increasing their strength and endurance noticeably. Isabel could sprint faster, leap farther, and run endlessly without tiring. But his blood did more than that; it also opened their senses to the wildness of the world in a way no ordinary mortal could ever know. She could smell the spice of rotting leaves beneath the frost, the fish in the creek, could hear a family of squirrels nesting high above in the treetops, could actually sense the pulse of life running beneath all things. *Ancient forces*, she thought, *older than the very dirt*. And when she ran like this—leaping and dashing through the woods like a deer, her heart and soul open to the spirit of the land—she found she could almost forget all that had been stolen from her.

They followed a creek beneath the highway, skirted a cluster of homes, then climbed up an embankment, coming out of the trees into a field behind the high school. The school looked the same to Isabel as it had when she'd attended over forty years ago. She stared at the dark windows and wondered if her son had gone there as well.

Makwa held up his hand and they stopped. He pointed toward the dark clouds. This time Isabel made out two specks circling about a mile away, near the elementary school, caught their distant calls. Her heart sped up. "He's still here!" Isabel felt her hopes rise. This time they knew the make of the man's truck, knew what he looked like. He wouldn't get away.

Makwa shook his head, looking troubled.

"What?" Isabel asked. "What's wrong now?"

"They call him. Call Santa Claus. He must be near."

The two brothers nodded their agreement.

"Oh, wonderful, that's just wonderful," Vernon said, his voice edging toward hysteria. "What do we do now?"

"We beat him there," Isabel stated.

"That's all well and good, but what if he already has it?"

"Then we take it from him," she said, not the least bit happy about it.

And that was the end of it; they all knew what she meant. Krampus had given them a direct command. He possessed them; the same blood that gave them the ability to run like deer also dominated their will. If Krampus should demand they chew open their own wrists while humming a tune, they'd be powerless to do anything but. They'd been commanded to bring back the sack at any cost, and so they'd expend their last breath trying, even if it meant going into the jaws of Santa's monsters to do it.

"We're wasting time," Isabel said, and dashed away. The Belsnickels followed.

She ran all out, and as she ran she took note of the beauty around her, the thousand shades of blue and purple, savored winter's twilight in its entire splendor as it fell across the mountains, knowing too well it may be her very last.

CHET CLIMBED OUT of his truck. "Why, I knew we could count on you, Jesse." He walked up to Jesse and gave him a slap on the back. "You're the man." Chet did a double take on Jesse's truck then tilted his head sideways. "What the fuck happened to your pickup?"

Lynyrd got out from the passenger side of Chet's Chevy and came up behind Jesse, grabbed him by the collar.

"Hey," Jesse cried. "Get your goddamn hands off of me."

"Cool it," Lynyrd said, and proceeded to pat Jesse down. He found the pistol in Jesse's jacket pocket and fished it out.

"What? You gonna take my gun? What the fuck?"

"Just calm down, man. You can have your shitty shooter back once we're done." Lynyrd sat the pistol on the hood of Jesse's truck. "Just wanna be sure you don't do nothing you're gonna regret."

"How's the hand?" Chet asked, and smiled.

Jesse glared at him, pressed his back up to the camper so he could keep an eye on both of them as well as the trees behind them.

"You nervous about something, Jesse?" Chet asked.

"Let's just get this over with."

"Well, damn. You don't sound very enthusiastic."

"I got better things to do then hang out with you two pricks."

Chet glanced over at Lynyrd and raised his eyebrows. "Jesse, I'm gonna ignore that on account you're too stupid to know better."

Jesse thought he caught movement in the bushes behind Lynyrd. Chet followed Jesse's eyes into the trees. "Relax," Chet said. "Nobody's out there. Besides, your good buddy Dillard's got us covered." Jesse sucked in a breath and fought to keep his nerves under control, did his best not to think about burning orange eyes.

"Oh, and hey," Chet said. "Thought you'd like to know . . . my nephew went batshit-crazy over that video game machine you gave me. I mean you should've seen his face. Thought he was gonna turn blue and piss himself right there on the carpet."

Jesse thought he was gonna piss himself if things didn't get moving. He wanted to scream at Chet to shut the fuck up and get on with it already before they were all eaten alive.

"Gave another one to his cousin. Did you know you can link those—"

"I'm so fucking happy," Jesse broke in, forcing a broad smile across his face.

"What?" Chet cut his eyes to Lynyrd. "Is it just me or is Jesse plain weird tonight?"

"Jesse is always weird," Lynyrd said.

Chet squinted at Jesse again, studied him like something escaped from the zoo. "Yeah, you're right on that one." Chet pulled out a tin of chew, twisted it open, dug out a plug, and stuffed it into his cheek. Jesse felt like the man moved in slow motion.

"Okay, sugar britches," Chet continued. "Here's the deal. Like I was telling you before, quick run up to Charleston. Same place as usual. It'll be Josh meeting you this time—his brother got another DUI and is still in jail. His wife won't pay his bail neither." Chet snorted. "I think she'd just as soon he stay in there, to tell you the truth. Anyhow Josh will be expecting you at nine. Do us all a favor and make sure you're on time. I don't want him bitching at me. I swear that man can carry on like an old woman sometimes. So don't be—"

"I'll be there on time," Jesse said, his eyes darting about in the shadows.

"Yeah . . . all right then." Chet paused. "You jacked up or something?"

"No."

Chet didn't look convinced. He nodded at Lynyrd, and Lynyrd unzipped his jacket, pulled out a large brown packet wrapped in duct tape.

"Josh will have six grand waiting for you."

"Six grand?" Jesse said, unable to hide his surprise.

Chet eyed Jesse, spat a wad of tobacco juice onto the snow. "Yeah, six grand. Don't you go getting any funny ideas. Just remember what the General said about your daughter. I mean it, Jesse. For her sake, you fly right."

Jesse's jaw tightened.

Chet jabbed a thumb toward Dillard's patrol car. "You're to follow Dillard as far as Leewood. Martin said he's on duty tonight. So the interstate shouldn't be a problem. He knows the make of your truck. So if you happen to notice the state patrol tailing you, don't sweat it none." Chet slapped Jesse on the shoulder. "See there, guitar man, we got you covered. And the General's bumping your bit up to three hundred. Y'know, to show there's no hard feelings on that there hole in your hand. That's three hundred bucks for doing just about nothing. You can send him a thank-you card if you want."

Lynyrd stepped up to the passenger side of Jesse's truck and popped the door open. The Santa sack tumbled out onto the ground. Loud cawing exploded from somewhere up above.

Lynyrd reached for the sack.

"Hey, leave that alone!" Jesse cried and leapt toward the sack.

Lynyrd had a big buck knife out in a heartbeat, had it pointed right at Jesse's chest. Lynyrd wasn't the biggest of the Boggses, but he was fast, scary fast. Jesse stopped, put his hands up. "Just getting the sack out of the mud."

"Why don't you just leave it be 'till I'm done," Lynyrd said.

Jesse backed off.

"Hell, Jesse," Chet said. "You need to calm the fuck down."

Lynyrd shoved the packet up under Jesse's seat.

"What the fuck is wrong with them birds tonight?" Chet said to no one in particular.

Lynyrd picked up the Santa sack and tossed it back into the cab without a second look.

"Hey," Chet said. "Is that a Santy Claus bag? It is. What the hell, Jesse? You been playing Santa?" He walked over for a closer look.

"Leave it be," Jesse said.

"Okay, sure. Relax, man," Chet said. "No one wants to steal your stupid Santa bag." Chet took a closer look at Jesse's face and seemed to reconsider. He squinted at the sack. "Whatcha got in there, anyway?" Chet patted the sack. "That's weird." He poked it. Watched the way the sack slowly reinflated. "Lynyrd, did you see that?"

Lynyrd grunted.

Chet pulled the sack back out. The cawing grew louder. "Fucking birds have done lost their minds?"

"Let it alone," Jesse said, taking a step forward.

Lynyrd grabbed him, shoved him up against the camper shell, flashed his knife in front of Jesse's face. "You're sure a slow learner, boy."

Chet whistled. "Look at him, man. He's all worked up. Must be something really good in here." He loosened the gold cord and peered in.

"Well?" Lynyrd asked.

Chet looked puzzled.

"What?" Lynyrd asked.

"That's really weird. It's like there's some sort of—"

A shadow slid from the trees and sprang for Chet. It was one of them—one of the devil men. It snatched the sack out of Chet's hands and knocked him sprawling across the snow.

Lynyrd reacted without a second's hesitation, launching himself at the creature, slashing out wildly with his big buck knife, catching the creature across the back of its shoulder. The devil man spun insanely fast, looking like some sort of rabid pillow-fighter as it swung the sack around in a tight arc, catching Lynyrd full in the chest and knocking him across the hood of Jesse's truck. Lynyrd snatched Jesse's pistol up off the hood, wheeled about, firing away. The first bullet went wild, the second caught the creature in the side of the face. The creature stumbled back and fell, but didn't let go of the sack.

Before Lynyrd could get off a third shot, a spear flew out of the dark, struck him in the chest, followed a half-second later by two more of the devil men. They leapt from the brush and smashed right into him, slamming him into the side of the truck with enough force to rattle the whole frame. One of them opened Lynyrd's throat with a quick slash of its knife, while the other tore the gun from his hand. Lynyrd crumpled to the ground, clutching the spear as blood gushed from the wide gash in his neck.

Two more of the devil beasts ran up, looking from the blood to the sack with wide, orange eyes. One of them grabbed the wounded devil and helped it to its feet, while the other took the sack.

"Who the fuck are you guys?" Chet cried from where he lay sprawled upon the ground. He glared up at Jesse. *"You set us up! You fucking set us up! You're dead! Your whole family's dead!"*

The ravens were right over their heads now, jumping around in the branches, cawing and cawing.

"Santa Claus. He is here," one of the devil men said, the tall one wearing the mangy hide. He pointed and they all looked across the street to a sloping field. Jesse did, as well, but saw nothing.

"Oh, dear God!" another of the devil men cried. He carried a busted-up shotgun but still looked scared to death.

Chet took the moment to scramble to his feet and run, sprinting for Dillard's patrol car, waving his arms, and screaming at the top of his lungs, *"IT'S A SETUP! IT'S A SETUP!"* None of the devil men gave him so much as another look, their orange eyes locked on the something across the way. They all seemed frozen in place.

"Get in the truck, now!" the one with the pistol shouted, and judging by the voice and slight build, Jesse guessed this one to be a woman or girl.

They moved.

She pointed the gun at Jesse. "You. Drive!" When Jesse didn't move fast enough, she shoved him in through the passenger door, sliding in next to him. "Get us out of here fast or we're all dead."

Jesse glanced at Lynyrd's body lying in the blood-drenched snow, knew these creatures, whatever they were, weren't to be toyed with. He cranked up the engine while the devil men piled into the camper with the Santa sack. He hit his headlights and saw a stout shape running toward them across the playground. It looked familiar.

"Go!" the devil woman shouted. "Go!"

Jesse hit the gas, heading for the lower exit of the parking lot.

A pair of headlights flashed on, blinding him. It was Dillard. The patrol car's big engine revved as Dillard accelerated to cut them off.

"Oh, fuck!" Jesse cried. Things were not going as he'd planned, not at all.

A gunshot rang out, then another, and Jesse's remaining side mirror shattered. Jesse gunned it, tried to press the pedal all the way through the floorboard, but there was nothing for it—Dillard would win the race.

Jesse caught sight of Dillard's mad grin, caught a muzzle flash, and a finger-size hole punched through the door frame and exited out the front windshield, followed a millisecond later by the report. Jesse knew this was just what Dillard wanted, probably sat there praying for—a chance to shoot him dead.

A man dashed into the beams of Jesse's headlights. The Santa man, eyes wild, teeth clenched in a fearsome grimace, carrying a sword and running directly for them. "Hey!" Jesse cried, and swerved, trying desperately not to hit the man. The Santa man swung the sword, striking the front of the truck, taking out the driver's-side headlight. The blade raked down the side of the truck as they barreled past, sending up a shower of sparks. The Santa man spun away and ended up directly in the path of Dillard's speeding cruiser. There came a tremendous wallop as the cruiser collided with the man, sending the vehicle veering away into the ditch and knocking the Santa man tumbling across the parking lot.

Jesse spun out onto the road, hit the brakes, looked back over his shoulder, hoping, praying, that he'd see Dillard's brains splattered onto the windshield of his cruiser. It just seemed fair that if everything else had to go so completely wrong, maybe this at least could go his way. Jesse had seen what a deer could do to the front end of a car, but the front of Dillard's cruiser was a step beyond that, more like what hitting a cow might do. He noticed the deployed airbag and his heart sank. "Dammit."

"Is he dead?" the devil woman asked. "Is he?"

Jesse realized she was talking about the Santa man, not Dillard.

"No," answered one of the devil men. "Don't think so."

Jesse scanned the parking lot, searching for a mangled body, was surprised to see the Santa man climb right back to his feet looking no worse for wear. The ravens squawked and swooped overhead. The Santa man turned, looking at something far up the road.

"They come," the tall devil man said. "See . . . see them!"

Jesse saw two dark shapes galloping toward them. He had no idea what they could be. They looked like shaggy dogs, wolves maybe, only huge, nearly the size of bulls, less than a hundred yards out and closing in fast.

"*Go!*" the woman shouted, they all did, "*Go! Go! Go!*"

Jesse got the message; whatever those things were, he had no desire to meet them up close. He pressed the accelerator firmly to the floor-board and the truck took off. The V8 roared and pinged, as the speed-ometer crept up: twenty . . . thirty . . . forty. "*C'mon!*" he shouted at the old F150. "*C'mon, baby! You can do it!*"

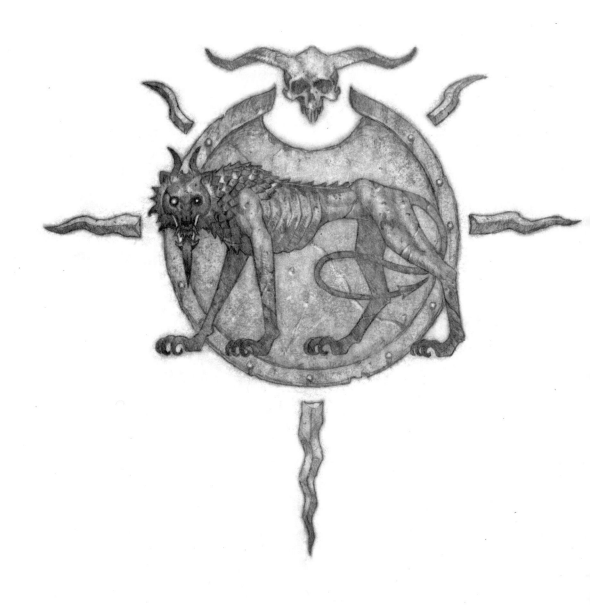

Chapter Five

MONSTERS

They'd lost sight of the wolves at least ten miles back, yet all the devil men kept their eyes fixed on the road behind them, no one speaking as they headed south on Route 3, following the Coal River through the isolated hill country.

No one had killed him yet, so Jesse felt he just might have a chance of getting out of this scrape alive. "So," Jesse said. "Where can I drop you and your friends off at?"

The she-devil studied him. The fire in her eyes had diminished, still holding their unnerving orange tint but not glowing as before. She pushed back the hood of her jacket, gave him a wry grin, and shook her head. Her hair was dark, matted, and greasy, cropped short, as if hacked away with a knife. Her gray skin with blotchy black patches made it difficult to gauge her age, but if Jesse had to guess he would've said somewhere in her late teens.

The window between the cab and the camper shell slid open and one of the devil men poked his head into the cab. He appeared to be older, his face heavily lined, late fifties perhaps, long, greasy hair and bristly, black beard. "We've lost them!"

"No," corrected the devil man seated next to him. It was the tall one, one of the ones with horns and draped in bear hides. His skin, like that of the two horned monsters next to him, appeared to be covered in black paint or tar perhaps, as though he'd purposely tried to darken it. The tall devil man crouched over, trying not to bump his horns on the camper roof. "You will never lose them. Not so long as the ravens follow." His speech was paced, a bit stilted; he sounded to Jesse like a Native American.

The woman rolled down her window; the cold wind buffeted the cab as she leaned her head out and scanned the night sky. She withdrew back in. "No sign of 'em. None that I could see no ways."

"They are there," the tall one said. "I feel them."

"I don't feel anything," the bearded man said. "How can you be so sure?"

The tall man gave him a pitying look.

"Don't give me that look. I hate that look." The bearded man was silent a minute. "Well . . . what're we going to do about them?"

"Do?" the woman said. "We got the sack. There's only one thing we can do."

"What?" the bearded man cried. "We're just going to go back to the cave? But that'll lead the monsters right to him. Not to mention right to us. Why, we'll be *trapped!*"

"We got no choice," she insisted. "That was his command."

"Well, then we better hope Old Tall and Ugly can get unhooked before they catch up with us, or we're all going to die horribly."

The creatures all fell quiet, the lone wiper beating out a squeaky rhythm as they watched the slushy road slipping away behind them in the glow of the taillights. Jesse noted the one that had been shot holding his face, blood spilling out between his fingers. He didn't think that one would be around for much longer. After seeing those wolves, he didn't think any of them would. "So," Jesse put in. "Given any thought as to where I should let you guys off?"

They ignored him.

"Are we even going the right way?" the woman asked.

"How the heck should I know," the bearded devil replied.

"Well, how about you ask Makwa."

The man's face wrinkled up in distaste, but he did just that and a heated discussion broke out accompanied by an arsenal of animated hand-gestures. He leaned back through the window. "Yes, we seem to be going the right way."

"You sure?" the woman asked.

"No, I'm not sure. But Big Chief Know-It-All sure seems to think so. And when was the last time he was wrong?"

The woman shrugged.

Makwa jabbed a finger into the cab, pointed ahead to a ridgeline barely visible in the night sky.

"Yeah, we got it," the bearded man said.

"Hey, I know where we're at," the woman said. "We should be coming up on the road in about a mile then." She looked at Jesse. "You got that? Turn up the next dirt road."

"Okay, that'll work. I'll just drop you off there."

"No, you'll do no such a thing." She looked at him sadly, her tone softening. "I'm mighty sorry, but you're tied up in this now. We're gonna need you to take us up the mountain as far as you can."

"Well, sweetheart," Jesse said. "I'm not really in the mood to go and get myself stuck up in them woods . . . not tonight. I'm gonna drop you guys off right here."

She poked the pistol against his ribs. "I'm not really in the mood to shoot you either, but I will."

Jesse gave her a quick, spiteful look.

"And my name's not Sweetheart. It's Isabel." After a long moment, she asked, "And you, you got a name?"

"Yeah, as a matter of fact, I do. It's Jesse."

"Well, Jesse, this here's Vernon."

The bearded devil smiled and stuck out his hand. "Good to make your acquaintance." From the way he spoke, Jesse knew he wasn't from around here, from somewhere up north maybe. Jesse looked at Vernon's extended hand as though it were covered in spit.

Vernon's smile withered and he withdrew his hand. "Yes, well . . . and this remarkably unrefined specimen here," he gestured to the tall devil in the bear hide, "is Makwa. Beside him is Wipi, and the unfortunate gentleman with the bullet hole in his face is his brother, Nipi."

Despite their appearance Jesse got the feeling that these creatures, or people, or whatever they might be, were more scared and desperate than menacing. On any account, they didn't seem to harbor him any ill will. Still he knew what they were capable of, couldn't get the image of Lynyrd's slit throat out of his mind, but decided maybe they weren't the murdering monsters he'd first thought. Either way, desperate people did dangerous things, and Jesse figured the sooner he got away, the better his chances of seeing another day.

"Just what are you guys supposed to be anyhow?"

"What'd you mean?" the girl asked.

"What'd you mean, what'd I mean? Are you werewolves, boogeymen, or just been out trick-or-treating?"

"Well," she replied, irritated. "I ain't any of those, thank you. I'm a person just like you."

Jesse laughed and not very kindly. "No. No, you most certainly are not."

"Krampus calls us Belsnickels," Vernon put in. "You'll have to ask him exactly what that means." His tone turned bitter. "But any way you want to put it, it means we're his servants . . . his slaves."

"I got another idea," Jesse said. "How about you let me out then? I'll just hitch a ride out of here. Take my chances."

Isabel shook her head. "I'm sorry, Jesse. But we can't do that."

"Why the hell not? I'm giving you my damn truck! What else do you need me for?"

No one answered.

"Well?"

"Can't none of us drive very well."

"What?" Jesse stared at her, then burst out laughing. "You gotta be shitting me."

Isabel frowned. "I wasn't but sixteen when I left home. And Mama didn't own a car no how."

"What about good old Vernon here, or them Injuns?"

Isabel smiled at that. "I'd like to see one of them Shawnee trying to drive. So long as I wasn't riding with 'em that is. And I'm guessing the last thing Vernon drove was hitched up to a horse."

Vernon sighed. "There weren't very many automobiles about when I was still human."

"What are you talking about?"

"Well," Vernon said. "We're a bit older than we might seem. I was forty-nine when I started surveying this part of the country. Was working for the Fairmont Coal Company at that time. That was about 1910. And Isabel, we found her around—"

"It was the winter of seventy-one. That'll put me somewhere in my fifties, I guess." Jesse caught a note of sadness in her voice. He glanced over. She was staring out the window into the darkness. She certainly didn't look in her fifties.

"That don't add up," Jesse said.

"I know it don't," Isabel said. "Not one bit. But that's the truth of it. It's Krampus . . . his magic that does it. And them Indians, hell, they been with Krampus nearly as long as he's been stuck in the cave. Going on near five hundred years I'd say."

Jesse noticed his fuel light was still on, wondered if he might be able to use that to his advantage. He thumped the fuel light. "'Bout out of fuel. Might should get some gas before we try and head up in the mountains."

"We'll make it," Isabel said.

"You sound rather sure."

"Just in my nature to be optimistic, I guess."

"Yes," Vernon said. "It's very annoying. Me, I say too much optimism will get you killed."

Makwa shoved his long arm into the cab. "There."

Jesse slowed down, caught sight of a reflector, then found the mouth of a small dirt road. The turnoff was overgrown with brambles and looked like it hadn't been used in ages. Jesse sat in the middle of the highway with the engine idling. "You got to be kidding?"

"Just turn."

Jesse contemplated opening the door and running for it, then remembered how quick these creatures were. "Dammit," Jesse said and pulled off the highway. The truck bottomed out in the ditch, the tail end making a terrible racket as it ground against the rocky grade. Branches scraped alongside the truck, the sound making Jesse's teeth hurt. The road followed a steep ledge upward—hard, tense going with just the one headlight. The truck bounded along the icy, washed-out ruts, and Jesse took a certain pleasure in hearing the devil men's heads hitting the roof of the camper. The trail—Jesse wouldn't call it a road at this point—zigzagged up the incline, fording the same creek at least a dozen times. After about half an hour the road abruptly ended in a wall of fallen rocks.

"Pull over there," Isabel said. "Beneath the trees."

"What for?"

"Just do it."

Jesse did, and the Belsnickels all scrambled out of the camper, Makwa carrying the Santa sack over his shoulder. Nipi, the one shot in the face, had tied a strip of cloth around his face, and the bleeding seemed to have stopped.

"Shut it off," Isabel said to Jesse.

"What?"

"You're coming with us."

"Like hell I am!"

She reached over, shut the truck off, and took the keys.

"Hey!"

She put the keys in her jacket pocket along with his pistol, got out, and came round to his door. "You don't want to be staying out here by yourself. Trust me."

"No, that ain't fair. We had a deal."

"You're right, it ain't fair. Not any of it. No one knows that better than we do. But we need that truck. And if we leave you here you'll get eaten. Then who's gonna drive us back down this mountain?"

Jesse wasn't big on the being eaten part at all.

She opened his door. "Don't make me drag you."

A distant caw came from somewhere far away. They all looked up.

"We need to hurry," Vernon urged.

"Fuck!" Jesse said, but shut off the light and got out of the truck.

The Belsnickels headed up the heavily wooded slope at a fast jog. Isabel pushed Jesse along after them. "You know what's after us, Jesse. Do your best to keep up. You hear?"

Jesse heard the cawing from somewhere far above them, heard the drumming in his chest, and wondered if he'd ever see Abigail again.

JESSE STUMBLED ALONG, clutching his side. The cold air seared his throat, his thighs burned, yet his fingers were numb from the cold. The hole in his hand throbbed. They'd been marching, climbing, and running up the mountainside for what Jesse guessed to be over half an hour. Isabel waited for him at the top of the trail. The rest of the Belsnickels were no longer in sight, had darted off as though unbothered by the cold and icy ground, three of them not even wearing shoes.

Jesse caught up with Isabel and stopped. He leaned heavily against a tree, gasping for air.

"Jesse," Isabel said. "We gotta keep moving."

Jesse shook his head, spat repeatedly, trying to clear the burn out of his throat. "I can't."

"Just a bit farther."

"Tell you what," he gasped. "Just leave me here for the wolves. I'd actually prefer to be eaten at this point."

She shook her head and managed a half smile. "Don't make me carry you." She grabbed his arm and tugged him along. She might be small but he could feel her strength, felt she really could carry him if she had to.

A lone caw echoed through the trees. It sounded far away, farther down the hill perhaps. Jesse glanced up, but couldn't see anything through the dense spruce limbs.

"I think maybe we've lost 'em," Isabel said.

"You already told me you were an optimist. I don't trust optimists."

They slid down a slight incline into a ravine. She pointed ahead. "There."

Jesse could just make out a cluster of boulders at the base of a cliff.

"Just where are you taking me?"

"You should be fine."

"*Should* be? What does that mean?"

"Just be careful what you say. Don't upset him."

"You mean the Grumpus guy?"

"It's Krampus."

"Just who's this—"

Isabel put a finger up. "Enough." She gave him a tug, led him into a recess between the boulders. They stooped down and entered a narrow cave. She guided him toward a faint flicker of light near the rear of the cavern. They stopped before a shaft. Jesse peered down, wrinkled his nose—it smelled of something dead, of decay, of a caged beast living in its own filth. A howl echoed up the shaft. It didn't sound like man or beast. Jesse took a step back, shaking his head. "No way."

Isabel grabbed his arm. "Jesse, there's no choice here." All the lightness had left her voice, what remained was cold and stern. Her eyes glowed, she looked wicked—like a devil—and Jesse knew now that she was leading him into a den of devils.

Jesse shook his arm loose, gave her a damning look, and started down. The flickering light below illuminated the shaft just enough that he could pick his way down the stones without falling to his death. A moment later, his foot hit the black sooty dirt. He turned and froze.

It was a cavern, not much larger than a standard living room, the floor littered with liquor bottles, bones, animal hides, and charred wood. Wads of blankets and hay nestled in the back recesses. Piles of newspapers and books were stacked nearly to the ceiling. Candles and oil lamps perched on every ledge and nook. There hung a large, yellowing map of the earth with what looked to Jesse like astrological symbols, charts, and lines plotted out in charcoal across the continents. Pictures of Santa Claus covered the soot-stained walls: newspaper clippings, magazine ads, children's books . . . and every single one had Santa's eyes poked out.

Jesse searched for the great Krampus, for the monster that held the Belsnickels in such dread, and almost overlooked the thing sitting cross-legged on the floor. It sat shivering in the ash and dirt, rocking back and forth, clutching the Santa sack. The stumps of two broken horns twisted out from its forehead and strings of matted hair curled down its gaunt, haggard face. It grinned, then snickered, revealing stained teeth and jagged canines. The creature appeared to be starved, so shriveled and frail, like a corpse, like death itself. Jesse could see every vein and tendon beneath its thin, liver-spotted skin. Something twitched behind it; for a second, Jesse thought it was a snake, a hairy snake, but then realized the thing actually had a tail.

It cradled the Santa sack to its bosom like a long-lost child, caressed it with quivering, arthritic fingers. It let out a laugh, then sobbed, then laughed some more, tears rolling from its slanted, filmy eyes. It lolled back its head and cackled wildly and Jesse noticed the thick manacle clamped around its neck. A chain ran from the manacle to the wall; the smooth metal glistening like no ore Jesse had ever seen. Jesse didn't know whether to be terrified or just feel pity for the wretched creature before him.

Isabel dropped down behind Jesse, strolled quickly over to the creature. "Krampus?"

The creature didn't look up.

The Belsnickels stood well away as though afraid to get too close, glancing nervously at one another and back up the shaft as though the wolves might come sliding down the shaft at any second.

"Krampus," Isabel said. "Santa Claus and his beasts . . . they found us. Can't be far behind."

Still the creature ignored her.

She laid a hand on his shoulder, gently shook him. "Krampus," she said softly. "The monsters, they'll be on us soon."

The creature didn't respond, only shivered, rocking back and forth with its sack.

KRAMPUS CLOSED HIS eyes and pressed his face against the sack, inhaled deeply. *Yes, I can still smell it, the fires of Hel, after all these centuries.* The smell reminded him of his mother, of blissful days when the dead danced around her throne and all things were right in the world. *I have suffered long, Mother.* He could see her face, a shimmering mirage floating in Hel's blue flames. The vision slowly evaporated. *No. Mother, don't leave me. Not now.* He shoved his nose deeper into the velvet, sniffed again. He jerked his face away as though bitten. *What is this?* He glared at the sack, his face a knot of hate and confusion. *His foulness.* The sack came into focus and he truly saw it, realized that it wasn't black as it should've been, but a deep dark crimson. *The color of blood.*

Krampus peeled back his lips. "You pervert all you touch," he growled in a deep, rumbling voice and then the horror of it struck him. *How? How had Santa mastered Loki's sack?* Such a feat should never have been possible, as the sack only answered to those of Loki's bloodline. "Such sorcery does not come without a price." His voice rose. "How many did it take? How much blood did you spill for such a prize?" Krampus shoved the sack away, stared at it as though it were evil itself. *How powerful he must be to do this. How his sorcery has grown.* And for the first time Krampus felt doubts. *While I rot and wither, he has grown ever so mighty.* Krampus pulled his knees to his chest, clutched his arms around his legs, and pressed his forehead against his knees. *There is much here to overcome.*

"Krampus?" The voice sounded far away.

"Krampus, they're coming. The monsters are coming. Krampus, please?"

He felt a hand on his shoulder.

Krampus looked up. *It is her. My Isabel of course. The girl with the heart of a lion.* "The monsters?" he said, more to himself.

She nodded.

"What form do they take?"

"We saw at least two creatures, wolves we think. Giant creatures as big as horses. The ravens are leading them to us. We should—"

"So Odin's great beasts live on. Then all of the old gods are not lost." This brought on a smile. "The ravens are Huginn and Muninn, and the wolves, Geri and Freki, mates for life . . . magnificent beasts." He grimaced. "How is it they came to serve Santa's hand?"

"Krampus, we should—"

"Hurry. Yes, I am only too aware. If he finds me, this time he will not leave me for the elements to erase. He will have me torn limb from limb and devoured by his monsters."

She looked anxiously at the sack. "Well?"

"You mean what am I waiting for?"

She picked up the sack and set it down before him. "The key. How long now have you been talking about that key? C'mon . . . grab it and let's get the heck out of here."

It should be just that easy. He should only have to envision the key while holding the sack, command it to seek it out, and the sack would open a doorway—a threshold between the here and the there—and the key would be waiting for him to reach in and take. For it was Loki's sack, after all, a trickster's sack, a sack created for the sole purpose of stealing. The very one Loki used to snatch what he pleased from the other gods. It was certainly never meant to be something as trivial as a gifting sack, to deliver toys to good little boys and girls. *Only Santa Claus could have so twisted its purpose.*

"What is the matter?" Isabel said. "Where is your fire?"

He looked at her, at the Belsnickels against the wall, could feel their mounting distress. *And why* do *I dally when all is so dire? Am I afraid? What if after all this the sack does not hear me? What if I cannot break Santa's spell? Then I will be left here to await my death with Loki's sack to mock me. The final proof that Santa bested me . . . and as such it would be this sack, this steward of my very salvation that would drive me into madness.*

Krampus pulled the sack to himself, opened it, and peered into its smoky depths. He didn't dare insert his hand, aware that the sack would still be open to the last place Santa had used it. *Probably his castle, a storehouse, someplace where he stored the toys he gave out at Christmas. Someplace where his magic would be strong, where my hand might be caught and I might become trapped. This door must be shut.*

He set both hands on the sack, took in a deep breath. "Loki, aid me." He closed his eyes and reached out, tried to find the sack's spirit, to touch it with his own. "See me. Hear your master's voice."

He felt nothing, nothing at all.

Again he searched for its spirit, focused all his will. The cavern and all his surroundings faded from awareness until it was only him and the sack. "It is Krampus, Lord of Yule, bloodline of the great Loki. Recognize your lord."

Nothing.

Krampus gasped and leaned heavily on his hands, breathing deeply and slowly, trying not to succumb to the exertion. He regarded the sack, contemplated its crimson sheen. "Blood," he said, and then laughed. "His spell is bound in blood, and so only blood can break it. Such should be obvious, but alas, I fear my mind is clouded."

He stuck his finger between his teeth and nipped the tip, watched a droplet of blood form. He pulled the sack into his lap and held his finger above it. One single drop fell onto the sack, beaded upon the plush velvet like a red pearl. "Honor my blood," he whispered and slowly rubbed the drop into the fabric.

Nothing happened.

"Loki, hear me." He waited and still nothing, nothing but the sound of his own labored breathing. And when he could stand it no longer, when he felt sure he would indeed go mad, the sack billowed ever so slightly, like a light breeze was blowing from the inside. A faint draft drifted from the opening, smelling of the wilds of Asgard. And he heard his name—faint and faraway.

"Loki?" Krampus asked in a hushed voice. "Loki . . . are you there?" The sack fell silent and stilled. Tears welled in Krampus's eyes. "Loki?" Krampus watched the dark stain of his blood bloom across the fabric, tendrils of swirling blackness swimming and intertwining like a nest of eels until at last the sack changed from crimson to black.

He wiped his eyes and smiled. "One drop. But one drop of my blood is all it took. How many casks of blood did it cost you, Santa Claus?" He laughed. *The sack remembered, because the sack wanted to remember. And the first wrong has been put right, the first of many. And the first drop of blood has been spilled, the first of many . . . the prelude to a flood.*

He swayed, noticed his hands were shaking, and his smile turned into a grimace. He clasped them together, tried to steady himself. He felt strong hands on him, propping him up. Isabel. "Will it work?" she asked. "Will the sack find the key?"

"I am the master of the sack. Let us just hope I have strength enough to command it."

He needed the sack to shift, to seek, to find the key, then open a new door. All of this had been so easy before, when he was a virile, robust spirit, but now, now the sack would exact a heavy toll, as such magic did not come without a price. He looked at his quivering hands, his frail, feeble arms and legs. *I have nothing left to give.* He realized the effort could very well end him. A wry smile crept across his face. *And if you do not retrieve the key? What then?*

He clasped the sack. "I am used up, my old friend. I need your help." He closed his eyes and envisioned the key, held it clearly in his mind. If he had known the location, then he could've steered the sack, made the finding easier, the cost less severe. But he only knew the key, and so the sack would have to search, and it would use his spirit, his energy, to do so.

He felt a charge and the sack pulsed faintly in his hand. He saw the cosmos, then clouds, then forest—shooting over them at the speed of a meteor—then trees, a vast lake, then its depths, finally the muddy lake bottom.

"The key . . . I see it!" Krampus cried, and opened his eyes. He swooned and slumped in Isabel's arms. The cave slipped in and out of focus as he fought to hold on to consciousness. He knew if he passed out now he wouldn't come back, not in time.

He reached for the sack, got his fingers around the mouth, and shoved in his hand. His hand entered water, cold water. He pushed deeper until his whole arm was in the bag. His fingers found the lake bed, clawed the mud and clay, pawing, digging, trying to locate the key. His hand bumped something rigid. He clutched the object and slid his arm from the sack.

His arm and hand were soaking wet. He opened his palm and there, among the mud and pebbles . . . a key. Krampus wiped away the clay, revealing the same ancient Dwarven symbols as those on the manacle. The key wasn't even tarnished; it, like the hated chain about his neck, was cast from healing ores, lost smithing arts of the Dwarven kingdom, metals that mended themselves. No matter how long one tried to cut through them, or grind them away, they always stayed whole. And none could attest to their powers more than he.

He kissed the key. "My freedom."

He clasped the manacle in one hand, found the lock, and tried to insert the key. His hand shook so badly that he fumbled and the key fell from his fingers.

"Here," Isabel said, and picked up the key. "Let me."

"*No!*" he cried, then softer. "I have waited five hundred years for this. Have dreamed of this moment ten thousand times. *I must be the one.*"

He took the key from her, hesitated, trying to steady himself as his vision blurred. He found the lock, inserted the key, and turned it. There came a simple, unremarkable click and the manacle popped open. Five hundred years of imprisonment ended with a simple click. He pulled it from around his neck, gave it a final, spiteful look, and chucked it to the dirt.

He looked around the cave, his prison, at the blackened walls that held him, at the maps he'd used to track Santa, at the thousand pictures of Santa Claus, at the filth, the bones, until his eyes fell on the Belsnickels. He smiled at them. "I am free," he said hoarsely. "*I am free.*" Then his eyes rolled up in his head and darkness took him.

"IS HE DEAD?" Vernon asked, sounding hopeful.

"I don't think so," Isabel said.

"No," Makwa added with absolute conviction.

"No?" Vernon's shoulders slumped. "No, of course not. Couldn't be that easy."

Krampus crumpled into a lifeless ball. Isabel shook him gently. He didn't respond. The creature looked dead to Jesse, more than dead, like something that had been in the ground a couple of months.

Isabel hopped to her feet, jumped over to a pile of tattered blankets, yanked one out, and brought it over to where Krampus lay. "What are you guys waiting for? Let's get him out of here." The three Shawnee leapt into action, wrapping Krampus in the blanket. Makwa hefted the creature up onto his shoulder and headed for the shaft.

Vernon shifted through a pile of tools, dug out two shotgun shells. "Is this all we have left?" No one seemed to have an answer. "Damn, I told all of you we needed something around here besides bows and arrows. Does anyone ever listen to me? Wait, I'll answer that. No, no they don't."

Isabel grabbed the velvet sack, pushed Jesse toward the shaft. "Time to skedaddle."

"Any idea what we're doing?" Vernon asked. "I mean, is there any sort of plan here?"

No one answered him.

"Didn't think so," Vernon sighed, pocketed the shells, and clambered up after them.

THE STARS GREETED Jesse as he crawled out from the boulders. The night had cleared and the moon cast shadows across the snow.

"I'm afraid those birds will have no problem spotting us now," Vernon said.

They skirted the edge of a large clearing and a wide expanse of sky opened up above them. "Stop," called a weak, raspy voice. Krampus opened his eyes; they were glassy like those of a man after a two-day drunk. "Mani." He sucked in a deep breath, lifted a shaky hand toward the moon as though he might be able to reach it, to caress it. "So sweet. So . . . sweet."

"Let's go," Isabel hissed.

"No . . . a moment. I need her magic." He lifted his chin, bathing in the moonbeam.

The Belsnickels shifted uneasily and searched the forest in every direction.

A cawing came from far overhead and Vernon started.

"We have been found," Makwa said.

"Yes." Krampus nodded.

Vernon pointed the shotgun skyward.

"Save the shells," Isabel said. "That gun don't have that kinda range."

Another caw and a howl came in answer, echoed up from the valley below, a long, deep howl, followed by another. Jesse couldn't gauge the distance.

"Freki and his mate, Geri," Krampus said with obvious affection. He smiled. "Sounds like they are on the hunt."

Vernon gave him a severe look. "They *are* on the hunt . . . they are hunting us, you idjit."

"Krampus," Isabel said. "We must—"

"Go," Krampus finished. "Yes." His eyes never left the moon. He smiled as tears slid down his cheeks. He reached for it one more time, then his arm dropped and his eyes again fell shut.

"Go!" Isabel said, and pushed the big Shawnee forward, and they sprinted away.

JESSE CAUGHT A glint of moonlight off chrome ahead; found the Belsnickels waiting for him and Isabel near the rear of his truck, alert and scanning the rocks and trees. The Shawnee all had their spears and knives at the ready.

Jesse had kept up better this time, the burden of Krampus slowing them all down. He fell against the side of his truck, gasping, trying to suck in enough oxygen to keep from fainting. He was spent, exhausted, covered in mud from a nasty fall, and desperately wanting a smoke. Jesse saw Krampus in the back of the camper. He lay wrapped in the blanket, curled up around the velvet sack, huddled in the fetal position, once again looking dead to the world.

Vernon came around the truck, carrying the old shotgun. "Hurry," he said, pointing upward. "They're leading them right to us."

Jesse searched the night sky, saw no sign of the ravens, but heard them cawing from somewhere high above.

Isabel tossed Jesse the keys and they climbed into the cab while the rest of them piled into the camper. The truck started on the second try and they were on their way, bouncing back down the mountain.

Jesse rode the gears to avoid burning out his brakes. The gas gauge flickered on and off and he bit his lip, trying not to think about what would happen if they ran out of gas now. He kept his eyes on the ruts, straining to see by the remaining headlight what lay ahead, expecting to find the huge beasts awaiting them around each and every turn. None of them spoke, all searching the surrounding trees, all too aware that they'd taken too long, that there was no way they'd reach the high-way before the wolves caught up with them.

As they neared the bottom of the mountain, the road began to level out, to widen a bit, and the going became smoother, faster. It was here that Jesse allowed himself to hope that maybe, just this once, God would cut him a break, allow them to reach the highway before the wolves found them. And, of course, as the joke always seemed to be on him, this was exactly when the wolves appeared.

"They're here. I feel them," Isabel said, her eyes wide. A second later they cleared a bend and there they stood, blocking the road not a hun-dred yards down the trail, big as horses, heads hung low, eyes glinting in the glow of the headlight. Jesse hit the brakes and slid to a stop.

"Turn around!" Vernon cried. "Go back!"

There is no going back, Jesse thought. No other way out. Even if there was, there'd be no turning around, not on this narrow lane.

The two wolves started forward at a stiff-legged trot.

"Oh, dear God," Vernon said. "We're going to be eaten alive."

"No," Jesse said under his breath. "Not me. Got too much business needing taking care of." He snatched the seat belt, drew it across his chest, and clicked it into place.

Isabel glanced at him. "What're you doing?"

"Going to go see Abigail." He stomped on the gas, the truck jumped forward.

Isabel braced herself against the dashboard as the truck picked up speed. "You're gonna get us killed!"

"Most likely."

The speedometer climbed from ten to twenty, then thirty, but that was all Jesse could handle on the narrow, rocky road without careening into a tree or down the steep ravine on their right. The wolves broke into a run, coming at them head-on. Jesse knew the chances of walking away from a head-on collision with such beasts were slim to none, hoped these monsters understood that as well. In the camper, Vernon and the Shawnee did their best to hang on, to keep Krampus from injury as the truck jostled them about. Vernon screamed at Jesse to stop, but Jesse didn't, he drove headlong toward the wolves, fighting to keep the truck on the path.

At the last possible instant, the wolves leapt from the road and up onto the embankment. Jesse lost sight of them as he struggled to make the curve, his right-side tires jouncing along the crumbling lip of the ravine. The truck tilted dangerously toward the ledge. Jesse thought they were goners, when the old Ford managed to regain traction and hold the road.

He no sooner had all four wheels onto level ground when a crash and a tremendous jolt rocked the truck. The back roof of the camper caved in as one of the wolves tore through the thin aluminum with its front paws. The weight of the beast bottomed out the rear shocks and the tail end thumped against the deep ruts, slowing the pickup considerably. The wolf hung on, snarling and snapping with its enormous jaws, trying to get to Krampus and the sack. Makwa kicked one of the garbage bags of video games into its face. It chomped into the bag, slinging it back and forth, tearing it apart, sending game consoles bouncing down the trail. Vernon swung the shotgun around at the beast, the truck hit a rut, and the gun bounced upward, going off with a loud blast, completely missing the wolf and blowing a hole through the top of the camper. The tailgate snapped beneath the weight of the wolf and the beast fell away, tumbling down the road.

The second wolf, the larger one, leapt over its mate and charged after them, quickly overtaking them. *"Oh, Christ!"* Jesse cried. There was no place to go, it had them. But the Shawnee were prepared this time. All three held their spears at ready and when the wolf leapt for the truck, they threw their weight behind their weapons, driving the spearheads deep into the wolf's chest. There came a horrible yowl, followed by a jolt as the wolf hit the truck. The wolf made a vain effort to scramble up into the truck bed, then collapsed, fell back onto the road, tumbled toward the ravine and disappeared over the ledge. Jesse heard splintering branches, another yowl, and that was all.

The pickup hit a steep grade. Jesse tapped the brakes, trying to keep control as the truck fishtailed back and forth. The left-side tires caught the ditch, causing the side of the truck to rake along the embankment; the truck came to a grinding halt and stalled.

The smaller wolf trotted into view about fifty yards back up the bend, but it wasn't looking at them, it peered over the ledge where its mate had fallen. It took one glance at them, then left the road, heading down into the ravine.

"What's it doing?" Isabel asked.

Jesse had no idea, but so long as it wasn't coming after them he didn't care.

"Whatever are you waiting for?" Vernon cried. "Go!"

Jesse twisted the key, the engine turned over, and the truck started up. Jesse eased on the gas, and the pickup slowly pulled out of the ditch and back onto the road.

They reached the highway about ten minutes later and heard a long howl coming from the hills behind them. Jesse pulled out onto the asphalt and sped away, heading south, heading away from the Santa man and his monsters.

PART II

KRAMPUS

Chapter Six

HEL

The wolf's howl echoed inside Krampus's head. *So much despair, so much pain.* His eyes flittered open. There came another howl, then another. He felt the forlorn cry in his heart, his soul. *I am not dreaming. One of them is dying. How did this happen?*

He caught the first signs of morning light and fought to keep his eyes open. *Too long I have been without dawn's sweet kiss.* Trees flew past in a blur; the cold wind buffeted the shredded canopy. *I am flying.* He inhaled deeply, felt some vestige of strength returning to him, the moon's rays, the stars, and forest air all like food for his starving soul.

"Why are you turning?" Isabel asked the man steering the carriage. "Where are you going?" Krampus didn't know the man, but assumed he was a prisoner, that the Belsnickels needed him.

"Can't stay on the highway," the man said. "Not after that fuckup last night. Too many folks are gonna be out looking for me, for this truck. Have to steer clear of the main roads."

"But we need to get far away from here . . . from those wolves, from whatever else might be after us."

"Look, you ought to know that them wolves aren't the only monsters after me. I got the General and his bunch looking to shoot me first chance they get. They'll kill me . . . kill you . . . and most certainly that ugly monster of yours. They got eyes everywhere. We keep heading down this highway in daylight and we won't make it out of the county. You understand?"

Isabel was silent.

"Fuck, and we gotta get some gas. Have to be running on fumes at this point. Any of you got any cash?"

"Yeah," she answered. "But it's back in the cave."

"What? You mean the cave we just left?"

"Uh-huh."

"Well, about how much good do you think that's gonna do us?"

More silence.

Krampus thought the man showed a lot of backbone, especially in the face of all that was going on, thought he might make a good Belsnickel. And he would need as many as he could sustain, because there'd be no telling what creatures Santa might send after them next. *I will have to claim him.* His eyes closed. He took in a deep breath. *But not now. It would be too much now. Later . . . perhaps when I am stronger.* His eyes shut and he drifted away into dreams of soaring through the clouds.

JESSE HEADED UP a gravel road; it was an old mining road and he felt pretty sure no one would be out this way. If he could find some shelter, it'd be a good place to hole up until dark, until they could get some gas and maybe by then he'd have figured out a way to escape this group of freaks.

Isabel rolled down her window, leaned out looking skyward. "Them birds is still following us."

Jesse hit the brakes, slid to a stop on the gray gravel.

"Whatcha doing?" Isabel asked.

"Taking care of something." Jesse unclipped his seat belt, hopped out of the truck, and headed across the road toward a clearing.

"Hey," Isabel called. "We can't stop here." She popped open her door and came after him. "We gotta keep moving."

Jesse shielded his eyes with his hand and searched for the birds, spotted both of them circling above in the cool early-morning light.

The Belsnickels slid out of the camper, looked from Jesse to Isabel.

"We need to get him back in the truck," Isabel said.

Makwa walked over and grabbed Jesse by the arm, gave him a tug back toward the pickup.

Jesse locked eyes with the big Shawnee. "I ain't running off." Jesse jerked his arm free and walked to the rear of the pickup. He stared at his father's truck, at the streaks of blood and clumps of fur stuck to the twisted aluminum of the shattered camper shell. The tailgate was gone altogether and the rear bumper all but dragged on the road.

Jesse set a knee on the truck bed and leaned in. The Krampus creature lay wrapped in the blanket near the cab, cradling his velvet sack. He was looking out the side window, up into the sky, his eyes far away and a half-smile on his face, like a drunk in a whorehouse. Jesse noticed his guitar, the big crack along the body and the missing frets. *"Damn,"* he whispered. His mother and father had given it to him for his twelfth birthday, and despite everything else that had happened, seeing it cracked like that still hit him hard. *Just one more thing to feel bad about . . . that's all.* Jesse pushed it aside, rolled the sleeping bag over to get at his father's hunting rifle. He grabbed it and the tackle box, slid them out.

Vernon caught the barrel, keeping it pointed at the dirt. "What the hell are you doing?"

"Let go."

"I'm not about to."

"Then we'll just sit here until them wolves come. Until that Santa fella tracks us down."

"Let him have it."

They both turned and found Krampus leaning against the side of the camper, staring up at the circling birds. Jesse noticed that the Krampus creature looked a touch better, closer now to a fresh cadaver, one that had only been in the ground say a week or so as opposed to a couple of months.

"Krampus, no," Vernon said. "That's a rifle . . . a gun. Do you know what—"

"I know what a rifle is," Krampus said in a voice deep and full of gravel.

"Well, then why in Hell would you let him have one? He'll just shoot us all!"

Krampus continued to stare up at the ravens, an odd, sad look in his eyes. "It must be done."

"What? No, that's a very bad idea. You can't trust a man like—"

"Give him the gun. That is a command."

Vernon made a face as though he'd sat on a tack, but relinquished hold on the rifle.

Jesse propped the rifle on his knee, flipped open the tackle box, and dug about until he found a carton of rounds. He pressed fifteen rounds into the magazine, cocked the lever, seating a bullet in the chamber, then crossed the road into the clearing.

He spotted the ravens, guessed they were about two hundred feet overhead, knew it would be an easy shot with them being so large, at least with this rifle. You handle a gun long enough and it becomes an extension of yourself, and Jesse had spent half his life with the old Henry .22. He'd once shot a bumblebee right out of the air with it. He seated the rifle against his shoulder, sighted one of the ravens, led the aim to compensate for distance, and fired. The gun kicked like a pat from an old friend, and a blast of feathers flittered away. It was a clean kill and the raven dropped from the sky. The remaining raven let out a piercing cry and began to flap furiously away, but Jesse already had a bead on it. He pulled the trigger twice in quick succession, the first shot missed but the second one caught the big bird in the wing, sending it spiraling earthward in a rain of feathers.

Jesse cocked another round into the chamber, turned, and leveled the gun on Krampus. "Get away from my truck. All of you."

The Belsnickels froze, all their eyes locked on Jesse. But Krampus didn't give him so much as a glance, only watched the big birds plummet earthward. One raven landed in the clearing, the other about fifty yards up the road. "Makwa, bring me the birds."

Makwa kept staring at Jesse, clenching and unclenching his powerful hands. Jesse could see the big Shawnee intended to tear him apart.

"Makwa?"

The Shawnee stiffened.

"It is a command."

Makwa gave Jesse one last look, one that promised a terrible death, then sprinted away up the road.

Jesse jabbed the gun at Krampus. "Get your stupid sack and get out of my truck. I'm not gonna say it twice."

The four remaining Belsnickels began to spread out, to encircle Jesse. Jesse raised the gun to his shoulder. "One more step and I will blow his head off. Go on, goddammit. I dare you."

"Leave him be," Krampus said calmly, his tone almost bored, even distracted, still looking at the birds. "Back away, that is a command."

The Belsnickels stopped, took a step back, and just stood there exchanging confused looks.

"Now get out of my truck," Jesse repeated.

"I thought you said you weren't going to say it twice?"

"Well, I sure as heck ain't gonna say it three times," Jesse growled. "That's for certain."

Krampus turned his face to Jesse and smiled. "We need your help."

"Don't care."

"From what I have heard you seem to have a lot of enemies."

"That don't concern you."

"Perhaps you need our help?" Krampus said. "Perhaps there are ways we can help each other."

"Don't think so."

"You have seen my Belsnickels at play. You know what they are capable of. What if they were to be at your command? If there is blood that needs to be spilt, they are very capable."

Jesse started to shake his head, then stopped, looked at the devil creatures, the Belsnickels, at their deadly fingernails, their terrifying orange eyes, thought about the way they'd attacked his truck, how quick and strong they were, how easily they'd taken out Chet and killed Lynyrd. *Stealthy night creatures . . . they could cut the General's boys down before they even knew they were there.* He knew that after the way things went down last night, the General would've already served his death warrant. He'd heard Chet screaming that it was a setup, no doubt that's how they'd all see it, and no amount of explaining on his part would ever change that. He also knew that the General would put a price on his head, offer a reward to anyone who'd report his whereabouts, would enlist every resource to track him down. But most of all, the General had made it clear that if Jesse ever crossed him, he'd hurt Abigail, would put her in a box. Jesse felt sure they'd probably already nabbed her, most likely taken her over to the compound. He couldn't help thinking about how scared she must be.

"Some bad folks is after my daughter," Jesse said. "I need to make sure she's safe."

Krampus nodded. "I understand."

"There's more to it than that. It's complicated. Need to make sure they won't ever hurt her again."

"Dead men cannot hurt anyone." And Krampus smiled.

Jesse thought about how good his odds would be if he showed up at the General's compound alone—his old hunting rifle against a dozen or more heavily armed men, men with automatic weapons.

"Punishing the wicked is something I'm very good at. We can cut them down . . . make them disappear." Krampus pointed into the camper, at the velvet sack.

"What do you mean?"

"I mean I am the sack's master. I can command it to open to any place I wish . . . of this world or of others. We can send your friends to the bottom of the ocean, into the realm of the dead if you so prefer." Krampus's smile turned sinister.

Jesse tried to get his mind around this. He'd not considered what would happen if you put something back into the sack, of where it might end up. He found the thought disturbing, but if it were true, if any of what this creature promised were true, it would sure simplify things, might even keep him out of prison. Only how did one go about trusting a devil? He gave Krampus a hard look.

"How can you trust me?"

Jesse was startled by how easily Krampus read him.

"You have already saved my life once. Why would I not help you?"

Jesse realized it all came down to risk. The odds of him successfully saving his daughter on his own against the odds that this creature, this devil, would truly come through for him. *Maybe this is an opportunity. Maybe it's at least worth a shot.*

Makwa returned, holding both birds by the neck. He gave Jesse a dark look. One of the ravens still lived and Krampus reached for it. Jesse had known the birds were large, much bigger than any raven he'd ever seen, but seeing it up close he was amazed. They were at least as large as a vulture or eagle. The bird struggled in Krampus's grasp, cawed, and tried to bite and peck him.

"Huginn," Krampus cooed softly to the bird. "Huginn, be brave." Krampus leaned his head and whispered softly, soothingly into its ear. The bird began to calm. Krampus cradled it, gently stroking its black feathers. The bird's breathing slowed and its eyes fell shut. Krampus kissed the top of its head. "It grieves me so to see you thus. You and your brother have both served Odin well."

He stroked the raven's beak, its head. It fluffed its feathers and leaned against his chest, and then Krampus slipped his fingers around its neck and gave a quick, hard twist. Jesse heard a snap and the bird fell still. Krampus hugged the bird and Jesse could see the heartbreak upon his face.

"So few of the ancient ones still live," Krampus said, almost to himself. "And now we have two less." His lips began to tremble. "This deed shall rest on your hands, Santa Claus. One more murder to add to your list, one more death to be avenged." Krampus kissed the top of the raven's head once more, then bit into the bird's skull.

"Oh, Jesus," Jesse said and took a step back.

Krampus chewed loudly, grinding the bones between his teeth. He swallowed and looked skyward. "Thank you, Odin. Thank you for this great gift . . . for this bounty of your blood in my time of need." He wiped his lips and took another bite, then another and another, as the raven's blood spilled down his chin and chest.

Jesse glanced about to see if the Belsnickels were as appalled as he was, but they acted as though nothing unusual was going on. Krampus ate not just the meat and guts of the bird, but also the beak, bones, and talons. He slipped off the tailgate, dropped to the ground, and picked up the other bird, sitting upon his haunches, gnawing and chewing until he'd consumed every feather.

The first rays of morning sun broke over the mountain, glistening off the snow. Krampus set back his head and basked in the sunlight. He let out a long, deep groan and Jesse noticed the change—the creature's skin gaining pigment right before his eyes, darkening from an almost lucent gray toward black. His flesh and bones appeared to be gaining substance.

Krampus grabbed hold of the bumper and pulled himself up onto unsteady feet, bracing himself against the truck. It was apparent that he was still far from health, but he was a much more formidable beast than the creature that'd been huddled in the blanket. He looked at Jesse, at the gun as though for the first time. "What were we discussing?"

"How you could help me get rid of some trash."

Krampus smiled, wiped his hand down his face, through his chin hairs, looked at the blood smeared across his fingers, offered the hand to Jesse. "There is no stronger pact than one sealed with blood."

Jesse stared at the blood. "What do you need me to do?"

"I need a place to hide away. A place where I can heal, can prepare. A face that is not pitch, eyes that do not glow to fetch us a few needed items. That is all."

"And for that you'll help me get my daughter? Will kill them men that took her?"

Krampus's eyes gleamed. "It has been long since I was terrible. I miss it dearly. It will be a great treat to see the fear in their eyes, to hear them beg for their lives, to feast on their blood and death cries."

"Feast on their death cries," Jesse said as though tasting the word. "I like the sound of that." He leaned the rifle against the truck, walked over, and took Krampus's extended hand.

Jesse was making a pact with the devil and he didn't mind one bit.

DILLARD'S CELL PHONE buzzed across the dashboard of his Suburban. He shoved his coffee into the cup holder, snatched up the phone, looked at the name of the incoming call, and contemplated not answering. It was the General, again, third time in the past hour. It buzzed again, again, then again. Dillard grimaced and flipped his phone open.

"What's the word?" the General asked, his voice raw and scratchy like he'd been doing a lot of yelling.

Dillard switched the phone to his left hand and turned off onto Coal River Road. "The word?"

"Yeah, what's the *fucking* word?"

There wasn't any word. Jesse and that piece-of-shit truck of his had disappeared. There were several hundred coal roads crisscrossing the mountains around Goodhope and almost as many old mining roads, most of which weren't on any maps. Even with all the General's crew out driving around they didn't have the manpower to search half of them. *Shit,* Dillard thought, *even if I had the entire state's police force it'd still take over a week.* Problem was, the General didn't want to hear that. "Noel's north, combing the hills around Elk Run right now. I put the word out county-wide to the folks I know I can count on. Let them know it's a personal matter between me and Jesse. They promised to keep an eye out."

"What about the troopers?"

"Have to be careful about them. Hard to get too many police outside the regulars involved without answering a bunch of questions. Things could get sticky if Jesse gets picked up by the sheriff. Just no telling what he might say, and the last thing we need is Sheriff Wright nosing around."

"As long as we got his little girl, he's gonna keep his mouth shut tight."

"Well, yeah, maybe. That being the case and all, it's hard for me to understand why he was in on that shit last night. Makes me believe someone put him up to it. I got a nagging suspicion this is about them Charleston boys we took care of. That they're playing Jesse to get back at us."

"There's a lot here I don't like," the General spat. "Don't like one bit. But one thing you can count on, I'm sure as hell gonna get to the bottom of it."

That makes two of us, Dillard thought. He was still trying to sort out just what had gone down last night. One second he'd been fiddling with the radio, the next there were gunshots and Chet running toward him screaming his head off. Those men, whoever they were, had killed Lynyrd . . . and with a fucking spear no less, stole the goods, and got clean away. They'd killed a Boggs. And the worst of it was it had happened right from under his damn nose. Now, on top of everything else, he had a murder to cover up. But the thing that bothered Dillard the most was that strange man, the one dressed up like Santa Claus. He'd hit him, slammed into him straight on. The car's crumpled front end proved it. Dillard couldn't remember exactly what happened after that. He rubbed the raw lump on his forehead; that damn airbag had just about knocked him out. Still, he'd never found a trace of the man. It was as though he'd imagined it. *But he was real. I know what I saw.*

"And about Lynyrd?" the General asked.

"Up to you."

The General didn't answer.

"Best not to take any chances," Dillard suggested. "Should get rid of *all* the evidence."

"Just can't stand the thought of dumping his body like that. Known that boy since he was a baby."

"Best to take him where I took the others."

"Yeah, I know it. Just really bothers me, that's all."

"You want to try and find a secluded spot somewhere up on your land?"

"No, don't bother me that much. Too risky."

"How about his sister? Think she'll raise a stink?"

"Naw," the General said. "Lynyrd's gone more than he's not. Gonna take a long time for anyone to notice."

They both fell silent. The snow began to pick up and Dillard clicked his wipers up. "Where's Jesse's little girl at?" the General asked. "She still over your place?"

"She's at her grandmother's."

"You think that's smart?"

"I plan on picking her up sometime this morning. Keeping her close."

"I'd like you to bring her on over here when you get the chance."

Dillard's grip tightened on the wheel. "Don't think that's such a good idea."

"Relax, I ain't gonna do nothing to her. What kind of a man do you think I am? Just want to make sure Jesse can't nab her."

"So your plan is to keep Abigail at the compound? Really? You're kidding me, right? Why, her mother would bring the devil down on both of us."

"Who am I talking to? Since when does Dillard Deaton let a woman, any woman, tell him how to run his business? I think Linda's pretty eyes are getting the better of you."

"Things are gonna be different with Linda."

The General snorted and Dillard prickled. "You're fooling yourself," the General said. "You mark my word, first time she gives you lip, you'll straighten her out, just like Ellen. See if you don't."

No, Dillard thought. He pulled off the highway onto the side of the road, sat there with the engine idling. *Not this time. I'm done hurting the folks I love. Devil's not getting the best of me, not ever again. Things is gonna work out with Linda. Gonna see to it.*

"Dillard, hello? Fuck, you still there?"

"Do you want to catch Jesse or babysit?"

"What?"

"Jesse might be up in the hills, might be in Charleston, hell, might be in goddamn Mexico for all we know. But one thing I'm sure of is at some point he's gonna come back around looking to get his daughter. Might be today, tomorrow, might be two weeks or even two months from now. You plan on keeping Abigail locked up in your office for two months?"

The General didn't answer.

"Abigail's the best chance we got of catching Jesse. If she's at the compound, he ain't gonna go for it. That boy might be stupid, but he ain't that stupid. But if she's here, at my place, he just might try something. And when he does, I'll get him. He won't make it out of Goodhope. I can tell you that."

"Yeah, well, what about them boys he's working with? What if they show up with him?"

"We're talking about Jesse here. He ain't calling the shots. Why would them Charleston boys risk their necks for his daughter? They got what they want. I wouldn't be the least surprised if they hadn't already poked Jesse full of holes and left him in a ditch somewhere."

"*I hope to hell not!*" the General shouted. "I want that boy alive. Gonna feed him his own pecker. Gonna douse his head in motor oil and set it on fire. Sure as shit I am! He's gonna talk, goddammit! Gonna tell me who these coons are he's been running with." The General's voice kept rising. "Gonna fucking cook them fucks alive! All of them! Let me tell you—"

Dillard pulled the phone away from his ear, sat it on the dashboard, and took another sip of coffee. The General sounded like an angry hornet trapped in a jar.

Here we go again, Dillard thought and wondered how jacked up the man was. He knew the General had a taste for amphetamines, but he was beginning to suspect that taste might be turning into a habit. Seems his behavior was becoming more and more erratic of late, paranoid, losing control of his temper at the drop of a hat, but worst of all he was getting sloppy.

Dillard rubbed the spot where the airbag had hit him, felt a headache coming on. Erratic and sloppy didn't sit well with him. He preferred things to be nice and tidy, like his Tupperware, all the bowls on one shelf, all the lids in the drawer below, each lid corresponding to the color of the matching bowl. But now, thanks to Jesse, nothing was nice and tidy, not anymore. The General was talking crazy and Dillard felt he was watching the man go down and didn't care much for the notion of going down with him. More and more, he found himself wishing he could wash his hands of all of it, just walk away. Only thing was, you didn't just walk away from the General, not unless you intended to walk all the way to Mexico. Even then there were no guarantees, not with Sampson Boggs, because no one carried a grudge like that man. Of course, there was another way. *It would sure be a shame if the General were to disappear.*

When the volume dropped a notch, Dillard placed the phone back to his ear.

"—You know what I'm fucking saying?" the General said. "Do you?"

"We'll get him. Just let me do my job."

"I'm not fucking around, Dillard. No one steals from me. No one kills a Boggs and lives to tell about it. I'm gonna see that boy dead. I don't care if it takes me the rest of my life to do it."

The connection ended and Dillard closed his phone. He pulled out, turned around, heading back up Route 3 toward Linda's mother's house. He didn't much like the way the General was acting, thought it might be prudent to go ahead and get Abigail now and bring her back to his place.

He let out a long sigh. *Well, one way or another Jesse's gonna be out of the picture. That should sure sweeten things up with Linda.*

LINDA HEARD THE front door open, sat down her coffee, and peered out from the kitchen. Dillard came in carrying Abigail in one arm. She was wrapped in her blanket, still in her pajamas, fast asleep against his chest.

Linda started to ask what on earth he was doing with Abigail at this hour in the morning, when another question hit her: had something happened to her mother?

Dillard put a finger to his lips, handed Abigail off to Linda. Abigail mumbled irritably, clutched her doll, and fell back asleep.

"Dillard," Linda whispered. "What?"

"Put her to bed. I'll explain."

Linda didn't care at all for the look on Dillard's face. She took Abigail to her room, tucked her in, and returned quickly. She found Dillard sitting at the table, warming his hands around a steaming cup of coffee.

"What's happened?"

Dillard tapped the chair next to him. "Have a seat, Linda. We need to talk."

The sternness of his voice caught her off guard. "Okay . . . sure." She sat down, braced herself, then noticed that he had her keys.

"Dillard, honey, you're scaring me. What's going on?"

"It's Jesse."

"Jesse?" This threw her for a moment. "Oh . . . oh, no. What's he gone and done now?"

"He threatened to kill you and Abigail."

"*What?*" She stood back up. "What are you talking about?"

Dillard took a sip of his coffee. "Jesse went on a rampage last night."

"Jesse? No. Is he all right? What happened? Dillard, is he okay?"

"It's not him you should be so worried about," Dillard said, a bite to his voice. "Seen this too many times before. Bitter split-ups leading to folks doing the worst sort of things to one another."

"Dillard, just tell me what happened."

"Jesse didn't take the news real good."

"What news? Dillard, what are—"

"About us getting married and all."

Linda sat back down. "Wait. How did he find out . . . you *told* him?"

Dillard looked at her as though she were a child, she hated that look. "Dillard . . . no! You weren't supposed to do that." She struggled to keep her temper in check. "You had no right. That was just between us." She glared at him. "Why, we haven't even firmed anything up. It wasn't your place to—"

He clamped a hand over her wrist. His eyes grew hard, his mouth tight. "It needed to be done, so I done it."

She started to respond then caught the look in his eye: a deep coldness, it scared her. His grip tightened. "Dillard, let go. You're hurting me." She pried his fingers loose and pulled her arm away. "Now, please tell me what happened."

He squeezed his eyes shut, inhaled deeply; when he reopened them he seemed back to himself. "Jesse met up with Chet and Lynyrd last night looking to do some work for the General. They said he seemed desperate and agitated, thought he might be jacked up on something. They told him the General was done with him and to go look for work someplace else. Well, Jesse didn't take that so well. Got on a rant cussing the General, cussing me, you, Jesus, and everyone else in Creation. When Chet and Lynyrd tried to calm him down he pulled out his gun, threatened to shoot them. Said he'd see you and Abigail dead before he'd let another man have you. Fired a few shots into the air, got in his truck, and drove off."

Linda covered her mouth.

"Chet called me last night and warned me. I've been up all night trying to track Jesse down."

"Oh, God." Linda planted both hands on the table to steady herself.

"Linda, this ain't the Jesse you once knew. He's upset, unstable. There's just no telling what he might do."

Linda shook her head, couldn't make herself believe any of it. Jesse had done a lot of crazy things, but he'd never raised so much as a finger to her or Abigail—or to anyone that she could recall, for that matter.

"Linda, I need you to help me out here. Need to know I can count on you."

She nodded quickly. "Of course, I'll do whatever I can. What—"

"I need you to stay in the house until I tell you otherwise. Can you do that?"

No, she thought. *I need to find Jesse. Need to talk to him.*

"I need to find Jesse before someone gets hurt," Dillard continued. "Before Jesse hurts himself, hurts you or the little girl of yours. Right now, I'm betting Jesse's in his truck somewhere sleeping off a bad drunk. I'd like to catch him before he gets his blood up again. Bring him in and let him cool off in a cell for a few days. Maybe that way no one will get hurt. Be a lot easier on me if I know you and Abigail are right here."

"Dillard, there's no need to worry about us. Jesse was just upset. I promise you he's full of talk, that's all. Jesse would never hurt Abi. *Never.*"

"Maybe, maybe not. But can you tell me he wouldn't grab Abigail and run off if he had the chance? Are you absolutely sure on that?"

Linda started to answer, then didn't, because she couldn't say for sure. "Just don't see why—"

Dillard was looking at her that way again, like she didn't know how to tie her own shoes. "Here, let me spell it out. I can't do my job if I'm worrying and wondering where you and Abigail might be." She could hear the growing aggravation in his voice. "You can't stay at your mother's, because she's too far out of town. Need you right here, where I can keep a close eye on you. Okay? You think you can do me that one little favor?"

She took a deep breath and tried to let it go. *He's upset, been up all night. Just worried about Abi and me. That's all, just let it go for now.* "Okay," Linda said. "Okay."

"Good." Dillard stood, tugged on his jacket, and headed for the door. "Just sit tight. Noel's casing the neighborhood, he'll have his eye on things till I'm back. So long as you stay put, all will be just fine."

He left the house, locking the door behind him. It wasn't until he'd driven off that Linda realized he'd taken her keys with him. She rubbed her wrist where he'd grabbed her, couldn't stop thinking about the way his eyes had gone so cold. She found herself wondering if maybe she'd rushed into things, if his nice house and new car had made it too easy to ignore the rumors about his first wife.

JESSE CAUGHT SIGHT of a short steeple peeking up above a thicket of trees and brush, and slowed down. He found a driveway—all but swallowed by bushes—and turned off the gravel road. Brambles and saplings scraped the side of the truck as he drove down a long drive to a small church. The structure had a slight lean to it, as though one more hard wind would see it over. The boards and siding were stripped of paint and weathered pale gray. A large wooden cross lay splintered upon the front steps, apparently having tumbled from its perch atop the steeple. The door and windows were boarded up, and Jesse found no sign that anyone had visited the place in ages.

They were well clear of the road, but Jesse didn't want to take any chances, so he pulled all the way behind the church, parking beneath a sprawling oak. He cut off the engine and got out. Isabel did the same and they came around as the Belsnickels helped Krampus from the camper. Krampus slung the sack over his shoulder and slid out. His skin and hair were even darker now, a true deep black, almost pitch, and his horns appeared to be growing back. He still had a slight hobble to his walk, but Jesse found it hard to believe that this was the same wretched creature he'd first seen in the cave.

A wire fence ran just the other side of the oak; three cows stood at the wire watching them with bored, unimpressed faces.

Krampus took a deep breath, seemed to inhale everything around him. "It is good to be alive this day."

Vernon rolled his eyes.

Krampus laughed, clapped Vernon on the back. "Open your soul my dear Vernon, and let Mother Earth sing you her song." Krampus's voice sounded stronger, fuller, deep and lyrical like a bass cello.

Jesse plucked a branch full of gray, withered leaves up out of the snow and headed back toward the road.

"Where you going?" Isabel asked.

"Snipe hunting."

"Snipe hunting? What's a snipe?"

Jesse looked at her as though she must be kidding. "Really?"

She frowned. "What? What is it?"

Jesse let out a snort.

Isabel's face clouded and Jesse couldn't help but laugh. Isabel set her hands on her hips. "Well, are you gonna tell me or not?"

Jesse just shook his head and kept walking up the drive.

Isabel stood for a moment longer before letting out a huff and following after him.

Jesse stopped where his tire tracks left the gravel road. He brushed the limb back and forth across the fresh snow, doing at least a passable job of obscuring the tracks. He tossed the limb away. "That'll have to do." He noted Isabel still looked perturbed. He smiled. "If we ever get out of this mess, I promise to take you snipe hunting."

Jesse scanned the horizon. The clouds were moving in again and the sky threatened snow. Jesse hoped it would hurry up, snow would cover their tracks. He headed back to the truck, slid out his guitar. The Belsnickels had broken in through the back door and Jesse followed Isabel inside.

There was no electricity, and it was hard to see with all the windows boarded up, but the dusty gloom didn't stop the Belsnickels. They were busy clearing stacks of junk and old boxes off the rows of pews, making room to sit and lie down. Vernon crouched in front of a cast-iron potbellied stove, stuffing it full of broken bits of cedar paneling, prepping it for a fire.

Jesse found several oil lamps lined up on a shelf. He consolidated the remnants of oil until he had one full lamp. He doused the wick, then plucked out his lighter and got it to burn, dialing down the flame. He walked over to Vernon and lent him his lighter, and soon the stove was producing heat.

The space wasn't much larger than a schoolroom and appeared to have been used only for storage for decades. A pulpit sat atop a small platform built against the far wall. A large, hand-carved cross bearing the suffering Son of God hung behind it. Krampus stood in front of it, staring up into the tortured eyes of Jesus, his tail twitching.

Isabel came by carrying an armful of dusty curtains. "Here." She tossed one at Jesse. "Not much, but it will help keep the chill off. There's a bunch more over by the stove if you need them." She moved on, handing them out to the rest of the Belsnickels.

Jesse carried the curtain over to a dilapidated upright piano covered in old dirt-dauber nests. He dropped the curtain on the floor next to the wall and stretched out, propping one boot atop the other. He leaned his head back, letting out a long, weary breath. *Feels damn good to stop moving for a bit.* It struck him he'd been running nonstop without sleep, and on only a few strips of jerky, for almost twenty-four hours. He sat the guitar across his lap, seeing if he could fix the loose frets. Broke or not, he still found it comforting just to hold. He softly strummed the strings while trying to get it back in tune. *"Damn,"* he whispered and winced, flexing his hand. It was getting hard to move his fingers. The wound had become red and inflamed and Jesse feared it might be infected. *Way things are going for me, probably have gangrene by morning.*

He noticed Krampus watching him. The creature hobbled over and took a seat next to him. Krampus looked worn out, yet there was a gleam in his eyes that hadn't been there before.

"A long day for all of us, indeed," Krampus said. "For me it is the end to five hundred years of long days." He pulled the sack into his lap and caressed it like a pet, as together they watched the Belsnickels situate themselves for sleep, all with the exception of Vernon, who paced relentlessly back and forth across the church, peeking out between the slats as though Santa was out there with his sword and a hungry pack of wolves.

Krampus tapped the guitar. "You have music in your heart."

Jesse nodded.

"I would have you play me a song."

Jesse opened his palm, showed Krampus the wound. "Can't . . . not till this thing heals up, anyhow." Then, almost to himself, "Maybe never again."

"Perhaps there is something for it." Krampus opened the sack, closed his eyes, and inserted his hand. Rapt concentration strained his features, then a smile broke. "Ah . . . all is not lost . . . some things have survived the great flame." Krampus pulled out a cone-shaped flask. It was covered in black ash, its long neck sealed in charred wax. He peeled away the wax and plucked out a rotting cork, then placed the bottle to his lips and took a long swig. "Ahh!" He wiped his mouth on the back of his arm. "All the sweeter for the long wait."

"Now, hold out your hand."

Jesse looked unsure.

"Fear not, this is not just any mead, but mead from Odin's own stores. This," Krampus held out the flask and marveled, "is from the cellars of Valhalla itself. It comes from the udders of Heidrun, who feeds on the foliage of the tree Laeraor. It will do your wound good. Now, cup your hand."

Jesse extended his hand. Krampus tilted the flask and Jesse braced himself for the sting of alcohol. An amber liquid flowed into Jesse's palm. It sparkled, Jesse felt warmth, then a pleasant tingling sensation as the liquid slowly soaked into his flesh. He flexed his hand. It did indeed feel a little better.

Krampus handed him the flask. "Here, a drink for your heart and soul."

Jesse took the bottle, put it up to his nose, and sniffed. It smelled like the sweetest day in spring.

"I hand you the mead of the gods and you sniff at it?" Krampus let out a snort. "Drink, fool."

Jesse took a tentative sip. It was as though someone had poured pure joy down his throat. The warmth spreading in his gullet, not the burn of whiskey but the way you feel when you're in love. He took another sip, a long one, and tried to take another when Krampus pulled the bottle from him.

"Careful," Krampus said. "It is not for mortals. Too much and you might sprout horns." He rapped his knuckles against his own broken horns, winked, and took a long swig.

Jesse laid his head back. The world around him lost its edges and he felt he was floating, drifting away from all his worries and fears.

"What do you dream of?" Krampus asked.

"Dream?"

"Your passions? What dreams take you off to sleep each night?"

Jesse thought for a minute. "Playing my songs. Those are my best dreams. The music and me come together, the melody is so clear . . . the crowd digs me." Jesse smiled. "They hold up their lighters and cell phones and sway to the tune. The encores go on *all* night long."

"So that is what you most want from life? To play your music?"

Jesse thought for a minute and nodded. "That'd be enough. It's the only time I truly feel connected . . . with myself, with people. When the music is good . . . it's . . . it's like I took a feeling right from my heart, took my deepest highs and lows, and shared 'em with folks. More like weaving a spell than playing. Don't care if it's just a bunch of drunks, neither. Don't matter. What matters is to be able to touch someone that way."

Krampus nodded. "Those dreams . . . they are your soul. You must live them to their fullest."

"Yeah, but they're just dreams, y'know. And the problem with dreams is you have to wake up."

"What do you mean?"

"I mean it's time for me to grow up . . . I guess. To give it up. Time to leave the dreams behind . . . because there's no room for dreams in the real world."

"No." Krampus's voice grew stern. "That is not true. Your dreams are your spirit, your soul, and without them you are dead." He made a fist. "You must guard your dreams. Always. Lest someone steal them from you. I know what it is to have your dreams stolen. I know what it is to be dead." His voice was almost a growl. "Guard your dreams. *Always guard your dreams.*"

They were both silent for a long while.

"How is the hand?" Krampus asked.

Jesse looked at the wound, most of the redness was gone. He wiggled his fingers, there was almost no pain.

"It is better?"

"Yeah," Jesse marveled. "It is."

"Good."

Vernon walked past, stooped, and peeked outside through the slats in the window next to them.

"Vernon," Krampus called. "Stop your fretting. It is helping no one."

Vernon threw up his hands. "How can you act so casual knowing those things are hunting us?"

"Vernon, come here."

Vernon stayed at the window, nervously twisting the ends of his beard. "You know, it's not like they were all that far back up the road."

"Come, Vernon. I command it."

Vernon came over.

Krampus held up the flask. "Drink."

Vernon pushed a long strand of greasy hair from his face and eyed the flask suspiciously.

"Mead."

Vernon's face brightened. "Oh." He took the flask, took a long sip, then another.

"Pass it around," Krampus said. "Give some to Nipi . . . he is in need."

Jesse noted that Nipi had removed the blood-soaked rag from his wound. The gunshot was red and swollen, but not raw, and actually appeared to be forming a scar already. Jesse might've been more amazed, but he'd seen enough wonders this day to understand some sort of magic was at play.

Vernon walked the flask over to Nipi. Nipi took a deep swig and passed it on. The bottle went round and round until all the Belsnickels were sitting or lying upon their makeshift beds, their faces mellow.

Jesse noticed Krampus staring out into space, gently caressing the velvet sack, a dreamy look upon his face. "So," Jesse asked, "what does a Krampus dream of then?"

Krampus stopped stroking the sack, didn't say anything for a long moment. "I dream of spreading the splendor of Yuletide once again across the land, of returning sweet Mother Earth to her glory. To see my temples and shrines all across the world. To have all the peoples pay me homage. That, Jesse, music-maker, that is my dream."

"All across the world, huh? Nothing wrong with shooting high, I guess."

Krampus nodded, his eyes still far away.

"Yuletide? Thought that was the same thing as Christmas."

"Christmas," Krampus spat. "No, Christmas is an abomination. A perversion! Yule is the true spirit of Mother Earth. Yule is the rebirth of the seasons. Without Yuletide, Mother Earth cannot heal herself . . . will wither and die. That is why it is so important that I reawaken the spirit within mankind. Help them to believe again. Because it is their power of belief, their love and devotion, that heals the land."

"And let me get this straight, that Santa Claus fella, I take it he's in your way somehow?"

"That name is a lie. A sham." Krampus's lip curled into a sneer. "His name is not Santa Claus. His name is . . . his true name is . . ." He hesitated, seemed incapable of saying more.

BALDR, KRAMPUS THOUGHT, then said it out loud. "Baldr. That is his true name."

"Santa Claus?" Jesse asked.

"Yes. His true name is Baldr." *There, it is said. After five hundred years his name again touches my tongue.* He scowled, hating the bitter taste of the word. "Vernon, bring me the mead."

Vernon hopped up, brought over the flask. Krampus drank deep, trying to wash the bitterness away.

"My grandfather, Loki, killed him once, long ago. Now I shall do so again." He clutched the velvet sack. "So tragic, Baldr's death. Fair and beautiful Baldr, beloved by all." Krampus sneered. "Or so it is told, as I knew him not before his death. I learned of those events from my mother, Hel, queen of the netherworld. She would tell this tale and so many others as I sat as a child upon the steps of her throne. Her sweet words, accompanied by the woeful singing of the dead."

"What's not to love about that?"

Krampus squinted at Jesse. "You are being sarcastic."

"Naw."

Krampus gave Jesse a disdainful look, but continued. "She spoke that all in Asgard loved Baldr, the second son of Odin. All praised Baldr, so fair of feature and so bright that light shone from him, fair-spoken and gracious. She told that they spoke of his charitable nature, his benevolence toward the downtrodden, going on and on about this gentle champion of the woeful and dispirited until one wished to hang oneself.

"But there was one not taken in by Baldr's charm and beauty. Loki, being the king of all tricksters, was quick to recognize deceit no matter how fair the package. He saw Baldr for the fraud he was and took it as a challenge to expose him before all, especially Odin, as there was no love between the two. And the opportunity to bring disgrace and shame to the house of Odin was too great a temptation to resist.

"His chance came when Baldr schemed to become more than a deity, but to have life and beauty everlasting. And to this means he spun a tale to play on his parents' great love. He told his father and his mother, Frigg, of his recurring nightmares, dreams that spoke of his impending death. His parents, not able to stand the thought of harm befalling their most beloved son, fell into Baldr's design. They traveled the nine worlds, sought and received an oath from everything in Creation not to harm Baldr. All, that is, but from a young, distant plant called Mistletoe, as Odin felt this weed to be too lowly and feeble to matter. And thus, Baldr gained his immortality."

Krampus snorted. "That is how the myths spin it, anyway. But myths are full of flowering fancy, and as much as I adore such tales, Hel told me the truth. Odin, being the great sorcerer that he was, concocted a spell and placed it upon Baldr. A spell that prevented any element of the nine worlds from ever harming him. Only the spell was contrived from the poison of Mistletoe, and thus, Mistletoe remained immune.

"Once Baldr had this wondrous gift, he did not wait to show it off, encouraging all comers to amuse themselves by trying to harm him with weapon of their choosing. Mother told that he made great sport of it, reveling in the attention, that the other gods loved the game, and as Baldr's popularity grew so did Loki's determination to expose him.

"Loki disguised himself as an old woman and tricked Frigg into revealing the secret of the Mistletoe. Armed with this knowledge, Loki sought out the plant and made from it an arrow, an alchemy of Mistletoe and ore. Loki took this arrow and the next time he found Baldr at play, he slipped in amongst the gathered crowd. There he found Baldr's blind brother Hoor. He asked Hoor why he did not participate. Hoor replied that this was no game for a blind man. Loki presented Hoor with a bow and the charmed arrow, offered to guide his hand. Hoor was thrilled to have a chance to play and pulled the bow with great vigor. The arrow hit Baldr in the chest, drove deep into his heart, and Baldr fell down dead right there before Frigg, before Odin. It is said that the silence was deafening. Poor Hoor could not see their fearsome gazes and Loki could not bear it. Loki fled.

"Odin's grief was bottomless and he had Hoor slain for the deed." Krampus shook his head. "I have always felt for Hoor. A pawn in a game of jealousy and spite. He carried the torment of killing his own beloved brother, then to be slain by his own father. Tragic indeed. Odin laid Baldr's body to rest upon the great ship *Hringhorni* and set it ablaze. It is said that Baldr's wife, Nanna, in her grief, threw herself into the flame to follow him into death."

Krampus took another swig. "But that was just the beginning, for Baldr's spirit fell into Hel, into the realm of the dead where even the great Odin had no right of rule. Though Odin and Frigg sent another of their sons, Hermod, to offer ransom and beg Baldr's release, my mother, Hel, would not give up Baldr's spirit. And it is known but to a very few that Hel played games with Odin to distract him while Loki sought a confession from Baldr. Told Baldr he would be Hel's slave, imprisoned until Ragnarok, unless he admitted of his scheme. Here is where Baldr surprised them, as he refused such bargain, chose to remain Hel's prisoner, to spend an age amongst the dead before exposing his own deceit.

"And that is how I first came to see him, as a prisoner in Hel. He was most curious to me as a child, this beautiful deity, there in his chamber with his dead wife. He looked such a desolate soul, appeared almost as stone. He would stand for days on end without moving, staring down into the bottomless chasms of the nether regions, listening to the songs of the dead and waiting, waiting, ever waiting for the end of the gods, for Ragnarok and its promise of freedom.

"I questioned Mother, 'How could one willing to make such sacrifice to keep his secrets truly be of low character?' She laughed and said not to confuse pride with nobleness, and warned me not to pity him. But I felt this being had suffered his share. Even then, at that young age, I could see that Loki's hatred and jealousy of Odin was at the heart of Baldr's fate. And so I did come to pity him, and that, my friend, was the beginning of my undoing. For a bitter lesson lay ahead and it is that a serpent is always a serpent, no matter the guise. I had no way of knowing then that there would come a day when I would be unable to utter his name, that I would dream of his blood on my hands a hundred thousand times over."

Krampus started to tell more, to tell the rest of the story. He glanced at Jesse, realized the music man was asleep.

Krampus let out a great sigh, tugged open the sack, peered into its murky depths. "Together we shall find Loki's arrow. Together we shall kill Baldr no matter what guise he might wear."

Chapter Seven

NAUGHTY LIST

Footsteps, heavy, stomping footfalls coming up the stairs. Jesse found himself in his childhood room. He was six, maybe seven years old, and it was Christmas. The banister was strung with tinsel and Christmas lights and they blinked and sparkled. A large shadow blocked out the lights as it marched up the stairs. "Ho, ho, ho," boomed a voice, one laced with judgment and condemnation. "Have you been naughty, Jesse? Hmm? Have you?" Jesse began to shake; he tugged the covers up to his neck. Santa pushed through the door, his burly figure so massive he barely fit through the frame. He crossed to Jesse's bedside, carrying a large sack, a blood-colored sack, slung across his shoulder. He stood there towering, looming, his tiny black eyes locked on Jesse as though weighing his soul.

Santa rolled the sack off his shoulder and onto the bed. The sack was moving, as though full of dogs and cats perhaps. Jesse heard what sounded like muffled mewing and cries, but knew it couldn't be, not coming from Santa's sack. Santa shook his head sadly. "You've been naughty, Jesse. Very, very naughty." Jesse tried to speak, tried to say that he was a good boy, but his mouth couldn't form the words.

Six hunched figures crept up behind Santa, glistening skin, dark as pitch, twisting horns protruding from their scalps and long red tongues lolling from between black teeth. They looked at Jesse as though he'd be good to eat.

Santa loosened the cord and opened the sack and now Jesse could clearly hear the cries, and they weren't from cats and dogs, but children, screaming and moaning as though in great pain.

Santa jabbed a chubby finger at Jesse. "He is on the naughty list. Put him in the sack." The devils all grinned, rubbed their long fingers together, and reached for Jesse.

Jesse opened his eyes and found himself still in a room with six devils; their hunched figures silhouetted by the flickering glow of the potbellied stove. The church was dark and he realized it was night, wondered how long he'd been asleep. Something smelled foul; he sniffed. *Blood?*

Jesse scanned the shadows and found huge, unblinking eyes staring back at him. He sat up.

A cow, or at least its head, sat atop a chest, blood dripping down its tongue onto the floor. *Whoa,* he thought. *Where'd that come from?* He spotted a large steel wash tub against the wall. He made out a rump, flank, and two legs jutting up. *Someone is gonna miss that cow.* Something else was new: mistletoe, several piles of it. It looked as though someone had been whittling spikes out of the branches.

He climbed to his feet, swayed, put out a hand to steady himself, still a bit light-headed from the mead. No headache, not like a hangover at all, just a slight buzz. His stomach growled. He hoped to find something to eat besides raw beef. He skirted around the mistletoe and came up behind the Belsnickels. They sat huddled around Krampus's sack.

"No, Krampus," Vernon grumbled. "That's not right."

Krampus held what appeared to be a black powder pistol. Jesse moved up for a closer look and noticed there were two swords, a shield, and an old, rusty revolver lying on the floor.

Jesse squatted next to Isabel. "What's going on?"

Vernon answered, "We're trying to get him to find us some acceptable weaponry. You know, in case, say, just by happenstance, a giant wolf or some other monstrosity should come along."

"He can pull anything out of there?" Jesse asked. "Not just toys?"

Krampus nodded distractedly.

Jesse agreed with Vernon, some updated weaponry would be very good to have indeed, and would certainly be in order when they stormed the General's compound. "You need some automatic weapons. A few assault rifles would do the trick."

"That's just what I was telling him," Vernon said, not hiding his annoyance. "Modern weapons, Krampus. You've seen pictures of them in the newspaper."

Krampus raised his hands in obvious frustration. "It is not so easy as that. One must first know what it is one is searching for."

"Might be able to help," Jesse put in.

Krampus looked up at him, considered. "Yes, maybe you can. Come here." He patted the floor next to him. "Sit."

Jesse came over and Krampus pulled the sack between them.

"The sack finds what I wish. But first I must know what it is that I seek. And further, it is easier if the sack knows where to look. Easier and far less draining, and until I have my strength back, I must ration my efforts."

"Okay, sure. What do I do?"

"You help me to seek. You are not of Loki's bloodline, so the sack will not obey you. Thus we must work together. We both must hold the sack. You will think of a location and an item and I will direct the sack to obey."

"I know how," Jesse said. "I used it before. Took a few toys out of it."

"That is not the same. You merely reached through a door that was already open."

"No, I thought of a certain toy and the sack found it."

Krampus raised an eyebrow. "That is indeed something. Perhaps there is a trace of Loki's spirit in you somewhere. But still, that is not opening doors. You could never do that, not on your own. But it says something that the sack would hear you at all." Krampus smiled. "That is good, it should make our task the easier."

"What-all are you looking for?"

"Guns," Vernon interjected. "Very good guns. Something that will punch enormous holes through giant wolves."

"Money," Isabel added. "There's things we'll need to buy—things we can't get with the sack. Least not until Krampus is stronger."

"Do you know of a place to find these things?" Krampus asked. "Keeping in mind the fewer doors I must open the better."

Jesse grinned. He did, he did indeed. He'd never actually been inside the General's office, but once, when Chet left the door open, he'd caught a pretty good peek, and the thing that stuck with him was the safe sitting in the corner. It was an old-fashioned safe, nearly as large as a washing machine, with a large brass dial set into its front. Jesse knew for certain the General stored guns in there, had to be cash as well, and no telling what-all else. *Sure would hate to steal from the General,* Jesse thought. *Be a real shame.* "Oh, I know a spot alright."

"Good," Krampus said. "Place your palms on the sack."

Jesse did.

"Close your eyes and seek."

"Seek?"

"Just close your eyes and it will come to you."

Jesse shrugged, closed his eyes, and imagined the compound, then the motor bay, then the General's upstairs office. Nothing special seemed to be happening. Then Krampus laid his hands atop of Jesse's and slowly the vision sharpened, details he'd never seen materialized. The safe sat in the corner. Jesse steered his mind toward it and the vision followed, it was just that easy, then he went into it and all was dark.

"This is the place?" Krampus asked. "Inside the chest?"

"Yup."

Krampus's hold tightened and Jesse felt a slight charge.

Krampus pulled their hands away. "It is done."

"That's it?"

"The sack responds well to you, Jesse." Krampus looked at him kindly, almost paternally. "Maybe a touch of Loki's blood does indeed run in your veins."

"So, I can just reach in there and take whatever I like?"

"You can, but be aware you are putting your hand into that other place. Your arm and hand will be visible to anyone who happens to be near. This can lead to trouble, to loss of limb, to even being pulled into the sack, into the very place you are robbing."

Jesse hesitated. "But it is a safe. No one will be in the safe."

"No, so long as the chest is closed, no one can see you."

Jesse loosened the mouth of the sack, peered into its smoky shadows. "All right, here goes." He inserted his hand until he bumped a wall. It felt right, like cold steel. He pushed downward until his fingers hit something hard, cylindrical. He grasped it, could tell by the weight it was a gun. He pulled his hand out, very pleased with what he found.

A minute later he had three machine pistols, several handguns, one sawed-off shotgun, a couple dozen boxes of ammunition, and stacks and stacks of hundred-dollar bills. But there were more surprises in the General's safe: an unopened bottle of aged bourbon; an assortment of pills—amphetamines, by the look of them; what appeared to be several grams of pure cocaine, not crack but the real deal; keys to who knew what; all sorts of contracts and promissory notes; an envelope full of Polaroids of some woman that looked an awful lot like Jesse's third-grade teacher, Mrs. Sawyer, in her birthday suit. Jesse wrinkled up his face but didn't stop until the safe was empty. It felt good to take something back from a man who'd stolen so much from him, and knowing he'd be using the General's own guns against him made the act all the sweeter. He grinned at Krampus.

Krampus grinned back. "You are enjoying yourself."

"It's empty."

"Then we're done."

Jesse looked over the loot, at the cash, at all the guns and ammo. He nodded and let out a deep breath, suddenly feeling drained.

"You are weary?"

"Need something to eat, that's all."

"It is the sack. It takes a toll."

Jesse wondered just what part of him the sack had taken that toll from.

"You should eat," Krampus said, nodding toward the tub holding the beef.

Jesse looked at the cow leg. He was just about hungry enough to eat it raw, but figured roasting a few strips over the stove would suit him better. He hopped up and started over, caught sight of the cow head and stopped. "Hey," Jesse called. "Is it possible to put something back? Back in the safe?"

Krampus raised an eyebrow. "Yes, it is possible. Once the door is open it will stay open until I open a new one."

Jesse lifted the cow head by the ear and brought it back. "That safe belongs to the man that put this hole through my hand."

Krampus nodded, grinned, and held the sack open. Jesse dropped the head inside. "Jesse, you are certainly a man after my own heart."

ISABEL WALKED WITH Jesse along the gravel road, glad to be out of the moldy-smelling church. It was night and they were headed to a mini-mart called Pepper's, which Jesse claimed to be about two miles back down on Route 3. They'd decided to walk instead of risking anyone seeing the truck or chance the vehicle running out of fuel. Jesse carried the empty gas can he'd retrieved out of the camper, gas being one of the things Krampus couldn't pull out of his sack.

"Man, what I wouldn't give to see the General's face when he comes eye-to-eye with that cow head," Jesse said with a laugh. "Over forty thousand dollars gone. Poof! That man is just gonna pee himself."

Isabel shook her head distractedly, scanning the shadows, keeping an ear out for any suspicious sounds, any sign or hint that Santa Claus or the wolves might be near.

Jesse gave her a light shove. "Hey, c'mon, it's funny. I'm telling you. You gotta understand that man's the biggest son of a whore in all of Boone County. Hell, maybe in all of West Virginia."

Isabel managed a smile. She liked it when he looked at her, liked his green eyes, the line of his jaw, but most of all she liked his laugh—kind and warm, and full of life. *It's nice,* she thought, *taking a walk with someone that's not as ancient as the hills. Don't hurt none that he's easy on the eyes,* she admitted. *No, not one bit.* She considered what it'd be like to hold his hand. It'd been a long time since she'd held hands with anyone. Not since her Daniel, and that had been over forty years ago now. But she knew this man wouldn't want to hold her hand; she knew what she looked like now.

"Okay, so you gotta help me out here," Jesse said. "Lord, where do I even start? None of this makes a lick of sense. Santa Claus, and giant wolves, and . . . shit, just what the hell is that Krampus guy? How in the heck did you ever end up with that devil?"

"He's not a devil."

Jesse halted. "Wait, did I get something wrong here? Aren't you his slave? Didn't he do this to you?" He gestured at her face. "Turn you into a monster?"

Isabel's cheeks burned. She looked away, surprised by how much his words stung. "He saved my life," she said, zipping up her jacket and pulling the hood over her head, hiding her face within its shadow. She walked on, leaving him standing there.

Jesse caught up.

"Well, that still doesn't give him the right to make you his slave."

"It's not like that. You wouldn't understand."

"That's 'cause it don't make any sense."

"And I ain't no monster. I'm a woman. If you weren't so thick you'd be able to see that."

Jesse put up his hands. "Didn't mean it like that."

Isabel walked faster, leaving him behind.

"Ah, c'mon, Isabel. Slow down. I'm sorry."

"I tried to kill myself, okay? Be bones in the ground, too, if weren't for Krampus."

"Kill yourself? Well, now why would you want to go and do a thing like that for?"

"That really ain't none of your business. Is it?"

Jesse frowned, nodded. "You're right, I'm sorry. It ain't none of my business."

She kept walking.

"Didn't mean to pry," he said. "Just trying to make sense of this whole thing. I mean it, I'm sorry."

Isabel slowed, sucked in a deep breath of the cold night air. "I'd got myself into a bad situation. Seemed things just kept getting worse. I guess I tried to take the easy way out, okay?"

"Isabel, you don't need to be explaining yourself to me."

They continued on in silence. Isabel wanted to say more, ached to talk to someone other than Vernon and the Shawnee, someone young, someone with clear, sympathetic eyes. But opening up had never come easy for her, and she didn't know this man. Just because he had a warm laugh and kind eyes didn't mean he could be trusted. And you didn't just start telling some stranger about how you got pregnant at sixteen, not unless you were prepared to have them look at you like you're some kind of hill trash. But it hadn't been some cheap hookup. Maybe if it had, the whole thing would've been easier. Isabel felt tears stinging her eyes and quickly blinked them away. *Don't you start. Just let it lie, girl.* It always caught her off guard how bad it still hurt, even after all these years. She tried not to think about her baby growing up without a mother. How maybe if she'd been stronger, she'd be with him right now.

"I was sixteen when I ran away from home, ran away from everything. I wasn't thinking straight, found myself up here in these hills. It was winter and cold, didn't know what to do. Couldn't see no way to fix the things I'd done. Walked out on a ledge and looked down at the rocks below and there was my answer . . . the answer to all the pain and heartache." Isabel found she was crying. "Wish I'd had better presence of mind. I just felt so bad about everything . . . so bad. Just wanted all that hurting to end." She wiped at her tears. "Dammit, didn't mean to start all this blubbering."

Jesse put an arm around her. Isabel had not had anyone touch her, not like that, not in over forty years. She covered her face and began to sob.

"I looked up into the stars," she said. "Begged the Good Lord to forgive me, and walked right off that ledge."

"Jesus, Isabel."

"Well, I should've picked a taller cliff, 'cause that fall . . . it didn't kill me." She let out a mean laugh. "Just broke a bunch of bones. I couldn't move. Just laid there crying and screaming. The pain was something awful." She moved away from Jesse and wiped her sleeve across her face. "Well, it was them Shawnee that found me. They brought me to Krampus. I'm guessing I broke something in my spine, 'cause I could move but one arm, couldn't feel a thing below my waist. Things were getting fuzzy. I believe I was dying. And that's when Krampus bit me."

"Bit you?"

"Uh-huh. That's how he does it. Turns people. Something to do with mixing his blood is the way he tells it. Whatever it is he does, it saved my life. Healed me right up. About two days later I was up and walking about. Only that wasn't all it done." She held out her hands, looked at the jagged black nails protruding from her scaly fingers. "Didn't always look like a monster y'know, used to have fair skin and long red hair. Owned a couple of pretty dresses, too."

They walked on a long time without either of them speaking.

"So that's why you stay, because he saved you?"

She looked up into the night, let the light snow hit her face. "No," she said, knowing she'd go looking for her son if she could. She knew her boy would be in his forties by now, wouldn't know her from Adam, and probably wouldn't want to, either, not after she'd abandoned him. But she would sure like to see who he turned into. See if he had his father's eyes. "I'd leave right this minute if I could."

"Well, what's stopping you?"

"Krampus forbid us from going into town. From going near folks when we can help it. Doesn't want anyone seeing us. Or at least he didn't. Y'know, back when he was all chained up. He'd send one of us into town every now and again to steal a newspaper, raid the library for any books on Santa Claus, or maybe if there was some other odd thing we needed that we couldn't make for ourselves."

"And, let me guess, there's some sort of reason you got to obey him? He's put a spell on you? Hypnotized you?"

She nodded. "That's pretty much so. Once we turned, when he gives us a direct command, we're powerless to do anything else. It's like becoming a puppet. You no longer think, you just do."

"And he's ordered you to stick around, I take it."

"He made us take this oath. Y'know, not to run off, to protect him, to take care of him, and other stuff like that."

"Don't leave much of a life for a young lady."

"I try not to think on it too much." She could see the mini-mart sign now, glowing not more than a quarter-mile ahead.

"What is he?" Jesse asked.

"Krampus?"

He laughed. "Who else would I be talking about?"

Isabel managed a smile. "Couldn't tell you for sure. The Shawnee think he's a forest god. Shoot, they're so goddamn infatuated with him there wasn't even need for him to have changed them. I guess he must've done it so they'd not grow old. Makwa told me that his whole tribe used to bring Krampus offerings since way back before the first white settlers even showed up."

"And Vernon, I'm guessing he didn't volunteer?"

She laughed. "He was surveying for the coal company sometime back first part of last century. He found Krampus by accident. Krampus, of course, wouldn't let him go after that. So lucky Vernon's been stuck with them stubborn Indians for company for going on nearly a century. And if you give him half the chance he'll be glad to chew on your ear about it, too, let me tell you."

They approached the store, skirting a mound of dirty snow piled along one end of the parking lot, and stopped in the shadow of a Dumpster. Isabel stared through the large front window at the goods inside the little mart. They sold a small selection of groceries and home basics, as well as local crafts and souvenirs: pecan rolls, jams, jellies, sausage and jerky, quilts, coon caps, key chains, magnets, and Indian jewelry made in China. She'd not been inside a store since before she was pregnant, and found herself mesmerized by the colorful displays and flashy packaging. *Wouldn't mind*, she thought, *spending a bit of time in there. Wouldn't mind at all.*

Jesse dug a roll of bills from his breast pocket. Flipped through them. "Shoot, it's all hundreds." He snorted. "Never thought there'd be a day when I'd catch myself complaining about having too many hundred-dollar bills. Ah, here we go." He peeled off a hundred and two twenties, put the rest away, and headed toward the store. Isabel remained in the shadow.

Jesse stopped, looked back. "Oh, yeah . . . guess you gotta stay out here?"

She nodded absently, her eyes fixed on the shelves of cheap trinkets.

He studied her for a moment. "Been awhile since you been inside a store, I bet."

She nodded again.

"Okay, gotta pay before I pump. It'll be a sec. Now, don't you go running off and leaving me." He winked at her and headed away. "Oh," he called over his shoulder. "And keep your eye out for snipes. A gal out this way lost a few toes to one just a couple of weeks ago." Isabel set her hands on her hips and watched him trot off.

About a minute after Jesse entered the store, a car came up the highway and pulled into the lot. Isabel withdrew into the shadows. Two teenage girls and an older boy climbed out, laughing over some shared joke. One of the girls jumped onto the boy's back and rode him piggyback into the store, all three hooting and carrying on as though life was one big carnival ride. *So carefree,* Isabel thought and tried to ignore the jealousy biting at her. "Life don't always go the way folks want," she muttered under her breath. "That's all."

Isabel watched them romp about in the store. Both girls had long, wavy hair. It bounced and shined, silky in the glow of the beer signs. *Something a man would want to run his fingers through,* Isabel thought, and touched her own cropped hair; it felt waxy, crusty. She hadn't had a chance to wash since fall; the creeks were too cold this time of year. The girls had on makeup, lipstick, and eyeliner, earrings. *All the things girls wore to pretty themselves up.* She wondered if there might be some makeup to cover up the blotchiness on her face. *Maybe a little lipstick? Might look a little bit more like a young woman than some cave monster.*

Jesse walked out; the gas can in one hand, a sack of groceries in the other. He nodded her way, headed to the pump, and began filling the canister with gas. The kids left the store a moment later. The boy shook his can of soda, popped it open, and sprayed it at the girls. Both of them let out wild screams, scooped up handfuls of snow, and threw it at him. He ducked, slipped on the ice, fell, dropping his soda. All three of them laughed so hard Isabel thought they would need medical aid. And all at once Isabel wanted them to stop. She didn't want to hear them, or see them. She clenched her hands into fists. Found she wanted to shut them up, wanted to tear their beautiful hair out of their heads, scratch their pretty faces, make them know what it is like to lose everything.

One of the girls tugged the boy to his feet. He slipped his hands around her waist, pulled her to him, and they embraced, kissed—a long kiss that only new love can share. Isabel put her fingers to her own lips, stared, hardly breathing. They piled back into the car and Isabel no longer wished them ill, no, only wished to join them, to climb into their car and go wherever it was that young boys and girls go these days to have fun. She tried to imagine what that would be like, to just have fun. She watched their taillights until they disappeared up the dark highway.

Jesse walked up to her. "Here. Can you take this?" He handed her a grocery sack and set the gas can down at her feet.

"I'll be right back. Need to make a quick call."

"Call? Wait. I don't know if you should."

"Isabel, I have to know if my little girl is okay. Just gonna call her grandmother. There's no way one phone call is going to endanger Krampus. So you're off the hook."

She bit her lip. If something wasn't obviously endangering Krampus or directly breaking one of his tenets, then her actions were her own.

"Isabel, I'm not asking. I'm going to make a phone call. I'll be right back."

"Yeah . . . okay."

He started toward the phone, then turned. "Oh, here. I bought you a little something." He pulled a plastic sack out of the grocery bag and handed it to her.

"What is it?"

"Why don't you take a look and find out?"

She watched him go to the phone booth, then peered into the sack, found a pack of watermelon bubble gum, a giant chocolate almond bar, and something fuzzy. She tugged it out. It was a toboggan cap, black and white and so frizzy. She held it up and realized it was shaped like a panda bear's head, complete with nose, ears, and big, droopy eyes. Two large fuzzy earflaps hung from each side. It was utterly ridiculous, but no one would ever, ever mistake it for a boy's cap. There was something else in the sack. She pulled out a box, popped it open, inside she found a charm bracelet with an attached oversize pink, heart-shaped locket. She let out a small cry, covered her mouth. Apparently, Jesse had as bad a taste in jewelry as he did in women's hats, but she couldn't stop smiling. She tore it out of the box and slipped it on her wrist. Just some ticky-tacky, she knew that, but it was still glittery and oh-so-girly. Not the sort of thing a guy would buy a monster, and for that second she felt like a girl again. She closed her eyes, savoring the feeling. A tear ran down her cheek, then another. She tried to remember the last time anyone had given her a gift. It had been her Daniel, it had been the ring, some forty years ago. She wiped at her eyes. "Stop that," she whispered. "Now's not the time to go all weepy-eyed."

Jesse hung up the phone and headed her way at a fast clip.

Isabel shoved her hood back and tugged on the toboggan, quickly tied the fuzzy earflaps beneath her chin. She hoped she looked as silly as she felt, couldn't wait to see his face.

Jesse snatched up the gas can. "We gotta get back." He headed up the gravel road without even looking her way, his face set and grim.

Isabel hesitated, confused, felt a sting of hurt. *What just happened?* She grabbed the groceries and sprinted to catch up with him.

"They're after Abigail," he said, his voice hard and tense.

Isabel didn't know what to say.

"Linda's mother asked me why Ash Boggs showed up at her place looking for Abi. That's all the old witch would say, wouldn't tell me a goddamn thing else. Just kept asking me what I'd done. You know what that means?"

Isabel shook her head.

"Means the General intends to make good on his threat, that's what that means. Fuck," his voice turned raw, cutting. *"Fuck!"*

Jesse's long legs ate up the road and Isabel had to jog to keep up.

"There's just no telling what the General might do," Jesse said, but it was more like he was talking to himself. "I gotta do something before it's too damn late."

ISABEL WATCHED JESSE empty the gas into his truck, then screw the cap back on and toss the canister into the camper. They found Vernon on the steps. He glanced at Isabel, his eyes going right to her cap. He let out a chuckle. "Why that is just adorable. I do hope you brought Makwa one." Jesse started past. Vernon put out his arm. "Hold up. I wouldn't go in there just now if I were you."

"Why?" Isabel asked. "What happened?"

"Nothing. Old Tall and Ugly is just in one of his moods. That's all."

Jesse pushed Vernon's arm aside and headed in. Isabel followed and they found Krampus sitting cross-legged in front of the stove, his eyes closed, his face deep in concentration, the sack before him, an assortment of arrows, gold, and bronze, all looking ancient, strewn about his feet. The Shawnee sat away from him, watching him, looking nervous. Wipi glanced over at them and gave a warning shake of the head.

"Now's not a good time," Isabel whispered.

Jesse ignored her, started forward.

Isabel grabbed his arm. "Wait."

Jesse shrugged her off, kept walking. "Krampus."

Krampus's brow tightened, but he didn't look up.

Jesse walked right up to the Yule Lord. "Krampus. We need to talk."

Krampus still didn't open his eyes, but raised a hand, shook it urgently. Isabel could see the rising frustration on the Yule Lord's face, knew what that could mean. She rushed to Jesse, put a restraining hand on his chest. "Jesse," she said in a low, harsh tone. "You gotta wait."

Krampus inserted his arm deep into the sack, appeared to be searching. This went on for several minutes. Isabel could feel the tension rising in Jesse with each passing second.

"Krampus," Jesse said, raising his voice. "It's urgent."

Krampus jerked his arm out, opened his eyes, stared at his empty hand, then let out a howl. "Damn Odin," he hissed. "Damn the Valkyries. Where did they hide it?" He locked eyes on Jesse and growled. "You *dare* interrupt me?"

Jesse didn't back down a step. "We need to go now. Get my daughter before it's too—"

"It will wait," Krampus said and waved him off. Isabel found herself surprised by his restraint, then saw his exhaustion.

"No," Jesse pressed. "You don't understand, the General will—"

"You are the one who does not understand. I must find Loki's arrow. Without it there is no way to stop him. Baldr will kill us all."

"Krampus, you have to—"

"*No*," Krampus cried, climbing to his feet, his tail snapping back and forth. "It is not your place to tell me what I must do!"

Isabel pulled Jesse back. "Stop it, Jesse."

Jesse jabbed a finger at Krampus. "My little girl's in trouble and I aim to do something about it. Tell you what, you just sit here, then. Me, I'm gonna go take care of this mess." He yanked his arm free from Isabel and marched over to a cardboard box where the cash and guns sat.

Krampus's face clenched into a knot, his nostrils flared, his breath came in short, hot bursts. Isabel knew what was next, watched helpless as his lips peeled back, revealing his long canines. His eyes flew open, red and glowing. She started to warn Jesse, but Krampus was on him in three quick strides. Jesse must've heard something for he started to turn; as he did, Krampus grabbed him, one hand around his neck, the other holding the front of his jacket. Krampus lifted Jesse off his feet and slammed him into the wall. The entire structure shook. "You will go nowhere 'less I give you leave."

Jesse gasped, forced the words out. "Fuck you. I'm not one of your slaves." Jesse grabbed Krampus's wrist, tried to twist free. Krampus threw him to the floor.

"Hold him," Krampus commanded and the Shawnee were on him, grabbing Jesse before he could get to his feet. Jesse flailed, landed a blow to the side of Makwa's face, then they had him pinned.

Krampus stomped over, towering above Jesse, a low growl coming from deep in his throat. Isabel knew Jesse had gone too far, knew Krampus would bite Jesse, would turn him.

"My patience is at an end," Krampus snapped. He squatted, grabbed Jesse's arm, held it taut. "You leave me no choice." He grinned, once again revealing his canines.

"*No!*" Isabel shouted. "Krampus, stop it!"

Krampus ignored her, opened his mouth to bite Jesse.

Isabel rushed in, pushed herself between them.

Krampus looked as though he might beat her to death with his bare fist.

"*You made an oath!*" Isabel cried. "*A blood oath!*"

Krampus shoved her away, sending her tumbling across the floor into one of the pews. Isabel rolled back to her feet and cried out, "*Does the word of the Yule Lord mean nothing? Then how are you any different than Santa Claus?*"

Krampus leapt to his feet, glaring at Isabel, and she could see he weighed her death, could see it burning in his eyes. He lifted his face upward, toward the rafters, let out a howl, gritted his teeth, and just stood there with his eyes shut, his chest heaving. Slowly, his breathing steadied. His shoulders slumped. "Isabel . . . my little lion. Your heart is bold and your words are true." He set eyes on Jesse. "You . . . should you ever dare to challenge me again . . . I will kill you." His words held absolute finality; he let out a long breath. "I will honor my oath. Those men will die, and die badly. But all in due time, for first there are more pressing matters." He turned and staggered back to the stove, stared down at the velvet sack.

"Bind him," Krampus said over his shoulder. "See to it he does not run off. I cannot risk him escaping. He is too unpredictable."

Makwa yanked Jesse around, shoved him hard against the floor, and put a knee in his back. He gestured toward several curtain rods leaning in the corner. Wipi hopped up, slid out his knife and cut the cords loose from the rods. Isabel intercepted him on his way back. "Give me those." She snatched the cords away from Wipi. Wipi looked at Makwa and shrugged. Isabel came over to Makwa. "Stop being such a brute. Now, get on off him."

Makwa scowled, said something in Shawnee, which Isabel knew to be unflattering, but he got off.

"Put your wrists out."

Jesse reluctantly did as he was told.

Isabel bound his wrists gently but securely. Jesse wouldn't look at her, just glared at Krampus the whole time.

Krampus took a seat next to the sack. He picked up one of the arrows, studied it. "Where are you hiding?"

SANTA CLAUS STOOD on the ledge and stared down at the wolves. The early-morning wind whipped his long beard. His breath steamed in the chill. One of the wolves looked up at him, then to her mate lying still on his side. She let out a whimper and pawed at her mate, but the mate didn't move. She barked up at the white-bearded man. Santa's face twitched but he did nothing but stare.

The man searched the sky, found no sign of the ravens, hadn't heard them since yesterday morning. He knew what that must mean. The trail was cold; without the ravens Krampus could be anywhere, could be a thousand miles away. He was wasting his time here.

He heard a horn, far away, from the east. He turned toward it, pulled out his own horn, and blew. The sound echoed across the valley, a sound most mortal ears would miss, a sound that could carry half-way across the world.

A few minutes later he caught sight of a sleigh flying toward him over the far ridgeline. It was smaller than his Christmas sleigh, drawn by two goats, Tanngrisni and Tanngnost. The goats were true Yule goats, the last of their breed, last of his ties to another age.

"The past should stay in the past," he growled. *So much had I managed to forget. Now, Krampus returns to resurrect old ghosts.* Santa looked heavenward. *Baldr is dead, by all the gods, and he needs to stay dead. Baldr paid for his misdeeds, his arrogance, his deceit, paid with his life, his soul . . . paid a hundred times over. How much is enough? When will I be allowed to forget?*

The sleigh floated down and came to a skidding stop on the rough road. Two elves hopped out, both armed with sword and pistol, dressed in woodland gear: thick jackets, britches, cloaks, and boots. They scanned the hills with keen eyes as they strolled up to Santa Claus—the top of their heads only reaching as high as his belt. They peered down the ravine at the two wolves.

"Is Freki dead?" Tahl, the younger of the two elves, asked.

"No," Santa replied. "But will be soon I am afraid."

"Can we do anything?"

"Not for Freki. He is too large to carry in the sleigh."

"'Tis a shame."

"Yes," Santa agreed, "and Geri will not leave his side. Not even in death. Their fates are one."

They watched Geri pace round her mate. She licked his fur and again looked to the white-bearded man. She barked, then her bark turned into a whine.

"We can't just leave them like this," Tahl said. "There has to be something we can do."

"It is sad, but they are of the past and like all the ancient ones, their time is done." Santa turned, mounted the sleigh. The older elf followed, but the younger one stayed, watching the doomed creatures.

"Come, Tahl," Santa Claus called. "Do not make this harder than it need be."

The elf bit his lip, left the ledge and the wolves behind, ran and leapt into the sleigh. The older elf snapped the reins; the two goats bleated and leapt skyward, pulling the sleigh up over the trees. Tahl watched the wolves become smaller and smaller, until they were just two tiny specks alone in the forest.

As the sleigh disappeared over the ridge, the wolf set back her head and howled; the mournful, forlorn sound echoed through the snow-covered hills.

Chapter Eight

AMBUSH

The howl pressed into Krampus's head, into his heart, so faint, not even a whisper, not even an echo's echo, yet so painful to bear.

Dawn's first glow peeked in through the window slats. The others slept undisturbed, but for Krampus it seemed there was no reprieve from the mournful call. *Such sorrow,* he thought. He clutched the sack, pulled it into his lap, and did his best to push the howls from his mind. *Loki's arrow,* he thought, *it must be found or I am defenseless.* He set his mind to the task, trying to picture it in all its possible manifestations. Only he had no idea what the fabled arrow looked like, where it might be, and had to rely on the sack not only to seek but to find, and the sack was taking its toll. *Where are you? Where are you?*

Legend told that Odin had it taken into Muspell, the realm of lava and fire, to be melted down and destroyed forever, but Hel had spoken otherwise. Krampus pressed his eyes shut, thought of Asgard, melded with the sack. The charred ruins of Valhalla appeared in his mind, the surrounding lands all scorched earth, all a graveyard of crumbling ash. Krampus wondered how much longer before the ghostly realm was lost forever. The bones of a ship appeared among a dry seabed. *"Hringhorni, Baldr's funeral vessel,"* Krampus whispered. *"It must be here. Look for the—"*

The howl—mournful and piercing.

The vision faded. Krampus opened his eyes, found himself staring about the church again, into the tortured face of the Christ hanging on the wall. He let out a long sigh, let the sack fall from his hands, the fatigue eating down to his very bones. He pushed himself to his feet and stepped to the window, peered out into the frosty morning and watched dawn's light dance among the icicles, heard the call of morning birds. He longed to just sit there the day long and watch Sol make her path across the winter landscape. But there would be no time for such frivolity, not for him, not so long as Baldr still drew breath.

Again, the howl.

Geri. Krampus felt sure. The language of animals was as his own, and with the ancients he shared a bond. The howl told of more than pain, it spoke of abandonment. Krampus shook his head. *He has left them behind. Odin's great pets left to die alone.* Krampus found his nails biting into his palm. *Odin would curse him ill for such deed.*

Another cry.

And blame is shared, for my hand is at play in these matters as well. That cannot be denied. Would I be as he then? Would I sit by and do nothing? Let them die? Allow those magnificent beasts to disappear from this world? He shook his head. *Something must be done.*

He turned, sure of course, then hesitated. *This could be one of his tricks. A trap. A ruse to draw me out.* Krampus took in a deep breath. *Perhaps . . . perhaps not. Some risks must be made.*

"Arise," Krampus called.

The Belsnickels raised their heads, sat up, looked about as though unsure where they were and how they'd arrived here. There was no such confusion on Jesse's face. He sat up quick, his hands still bound and his leg tied to the pew. Krampus could read his focus, his hatred; the man made no effort to hide it. Krampus thought how surprised Jesse would find it if he knew how much he, Krampus, understood that hatred. He liked this man's spirit, wanted to tell him to hold fast, that he, the Yule Lord, would make good on his promise, but knew such words would be lost on the man while he resided in such a dark place.

"We go. Load up into the carriage. I have an errand."

They looked at him confused.

"We must find the wolf."

"THIS IS JUST plain stupid," Jesse said, keeping a tight eye on the icy rut road as he patted his pockets in the hopes of finding a stray cigarette.

"Stupid or not," Isabel replied, "his mind's made up." She still wore that confounded panda cap he'd bought her, hadn't taken it off since first putting it on, and it made it hard to be mad at her.

Jesse slowed the truck down to a crawl as they forded a small creek. He shook his head. They'd been lucky on the highway, the only traffic was two out-of-state semis. But it was early, traffic would pick up soon, and there was no guarantee their luck would hold when they tried to head back. "He's gonna get us all killed. This is stupid, stupid, stupid."

"He can be a hard one to figure sometimes," Isabel said. "Talking murder one minute then crying over some dead birds the next."

"Well, one run-in with those wolves was enough for me." Jesse glanced into the rearview at Krampus and the Belsnickels sitting beneath the torn-up camper shell, all of them watching the woods, searching the trees for any sign of the wolves, Santa Claus, who knew what else. The Belsnickels held everything, from spears and knives to a machine pistol, while Krampus clung to that sack like a child to its blanket, his eyes drinking in the scenery.

They came across the video-game boxes scattered all across the dirt road and Vernon tapped the glass. "Krampus wants you to turn around. He believes we've passed them."

Jesse found a wide spot, turned around, and headed slowly back down the mountain. About a quarter-mile later, Krampus raised his hand. Jesse gently tapped the brakes, careful of the ice, and they rolled to a stop.

"He wants you to turn off the engine," Vernon said in a hushed voice, as though the wolves might be hiding under the truck.

Jesse thought this was a bad move. He wanted to be able to stomp the accelerator and go, should either of the wolves appear, and you couldn't always count on the old V-8 to start right up, even when it was warm. "I don't know if I—"

"Shush," Vernon said, putting a finger to his lips. "He's listening for them."

Jesse rolled his eyes and shut off the engine.

Krampus slid out of the truck, followed by the Belsnickels. The Shawnee wore their pistols and knives in their belts and held their spears at the ready, scanning the woods in all directions. Vernon walked up to Jesse's window, fiddling with the converted Mac-10 he'd brought along, oblivious to the fact that he was pointing it at Jesse while he did. "Hey," he whispered. "How do you cock this thing, again?"

Jesse pushed the barrel toward the ground. He had little faith in Vernon's abilities to use the weapon without shooting himself, or his pals, and just hoped he wasn't anywhere near the man if he did decide to use it. "When you get ready to use it, slide this bolt back." Jesse had never shot a machine pistol before, but it was a simple enough gun. By the way Vernon handled it, he wondered if Vernon had ever shot any gun before. "Don't pull the bolt back until you're ready to shoot, or the gun could go off in your hand."

Vernon pulled the bolt back.

"No, Vernon, not until you're ready to shoot."

"I am ready," Vernon said, inadvertently pointing the gun right at Jesse as he did.

"Shit, Vernon," Jesse snapped, shoving the barrel away from his face. "Look, man, you gotta watch where you're pointing that thing. Okay?"

"Oh, yes. I'm sorry."

Krampus and the Shawnee stood at the ledge, scanning the gorge below, when a low howl echoed up the valley. Jesse's skin prickled. It sounded nearby.

Makwa sprinted up the road a piece, stopped, and pointed below.

"They found something," Vernon said.

"Let's go see," Isabel said, and started to get out of the truck, stopped, and looked at Jesse.

"I'm good right here," Jesse said.

Isabel shook her head. "I don't think so."

Jesse let out a grunt, put on the emergency brake, and climbed out. "Look, ain't someone gonna at least give me a weapon?" No one paid him any attention. "Fine," he said and followed Isabel and Vernon to the ledge.

He could see the wolves, both of them, about fifty yards below. One of them lay on its side. It looked dead to Jesse. The other stood guard beside it. It stared up at them, growling, its fur bristling. *Need to just leave that thing be.*

Krampus and the wolf watched each other for several minutes, both of their tails twitching. Finally, Krampus spoke. "None of you are to use your weapons without my order. That is a command. Now, wait here." He walked back to the truck, reached into the camper, and pulled out his sack.

"What's he up to?" Vernon asked no one in particular.

Krampus closed his eyes, clutched the sack, then reopened his eyes. He inserted his arm into the sack and withdrew a chunk of something. Krampus tossed the sack back into the truck bed and headed their way.

"It's the leg of beef," Vernon said. "He's planning on feeding the damn things. Isn't he? He's mad, completely mad."

Jesse realized Krampus must've opened a door back to the church and simply pulled the meat out of the wash tub. "Maybe he'll let you feed them, Vernon."

But Krampus passed them by without a word and started down the rocky embankment. He slid and scrambled his way to the bottom of the ravine, then leapt deftly from boulder to boulder until he was about twenty yards from the wolves. The huge wolf bared its teeth and stood its ground. They could hear the low rumble of its growl all the way up the ravine.

"My friends," Vernon said, making no effort to hide the pleasure in his voice. "Lord Krampus is about to be devoured before our very eyes."

The Shawnee cut him a dark look.

"Do not *even* frown at me, you bunch of heathens. Not everyone is having a gosh-darn good time here. God or not, he has finally gone completely cuckoo." Vernon smiled. "'Sooner he's dead, the sooner I get to wake up from this nightmare."

Krampus took a step, then another, slowly moving closer and closer to the wolf. The wolf showed no sign of backing down, its growl increasing in volume. Jesse found he shared Vernon's sentiment; Krampus had indeed lost hold of his senses. Even the Shawnee looked unsure, clutching their weapons and exchanging nervous glances.

Krampus stepped upon the ledge with the giant wolves. He held the chunk of beef out before him and spoke to the wolf. It was impossible to make out the words from that distance, yet somehow Jesse caught his low, soothing tone, as though the Yule Lord was reaching out in other ways.

The wolf took a step back, then another. Krampus laid the beef down in front of it. The wolf sniffed, appeared confused—growling then whining, growling then whining.

Krampus stepped over to the injured wolf, squatted on his haunches. He tore off a strip of beef, held it before the prone wolf. It raised its head, sniffed, licked the beef, then took it. Krampus fed it another strip and another, stroking its fur, all while its mate looked on. Finally, its mate took a timid step over, its tail down, sniffing. Krampus nudged the beef toward it. It licked, then bit into the meat—chewing greedily. Jesse wondered how long it had been since it had last eaten.

Krampus kept speaking to them in that low, soothing tone; whatever he was saying seemed to be working. Krampus was soon petting both animals and Jesse watched in disbelief as the standing wolf licked Krampus's hand then actually nuzzled the Yule Lord.

"Looks like today's not your lucky day after all, Vernon," Jesse said.

"Yes, it appears madness wins," Vernon said with a sigh.

Krampus stood and waved to them.

"Now what?" Vernon moaned.

"He wants us to come down," Isabel said. "I got a good idea he's gonna want us to tote that lame wolf back up to the truck."

Vernon let out a long groan.

The Shawnee started down, but Isabel paused. "Vernon, need you to stay put and watch the truck. Krampus's sack's in the back, remember? Shout if you hear anyone coming."

Vernon smiled. "That works for me."

She glanced at Jesse. "And don't let Jesse out of your sight."

The four Belsnickels slid down the embankment, made their way over the boulders, and cautiously approached the wolves.

Jesse blew into his cupped hands, trying to warm his fingers, then shoved them into his pockets. He felt the keys and his heart sped up. He'd forgotten he had them; his mind had been on the wolves—if and when they were going to leap out of the trees and rip them all apart. In his fear and excitement, he'd not even considered escaping, and now realized he wasn't the only one preoccupied, that no one else had thought of the keys, either.

He snuck a quick glance toward the truck; it sat just waiting for him to run and jump in. He considered Vernon standing there on the ledge. *One quick push is all it'd take.* Jesse clutched the keys. *Might be my only chance.*

"Oh, this is just rich," Vernon said, completely transfixed by the drama unfolding below.

Jesse took a step closer to Vernon.

Vernon looked at him, and Jesse froze. "What are you doing?"

Jesse opened his mouth, couldn't find any words, shrugged.

"Well here, look. You're going to miss it."

The standing wolf bristled as the Belsnickels neared, began to growl again. The Belsnickels stopped in their tracks.

"Just hate to see one of them dunderheaded savages get their arm bit off." Vernon chuckled. "Why, that would just be horrible."

Jesse looked at all the rocks and roots below. He sure didn't want to kill the man, just get away. *Sorry,* Jesse thought and gave Vernon a shove, catching the Belsnickel completely by surprise.

Vernon flew off the ledge and Jesse didn't wait around to see what happened next. He dashed for the truck, leapt in the door, and slammed the key in the ignition. He turned the key, the engine whined, then nothing. Jesse pictured the Belsnickels all scrambling up the ledge, he knew he had only seconds. He tried again, lightly pumping the gas, trying not to flood it in his excitement. This time the engine turned over, the muffler coughed, and black smoke shot out the back. Jesse slammed it into gear and punched the accelerator.

He bounced down the rut road. Howls came from somewhere behind him. He dared not so much as a glance back, all his attention on keeping the truck from sliding off the icy track. A minute later he shot through the brambles, and the front wheels of the old Ford actually left the ground as he flew out onto the highway. A horn blared, followed by the squeal of brakes. Jesse spun halfway around and just missed an oncoming semi. He straightened up, hit the gas, and headed up Route 3 toward Goodhope.

JUST BEFORE TOWN, Jesse pulled down the long gravel road leading to Linda's mother's, then into the turnaround beside the creek. He left the motor running, hopped out, and unscrewed the four pins holding what was left of the camper to his truck. He shoved the camper off into the bushes. He couldn't remember ever seeing the truck without the shell, almost didn't recognize it, hoped no one else would either.

He set his knee on what was left of the tailgate, shoved the sack aside, and pulled out the .22. *Not much, but might be all I need if Abigail is still at Dillard's.* "Wait a minute." He looked at the sack, recalled Krampus pulling the beef from the sack, and his pulse quickened. "The church? Yes, gotta be. It should still be opened to the church. And what's in the church?" He let out a laugh.

He snatched the sack over to him. Stared at it a long minute. "Okay, let's see what you got." He opened the cord, closed his eyes, thought of the machine pistols, and stuck in his arm. His hand waved in empty space and there came a prolonged second when he thought the door had shut, then his hand hit what felt like cardboard, then cold, hard steel. He withdrew his arm and smiled—one of the Mac-10s, it looked like the most beautiful object on earth to him at that moment. He thought of the clips, pictured them in his mind, reached back in, and they were right there. He plucked out two of them. "This should even up the odds a bit."

Jesse tossed Krampus's sack in the passenger's seat and climbed back in. He held the gun up and looked heavenward. "Thank you, Lord." He kissed the gun. "Gonna take this as a sign you're pulling for me."

JESSE TURNED UP Linda's mother's driveway, pulled all the way around to the rear of the house. He slung the gun over his shoulder, jumped out, and ran up the back steps, not bothering to knock, just barging in. He rushed through the house, looking for any sign of Linda or Abigail.

"Linda!" he shouted. *"Abi!"*

"Jesse?" Polly peered down the staircase, clutching her house robe.

He dashed up the stairs; she saw the gun over his shoulder and backed away.

"Where are they?" he asked, his voice frantic. "Where's Abigail?"

"They're not here."

He pushed past, took a quick look into both bedrooms.

"Jesse, what's gotten into you? You don't just come into someone's house and—"

"Have you talked to Linda again? Have you heard anything?"

"She said you were in trouble. Jesse, what kind of trouble are you in?"

He set desperate eyes on her. "Abigail's life's at stake, if you know anything please tell me."

"Only thing I know is that Dillard wants them to stay put at his place. Linda won't say more than that. Said I wasn't to come over." Polly's eyes began to water. "I'm so scared. Jesse, please tell me what's going on."

"Maybe they're still safe then." He ran back downstairs.

Polly caught up with him in the hall. "Why won't anyone tell me what's going on?"

Jesse lifted the phone off the cradle, an old rotary dial. "What's Dillard's number?"

"Nuh-uh. No, sir. I ain't telling. You're just gonna stir things up."

"I'm just gonna see if she's there. Not gonna say a thing."

"You'll just make it worse."

"It can't get no worse. They're out to hurt them . . . Linda and Abigail both."

"Jesse, you got her in this spot didn't you? If—"

"I fucked up, Mrs. Collins. I know that. But I'm willing to die if that's what it takes to fix things. Does that mean anything to you?"

And for a second her stern face weakened and he could see the pain, the fear, then the stubborn came back. "I ain't telling."

"You better, goddammit!" he shouted.

She crossed her arms and he knew unless he was willing to tear her fingernails off one by one, he wasn't getting that number. He yanked the receiver, ripping the cord right out from the phone.

"What in the hell is wrong with you?" she cried.

"Sorry about your phone, Mrs. Collins. Just don't want you telling anyone I was here, at least for a bit."

He headed out the back, taking the receiver with him. Polly followed onto the steps, watched him climb into his truck.

"If anything happens to my babies," she shouted, *"I swear I'll—"*

"You won't have to, Mrs. Collins," Jesse shouted back. *"I'll be dead."*

Her mouth drew into a tight line.

THE PHONE RANG. Dillard reached across the nightstand, knocking over a bottle of Excedrin, spilling pills all over the floor. "Fuck." Another ring. "Hello." He heard a woman breathing. "Polly, is that you again? Damn it, Polly, we told you to stop calling all the—"

"He's on his way over there," Polly snapped.

Dillard sat up. "You mean Jesse?"

"Yeah I mean Jesse. He's got a gun and is out of his gourd. Tore my phone right out the wall, had to walk all the way down to Berta's just to call you. He really scared me, Dillard." She was crying. "What's going on? Would you please just tell me?"

Dillard switched on the table lamp. "Calm down, Polly. It'll all get worked out." Linda sat up, squinting into the light, looking confused. "Here, I want you to tell Linda what you just told me." He handed Linda the phone and got up, slipping on his pants, shirt, and boots. He snatched his pistol, cuffs, and cell phone off the nightstand and headed down the hall. He could hear Linda trying to calm her mother, hoped Polly would convince Linda that Jesse was unstable. *Getting tired of hearing her defend that cocksucker.*

Dillard flipped open his cell phone and made a call.

"What?" a groggy voice answered.

"Chet?"

"Dillard?"

"Yeah. Get on over to my place. Got a present for you."

"Jesse?"

"He'll be here any minute, so you might want to hurry."

Dillard snapped the phone shut, slipped it into his pocket, then walked through the house turning off any lights and closing all the drapes. He stationed himself in the den and peeked out through the blinds. He wondered if Jesse would be stupid enough to pull right into the driveway, or if he'd park down the road and try to sneak up. *Might get tricky if he does. Be a hell of a lot easier if I could just shoot him dead.* But Dillard didn't want to do that, the General wanted him alive, there were a lot of questions needing to be answered.

Dillard pushed the safety off on his gun. He knew Jesse was a loser, but he didn't allow himself to believe for a second that a loser couldn't get lucky, he'd been on the job far too long, seen too much go wrong. *Ain't no easy way to take a gun away from a man without killing him first.*

Linda came running into the room in her jeans and socked feet, buttoning up the front of her blouse. She saw the gun and her mouth tightened. "Let me talk to him."

Dillard gave her a hard look. *When was she gonna learn?* "No. That ain't gonna happen. I want you to go down the hall and wait with Abigail until I tell you otherwise. You got it?"

"Please."

"You need to stay out of my way and let me do my job."

"Dillard, I know how to talk to him. There ain't no need for this."

He felt his temper heating up. "Did you not hear your mother? Does that sound like the Jesse you once knew?"

"I'm not gonna stand here and let you shoot him dead."

"Goddammit, Linda." He took a step toward her, intent on straightening her out one way or another, when it struck him that she might be just the trick. He let out a long breath. "Okay, Linda, you wanna save Jesse? You get him to put that gun down. Think you can do that?"

Linda nodded without hesitation.

"Understand me, as long as he has that gun there's a very good chance he's gonna end up dead."

"I know."

Dillard wiped his hand across his mouth. "Let him in, distract him and—" Dillard heard a vehicle approaching, recognized the sound of

Jesse's busted muffler. The engine cut off a moment later and Dillard assumed Jesse must've parked just beyond the rise.

He met Linda's eyes, they were wide and anxious. "You ready?"

She nodded, but he could see her hands were shaking.

JESSE HEFTED THE Mac-10, loaded a clip. He shoved the extra clips in his pocket, opened the door, and got out. He pushed the door to without slamming it and glanced up and down the wooded road. The homes along this stretch were few and far between, the next nearest mailbox at least a hundred yards back. He slipped the gun strap around his neck, setting the machine pistol beneath his arm. The light snow had turned into a miserable drizzle. He flipped up his jacket collar and, sticking to the trees, headed over the rise toward Dillard's.

Jesse hunkered down in the bushes at the edge of Dillard's yard, wishing he had a cigarette or something to calm his nerves. The cruiser was gone, which meant there was a real good chance Dillard was, too. And if Dillard happened to be home, hopefully he'd still be in bed, giving Jesse some chance at catching him by surprise. *Are you prepared to shoot him?* Jesse recalled the last time he had had to make that choice. *This is different. This isn't about me. This is about Abigail. I* will *shoot him if I have to.* He took a deep breath, pulled the bolt back on the Mac, hoping to hell he wouldn't have to shoot anybody. He broke cover and headed down the slope.

Jesse crept along the front of the house, trying to peek into the windows, looking for lights, any clue to who might be inside. He started to climb onto the front porch when the door opened. Jesse jumped, jerked the gun up, finger on the trigger.

Linda stood in the crack of the door, and for a moment he forgot about Dillard, the General, even Krampus, only felt the ache in his heart.

"Jesse," Linda said, looking shocked. "What are you doing here?"

He darted up the steps, trying to see inside, keeping the gun ready. "Is he here?" he hissed. "Is Dillard here?"

She shook her head and a rush of relief washed through him.

Linda glanced up and down the road. "Quick, get in here before someone sees you."

Jesse ducked inside the foyer. "Where's Abigail?"

She looked him over and he could see in her eyes what a mess he must be.

"Jesse, I'm so worried about you. What is—"

"Is she here? Is Abigail here?"

"Jesse, would you please put that gun away." He caught the quiver in her voice, noticed she was talking to him carefully, the way you'd talk to a crazy person.

"Please," she said. "Just put it down and talk to me, Jesse. Please."

He saw it then, the fear in her eyes. "Oh, Linda. Oh, no . . . you got it all wrong." He yanked the gun strap from around his neck, sat the weapon on the hall table beneath an oval mirror, and stepped toward her. "Baby, last thing I meant to do was scare you."

She backed away.

He couldn't stand the pain in her eyes. He reached for her, taking another step. "Linda, please just listen. I can explain every—"

From the corner of his eye, he caught sight of a shadow rushing out from the dark den. It hit him before he could turn, driving him into the wall with a tremendous thud. His feet were kicked out from under him and he hit the floor, his head bouncing off the river-rock tile. For a moment everything went bright-white and syrupy. A crushing weight landed on his back, hard hands twisted his arms behind him, and cold steel clamped around his wrists. He was patted down, then a big boot kicked him over. When things came back into focus, he found himself staring up into Dillard's cold eyes.

"That ought to take some of the spit out of you," Dillard said.

Jesse searched for Linda, found her clutching her face in her hands. "Linda . . . why?"

"Jesse, I'm so sorry. I . . . just . . . I thought . . . just wanted to do what was best. I was scared you were gonna end up getting hurt. Scared you might hurt somebody. Scared for Abi." She gave him a pleading look; opened her mouth to say more, then burst into tears. She hid her face in her hands and sobbed.

For Abi? Then it hit him: Linda had no idea. "Linda, no. You got it all wrong. It's the General that means to hurt Abi. Don't you see, baby? Dillard, too, they're all in on it. They're playing you to—"

Dillard drove his boot into Jesse's stomach. Jesse doubled up, groaning.

"*Stop it!*" Linda shouted.

Dillard ignored her, picked the Mac-10 up off the table. "How'd you come by this?"

Jesse glared at Dillard, but didn't answer.

"I asked you where this goddamn gun came from."

"*Pulled it out of my ass!*" Jesse shouted.

Dillard leaned over, grabbed a handful of Jesse's hair, and slammed his face into the floor. Jesse felt something snap in his nose and his head exploded in a burst of bright pain.

"*Stop!*" Linda screamed and grabbed Dillard by the arm. "*Stop it!*"

Dillard stood up, locked his stony-gray eyes on her. She fell back a step. "Linda, I'm gonna tell you this one time." His voice cold, void of emotion. "Go down the hall to Abigail's room and stay there."

Linda's lips tightened; she was shaking. "No, I won't."

Dillard tilted his head as though he weren't hearing right, then sat the Mac-10 back on the table and took a step toward her.

A vehicle—a truck, by the sound of it—pulled up outside. Jesse heard doors slamming, excited voices, then the drumming of feet on the porch. The front door burst open and Chet and Ash Boggs rushed in, weapons leveled. Chet carried a pistol and Ash a scattergun. They saw Jesse on the floor, grinned, and lowered their weapons.

Ash let out a whoop and all three hundred pounds of him practically danced over to where Jesse lay. He jabbed a finger at Jesse and said, "Picked the wrong son'bitch to steal from. Didn't you, cocksucker? Why, the General's gonna boil you alive, boy."

Linda's eyes shot to Dillard. "What's he talking about?"

"Ash," Dillard said. "Why don't you shut up."

"Dillard?" Linda pressed.

"They threatened to kill Abi," Jesse spat. "Dillard's part of it! Open your eyes, Linda, before it's too—"

Dillard kicked him again.

"*Dillard!*" Linda cried. "What's he talking about?"

Dillard didn't answer.

"He's not going with them," Linda said, and Jesse saw the stubborn, take-no-shit-off-no-one gal he'd fallen in love with. "I won't let 'em take him. I'll call the sheriff if I have to. But he's not going anywhere with them."

Chet and Ash exchanged a glance.

Dillard stared at Jesse, his eyes burned into him, nodding to himself. Slowly, he lifted his head, fixing those burning eyes on Linda. "Linda," he said, his tone tight and strained. "Leave."

"I won't."

Dillard closed his eyes and Jesse started to shout, tried to warn Linda, but Dillard was already on the move. He swung, caught her in the face with his open palm, spinning her around. Her feet tangled and she tumbled into the living room.

"You fucking piece of shit!" Jesse cried and tried to make his feet. Ash, a man easily double Jesse's weight, dropped atop of Jesse, pinning him with his knees.

Linda sat up, touched her busted lip, and looked at the blood on her fingers.

"Mommy?" Abigail stood in the hallway in her pajamas. She clutched her doll, her eyes confused. She saw Jesse. "Daddy? *Daddy!*" she cried, and dashed toward him. Dillard grabbed for her arm, missed, and caught hold of her hair, yanking her back. Abigail screamed, a sound full of terror and pain.

"Fuck!" Jesse cried, kicking and bucking, not even feeling the cuffs biting into his wrists as he fought to dislodge Ash.

"Oh, no you don't," Ash said and hammered a fist into the back of Jesse's head. Jesse's vision blurred again, but he could still hear Abigail crying.

Dillard, still clutching Abigail by the hair, dragged her over to a door on the far side of the living room and opened it. It appeared to lead down into the basement. "Linda," he snapped. "If you don't want her getting hurt, you're gonna take her downstairs . . . *now.*"

Linda climbed to her feet and rushed over to Abigail, picking her up. Abigail clung to her neck, wailing. Jesse caught one last terrified look from Linda as she and Abigail disappeared down the stairwell.

"Dammit," Chet said under his breath. "Didn't I warn you, Jesse? Didn't I tell you not to fuck with him?"

Dillard slammed the door shut and turned the bolt, locking the girls in. He stood there a minute longer, taking long, deep breaths. Slowly, he turned to Jesse, walked back into the hall, and plucked the Mac-10 back up. He squatted on one knee and grabbed Jesse by the hair, pointing the machine pistol into Jesse's face. "Where'd you get this gun?"

Blood ran from Jesse's nose into his mouth and down his chin. "Shoot me, asshole," Jesse spat, and meant it. He knew he was done for, one way or another, and just wanted Abigail's heart-wrenching scream gone from his head. He couldn't bear to think what might happen to Linda and Abigail now. Dillard had been right, he was a loser. He'd not just failed, he'd made everything worse for everyone.

Dillard pressed the gun against Jesse's temple, rested his finger on the trigger. Both Chet and Ash moved back. The foyer fell dead quiet and Jesse clenched his eyes shut, waiting.

"Ah . . . hey, Dillard," Chet said softly. "General said we're supposed to bring him in alive. Y'know? I'm just saying."

Dillard didn't move, seemed to be made of stone.

"Dillard . . . man. C'mon. None of us need the General on our asses."

Dillard let out a long sigh, handed the Mac-10 to Chet, leaned over, and spoke into Jesse's ear. "You fucked everything up. For me, for you, for Linda and Abigail." A tremor crept into his voice, he sounded on the verge of tears. "I made you a promise last time we spoke. You remember? I told you what would happen if you set foot on my property again." He grabbed hold of Jesse's pinkie, gave it a quick twist, bent the finger all the way backward. Jesse felt a snap and a shot of pain rocketed up his arm. He screamed.

Dillard moved to the next finger, then the next. Twisting and snapping each finger on Jesse's left hand, not just dislocating them, but breaking them. Jesse screamed and bucked, tried to understand how anything could hurt so bad. The world began to spin, all bright lights and the taste of the stone tile against his teeth. With a final twist, Dillard snapped Jesse's thumb. Mercifully, Jesse lost consciousness and the world swam into darkness.

Chapter Nine

BLOOD BATH

From the rear seat of Chet's Chevy Avalanche, Jesse watched the gate grind open along its rusty track. The rain had picked up, and the darkening sky painted everything gray. Chet pulled into the General's compound and up to the motor bay followed by Ash in Jesse's truck. The gate rattled shut with a clang that echoed in Jesse's head like a death decree. Cinder-block walls, barbed wire, steel outbuildings, rusting diesel parts, and dirty snow—Jesse couldn't picture a more desolate setting to meet his end. He watched the water drops gather and slide down the windshield, remembered how as a child he'd pretend they were eating each other, tried to pretend he was sitting in the back of his daddy's car now heading over to Grandma's for dinner. He fought to control his shaking, the fear in the pit of his stomach. The fear came not from knowledge of his impending death; he was more than ready for that. He'd lost everything, Abigail, Linda, and now the only thing he had left—his music. His left hand was utterly ruined; he would never play again. His fear came instead from knowing his death was going to be long and bad . . . very, very bad. He squeezed his eyes shut. *Please God, make it quick. I don't have the strength for this. You know I don't.*

Chet got out, came around, and opened Jesse's door. He dug Dillard's keys out from his jacket and uncuffed Jesse from the armrest. Chet tucked the cuffs away and hauled Jesse out, bumping his injured hand. A fresh jolt of pain shot up Jesse's arm and he fought not to cry out.

"Get used to hurting," Chet said. "'Cause you got a world of it ahead of you. As a matter of fact I can without a doubt state you are the very last person I'd care to be right now." Jesse saw Chet meant it, caught genuine pity on his face.

There came a click, an electrical hum, and the bay door rattled upward, revealing first boots, then legs, and finally a row of men. The General stood, his arms across his chest, eyes set on Jesse, his face stone, staring so hard as to appear never to blink. Behind him stood close to a dozen men, all Boggses and Smootses, all the General's kin of one sort or another. *The whole clan turned out,* Jesse thought. *A family reunion just for me.* And the reason why wasn't lost on him. He knew the General meant to make an example of him, to show these men what happens when someone betrays Sampson Ulysses Boggs.

"Bring him on in," the General said, his voice dry and dead as his face.

Chet and Ash each grabbed one of Jesse's arms. "You're in a world of shit, Jesse," Ash said. "A world of shit." They dragged him into the auto bay. The men moved aside, revealing a single steel office chair in the middle of the room. They sat him down.

The General plucked a roll of gray duct tape off the peg board, tossed it to Chet. "Make sure he can't squirm loose."

Jesse made to rise, and two sets of hands sat him back down hard, held him tight while Chet strapped his ankles to the front legs of the chair and his arms to the back.

Ash came in, carrying the Mac-10 Dillard had taken from Jesse. He handed it to the General along with the additional clips and cash they'd found in Jesse's jacket.

The General looked the gun over, nodded. "You're right, Chet. It's one of mine." He sat the gun down on a tool cart and began to count the cash.

"There's eight hundred dollars there," Chet said.

"Eight, huh," the General said, scratching at his thick beard. "I believe that's at least forty thousand short." He looked at Jesse, wagged the cash at him. "Someone stole this out of my safe . . . without even opening it. Can't wait to hear the secret to that trick.

KRAMPUS

"Ash. Shut the bay will you?"

Ash hit the switch. The bay door rolled down and Jesse watched the gray day slowly disappear from view, and it felt to him as though someone was closing the lid on his coffin.

Everybody stood in silence, waiting for the General's next move. Jesse never felt more alone in his life. He heard a muffled train whistle from somewhere far off and wondered if Abigail could hear that same whistle, realized he didn't even get to tell her good-bye, to tell her one last time how much he loved her. He could still hear that scream, his sweet little girl screaming with fear and pain all because of him, and it burned into him like a brand. He gritted his teeth, blinked back hot tears. He was ready, ready for it to all be done.

Chet rolled over a tool cart. An array of tools sat along the two shelves: saws, hammers, pliers, a hand drill, a nail gun, and even a blowtorch. Jesse did his best not to look at any of it.

"Don't much care for the way Dillard's treating Linda and Abigail," Chet said, speaking to the General.

"Why, what'd he do?"

"Bloodied Linda up a bit."

"That so?" the General said.

"Yanking that little girl around by the hair."

"I guess them girls is his business now."

"Don't make it right," Chet growled.

"There's a lot not right around here," the General said and set eyes on Jesse. "A lot of shit needs getting to the bottom of." He pulled a shop stool over and took a seat in front of Jesse. "Jesse you're already dead. You know that and I know that. So you're probably asking yourself why you should bother answering any of my questions. I think your answer depends on how bad a death you wanna have." He pulled a silver snubnose revolver out of his belt, leveled it at Jesse. "You answer my questions straight up, then I'll take this here gun and shoot you in the head and it'll all be over. You have my word on it. And you know I'm good for my word." He sat the gun down on top of the tool cart, leaned over, and tugged something out from the bottom shelf. He held it up and Jesse found himself staring into the milky, dead eyes of the severed cow head. The General dropped it on Jesse's lap; the cold wetness soaked into his pants, the stink saturating his nostrils.

The General flipped off his hat and the overhead fluorescent gleamed off his bald scalp. He set the hat on the tool cart and picked up the nail gun. Held it in front of Jesse's face. "Now, on the other hand, if you give me the runaround, lie to me even once, then things are gonna get real ugly, real fast." The General pointed the nail gun at the floor and hit the trigger. A nail blasted out of the front and bounced off the concrete floor with a spark and a loud ting.

The General pressed the nail gun against Jesse's kneecap. "Now, tell me, Jesse Walker. Just how did that there cow head come to find its way into my safe?"

Jesse closed his eyes, tried to prepare himself for the pain, because he knew whatever he said would be the wrong thing, that he'd never be able to convince them of the truth, and there was no lie he could possibly come up with that would make any sense. There was no way out, and no one to hear his screams, not out here, and if they did, they'd know better than to call the police about it. *I'm fucked and that's all there is to it.*

"I got twenty-four-hour surveillance," the General said. "I watched the tapes, and from the time I left till the time I came in the next morning, weren't no one anywhere near this place, let alone in my office. That safe weren't broke into and nobody knows that combination but me. So tell me Jesse . . . tell me how you done it?"

Jesse opened his mouth, tried to come up with something, anything.

The General tapped the nail gun against his knee. "Now think real hard before you answer, because you want to get this right the first time. Trust me on that."

"I used the Santa sack."

The bay fell dead quiet.

Chet let out a snort.

"Come again," the General said.

"The sack. The fucking Santa sack. The one in my truck." Jesse's voice kept rising. "I used it to empty your safe. It's magic, all right? *All right!*" he yelled. *"You can fucking believe me or fucking not!"*

The nail gun hissed. Jesse felt the kick as the piston drove the nail deep into his kneecap. A half-second later the pain hit. *"Fuck!"* Jesse cried. *"Fuck!"* The General bounced the nail gun up Jesse's thigh, hit the trigger again, and again, and again, driving three more nails into

Jesse's leg. Jesse screamed, bucked, would've knocked the chair over backward had Chet not caught him and set him up straight.

The General grabbed the cow's head by the ear, tossed it aside, shoved the nail gun hard into Jesse's crotch. Jesse groaned.

"Jesse, do you really want to spend the entire evening doing this? I know I don't. I just want some answers. Want to know about this gang you been running with. Who they are? Where they live? So here's the place where I give you one more chance. You work with me here, and this can all be over. I can go home and watch some TV and you can be dead. Now tell me Jesse. How'd you get into my safe?"

"Look . . ." Jesse said, barely able to get the words out. "Just . . . bring me the sack. I . . . can show you."

The General shook his head, pulled the trigger. Jesse felt the nail tear into his groin. *"No!"* Jesse screamed as the General punched two more into his gut, the nails penetrating deep into his lower abdomen.

"Oh, God!" Jesse screamed. *"Oh, for fuck's sake! Stop! Stop it!"* He swooned, almost blacked out. "Listen," he gasped, trying to get the words out between sobs. "Listen . . . hear me out. You want your fucking money back, right?" He gritted his teeth, tried to focus through the pain. "I can . . . get it back. Your drugs . . . all of it. Right now. But you gotta hear me out. God, what the fuck you got to lose? Just hear me out."

No one spoke; the only sound in the bay was Jesse's groans. Jesse watched the blood darkening his pants along his leg and crotch. Tried not to think of the nails inside his gut, the holes they'd punched into his lower intestines. He'd always heard a gut wound was the worst way to go, slow and painful, he could certainly attest to the pain.

"Okay, son. Shoot."

Jesse raised his head, tried to blink away the tears, tried to hold the General's gaze. "Your drugs . . . are still under . . . fuck . . . under the front seat of my truck. Exactly where your dumbass nephew . . . left them. I can get your money back . . . but I'll need the sack. I know you think I'm full of shit. Look . . . look at me. Do I look like I'm fucking around?" Sharp pain made Jesse squeeze his eyes shut, he let out a deep grunt, opened them again. "What the hell do you have to lose? Just bring me the goddamn sack and I'll show you."

The General paused, seemed to mull it over, and Jesse dared to hope that he just might have a chance. The sack was open to the church, the money was there, but more important, so was the rest of the General's guns.

"Chet, go get that stupid sack."

"What? Really, I mean how the fuck can a sack—"

"Shut up and just go get the damn sack."

"Ash," Chet said. "Go get that damn sack."

"No, Chet," the General said. "I told you to get it. I'm the one that gives the orders around here."

Chet gave Jesse a dark look, then headed toward the side door.

"And the drugs," the General called. "See if the drugs are there."

The men waited, shifting uncomfortably from foot to foot, looking at the tools, at the overhead fluorescents, at the flickering Christmas lights over on the stairs, anywhere but at Jesse, at the nails protruding out of his leg and gut.

Jesse fixed on the sack, trying to push the pain from his mind by thinking about what he'd do if he could just get a hold of one of those guns. *God, if you were to grant me a last wish. Please, give me the chance to send as many of these motherfuckers to Hell as I can.*

"Praying ain't gonna save you, son," the General said.

Jesse started, wondered for a second if he'd been thinking out loud.

The General sat the nail gun down. "The truth. That's your only salvation."

Chet came in, carrying the sack over his shoulder and the packet wrapped in duct tape. "Well, I'll be damned. He weren't lying about the drugs. Here they are."

The General's brow tightened. "That don't make no sense. Why—" He paused. "Shit, ain't nothing making sense. Here, hand me that blasted sack. We're gonna get to the bottom of this nonsense, and right now."

The General held the sack, seemed to weigh it. "Not much to it." He laid it on the floor, stepped on it, watched it slowly reinflate. "Tell me that ain't strange." He pulled it open. All the men stepped forward, leaned in, trying to get a look. "Can't really see nothing." He pulled the mouth of the sack open as wide as he could, tried to angle it so the overhead fluorescence would illuminate the insides. "Kinda smoky, huh?" The General looked up and the other men all nodded.

"Chet, here. Reach in and make sure he's not hiding nothing in there."

"Are you fucking nuts? I ain't sticking my hand in there. No telling what's in there. That smoky stuff could be some sort of poison."

The General scratched his beard and looked around; there were no volunteers. "Well, it is a bit creepy I guess." He held the sack upside down and shook it. Nothing fell out. He took the sack and pushed the air out of it, folded it once, started rolling it up, tighter and tighter, until it was as tight as a bedroll. "Don't think you could hide any sort of weapon in that. Couldn't hide much of nothing." He set hard eyes on Jesse. "This better not be a game. If it is . . . I can guarantee you'll regret it something awful." He dropped the sack on the ground in front of Jesse. Everyone watched as it slowly regained its shape.

"Now, tell me how to make it work."

"Can't."

"Can't?"

"No, it won't work for you. It's like a magic hat, you have to know the trick. I have to show you."

The General squinted at him. "You're trying to tell me you used a magic trick to steal from my safe."

"Yes."

"That's a bunch of bullsnot," Chet put in. "He's just trying to make us look stupid."

"You're telling me if I let you stick your hand in here," the General continued, "you can pull out my cash?"

Jesse nodded.

"Well," the General said. "That's one magic trick I wouldn't miss for the world. Cut his arms loose."

Chet let out a disagreeable grunt but slipped his knife out from the holster on his belt and slit the tape. Jesse freed his arms, cradled them to his chest, careful to avoid touching his lap or leg.

"Don't you try nothing," Chet said and pressed the knife against his neck.

"Hell, Chet," Ash said. "What's he gonna do, get blood on your shirt?" Ash snickered. "Christ, if you don't sound like a little girl sometimes."

The men chuckled and Chet turned red. "Fuck you, Ash. Hell, if you don't sound like a little bitch when you're choking on my goddamn pecker."

"Both of you shut up," the General said. "And Chet put that knife away before you hurt yourself." The General picked up the sack and sat it beside Jesse. "Okay, son. We're all waiting."

Jesse tugged the sack up and balanced it on his good leg. He held it in place with his left arm, careful not to let it bump his broken fingers. The men watched his every move. He swallowed. *Okay, God, time to pick your team.* He closed his eyes, thought of the guns, and inserted his good hand. No delay this time, the sack was still open to exactly where he'd last been; his hand hit the stack of cash, he patted over and bumped metal—one of the .45s. He opened his eyes, found everyone leaning in, all trying to see what he was up to. He pushed the safety off and slipped his fingers around the grip, licked his lips, his mouth suddenly dry. He started to slide his arm out and felt Chet's hand on his shoulder, his knife against his back. "I'm watching you." And this time no one gave Chet a hard time, the mood had changed; Jesse could sense their nervousness.

Shit, Jesse thought, *this won't work.* He almost pulled the handgun out anyway, just went for it, but stopped. *No, if you do this right, you just might get out of here.* He sat the .45 down, picked up as many bills as he could hold, and slowly inched his arm from the sack.

"That's it," Chet said. "Nice and slow."

Jesse eased his hand out, revealing the rolls of bills. There came several audible gasps, and Jesse felt every bit the stage magician. He handed them to the General.

The General scrutinized the cash, shook his head, and smiled. "Well, slap me silly!"

Grunts and grins of approval, someone even clapped; Jesse wondered if he should bow. Instead he slipped his hand back in and pulled out another handful, then another, dropping the cash onto the floor, watching, waiting until they were all taken in by the trick, discussing, joking, and staring at the money. He felt the knife leave his back, saw Chet staring in stupid wonder. *Now,* Jesse thought and found the gun again, wrapped his hand around the grip, his finger on the trigger. He twisted round, bringing the handgun up quick, intent on dropping Chet before he could stab him. But the gun sight snagged on the lip of the sack, causing Jesse to fire before the revolver cleared the sack. There came two muffled reports, but the bullets didn't punch through the velvet and Jesse understood with horrifying clarity that he wasn't firing at Chet at all, but into the church.

"*Oh, fuck!*" Chet cried as Jesse shook the gun free. Chet drove his knife into Jesse's back, shoved Jesse, chair and all, forward, toward the pile of money. Jesse landed face-first into the cash, Chet already on top of him, stomping down on his hand before he could raise the gun, crushing the weapon and Jesse's fingers beneath his boot. The gun went off, two rounds hitting the concrete floor. Men scattered as sparks and ricochets bounced about the bay. Chet stomped again. Jesse heard his fingers snap, and on top of all his other pain, his brain found room to bear this fresh assault in full glory. Jesse screamed and lost hold of the gun. Chet kicked the weapon across the room.

Jesse lay in the pile of money, his legs still strapped to the toppled chair, cradling both his broken hands to his chest. Someone was yelling, but it was hard to make out over the ringing in his ears. Chet yanked the knife out of his back and Jesse gasped, choking as he struggled to breathe.

I'm dying, Jesse thought, and found great comfort in this.

"*HOLY SHIT!*" CHET yelled. "*Holy freaking, fucking shit!*"

The General sat on the stool staring at Jesse, at the sack, the cash, the gun, trying hard to make sense of any of it, of any of the strange events over the last couple of days. He wished Chet would shut up and stop stomping around. The General leaned forward, tugged the sack out from under Jesse. There was blood all over the sack. The General felt sure the kid was on his way out.

"*What do you want to do about this turd?*" Chet cried.

"Stop yelling, Chet," the General said. "I'm right here."

"Fucker almost killed me! Almost killed everyone!"

"Yep," the General nodded as he pulled the sack open and peered into its smoking depths.

"Hey, you ain't thinking about sticking your arm in there are yah?"

The General nodded absently. "I think I am."

The men began to pick themselves off the ground, checking themselves for holes. Apparently, no one caught any of the ricochets and they gathered back around, all eyes glued on the sack.

The General slipped his hand in, all the way up to the wrist, waited. The air in the sack felt cooler, but other than that nothing happened. He pushed his whole arm in. His hand hit something. He gave it a light pat, knew exactly what it was. He pulled out a handful of hundreds. "If that don't beat all." He grinned. Shoved his hand back in, only this time his hand didn't find any cash—instead, something found his hand. The General's grin fell from his face. His eyes grew large. Something had a hold of him.

"What?" Chet asked. "What the fuck now?"

The General let out a yelp, tried to yank his arm free, when that something gave him a tug, pulled his arm, shoulder, and entire head into the sack. There came a blink of darkness, then he found himself face-to-face with . . . *the devil.* The General screamed. The devil pressed its nose right up against his, grinned, its hot breath coming through jagged teeth, its eyes, its red, glowing eyes staring right into him. The General screamed again, felt hands grab hold of his legs and waist, hauling him back into the bay. Only the devil didn't let go; no, it held tight to his arm and came right along with him.

"What the fuck is that!" Chet yelled.

The devil was halfway out of the bag, halfway into the room, looking like a kid in a sack race. It let go of the General and stepped out of the sack.

The General tried to scream again, but had no air left in his lungs and emitted a pathetic squawk.

The thing stood to its full height, towering above them, at least seven feet tall, all wiry muscles and veins and black, glistening skin and fur. A wild mane of ink-black hair framed twisting horns as wide as its shoulders. It looked around at the men, grinning from ear to ear, its red, slanted eyes gleaming. It began to chuckle.

Everyone froze.

"Time to be terrible," the devil said, and snapped its tail like a whip. The men stumbled back and the beast let loose a roar. The booming sound shook the steel walls.

Chet snatched the General's snub-nosed pistol off the tool tray, but the beast moved almost faster than the General could see, slashed its claws across Chet's chest, opened him up to the bone, and sent him tumbling into the men.

Men scrambled in every direction, into each other, into the tool carts, into chaos. A gun shot went off and another, but the beast was gone, leaping across the room. It hit the overhead fluorescents and the tubes exploded in a shower of sparks, throwing the room into the red glow of the Christmas lights. More gunshots, and in the muzzle flashes the General saw the beast tearing men apart, slashing and ripping. Men were screaming, crying, bawling.

The General crawled on his hands and knees toward the door, his hands slipping and sliding in the blood—in all the blood. He climbed over two bodies, his hand tangling in something warm and squishy—a man's stomach, his very guts. A bullet caught the General in the leg. He let out a cry and crumpled. Someone fell atop of him—Ash, clutching his neck as blood spurted between his fingers. Howls echoed, coming from everywhere, crawling beneath the General's skin. The General pulled his knees up to his chest, hugged them tight, squeezed his eyes shut. *"Please, God, please, Jesus,"* he whimpered. *"Please, don't let Satan take me."*

JESSE TRIED TO reach his ankles, tried to tear the tape off, but his broken fingers couldn't do the trick. He grunted, let out a groan, and fell back. The pain in his stomach, legs, hands, back, it all made the slightest movement unbearable. His eyes grew accustomed to the dim glow of the Christmas lights, their shine casting long shadows across the dead and dying. He focused on the carnage, on Krampus, trying to push the pain from his mind.

Krampus straddled Ash's quivering body. The Yule Lord was taller, larger, and so much more imposing than when Jesse had seen him last. His horns were now mighty weapons, unbroken and curling upward from his head, his eyes glowed boldly, his movements quick and powerful. Krampus punched his hand into Ash's chest, cracking bones and tearing tissue, to come away with something Jesse guessed must be the man's heart. Krampus held the organ heavenward and let out a triumphant howl. Squeezed the heart and let the blood run down his arm and drip into his mouth. His chest heaved and a deep growl full of strength, of vitality, of life escaped his throat.

The Yule Lord tossed the heart away, surveyed the room, the carnage, cocked his head this way and that to better take in the moans of the mangled and dying. And he was grinning; even in the gloom Jesse could clearly see that grin. His slanted eyes fell on Jesse. "It is good . . . good to be terrible," Krampus said, licking the blood from his hand.

Jesse shook his head, focused on breathing.

The Yule Lord frowned. "You do not look well."

"Been . . . better." Jesse coughed. "Think I'm dying."

Krampus walked over, knelt down next to him, looked at the growing pool of blood beneath him. "Yes, I believe you are." He cut the tape loose with a quick slash of his fingernail, gently propped Jesse up against the tool cart. "You've been very naughty."

Jesse nodded. "Yeah. I have at that."

Krampus smiled. "You may be dying, but you still have your spirit."

Someone moved behind Krampus—Chet, struggling to sit up near the door. He still had the snub-nose, held it in his shaking hands, trying to level it at Krampus. Jesse opened his mouth to utter a warning when the pistol went off with a deafening bang. The bullet hit Krampus in the horn. Krampus leapt to his feet. The gun went off again, the bullet sparking off the concrete floor several feet to their left. Chet's arms fell; he slumped against the door frame, dropping the gun into his lap. Krampus strolled over, squatted before him.

"Fuck, fucking devil, fucker fuck!" Chet spat, blood running from his mouth. He tried again and again to lift the gun but couldn't.

Krampus glanced over his shoulder at Jesse. "This one has spirit as well. Might make a good soldier." Krampus plucked the gun from Chet's hand and tossed it away. Grabbed hold of the man's arm and bit him on the wrist.

Chet let out a howl, yanked his arm away. "You bit me! What the hell is that shit?" He stared at the bite. Even in the dim light Jesse could see the skin around the bite darkening, the stain spreading up Chet's arm, and understood that Krampus had turned him.

"You are mine now. You will sit here and wait until I tell you otherwise."

"Fuck you!"

Krampus left Chet leaning against the wall, rubbing his arm and slowly turning black all over. He walked to the sack and picked it up. "You deserted me," he said to Jesse. "You broke your oath. I owe you nothing now."

"I know."

Krampus held up the sack. "You took something that did not belong to you."

"Sorry about that."

"I should kill you."

"Too . . . late." Jesse tried to laugh, but choked on his own blood.

"Yet, I bear you no grudge."

Jesse shook his head and rolled his eyes.

"I am being sincere. Your distractions have made the difference, for all I know they have made all the difference. See, I was trapped in a riddle." He closed his eyes, his face falling into deep concentration. He inserted his hand into the sack. "There . . . the ship. All is burned . . . the bones, boards, masts, and treasure. And, and, yes." He smiled. "The answer, so plain I could not see it." He withdrew his arm and pulled out a spear, broken midway along its shaft and blackened from age and fire. "I was searching for an arrow all this time. So fixated I could see nothing else. Pushing the sack to find a thing that did not exist. But now you see . . . it was not an arrow." He wiped the spearhead clean of the soot and grime and it gleamed gold, like the strange ore of Krampus's chains back in the cave. He walked over to Jesse so that he could see the mistletoe leaves and berries delicately inlayed along the blade. "See . . . see the answer? It is a spear, not an arrow." He let out a great sigh. "The answers to all riddles seem obvious once you know them."

He turned the blade round and round, as though transfixed. "Baldr," he whispered. "It is death I hold in my hand. Your death."

Jesse tried to clear his throat, worked to breathe. Coughed and spat up more blood. The pain all but blinded him, forced him to nearly double over.

Krampus sat down next to him, lay the spear across his lap, and pulled the sack over. He reached in and a moment later held one of the ancient flasks. He tore off the wax.

"Odin's mead I hope?" Jesse forced a smile.

"Yes, mead. Now drink." He lifted it to Jesse's lips. "It will not save you. But it will make the dying easier."

Jesse drank, several deep gulps—the mead warm and soothing. His vision became fuzzy, dreamlike, his breathing easier, and the pain receded. His eyelids grew heavy, he leaned his head back against the cart, looked at all the dead men. *Too bad,* he thought. *Too bad Dillard hadn't been here.* He forced his head up, clutched Krampus's arm. "Dillard . . . he still has them!"

"Dillard?"

"He's got my wife . . . my little girl. He's a murderer." Jesse tried to hold the thought, he needed to make Krampus understand, but things were becoming murky, his thoughts befuddled. "He'll hurt them . . . I know it. We gotta do something, gotta stop him. Krampus . . . I'm begging you . . . go kill that bastard."

Krampus admired the spear. "Perhaps one day," he said distractedly. "But this day there is another villain that needs to be dealt with."

KRAMPUS RAN HIS finger along the blade, watched the red Christmas lights flicker off its edge, thought of the high sorcery that went into the crafting of such a weapon. "Still as sharp as the day it was forged." He held it out for Jesse to see. Jesse's eyes were closed, his chin down. Krampus tapped him lightly on the shoulder with the spear.

Jesse's eyes fluttered open. "What?"

"The blade, see. It still holds its edge."

Jesse squinted at the blade. "That's . . . fucking wonderful." His words were slow, slurred.

"Soon, it shall put an end to this Santa Claus charade forever."

"Why . . . why the hell you wanna go and kill Santa Claus for . . . anyhow?" Jesse muttered, his words barely comprehensible. "He's fucking Santa Claus. Hands out presents to children . . . bunch of nice shit like that." He coughed. "Fuck. Give me another swig of that stuff."

"He is *not* Santa Claus," Krampus said, lifting the flask to Jesse's lips. "Santa Claus is a lie. He is Baldr. I told you that. Do you not remember?"

"Yeah, Baldr. Okay."

"You do not understand. You know nothing of him, nothing of his treachery." Krampus felt his blood rising. "His treachery to me, to all of Asgard. How he brought ruin to all." Krampus fell silent, listening to Jesse's labored breathing. "Are you not curious?"

"What?"

"Of Baldr's treachery?"

"No . . . not so much."

"Well, you should know. Everyone should know." Krampus took a deep drink from the flask, wiped his mouth on the back of his arm. "His villainy, his real villainy . . . it began when he came back, after his rebirth, just after Ragnarok swept through Odin's realm, somewhere around eleven hundred years after the Christ child was born. Are you listening?"

Jesse shook his head.

"That was when Asgard fell beneath war and flame, when all the old gods perished. But no thundering apocalypse consumed the earth as foretold. No, mankind had their new gods by then and barely noticed the passing of the old. And us earthbound spirits found ourselves abandoned and alone in a world that had turned unfriendly to our kind. Over the next several hundred years, men were taught to fear us, to drive us or those who still worshipped us away. Our shrines were burned and desecrated. Without tributes and offerings most gave up, faded, were forgotten, and to be forgotten is death . . . the only true death for my kind.

"My shrines were abandoned as well. By the early 1300s, a new tradition by the name of Christmas had wormed its way across the land and as more and more turned to celebrating this miserable holiday, Yule and Winter Solstice were becoming lost. I could see that soon I, too, would be lost." Krampus took in a deep breath. "And I almost gave up. But as I walked amongst the winter nights, seeing the splendor of Yuletide perverted by the new religion, my blood began to burn. I was Krampus, the great and terrible Yule Lord, and I vowed that I would no longer suffer such insult, that I would remind them that I was still here, that I would make them believe. And thus began my rebirth. I humbled myself by traveling from house to house. Loki had left to me his sack and I brought it along, offering rewards to those who remembered, who honored me properly. But for those who did not . . . well, for those I was terrible." Krampus grinned. "I would thrash them with birch rods and for those that would commit evil upon my fold, those I would put in Loki's sack and beat them until they could not walk.

"And the name Krampus began to mean something again. And if Baldr had not come along, who knows . . . maybe it would be my face on all those cola ads, my balloon floating along on the Yule Day Parade, my Belsnickels ringing bells on the street, demanding tribute, or sitting in department stores and making promises to little boys and girls that will never be kept. Maybe, maybe, but only if I had not taken pity on that soulless creature."

He glanced at Jesse. Jesse's chin was back down on his chest. "Jesse?"

Jesse didn't respond.

Krampus reached over and wiggled one of the nails protruding from Jesse's leg.

"Ow, fuck!" Jesse cried. "Watch it. Goddamn, what's wrong with you?"

"You still live."

"Yeah . . . I still live. Lucky me."

Krampus nodded. "Good . . . now, where was I? Ah yes, Baldr's rebirth. It had been prophesied that Baldr would be reborn onto the earth realm after Ragnarok, an earth cleansed of darkness by an all-consuming fire, Baldr reborn a god of light and peace, a just god, to watch over the world of men. But of course there came no cleansing flame and the Baldr I found stumbling in my forests did not even know his own name. Draped in filthy rags, he looked lost, starved. And being that there were so few of us left from the old lineage, I felt a kinship, a responsibility. So I brought him into my domain, dressed him, fed him, plied him with drink. Yet never did I see him smile, not then. But there were times when I would catch him staring at me, his face dark, as though blaming me for all his woes. I should have taken heed to this, but the truth of it was I harbored guilt, guilt for what my mother and grandfather had done to him. I suffered under the delusion that my charity might in some way absolve my lineage of these crimes.

"I offered him brotherhood, gave him a place at my side. Together we took the task of spreading Yuletide. But he seemed ever in a state of brooding, and made only a halfhearted effort at best. One night, as I ravished a house honoring Saint Nicholas, I saw Baldr pocket a small book bearing the saint's mark upon its cover. I should have taken it from him, thrown it into the fire, but my pity made me weak. It was not too long thereafter that he began to don the red and white, to mimic Saint Nicholas in dress. Still I held my tongue, hoped it was but a passing fancy. Then I found the cross. It sat brazenly upon the mantelpiece in his room, the sight hitting me as a slap to the face—the very symbol of my torment in my house! This was more than I could bear. I stormed into his room and threw the cursed item into the fireplace. I tore open his coffer, intent on finding and destroying this book. I did not find that book, but I did find a treasure trove of artifacts and scrolls filled with the dead saint's teachings. I tore them apart, threw the shards at his feet, and demanded explanation. Asked him how he could embrace such evil. He showed no emotion, his face like stone as always. He told me then that the old ways were dead. That I was too blind to see that the ancients' time upon earth had passed. He snatched the smothering cross from out of the fireplace, held it before me as though it were a great talisman. 'Here,' he said. 'Here is the world we now live in. And unless you learn to serve it you will soon be a relic.'

"I knocked that cross from his hand and slapped him across his face. He hardly flinched, just stared at me with those cold eyes. Enraged, I hit him again, a blow that would have felled an ox. Nothing, it was as though he did not even feel it, and it was then that I did first see him smile. A smile of pity. *Pity*, for me. The way one would look at a misguided child! This disparaging look, it burned into me and so I snatched up the iron poker from the fireplace and struck him soundly across the face. He laughed, a sound that I can still hear to this day. It went into my brain and drove out all sane thought. I struck him again and again, meaning to murder him . . . yet I made no mark. It was as if I were beating stone and still he laughed, the sound seeming to multiply in my head. It was then that I truly saw him for the monster that he was, that I understood that he had been playing me all along, that even though he had been reborn into flesh, Odin's spell still held protective power over him. Still I would not stop; I beat him until I could lift the poker no more. He took the poker from me as easily as from a child, knocked me to the floor, kicked me and struck me upon my head until all began to fade. I fell into darkness with his laughter ringing in my ears."

Jesse coughed, leaned forward, clutching his stomach.

"Yes, it is a hard story to hear. I know."

"What?" Jesse muttered.

"Here, another sip." Krampus held the flask for Jesse. "Drink yourself silly. There are worse ways to pass on to the afterlife."

Jesse sipped. "God, you . . . sure like to . . . talk."

"What?"

Jesse grimaced, closed his eyes.

"Talk? Yes, at times." Krampus took another sip as well and continued. "I awoke in my own cellar with chains around wrist and ankle, shackled to a great oak beam. He sat upon a chair, my chair, staring at me with that stone look upon his face. Loki's sack sat in his lap like a trophy. He offered me my freedom if I would but teach him the secret of the sack. As you know there is no secret, one has to be of Loki's direct blood. I knew of no other way, the sack was not my magic but Loki's great sorcery. I did not reveal this, as I feared it would spell my doom, instead acted as though unwilling to tell.

"He took my great house in the forest for his own, left me in the cellar to rot without sun or moon in hopes that time would change my mind. Decades crawled by with nothing for nourishment but slugs and stagnant water. I withered, became but a frail shadow of myself, but my spirit held. I knew even then that if I could but hold on, that the time would come for my revenge.

"He did not wait for the sack to pursue his ambitions. His obsession with the saint grew, and though Saint Nicholas had died over a thousand years before, Baldr took his mantle, stole his name, growing long his white hair and beard, dressing and adorning his robes all in ridiculous imitation of the dead saint.

"His betrayal of the ancient ones, of his own heritage, seemed to know no limits. Even with my captivity, Yuletide still held its place in the land, but that all began to change once Baldr started his reign, began to visit homes far and wide on Christmas Day in the guise of Saint Nicholas, handing out gifts and charity, preaching his gospel of lies. It was not enough for him to simply usurp Winter Solstice—he was not happy until all things Yule were buried, lost. He was trying to make the people forget, forget where the traditions came from, forget Yule and the Yule Lord.

"And how easily he fooled them, how easily he had them eating poison from his hand. For when Baldr was out amongst the people he did play the role of the kindly saint as though born to it. They flocked to him, could not resist his charm, his gracious manner, embraced his words of kindness and charity as he played on the popularity of the Christ God. He became a master of public manipulation. He printed and distributed glorified fables of his charitable deeds and soon his fame spread far and wide, as did the popularity of Christmas.

"But it was all lies, one great ruse, for even as he preached Christian virtues he was delving into the sorcery of the ancients. From my cell I watched him unearthing the dark arts, secretly pursuing the very things he publicly condemned as heresy and demonography. Trying, always trying to break the spell of Loki's sack. Even then on the track of blood, as he bled me almost dry in hopes of manipulating the spell with my blood. He tracked down the last of the old peoples, mostly elves, a few dwarves; put them to work serving his purpose. They fortified my forest home with buttress and stonework walls topped with spikes, dug out the cellar into a great vault from which he pursued his sorcery and wicked ambitions. And while leaving me to rot in that cellar, he went—"

Krampus's voice trailed off, he glanced at Jesse. Jesse's head lay on his shoulder, his eyes closed; there came no sign of breath.

"It appears I am talking to myself." Krampus crossed his arms atop his chest and grunted. He looked around at the dead, inhaled deeply, drank in the smell of blood. It had felt good to kill the wicked. He had not felt so alive in over a thousand years. He thought of the bad man Jesse had spoken of. *Who is this wicked man, Jesse? This Dillard? Do his deeds truly merit death? I, for one, would like to know.*

He poked Jesse. Jesse didn't respond. Krampus leaned over, sniffed him, and smiled. "Jesse, your spirit is strong. You hold on when you should be dead." He looked at the man's mangled hands. *It would be a shame to lose one gifted with song.*

"Would you like to come along with me? Would you like to kill the Dillard yourself?"

There came no response from Jesse.

Krampus drummed his long fingers on the spearhead. "I think you would. Yes, most certainly." He lifted Jesse's arm and bit him on the wrist.

Chapter Ten

IN THE BONES

A song . . . far away . . . "Achy Breaky Heart." Jesse decided he must've ended up in Hell, because there was no way they'd play that god-awful song in Heaven. He opened his eyes. Hell looked a lot like the crew cab of a truck. Jesse sat up fast, too fast, and the world began to spin. He braced himself against the seat and let out a moan.

"You will feel better soon."

Jesse found Krampus sitting next to him, a mischievous grin upon his face. "Fuck," Jesse said, trying to focus his eyes. "You're still here." He tried not to swoon, thought maybe he was still a bit drunk, noticed the sack and spear across the Yule Lord's lap. "You're not wearing your seat belt."

"Seat belt?"

"Where are we going?"

"To kill Baldr. Your friends have decided to join us."

Jesse blinked, rubbed his eyes, and saw Chet driving. Only Chet wasn't exactly Chet. Chet was a Belsnickel, or well on his way to being one, at least, as his skin was spotted charcoal gray. Someone, Jesse wasn't sure who, was riding shotgun. The man looked back at Jesse and Jesse realized it was the General, his skin changing also, his eyes orange. He looked terrified.

"Too bad for you, motherfucker," Jesse said and laughed.

Krampus laughed, too. "Found the short one peeping out from beneath a dead man. He looked lost and scared, so I brought him along. What do you say, little peeper? How about you and Chet sing me a song?"

The General didn't answer, just stared at Krampus with haunted eyes, like a man who wanted to wake up from a bad dream but couldn't.

"General, I command you and Chet to sing me 'Jingle Bells' . . . soft and sweet please. On the count of three: one, and a two, and a three . . ."

They both began to sing, a sad mumbling chorus, out of synch and out of tune.

Jesse laughed again and felt a deep discomfort in his back and chest. He fell quiet. *I was stabbed.* And through the haze of the mead it came back to him. He touched his stomach, his leg. The nails, they were gone, as was the pain, most of it anyway. *I'm still alive!* He slowly tugged up his sleeve, afraid to look, knowing too well what he'd find. His skin, it was speckled gray and black. "No," he said. "No, you didn't!" He glared at Krampus. Krampus nodded, smiling. Jesse pulled up the front of his shirt, exposing his stomach. He could see where the nails had been, the wounds were still there, not oozing blood, as they should've been, but well on the mend.

"I have granted you a life," Krampus said.

"You've turned me into a monster."

"Of sorts."

Jesse held up his hands, wiggled his fingers, and winced. They were stiff and sore, but he could hardly tell they'd been broken. "How . . . can this be?"

"My blood will do that," Krampus said with obvious pride.

"This is wonderful. I think. Now change me back."

Krampus frowned. "Why would I wish to do that?"

"Because I'm telling you to."

"Enough song," Krampus called and both men ceased singing. "Jesse, you are confused. There is only one of us that gives orders and I am afraid it is not you."

Jesse grabbed Krampus by the arm. "No, fuck that. You're gonna change me back. Now!"

"Release my arm, I command it."

KRAMPUS

jesse

ISABEL

SANTA CLAUS

PERCHTA

WIPI

ꡥꡦꡤꡦ

MAKWA

And, to Jesse's surprise, his body did exactly as told, as though someone else was driving while he watched. Jesse's eyes grew wide. "Oh, that's some shit."

Someone snickered and he saw Chet smirking at him in the rearview mirror.

"What the fuck are you looking at?"

"Welcome to the club, dumbass," Chet said.

"You can't do this," Jesse said to Krampus.

"You prefer death?"

Jesse started to say yes, found he wasn't sure. "Just turn me back."

"I cannot."

"Can't or won't?"

Krampus shrugged.

"You son of a bitch."

"We have great wrongs to right. Both of us. We go to kill Santa. When that deed is done, then perhaps, if you serve me well, then we can go take care of this other evil, this Dillard if you so wish it."

Jesse fell silent. He so wished it alright, but what did it mean to be a Belsnickel? Had he been condemned to a life of slavery? Did he truly believe Krampus would make good on his offer? No way to know. He did know that for now he'd been given another life, perhaps another chance to take care of Dillard, to kill him if it came to that, to save his Abigail, and that was what mattered.

CHET DROVE THEM down the narrow drive and pulled up behind the church. A giant wolf stood next to the great oak, its fur bristling. "Oh, what in the shit now?" Chet asked.

A moment later all three Shawnee dashed from the church, clutching spears and pistols. Krampus opened his door and stepped from the vehicle. The Shawnee let out a whoop. The wolf's fur settled and it came trotting over. It licked Krampus's hand and the Yule Lord rubbed it behind the ears. Its tail began to wag.

"Out, all of you," Krampus commanded and Chet, Jesse, and the General opened their doors and climbed out.

Jesse stepped down into the snow and realized he'd lost a boot somewhere along the way. He could feel the frost on his bare foot, but, oddly, it had no bite and though it was certainly below freezing out, he hardly noticed the chill. He became aware that he could actually smell the snow, the dead leaves beneath the snow. He inhaled deeply; it seemed everything was crisper: smells, sounds, colors, and he assumed all these sensations must be some effect of Krampus's blood.

Chet and the General clung to the Chevy, their eyes shifting back and forth between the Shawnee and the wolf as though they were about to be eaten.

Isabel came out onto the back steps, saw Jesse, and let out a cry. "Krampus! No! You promised. Your oath."

"Save your temper, little lion. It was he that broke the oath. Not I."

Isabel walked down the steps and over to Jesse, touched his face with the back of her fingers. "Oh, Jesse. I'm so sorry."

"Things could be worse," Jesse said, surprised to find he pretty much meant it.

"Come," Krampus said, and headed into the church, his tail swishing excitedly.

Chet and the General remained next to the truck as though frozen in place. Makwa gestured toward the steps with his spear. Chet and the General exchanged a fretful look and then tromped along after Krampus as though being marched through the gates of Hell.

Jesse entered the church, found the second wolf, the larger one, lying upon its side. It lifted its head, keeping a watchful eye on the newcomers. The smaller wolf came over and began licking its face. Isabel picked up one of the mead flasks, poured some into a pie pan in front of the wolf. The wolf lapped at it. "This is Freki," Isabel said, stroking its fur. "He's doing a lot better."

"And no thanks to you," someone said with open hostility. Jesse found Vernon glaring at him. "We had to carry him out of that ravine. Damnable beast weighed a ton." Vernon walked over to Jesse, looked up at him, his eyes two angry slits. "You pushed me."

"Yup, that I did."

"You're a son of a bitch. You know that?"

"Yes, I most certainly do."

"Must've walked ten miles through the woods to get back here. Had to carry him all that way. All the way. That's a long way to carry a giant canine."

"Vernon," Isabel said. "Quit your bellyaching. You've been going on about it nonstop. Starting to get on everybody's nerves."

"Yes, well, you're not the one who was shoved down the side of a mountain. Now were you?"

"You didn't fall down no mountain. You got stuck up in a tree." She laughed. "Looked just like a treed coon."

Vernon gave her a thunderous scowl, shook his head, and walked away. "One day I'm gonna wake up from this goddamn nightmare. One day, and it can't be too soon."

Krampus dropped the sack in the middle of the room. "All of you . . . here to me." He held the spear out. "I have it!" The Shawnee gathered round. "The day we have waited centuries for is at hand. Today is the day I face Baldr. Today is the day I make him pay for all his crimes!"

He looked from face to face, eyes gleaming. "Let me tell you why you must never make the same mistake as I and pity this monster. Why he must be put down like some rabid dog."

Krampus sat a hand on Jesse's shoulder. "Jesse, I told you of his guise, his worship of Saint Nicholas, but there was no end to his deceit. Let me finish the tale, let me share with you the rest of the story."

Jesse shook his head. "Can't really stop you, now can I?"

The Yule Lord's brow furrowed and Jesse thought he might've overstepped, then slowly a smile crept across Krampus's face. "No . . . no, you can't. No one can. Not anymore. This story will be told . . . told again and again, until the whole world knows the truth behind the lie."

Krampus clutched the spear in both hands. "His is a story of betrayal, of a foul creature having no conscience, no regard for anything except his own blind ambitions. For even after I brought him into my own house, even after I showed him brotherhood, after all my charity, still he betrayed me, betrayed all Asgard." Krampus's eyes glowed. "He stole everything from me, locked me away in his dungeon. Was that enough for him? No. He wanted more, wanted my name erased from the land. He thought he could make them forget . . . forget Yule and the Yule Lord." Krampus laughed. "But he underestimated my great spirit, and even into the 1400s, there were those who still held to the old traditions, still paid me tribute.

"This did not sit well with our beloved Baldr. He decided something should be done. Come that Christmas, he had me shackled and carried from the fortress, set upon a throne of rotting vegetables atop a cart drawn by goats. He bound a pitchfork to my arm and draped a necklace of goat tongues about my neck. He dressed his slaves in coats of filthy fur, wearing horned masks and chains. They paraded me along the countryside and through the towns and villages, dancing and prancing, hissing and growling like silly beasts, ridiculing me and all I stood for. And Baldr, in his guise of Saint Nicholas, would cry out, 'Behold, it is the devil, Krampus. Not but a silly old fart.' The villagers would throw clod and manure, while the children would prod me with sticks. I was too weak and frail to do more than hang my head. He went further, knowing well the power of lies. He printed posters that portrayed me, the great Yule Lord, as nothing more than a wicked imp, an evil buffoon, and pasted them across the land. Year after year this continued and he promised no end unless . . . unless I should reveal the secret of the sack.

"But it did stop, sometime around the early 1500s, I would guess, hard to say as by then I was losing any sense of the passing years. Just when I thought he had forgotten about me, he showed up in front of my cell. Only I did not recognize him, not at first. Gone was the guise of the lean, pious saint, what stood before me now was a robust figure, one dressed in some ridiculous costume. He was cloaked in a floor-length cape over a robe, all crimson velvet trimmed in white fur, a wide black belt strapped across his middle and a tall, pointed cap dotted with golden stars atop his head. His hair and beard had grown so full and long as to hide even his shoulders. He looked as some demented wizard.

"He introduced himself as Father Christmas, told me that he had mastered Loki's sack and had no more need of the devil . . . that it was time for Krampus to be utterly forgotten. He had his servants bind me and set me in his sleigh. He flew me across the great ocean to the newly discovered continent of America, into the deepest, darkest mountains, and chained me in a cave far below the rocks, where none would ever find me, left me there to rot away."

Krampus slowly shook his head. "But I did not rot away. No, for I sang my song to the forest and the forest listened." He gestured to the Shawnee. "The great Shawnee people found me and saw to my needs.

And I waited. Sat there for five hundred years waiting for one thing. The day I would be free, the day I would kill Baldr."

Krampus spoke directly to Jesse. "And every one of those days I pondered the how of it. How I would escape, how I would kill a being that could not be killed. As time passed and the Europeans marched across the Americas, I had my Belsnickels bring me newspapers and books, and from these I kept up with his doings, watched as his fraud spread across the globe. I made charts, mapped and plotted his course until I came to understand his method, his path. And finally all lined up and when he came at last to Goodhope, I was *ready*. Yes . . . indeed.

"And now I am ready to end it, to end his reign of lies. Ready to take back what is *mine!*"

Krampus pointed the spear heavenward and howled. The Shawnee threw back their heads and added their voices, and then the wolves joined in. The ghoulish, unearthly sound echoed to the rafters of the old church, making the hair on the back of Jesse's neck stand on end. Chet, the General, and Vernon looked on miserably.

Jesse couldn't control a shudder. *Are we really going to kill Santa Claus?*

KRAMPUS STOOD OVER Loki's sack, the Belsnickels forming a circle around him. *Nine hearts beating my blood, nine is the magical number. I have never felt so alive.*

He inspected his warriors. The Shawnee armed with knives, pistols, and spears, ever proud and dependable, their skin stained pitch, wearing horns and masks and furry hides, all in honor of him. Isabel, his brave little lion, carrying a shotgun and managing to look fierce even while wearing that ridiculous cap. Vernon held one of the new machine weapons and appeared glum as always, but not as miserable as the two criminals. Jesse stood there without shoes, his pants and shirt torn and covered in his own blood. Yet the song-maker appeared almost eager, though Krampus was sure it was not for the adventure ahead but for the man he called Dillard. There was something about Jesse's spirit that Krampus liked, his gall, perhaps that glint of mischief in his eyes when he smiled. He hoped the young man would return alive, but there could be no guarantees. Krampus had never been to Baldr's castle, had no idea what lay in wait. Would Baldr be expecting them? Most likely. There could be no telling what tricks and traps he might have in store. But would Baldr know about the spear? Krampus tightened his grip on the weapon. *No. That will be quite the surprise.*

Krampus set eyes on Jesse, Chet, and the General. "I command you to raise your hands." All three obeyed. "My blood runs in your veins. I am your master. I command you to do your utmost to follow my will, to stay by my side, to protect me at all cost, even if it should cost your life to do so. Now swear it."

They did, they had no choice.

"Good," Krampus said and handed Chet and the General each a handgun. He handed Jesse a pistol and his rifle.

"It is time to go."

"Where?" Vernon asked.

"Spain."

"Spain?" Jesse said and glanced about at the others, but they looked equally perplexed. "Spain?"

"Yes, to Baldr's castle. Where did you think he lived? The North Pole?" Krampus scoffed. "How easily people fall for his lies. Our jolly old elf has no temperament for the Arctic. He has lived on the coast where the warm sea blows, has lived there for centuries. But not after today, not after we burn it to the ground."

"That's a pretty long walk," Jesse said.

Krampus smiled. "Always with the jests, you. We do not walk." He nodded toward the sack. "I will open a door and we will travel through the sack."

It took them a moment, some longer than others. But he saw most of them understood.

"It will be night there and darkness is our friend. I will send you through one by one, and then will follow, and together we will destroy all that is his. He may have guards: elves, beasts, things I cannot know. If they spot you, kill them. Show no mercy, for none will be shown for you. Failure means death for us all, as there can be no retreat, for the sack will have to remain behind."

They all stared at the sack. *Yes, there shall be no quarter from Baldr, not this time.* Krampus took in a deep breath. *I am ready. One way or another I am ready for this to be done.* Krampus picked up the sack, pulled out a bottle of mead, broke off the wax, and drank deep. He wiped his arm across his lips and offered the bottle. The Belsnickels passed it around.

He held the sack open, stared down into its shadowy depths. *Time to open the door.* Only he didn't know to where. He'd never been to the castle. He needed an object, something to fix on, to direct the sack to, something that wouldn't put them in the line of danger, wouldn't give them away.

"There a plan on getting back?" Jesse asked.

"We will fly back in the sleigh," Krampus replied and realized almost at once that the sleigh was his answer. *Yes. I will have the sack find the sleigh. The old one, the one he brought me to the Americas in. It would most likely be in the stables, which would be a good place to begin.* He wondered if the sleigh even still existed. *There is but one way to find out.*

He closed his eyes, connected with the sack, could feel its pulse. It was so easy now that he had his strength, almost effortless. He thought of the ancient sleigh, pictured it in his mind, and the sack responded. He saw the sky and ocean streak by, a fortification, just a glimpse, but enough to see this was not a place of candy canes and snowmen, but instead imposing walls of stately white stone. *There it is . . . the sleigh!* Krampus opened his eyes. "The door is open."

Krampus left the circle, walked over to where the two wolves lay side by side. He squatted, stroked their thick pelts. "Geri, Freki, we must go now. Guard the sack. Let none take it. If you smell him coming, then we have failed." Geri let out a low whine. "It is my wish that you should then tear the sack to shreds. Understand?" Freki barked.

Krampus stood, stared at the sack. All was in play. He picked up the spear, ran his finger along the edge of the blade, testing its sharpness for the hundredth time, took in a deep breath. *It is time to take back that which is mine.*

SANTA CLAUS REMOVED a small, leather-bound book from the shelf in his study, carefully sat it upon his desk, and touched the mark inlaid upon its cover. He caressed the frayed edges and cracked binding, opened the book, carefully turning the brittle parchment until he reached a crude ink drawing of a thin, stern-faced, bearded man holding a shepherd's hook. Santa Claus ran his finger across the rough parchment, lightly tracing the inscription below. *"Charity unto others brings its own reward,"* he whispered.

He looked out from his window, out across the Mediterranean Sea. The last vestiges of sunlight glittering across the waves. He closed his eyes, inhaled the warm, salty air, and made himself remember, remember the flame as his prison burned, remember the screams as Ragnarok consumed all in Hel, all in Asgard, remember his wife's very soul burning before his eyes.

"The flame licked my flesh," he whispered, talking to the book. *"But there came no end, no relief from my torment. I watched until all was consumed, until I stood alone, the only soul amongst a world turned to ash and blackened bone.*

"God, the One God above all, sent down her angels, the Valkyries, and they carried me away to Midgard, left me naked to roam the earth. For years I wandered aimlessly. I forewent food and drink, bore the elements, all in the hope I would perish. Even threw myself from great cliffs, all in vain, for my flesh would not die.

"Krampus found me, forced me into servitude—me, the son of Odin, a slave to a low-cast demon. I did not care, did not feel. Hollow of heart and soul, I came to believe this to be my fate, my penance, that I had been spared to bear torment not just for my own vanity and arrogance, but for that of all my forebears.

"I was lost, dead in all but flesh." He gently closed the book and clutched it to his chest. *"Your words, Saint Nicholas, your words found my soul, reminding me of the days before Ragnarok, before Hel, before all the scheming, treachery, and petty games of the gods. Of a time when I roamed the land, charitable and gracious, seeking the simple joy of raising the spirits of the downtrodden. The only time I ever truly knew happiness."*

"I thought I would find you here."

Santa turned.

A thin woman with flowing white hair and ageless eyes entered the room. She wore a dress of dark crimson trimmed in gold. She took the book from him, sat it back upon the shelf. "You need not the teachings of a dead saint to show you what is in your heart."

"Sometimes I forget," Santa replied. "The play of gods makes one yearn for a simpler time."

She touched his hand. "Your charity is not to please the gods. It is your nature."

"True. I know no joy greater than spreading hope and cheer. But do I also enjoy hearing my name in song, seeing my image celebrated in every corner of this earth? Yes. I must admit I crave such, that my heart will not be content until everyone sings my songs."

"Charity is your vanity. So what of it? No one has put it upon you to be a saint. Charity is its own nobility, regardless of purpose."

"The only truth I know for certain is that when I fly around the world giving gifts, helping those in need, it is only then that I forget the pain of my past. Beyond that, beyond the gods and where I might fit in their great designs, it matters not."

"He is coming."

"Krampus?"

She nodded. "The signs are in the bones."

"I knew he would."

"I believe it will be soon."

"I am ready." Santa Claus hefted his broadsword from the corner, sat it on the desk. "Did the bones give away any other secrets?"

"No. Do you fear him?"

"He can do me no injury. The gods have seen to that."

"Why then do I read worry upon your brow?"

"It is the sack I fret over. He could bring it harm. I do not know where I could ever find another of its like."

"Then you must see he does not escape."

"He will not. Not this time. This last of Loki's treachery will die with him."

Chapter Eleven

DARK ARTS

Krampus held the sack wide-open; Jesse watched the darkness shift and swirl. The Yule Lord nodded and Makwa set one foot in, then the other, slid down to his waist. Krampus tugged the sack up over his head and just like that, the big man was gone. The brothers, Wipi and Nipi, followed without hesitation, needing no command. Isabel went next, and Vernon, who gave Krampus a look of utter contempt but went in without a word.

Krampus looked at Chet and the General. The General took a step back, his fear plain on his face. He shook his head. "No, sir, I ain't going in there."

"You're all hot air, ain't you?" Jesse said with a sneer. "Always figured you weren't much of nothing without your kin backing you up."

The General seemed not even to hear him, just stared at the sack.

Jesse shoved the General aside and stepped up, ready to get this show done and over with. The mead warmed his blood, making him feel a bit crazy, a bit mad, and he liked the feeling. He stuck a foot in, sucked in a deep breath—he was still having a bit of trouble breathing, but the pain was fading. He slipped in the other foot.

Krampus sat a hand on Jesse's shoulder. "Time to put things to right."

"Just don't get us killed," Jesse said and slid down into the sack. There came a moment when he felt nothing below his feet, a sensation not of falling but more like sliding down a velvet chute. A second later he found himself on his butt in soft dirt and scattered hay. He blinked and the world came into focus. It was night, the air warm. Jesse had never been to the ocean, but knew that must be what he now smelled. He heard the distant sound of waves crashing on rocks and stood up.

"Get down," Isabel whispered, grabbed his arm, and tugged him into a stall. The Belsnickels were crouched against the inside wall, sharing the stall with an old green sleigh. They peered out into a court-yard surrounded by white stone walls, at least twenty feet high. They saw not a soul, but there were gas lanterns flickering about every fifty feet along the wall. The stall butted up against a larger structure. Jesse smelled hay and manure and guessed it to be a stable. Across the court-yard stood a stately house of arches and turrets, built of the same white stone as the walls and stable but topped with a red-tiled roof.

A cowboy boot connected to a leg suddenly appeared out of thin air right in front of Jesse. A moment later the General sat on his back-side in the dirt. The General glanced around wild-eyed, pointing his handgun in this direction and that. Jesse, fearing the man would begin shooting randomly at any second, leapt forward, pulled him into the stall. Shortly after, Chet and Krampus arrived. Krampus stood tall, right out in the open, hands on hips, surveying the courtyard. He spot-ted the old sleigh, walked into the stall, and ran a hand along its weath-ered sideboard.

"This is mine," he said in a low tone. "He stole it. One of many things he stole. One of many things I have come to reclaim. Come." He left the stall and walked along a cobblestone path; the Belsnickels followed. He stopped in front of the stable, looked it up and down. "This will do." He slid one side of the tall carriage doors open a crack and peered in. "Yes, perfect. Chet, I want you and your little troll friend to stand guard out here. Give us warning if any should come. It is my command."

Chet nodded, but the General seemed lost, his eyes shifting this way and that. Jesse felt sure the man was going to blow the whole opera-tion, couldn't understand why Krampus would leave these two out here alone.

Krampus entered the stable; Jesse, the Shawnee, Isabel, and Vernon all followed. Two gas lanterns flitted from their perch inside, casting long shadows down the stalls. A second-story loft, stacked with hay, ran the length of the structure. The middle lay opened all the way up to the ceiling. The stalls began about midway in, leaving a large, open space for loading, unloading, hitching, and other tasks. Krampus strolled into the middle of this space and, standing there, spear in hand, he struck Jesse as some devilish gladiator awaiting challenge.

"Find cover," Krampus said, pointing with his spear to a set of stalls. "All on one side, so as to avoid shooting one another." Jesse got the feeling Krampus had things more planned out than he let on. He hoped so, anyway. Jesse started to follow the other Belsnickels when he caught movement in the loft above. He squinted into the shadows, found his newly acquired ability to pierce the darkness amazing, but still saw nothing or no one. He glanced at Krampus. Krampus nodded. "There are eyes on us. Have been since we first arrived." Jesse swallowed. Things were getting very real, very fast.

Jesse slid behind a large wall post and waited, having no idea for what or for how long. Isabel and Vernon found cover behind a stack of crates, and the Shawnee crouched in an empty stall next to Jesse. Somewhere a goat bleated. Jesse glanced behind him. Several reindeer looked back at him from their stalls, snorting and stomping in agitation. Jesse leaned his rifle against the post in easy reach, pulled the revolver from his belt, started to check the chamber, when a blast of gunfire came from outside, followed by a scream. Jesse jumped, almost dropping his pistol. He managed to get a hold of the grip and pointed it toward the door just as another round of shots rang out. A second later something hit the doors with a loud thud. Chet rushed in, fell, and tumbled across the ground, losing hold of his weapon. *"Fuck,"* he screamed, snatching his gun back up as he scrambled to his feet. Krampus grabbed him, held him.

"He's out there!" Chet cried, looking backward over his shoulder, trying to twist away from Krampus. "Shot him. We both did. Shot him right in the chest . . . in the head. Didn't do a thing! Not a fucking thing! Didn't even slow him down!"

"Go, stand with the others," Krampus said and let him loose. Jesse was struck by how calm Krampus sounded. Chet dashed for the stables, slid in behind the giant post next to Jesse. "We're fucked, man,"

Chet said, his chest heaving, his breath coming hard and fast. "That thing, there's no stopping it. It's a monster. A real live monster!"

Jesse found his own breath speeding up, found himself badly in need of another shot of mead. He heard the patter of little feet above them, caught sight of a few boyish figures dashing about in the rafters.

"Shit," he said, switching to his rifle. "They'll get the drop on us."

But no fire came from above, only the occasional eyes peeping down at them.

"Don't like this," Jesse said, keeping a bead on them. "Not one bit."

Something flew through the door, hit the ground, and rolled across the straw-littered dirt, coming to a stop at Krampus's feet. It was the General's head—the neck cut clean, the eyes gone. Jesse's mouth became dry, his heart drummed in his chest, he forgot about the figures above, could only stare at the gory sockets that used to be the General's eyes.

"Fuck me," Chet whimpered.

"Krampus," a voice thundered from outside. "Your time is done."

Krampus smiled, glanced back over his shoulder. "Hold your places. Watch the rafters. And don't waste any bullets on our dear old friend Santy Claus."

Jesse caught sight of a dark shape approaching the carriage doors. Far too wide to slip through the gap, it gripped the massive doors and effortlessly shoved them apart to arm's length. It was him, there could be no doubt, Santa Claus, *Baldr*. He stood there in the flickering lantern light with a look of supreme confidence on his face. Not as a man coming to battle for his life, but a man coming to stomp upon vermin. He was as far from the image of the plump, jolly Santa Claus of vintage Coca-Cola ads as Jesse could imagine. Jesse even had a hard time making this be the same man he saw running across the snow so long ago in the trailer park. This man looked more like a Viking lord. Gold hoops in his ears, his white hair tied into a topknot, his long beard braided and running down his bare barrel of a chest. He wore red leather britches with stockings and curled-toed shoes adorned with big brass buckles, thick leather wristbands, and a wide harness studded with brass rings atop white fur. Much shorter than Krampus, but stout, solid, hard-packed muscle like a bull, thick through the neck, wrist, and ankle. Hands and forearms that looked able to easily tear apart phone books. He held a broadsword, blood dripping from its long, wide blade. Jesse could see the smoke burns from the gunfire, they ran across his chest, his face, but found no trace of any wound.

Santa Claus slid the heavy doors shut behind him, pulled the slide bar in place, barring them all in. He shook his head, a look upon his face of a man who has a distasteful chore before him. "Krampus, you have become most tiresome."

DILLARD FLIPPED THE deadbolt and opened the basement door. Linda sat midway down the stairwell, her back to him with Abigail sleeping in her arms. Her lip was swollen and an ugly bruise was blooming along her cheek. He tried not to look at it, tried to pretend it wasn't there. He let out a deep sigh. "How about we give this another try? What'd you say?"

She didn't answer, just slowly got to her feet, cradling Abigail. Abigail woke, saw Dillard, and pressed her face into her mother's chest. Linda marched up the steps, tried to push past him.

Dillard didn't budge.

"Move!" she hissed.

"I think it'd be good if we talked."

She pressed her back to the wall, refusing to look at him. He could see her trembling, fighting to control her temper.

"I need you to understand I done what I done because I had to . . . to protect you, to protect that little girl of yours. Jesse, now he's the one that fucked up. What he got, he done to himself. You know it. He crossed a line with the General. That's done and over with . . . ain't nothing you, nor me, nor anybody but Jesus can do for Jesse now. Time to think about what's best for you and Abigail."

He reached out, stroked Abigail's hair. "Linda, you need to understand that the only reason that little girl of yours is here safe and sound is because of me. The General, well, he had other plans, wanted to use her to get at Jesse for what he'd done, and it weren't easy to convince him otherwise."

Linda glared at him. Dillard saw the fire and blinked. "What you done," she said, "amounts to murder. No different than if you done it yourself."

Dillard ground his teeth, fought down the heat rising in his chest. "I need to make something clear to you . . . absolutely crystal-clear. The General, he gets dangerous when he thinks someone might start gabbing about his business. And if you were to get it into your head to talk about what went down with Jesse, so much as a single word, there wouldn't be a goddamn thing I could do to keep you and Abigail safe. And after what you said in front of Chet and Ash, about the sheriff, they'll be watching you, you can count on it."

She stared at the wall, shaking her head.

"Christ, Linda. Can't you see I'm doing my damnedest here to keep you two safe? Can you not try and understand?"

He waited for a response, some sign that all was not lost, but she continued to stare at the wall as though he wasn't there.

"Why are you making this so hard?" he asked.

"Really? Are you kidding me?" The venom in her voice surprised him.

Dillard made himself look at her swollen lip. *Why do things always have to go this way with me?* "I'm . . . sorry," he said. "Sorry I lost my temper. About as sorry as I can be. Do anything I could to take that back. I mean it, Linda. Things got out of hand . . . won't ever happen again. I swear it. Swear to God."

Linda's lip began to tremble and she wiped at her eyes.

Dillard thought maybe some part of her understood. He hoped so. "You got every right to hate me right now. But I'm hoping you won't. That maybe after a bit you'll come to forgive me. All I ask is that you try and remember I made my decisions, right or wrong, for you, baby."

He gave her another minute, hoping she would say something. She didn't.

"Listen," he said. "However you might feel about me, I still need you to stick close for a few days . . . until things with the General calm down a notch. That will give me a little time to convince him you understand the ways things are. If you want to leave me after that . . . well . . . I won't stand in your way. But, Linda . . . I'm hoping you won't. I'm still hoping we can build a life together."

Linda's face was stone, he saw nothing for him in her eyes, nothing.

Ellen had worn that same look, like part of her was turned off, dead. He couldn't stand it another minute, afraid he'd start tearing up. "I have to go out. I won't be far. If you see any of the Boggses driving by, you be sure to call me right away."

Dillard left them on the stairs, slipping on his jacket. He patted the pocket, making sure Linda's keys were still there, and headed out the door.

"WHY DO YOU come here?" Santa Claus asked, his voice deep and low.

"You know too well the answer to that, my dear old friend," Krampus said, his tail swishing back and forth like that of a cat on the hunt.

"You could have lost yourself in the wilds. Lived out your existence in the forest." Santa spoke softly, but his words resonated. "Instead you must make a nuisance of yourself . . . force my hand. Make me kill you when I have no desire to do so."

"Kill me? That sounds a bit presumptuous. Would you not agree?"

Santa shook his head. "Why does the blood of Loki know only vileness? I showed you charity, tried to show you the truth, tried to save you from yourself. Gave you every chance."

"Being chained beneath the earth did not feel very charitable."

"Pity made me weak. I see now that I should have killed you and put an end to your suffering. But, you see, I spent an age in your mother's prison. That time in Hel gave me the chance to better understand myself, to meditate on the consequences of my choices. My hopes were that solitude would give you that same chance. A chance to see beyond yourself for once."

"Shit spews from your lips as from the ass of a pig. You did not *find* yourself in Hel, you were lost. It was I who tried to save *you*, that brought you into my very home, tried to give you purpose, to heal the great wounds in your heart. The truth is you chained me in that pit for one reason, the hope that I would be forgotten and fade away, and the spirit of Yule would fade away with me."

Santa shrugged. "Yule is dead. It is the past. Men need a path to enlightenment, to be set free from trivial earthbound concerns, to see beyond the limitations of flesh and blood. Life is fleeting, but the hereafter is eternal. I see no greater calling than to help illuminate that path. I offered you a chance to assist."

"You worship death. You and all the One Gods. They seduce mankind with their promises of glory attained in the hereafter, thus blinding men to the splendor before them here on earth. One can never expect to achieve enlightenment if one does not first live life to its fullest."

"Your words only serve as proof that there is no longer a place for you on God's earth."

"Earth belongs to *no* god! Mother Earth is god. Have you forgotten everything? Do you pretend not to see that she is dying beneath your feet? Or do you not care? She needs rebirth, needs the spirit of Yule to heal her. You talk of enlightening men, but there will be no men without her!"

"Foolish beast, earth is nothing more than a rock in space." Santa shook his head. "The world has moved on and left you behind. You have become nothing but a pathetic relic of days long dead. What I must do now is a mercy, so let us not prolong this. I have you, there is no escape. Kneel now before me and I will give you a quick death."

"A very gracious and tempting offer, indeed," Krampus chuckled. "But I believe it is you that should kneel."

"This is madness, you know you cannot harm me."

Krampus laughed.

Santa frowned. Krampus could see his mirth annoyed his rival, and laughed the harder.

"It appears five hundred years in that pit has addled your mind."

Krampus sneered. "Five hundred years in that pit has made all things clear. Clear as spring water in Asgard. Or have you forgotten Asgard? Forgotten the face of your mother, your father? Forgotten your own name? Well, I have come to help you remember."

Santa's mouth tightened.

"You have blood on your hands," Krampus said. "How much? How many did you murder in order to bend Loki's sack to your will?"

"I have grown weary of your prattle," Santa said and sprung forward, brought the great sword to bear, swung it high and down hard, a strike meant to cleave Krampus's head from his shoulders. Krampus skipped aside, the blow intended for his neck instead striking deep into the soft dirt.

Santa appeared surprised by Krampus's agility. He yanked the blade free, hefted it, ready to strike again.

Krampus made no move to retreat; he pointed the spear at Santa. "It is time I reminded you who you are."

Santa shook his head, appeared almost bored. "Why must you put us through this? Surely you know your efforts are futile? Save yourself some dignity."

"You have much to learn," Krampus hissed. "Much to answer for. I am here to see that you do. For Huginn and Muninn, Geri and Freki, for all those you used then tossed aside, all those you betrayed, who bled for your ambitions. But most of all . . . for *me*."

Santa charged, a great sweep of the blade. Krampus ducked, swept beneath the sword, came up as Santa went barreling past, lashed out, one quick strike, and slipped away.

Santa turned, prepared for another lunge, then hesitated, appeared unsure, his face twisting into something approaching befuddlement. He lowered his sword, looked at his arm. A small red line ran just beneath his shoulder, growing thicker as he stared at it. A crimson drop pooled and slid down his arm. Santa touched the cut, looked at the blood on his fingers. "What trickery is this?"

"Your face," Krampus said. "It is worth all my days below the earth."

Santa tasted the blood. "Impossible."

"A house built on lies has a weak foundation, my dear old friend."

Santa looked at him, still not comprehending.

"You do not see? Have you lied to yourself for so long that you have forgotten the truth? Think. Remember."

Krampus saw it, confusion turning to alarm. "Yes. Yes," Krampus jeered. "Santa Claus might be untouchable, but . . . *Baldr* . . . he is not." Krampus held the spearhead up so that the lantern light caught the ancient ore and flickered across Santa's face. "You can fool the world, you can fool yourself, but you cannot fool this."

Santa squinted at the weapon, his brow tightened. "How? It was destroyed. Odin ordered it destroyed."

"Apparently, he did not. I found it at the bottom of the sea, there amongst your bones. Amongst Baldr's bones."

Santa's eyes grew wide, confusion turning to betrayal, and then, for the first time ever, Krampus saw fear on Santa's face. Santa fell back a step, glanced toward the great doors.

Krampus laughed, loud and full. *"Who? Who is trapped now?"* The Yule Lord raised himself to his full height, inhaled deeply, felt his heart drum with the sweetness of his own wrath. He peeled back black lips, exposing long, sharp teeth. His tongue flashed from his mouth, he snapped his tail back and forth. His laugh turned into a snarl as he leapt at the white-bearded man.

Santa seemed to be in shock, a man in deep water who has just forgotten how to swim. He raised his sword, but too late; Krampus drove past his guard and caught him across the forearm, not a nick this time but a deep slash, cutting all the way down to the bone.

Santa let loose a howl, a sound of outrage, of complete incredulity, and stumbled against the railing, struggling to keep hold of his sword.

Krampus spun away, almost dancing. "How sweet the taste of revenge. How very, very sweet!"

Santa clutched the wound, face aghast at all the blood pumping from between his fingers.

Krampus hopped from foot to foot, prancing on his toes, grinning and tittering.

Santa kept his sword pointed at Krampus as he backed away, edging toward the double doors. Krampus followed, stalked him around the ring, allowing him to reach the door. Santa struggled to maintain his guard while attempting to slide the latch with his injured arm.

"Where are you going?" Krampus asked. Santa wet his lips, sweat beading on his forehead as he inched the slide over.

"You are a beast!" Santa cried. "Not but a low-caste demon. And that is all you shall ever be!"

The Yule Lord snorted and feigned attack. Santa lashed out with his sword, a wild, aimless swing, catching nothing but air. Krampus dashed forward, striking Santa atop the wrist and knocking the sword from his hand. The sword landed in the dirt between them. Santa made to grab for it when Krampus slashed the spearhead across Santa's thigh, the mythical blade cutting easily through his britches and muscle, biting into the bone. Krampus yanked the blade free and Santa collapsed onto one knee, cradling his leg as he screamed through clenched teeth.

Blood from his forearm, his wrist, and the deep slash to his leg spilled onto the ground and turned the blond straw red.

Krampus kicked the sword away, stepped up to Santa. "It is time you faced yourself." All the play left Krampus's voice, his tone became somber. He pressed the spearhead against Santa's neck. "What is your name?"

Santa closed his eyes, began to shake.

"What is your name?"

"Santa Claus," he mumbled.

Krampus kicked him, knocked him onto his side, planted his foot on his neck and set the spear into his gut. "No, it is not Santa Claus, it is not Kris Kringle, not Father Christmas, nor is it Saint Nicholas." He pressed the blade into Santa's flesh, an inch—two inches. Blood pooled beneath the spear tip. "What is your true name?"

"Santa Claus!" Santa cried. "My true name is Santa Claus!"

Krampus kicked him hard in the stomach. *"No!"* he yelled, unable to hide his outrage. "The charade is over! Your name is Baldr, the son who betrayed his own mother and father. Betrayed all the ancients. Claim your true title—Baldr the thief, Baldr the liar, Baldr the traitor, Baldr the murderer. That is who you are! Now you *will* claim it!"

Santa opened his eyes, glared up at Krampus, a steady resolve set into his face. "No, I am not Baldr. Baldr and all Baldr was is dead. I am Santa Claus. I serve a god of peace and love."

Krampus squinted at him. "You serve only yourself. A world of lies contrived to hide your wicked deeds."

"Whoever I might once have been, that person is dead, has been left behind. I have been reborn and have found my redemption through compassion and charity to others."

"No!" Krampus spat. "No! No! No! What utter bile. One does not get to forgive one's self. You cannot just walk away from your guilt. Forgiveness can come only from those against whom you have trespassed. Only they can absolve you of your crimes. Perhaps in the afterlife, after they have ripped the skin from your bones a thousand times, then and only then may you beg their forgiveness. And now, unless you claim your name, beg *my* forgiveness, then I will send you to them here and now."

"I am Santa Claus. I answer only to God."

Krampus stuck the blade into Santa's chest, pressed slowly downward, toward his heart. "Claim your name."

Santa grasped the blade, the edge cutting into his fingers. "Your efforts are in vain," he gasped. "Santa Claus cannot die . . . he lives forever."

Krampus saw that Santa believed it, believed it to his very soul. Krampus hated the solace it seemed to give him. "We shall see," Krampus sneered, gave the blade a heavy shove, felt ribs snap and flesh rip, watched the blade sink deep into Santa's chest.

Santa's eyes grew wide, blood bubbled from his lips. "God will be wrathful, there will be . . . no place . . . you can hide." Santa Claus fell still, his eyes staring ever upward toward the heavens.

Krampus yanked the blade free. "There. There. You are dead!" he spat. "And this time you shall stay dead!" He raised the blade, brought it down with all his might onto Santa's neck, over and over he hacked—blood and gore spattering across his face with each strike. He hacked until Santa's head rolled away from its body. The Yule Lord jabbed the spear into Santa's skull, lifted it skyward, and shook it. "Where is your great god now? Where is his wrath? Nothing! For you are nothing but one monstrous *lie!*"

KRAMPUS THREW SANTA'S head into the courtyard, watched it bounce across the lawn, and then just stood there in the doorway for a long time, studying the stars.

Jesse stared at the body, tried to accept what he had seen, what he had been through, all of it, any of it—that there could truly be a Santa Claus at all and, if so, that this headless body lying in the dirt could be him. *And if not Santa then what? He knew he should be shocked, horrified, but felt only a grim numbness. He'd seen too much, been through too much, knew on some level if he looked too hard he would have to question his own sanity, and for now all he wanted was to hold it together long enough to get through this madness and somehow make it back to Abigail.*

He caught movement in the rafters. The little people, whom Jesse assumed to be elves, had left their hiding places and were peering down in horror and disbelief. Jesse glanced around, found Vernon, Isabel, Chet, all with the same shell-shocked expressions upon their faces.

Makwa left the stall, walked over to Krampus, and pointed to the elves. "What of them?"

Krampus strolled back into the stable, called up to the elves. "You are free. Return home to the wilds where you belong. Reclaim your spirit. But do so now, as I intend to burn this stable—and all that belonged to the traitor—to the ground."

The little people glanced about uneasily but, one by one, began to slip away.

"Jesse," Krampus called. "Open the stalls, free all the beasts. The rest of you, move those bails there, the barrels, that cart, anything that will burn, against the center post."

While Jesse freed the reindeer, Krampus walked down the length of the stable, peering into each stall, stopping near the back. He opened a gate and led two goats out. "Jesse, bring those two harnesses there and follow me." Krampus led Jesse and the goats outside to the green sleigh. He strapped on their harness, speaking kindly to them as he hitched them up. He guided them well away from the structures and tied them to a bench near a garden.

Krampus returned to the stable, looked over the pile of wood and hay, appeared satisfied, then grabbed Santa's body by the leg and dragged him over. Together with Makwa, he tossed the body onto the pile like one more scrap of wood.

Krampus lifted one of the oil lamps from its post, threw it atop the pile. The lantern shattered, setting the wood and hay ablaze. The fire crackled and spread.

"Come," Krampus called and led them out. They crossed the courtyard, went through a topiary full of shrubs cut to resemble mythological creatures, then across the garden surrounding the main house. Jesse watched the reindeer joyfully munching on the rows of flowers. Krampus stopped in front of a single-story building that ran the entire length of the main house. Two statues of rearing white horses stood astride a wide, double-door entrance. Krampus walked up to the doors and gave them a tug. The doors were unlocked and they entered.

It appeared to be a warehouse of sorts, with rows of shelves all the way to the ceiling and stacked with all manner of items, mostly toys, but Jesse also noted rows of children's shoes, coats, and other articles of clothing, even a row of crutches and basic medical supplies. It took him a moment to put together that this must be where the sack had been open to, back when he'd first put his hand into it. He shuddered to think what might've happened if he'd been caught and pulled through.

Krampus ignored the toys, walking along the wall, opening each and every door he came to. Jesse had no idea what he might be looking for. Krampus opened one door, shut it, then paused, seemed to reconsider. He walked back, reopened it, and went in, came out a moment later with a bundle of colorful clothes. He tossed them onto the floor, and then brought out more. Shirts, pants, jackets, boots, all made from fine leathers and fabrics, in deep emerald greens, golden ochers, and dark crimson reds. "Lose your drab rags and don this finery. Those that serve the Yule Lord shall hide in shadows no longer."

The Shawnee weren't the least interested, but Isabel appeared delighted. She dug into the pile with obvious spirit, admiring one piece after another, holding the rich textiles up against her small frame for fit. Jesse guessed it must've been tough on her, spending the last forty years wearing nothing but grungy, ill-fitting pants and jackets.

Some of the items appeared to be well-worn work clothes, but most were flamboyant and ornate, rich velvets and corduroys, they reminded Jesse of movie costumes, the sort of thing they wore back in the seventeenth or eighteenth century, or whatever century men used to prance about in ruffles and powdered wigs.

Vernon seemed glad to shed his ragged coat and filthy pants, had no trouble finding suitable replacements for his small build.

Jesse had lost his boots and jacket at the General's, his shirt and pants were torn and covered in dried blood. He wasn't too sure about the selection, but at this point most anything would do. He quickly realized most of the items were too small, sized to fit children or elves perhaps, but he managed to find a shirt and a pair of leather britches that laced around the calves, and quickly slipped into them. He dug through the shoes until he found a pair of boots that fit, they came almost to his knees but he didn't care, it was good just to have something on his feet again. The only coat he could find that fit was long-tailed ·

with a high velvet collar, burned gold in color with copper buttons running up the lapel and along the oversized cuffs.

"Oh," Isabel said. "That's very romantic."

Jesse groaned.

"No, really. You look dashing."

Chet snickered. "You look like a queer."

"Chet," Jesse said. "You have a way of growing on people . . . about like a fucking wart."

Isabel ended up in a fancy turquoise velvet long coat, the sort of thing a pirate might wear. Jesse felt her panda cap gave her costume that last needed touch of lunacy.

Krampus picked up a lavender crushed velvet coat with swirling gold trim, something that would've been right at home in any glam rock band. "This one is simply splendid," he said and held it out to Makwa. "Do you not agree?"

Makwa crossed his arms over his chest and looked in the other direction. Krampus pushed it toward the brothers and they both stepped back as though from a snake. Chet snickered, and Krampus's eyes fell on him. He held the lavender coat out to Chet.

Chet shook his head. "Oh, hell no. I ain't wearing that."

"Put it on. It is a command."

"Fuck," Chet said, and did as he was told, making a face like he'd been made to eat mothballs.

Jesse snorted and Chet locked eyes on him. "Say something, you little twat," Chet growled. "Go on. Break your fucking jaw. See if I don't."

Jesse blew him a kiss.

Chet's lip curled and he started toward Jesse, murder in his eye.

"Stop," Krampus commanded. "This is not the place."

Chet halted, glaring at Jesse.

Jesse gave him the finger and grinned. Chet's face turned red, looked fit to burst.

Krampus found a red ribbon and tied his long hair back out of his eyes, and inspected his Belsnickels. He nodded and smiled. "Yes, elegant, dashing . . . as servants of the Yule Lord should look."

From where Jesse stood, he couldn't figure how they could've possibly looked any more ridiculous.

Krampus continued down the building until they came to an archway containing a door of solid iron. Krampus twisted the handle and gave it a shove. The heavy door slid inward, revealing a short hallway that emptied into darkness.

"Fetch me a lantern," Krampus said.

Isabel pushed past, hit a switch on the wall, and the hall and the room beyond flooded with light. She smiled at Krampus. "Some things *have* changed for the better."

Krampus examined the switch, flipped it off and on a couple of times. "Perhaps."

The short hall opened into a large oval room with a beamed cathedral ceiling. They entered. Jesse glanced around and immediately thought of a mad scientist's laboratory, the sort of place where Doctor Frankenstein might go about bringing the dead back to life.

Krampus moved down the rows of wooden tables, past beakers and flasks filled with iridescent liquids, past tall shelves of jars containing all manner of dried creatures: frogs, lizards, snakes, squid, metallic colored beetles, jar after jar of powders, leaves, herbs, roots, and mushrooms. The Yule Lord pulled at his chin hairs as he peered into sinks, trays, flipped through books, poked, prodded, sniffed, and tasted his way from one station to the next. He stirred his finger through a tray of sprouting crystals, plucked out a few of the larger specimens and held them up to the light. "Alchemy." Krampus appeared impressed. "Diamonds, rubies, sapphires. All of the highest grade. Someone has uncovered many of the ancient secrets."

Krampus dropped the gems back into the tray and moved on, losing himself in a ragged book of hand-scrawled symbols and runes, leaving the Belsnickels standing about gawking like children in a curiosity shop. Jesse peered into the hollow eye sockets of what appeared to be a baboon skull, painted red and stuck full of nails. Jesse decided that jolly old Saint Nick wasn't exactly the person he'd always believed him to be.

Chet slid over to the tray of gems, scooped up a handful, and slipped them into his coat pocket. Jesse started to follow suit when Isabel nudged him. "Wouldn't do that if I were you."

"What? Why not?"

"Might be poisonous."

Jesse took a closer look at the dusty gems, bit his lip, and started to take a few anyway when Krampus slapped the book shut with a loud clap. Jesse jumped and snatched his hand back from the tray.

"Here, look here," Krampus called, leading them all over to a tall shelf. The Yule Lord hefted a cotton sack about the size of a bag of sugar, untied the sash, and scooped out a handful of brown grit, letting the fine grains sift through his fingers and back into the sack.

"Sleeping sand. Baldr used it to keep nosy parents and bratty children from interfering with his pursuits." He tied the sack closed, pulled a second one off the shelf, and handed both of them to Vernon. "Carry these. Be sure not to get them near your face, or you might be in for a long nap." Vernon looked even less pleased than usual.

"And here, look here. See this?" Krampus plucked a key ring off a hook. Six keys of various sizes and shapes hung from the ring. "Skeleton keys," Krampus said, delighted. "They can open most any key lock. They were mine, a gift from Loki. They are mine again." He looked closer. "Interesting." He examined the smaller, more modern-looking designs. "There are three new ones. Jesse, come here."

Jesse did as he was bidden.

"You shall be my key-bearer." The Yule Lord slipped the keys into Jesse's coat pocket and gave them a pat. "Seems dear old Saint Nick was not sliding down chimneys after all—"

Krampus stopped. His face grew stern. He walked over to a table upon which sat a goat skull, its horns cut off at the base. The horns and what must be its bones, fur, and hooves were stacked beside it, all cleaned and dried. Next to them stood a device with a large crank; it reminded Jesse of a sausage-grinder. Krampus gave it a crank and chunks of finely ground gray matter fell from the bottom and into a waiting bowl. He pinched the grounds, put them to his nose.

"This is dark magic," Krampus growled, his face grave. "These bones are those of a Yule goat. So few remain and now we have one less, nothing more to dear *Santa Claus* than ingredients for his potions. The Yule goats were beasts of the gods and flew of their own magic. He has butchered them for that magic. I suspect it is from this that his flamboyant display of flying reindeer have come."

Krampus snatched up a large flask and hurled it across the room, crashing into the wall of jars, startling them all. *"Is it not enough that you stole my traditions!"* he cried. *"Distorted them for your own selfish design. Now you twist the very life, murder the very soul of Yule itself for your own glory!"* His voice dropped, little more than a whisper. "There is so precious little magic left in this world . . . so little. Why must your ambitions come at such a cost?"

He picked up another flask and threw it after the first, another, and another. "Blood, bones, and death . . . that is the truth behind Santa's Christmas magic!" The jars shattered and crashed to the floor, the ingredients spilled and mixed together, sizzling and bubbling. Flames bloomed and spread, noxious smells and fumes of colorful gas began to curl upward into the rafters.

· *"I am done with his depravity . . . the world is done!"* Krampus shouted and led them from the room, down the long rows of toys and back out into the night. "All is not lost. There is still time to undo his great injury. Time for me to bring back Yuletide, to spread its magic and heal Mother Earth!" He grinned, his teeth set in a grimace, eyes afire. "Time to help mankind find its spirit and remember whence it came. Yuletide shall reign once again, and I . . . I the Yule Lord shall lead the way."

They crossed through the garden and into the courtyard, back to where the two Yule goats stood tied. The stables were now completely engulfed in fire. Giant flames leapt skyward, bathing the entire compound in an orange glow. They stood and watched the cinders spin and dance about them.

"Beast! You shall burn in Hell!" came a sharp cry from behind them.

Jesse started, spun round. They all did, and found six women standing within the wide arch leading into the topiary garden. Five of them were dressed in flowing white gowns, young, plump women with long hair and full, curvy figures. They watched the flames, tears streaming down their faces. The sixth one was not crying. She stood in front, whip-thin, hard of face and mouth drawn. Impossible to gauge her age, but something in her eyes made it plain she was older, much older. She wore a full-length dress of dark crimson trimmed in gold swirling snakes, and her wavy white hair flowed down past her hips, billowing about her.

"And who might that be?" Vernon asked.

Isabel shrugged.

"Maybe it's his wife?" Jesse said. "Y'know, Mrs. Claus." And if indeed she was, Jesse thought she was a far shout from the sweet grandmotherly soul he'd always imagined. This woman looked like she would cut out your liver and eat it raw.

"What about them?" Vernon gestured at the girls. "Think those are his daughters?"

"Daughters." Krampus snickered. "Those are all his wives. Baldr was a man of large appetites."

"Wives?" Vernon marveled.

The plump women pointed at Krampus and began to wail, their volume rising to shrieks, screaming in tongues the way Jesse had heard the Pentecostal women do. Except he decided these weren't prayers but curses.

Krampus pulled the whip from the sleigh and smiled, baring his teeth. "It has been a long, long time since I have had the pleasure of spanking a few bratty bottoms." He cracked the whip and took a step toward them. The shrieking dropped down to hysterical sobbing and the girls fell back, but the woman—she did not flinch. Krampus took another step, cracked the whip again. Still the white-haired woman held her place. She raised an accusing finger. "Beast, you dare sully these grounds with your foulness? Bring murder to this house? Santa Claus is the beloved son of the gods. Cherished for his grace and self-lessness, a noble knight of charity, a celebrated stalwart of—"

"Poppycock."

"*It is truth!*" she cried. "You saw his warehouse, not just toys, but shoes, clothes, basic necessities for those without. He toiled every day into the late hours to make Christmas more than just a festival, but a magical time of hope. He traveled the globe spreading charity in the wish that his example would inspire people to be kind to one another, that this kindness would spread, would elevate their souls."

She appeared to grow taller. Jesse realized she was floating, looking down at them with glaring, glowing eyes. The snake designs in her dress came to life, began to hiss, swirling about her, snapping at them with dripping fangs. Jesse fell back.

"Santa Claus spreads hope," she hissed, her voice the same as the snakes, echoing about the grounds; the very air felt alive, chilling Jesse's skin. "What do you bring, demon? You wallow in flesh and debauchery, demand tribute and sacrifice in your name. Death and blood is all you know!"

Krampus snapped the whip, catching her across the cheek. "Enough of your deceit."

Jesse blinked, and the snakes were just designs once more, the woman firmly on the ground, clutching her hand to her cheek.

"I have seen enough of his charity this night," Krampus growled. "There is blood and murder aplenty in his laboratory. Or do you pretend not to see?"

Her eyes burned. "Everything comes with a cost, as you are soon to find out. God will not sit back and allow such a wicked deed to go unpunished."

Krampus laughed. "Baldr is dead. It is the end of it."

"He has died before."

The mirth left Krampus's face.

"He is God's chosen servant." She stepped forward, her finger and entire arm shaking with her wrath. "The Lord will send the Valkyrie and Santa Claus shall rise again before morning. And," she cried, "together they will hunt you down and slay you, beast!"

Now Krampus was the one who fell back, and for the first time that Jesse could remember, the Yule Lord looked unsure.

The woman spun about and stormed away, the girls trailing in her wake.

Krampus stared after her until she disappeared from sight. "This place is full of wickedness."

The warehouse now burned as well, the flames spreading toward the main house. Jesse and the other Belsnickels batted the raining embers from their clothes and hair. Krampus appeared in a trance.

"We should go," Isabel urged. "Don't you think?" She touched Krampus on the arm.

"Yes," Krampus said. "Just one last thing." He walked rapidly out into the courtyard, stooped, and retrieved something off the ground. He returned, carrying Santa's head in one hand, the spear in the other. "He will never return so long as I possess these." He slid the spear into the whip mount and mounted the head atop the blade.

"Load up," Krampus called and they did, all squeezing into the small sleigh. Krampus stepped up onto the front bench, stood a moment longer, scanning the flames and destruction. "It is good to be terrible," he said and patted Santa's head.

"Away, Tanngnost! Away, Tanngrisni!" Krampus cried and the goats pulled the sleigh forward step by step, and all at once Jesse realized they were climbing skyward. He clutched tightly to the rail as the sleigh rose above the flames. They circled the inferno once and then headed out over the sea, the wind buffeting the small craft as the Yule goats picked up speed. They skimmed along the waves heading west, the bright moonlight glistening off the whitecaps below.

"It is Yuletide!" Krampus bellowed. "It is time for the world to celebrate the return of the Yule Lord!"

He set back his head and laughed and laughed as they chased the night across the Atlantic.

PART III

yuletide

Chapter Twelve

YULE CHEER

Geri greeted them at the door. If a wolf could smile, Jesse felt sure this one was smiling now. Krampus hopped out of the sleigh, bounded over, and caught the wolf in a bear hug. "Happy Yuletide!" Krampus cried, and pranced into the church. He plucked up the sack, spun around in a circle. "We go! We go!"

"What? Where?" Vernon asked, setting down the two sacks of sleeping sand. "Tonight? You can't possibly mean tonight. Besides, Christmas is over for this season."

"We are not celebrating Christmas, you fool!" Krampus cried. "Christmas is dead! We are celebrating Yule. Yuletide runs for many weeks, and this year, it shall run as long as I deem necessary to spread my word."

The Shawnee glanced excitedly at one another, but Vernon moaned, plopped down into one of the pews. "I'm tired and I'm hungry."

Krampus made a sputtering, dismissive sound. "It is festive season, there will be food aplenty. Now, up with you. Take the sleeping sand and put a handful into pouches and bring them along."

"Pouches?" Vernon whined. "Where am I supposed to find pouches?"

Wipi pulled out his knife and began hacking at one of the curtains. He cut out three pieces, folded them, and used part of the cords as ties. Within a few minutes, he'd made three pouches, handed them to Vernon.

"Oh, don't look so damn smug," Vernon said, taking the bags.

Isabel headed over to the injured wolf, Freki. A few well-gnawed cow bones lay near his bedding. Freki managed to get to his feet and greet her, standing unsteadily as Isabel ruffled his great mane. She appeared so tiny before the great beast that could so easily take off her head with one chomp. He nuzzled her hair as she poured more mead into his pie pan.

"All right, enough delay, let us go." Krampus sounded like a child wanting to open his birthday presents. "Come now. Out . . . all of you!" They headed for the door. "Wait!" he looked them over, frowning. He snatched a spear from Makwa, the handgun from Chet, tossed them into the cardboard box with the cash. "Other than your knives, there shall be no weapons, not on a Yule run." The Shawnee didn't look pleased with this at all, but all the Belsnickels dropped their weapons into the box.

They followed Krampus outside, where the Yule Lord found a birch tree and commenced snapping off several long, thin branches until he had a handful. He pulled the satin ribbon from his hair and bound the twigs together. He swished them through the air, seemed pleased with the whistle, and gave Isabel a light swat on her rump. "Hey," she yelled. "Cut it out!"

Krampus laughed. "This will do. Will do just fine."

The Yule Lord took his place in the front of the sleigh, Isabel on the bench next to him, holding the sack and switches, Jesse beside her. Vernon, Chet, and the three Shawnee squeezed into the compartment in the back.

Krampus lifted the reins, hesitated, his eyes fixed on Santa's bloody head atop the spear. "You were a very naughty boy. You do not get to come along." He snatched it up by the hair and chucked it. It rolled across the snow and bumped up against the fallen downspout, lying there on its cheek, its dead eyes staring back at them.

"Away," Krampus called and popped the reins. The goats leapt forward, climbing up over the treetops and into the clear night sky. They followed the valley north toward a cluster of lights, toward Goodhope.

Jesse could see the occasional home or trailer not too far below, the headlights of cars going about their way. He thought of Abigail and Linda somewhere down there. He'd lost all sense of time and wondered if they were still awake, if everything was okay. He wanted to go to them now, ached to see them again, but knew there'd be no chance of it, not tonight, not while Krampus was in such a state.

KRAMPUS DROPPED DOWN until they were skimming the tree line. He found a dead-end street on the edge of town with only a handful of homes, circled once, and landed, sliding to a stop beneath a leaning streetlight.

Krampus hopped from the sleigh, looked around at the homes, at the blinking Christmas lights. He took a deep breath, appeared to drink in the cold night air. "I am finally here." He closed his eyes. "At last . . . it is over. Baldr is no more and I am free to return to spreading Yuletide blessings, to chasing dark spirits from the land." He opened his eyes, wiped them. "My apologies, the moment overwhelms me." He looked at them. "You each played your part and for that I thank you. In your honor I shall make this a night to remember, that I promise."

Krampus held out his hand. "Vernon, the sleeping sand." Vernon gave him the pouches. Krampus handed one to Isabel, one to Jesse, started to give one to Makwa, reconsidered and gave the last one back to Vernon. "In case we run into those that are not in a festive mood. A few grains dashed to the face will have them sleeping like babies. Now follow my lead, try not to bring harm upon any, 'less they threaten violence."

Jesse slipped the pouch into his front breast pocket for easy access.

"Remember," Krampus said. "We are here for the children, to teach them to honor the Yule Lord, to make them *believe*." He started across the street toward the nearest house.

"Wait," Isabel said, and grabbed his arm.

"What is it now?"

"Not that one."

"Why not?"

"They don't have kids."

"How can you know that?"

"Look . . . no toys or bikes in the yard. No swing sets either. You want that one." She pointed to the next house up, where a tricycle lay on its side next to a brightly colored plastic play gym.

Krampus gave her a nod and patted her on the head. "Isabel, my little lion. You are full of surprises." He headed for the house, the Belsnickels falling in line behind him.

"Little lion," Jesse snickered, and patted Isabel on the head. Isabel socked him.

Krampus spied a large plastic Santa on the porch as they headed up the walkway. He sneered. "This home looks like it needs reminding of what Yuletide is truly about." Krampus stepped up onto the porch, picked up the plastic Santa and chucked it out into the yard.

"We're gonna get shot," Chet mumbled. And for once Jesse found himself in full agreement with the man. Jesse felt sure that before the night was over, one of them, or maybe all of them, would be lying on someone's living-room floor full of buckshot. Jesse hardly knew a soul around this part of the county who didn't own at least one gun—and three or four, more likely than not.

Krampus knocked on the door. They stood and waited, Krampus with the black sack over his shoulder and clutching a handful of switches, the Belsnickels standing around him like a confused band of trick-or-treaters. Jesse could hear a television blaring from somewhere in the house and exchanged a worried glance with Isabel. Krampus knocked again, louder.

A woman yelled from somewhere in the house, "The door, Joe. I think someone's at the door!"

The volume of the TV dropped. "What's that?"

"I thought I heard the door."

"Well, for crying out loud, you done forgot how to answer a door?" There followed a long minute of silence. "Ah for fuck sakes," the man cried. "All right, I guess I'll get the goddamn door. Wouldn't want you to ever have to get up off your fat ass." They heard slippers clomping toward the door; a moment later, the porch light came on and the door popped open. A middle-aged man in a red flannel hunting shirt over a pair of gray sweatpants leaned against the door, holding a beer and a cigarette in one hand. The man was drunk, but not too drunk to see that Krampus wasn't who he'd been expecting.

"Are there any good children in this dwelling?" Krampus asked.

The man's eyes grew wide, he stumbled back several steps, losing both the beer and the cigarette. All at once he appeared to sober up and made to slam the door shut. Krampus extended his hand, knocked the door back and the man to the linoleum.

"Yule cheer to one and all!" Krampus called and pushed in, stepping over the man and heading down the hall.

The Shawnee pounced on the man, pinned him. The man started hollering and Makwa raised a fist. Isabel grabbed Makwa's arm before he could land a blow. "No! Bad!" Isabel cried. "Stop it!" Jesse fumbled for his sleeping sand, but Vernon beat him to it, tossing a pinch of the sand into the man's face. The man squinted, looked as though about to sneeze, then his head lolled over and he was out. The Shawnee appeared disappointed.

Jesse managed to let out half a breath before a woman's scream came down the hallway. Isabel and Jesse shoved their way past the Shawnee, intent on beating them to whatever trouble Krampus had got into now.

It was a woman, about the same age as the man, wearing an almost identical outfit of a red flannel hunting shirt and sweatpants. Krampus had her trapped over in one corner of the room, behind the Christmas tree. The Yule Lord was plucking ornaments off the tree and smashing them into the fireplace. He held up a sparkling glass Santa. "No, no, no," he scolded, and threw it at her. It smashed to pieces against the wall and she let out another cry. "No more Santa Claus. Ever! You want to know why?" He didn't wait for her to answer. "Because he is dead!" he snarled. "I cut off his head and if you doubt me, why, I can show it to you. Would you like to see it?" The woman shook her head. Krampus spied the beautiful blown-glass cross sitting on the top of the tree and his face knotted up. "This will not do. You are not to put Christian totems on a Yule tree." He plucked it off, shook it at her as though she might be a vampire. "No crosses! No Santas! Is that understood?" He raised his arm as though to throw it.

"No!" she screamed, actually coming forward and reaching for it. "Please, no. That was my mother's!"

Krampus raised the ornament up beyond her reach.

"Please, please."

"Only if you promise never to put it on my tree again."

The woman nodded adamantly.

"Swear it."

"I swear it!"

He held it out and she snatched it, clutched it to her breast, and began sobbing.

"Where are the remains of your feast?" Krampus asked.

She looked at him and blinked several times. "Feast?"

"Yes."

"You mean . . . the leftovers? They're in the fridge. Where else would they be?"

"And do you offer them in tribute?"

"Do I what?"

"Offer your fare to the Lord of Yule?"

"You want my leftovers?" She appeared unsure whether to laugh or cry, but undoubtedly wanted to say whatever might send this demented demon away from her. "Sure . . . you go right ahead. Kitchen's that way." She pointed. "Knock yourself out."

"Good. Your Yuletide offerings will bring you many blessings for the coming year." Krampus headed toward the kitchen, leaving the lady trembling in the corner, still clutching her mother's ornament.

Isabel and Jesse scooted over to the woman. "Sit down," Isabel said.

"What? Why? Are you gonna hurt me?"

"No," Isabel said. "Nobody's gonna hurt you. Now, just sit."

The lady did and Isabel tossed a pinch of sleeping sand in her face. A few seconds later she was out. Isabel gingerly plucked the ornament from her arms and set it on the mantel.

Something crashed in the kitchen.

"What now?" Isabel asked.

"He did promise us a night to remember."

"Yes, sir, I'm afraid he did at that."

The two of them peered into the kitchen. The refrigerator stood wide-open, Wipi was pulling dishes from the fridge and handing them to Nipi. A large ceramic tray sat on the counter, the tin foil peeled back, exposing a half-carved turkey on a bed of cornbread dressing. Makwa,

Chet, and Vernon were shoveling handfuls into their mouths, not even bothering with utensils. Vernon glanced up, a guilty look upon his face. "What? I'm starving. Christ, we haven't eaten since . . . what . . . yesterday, or was it the day before?"

Jesse found a clock, it was ten till midnight. He tried to figure out how long they'd been up, but between the two continents he had no idea.

"Where's Krampus?" Isabel asked.

"Went down the hall," Chet said through a mouthful of dressing.

"Down the hall?" Isabel said. "You let him out of your sight?"

"Hey," Chet said. "I sure as shit ain't his babysitter."

They heard a scream, a child's scream.

"Oh, for Christ's sake," Isabel said and darted down the hall. Jesse took off after her.

Krampus stood in the middle of the room between two beds. One bed was empty, two girls huddled together in the other. Jesse guessed one child to be nine or ten years old, the younger one about the same age as his Abigail. The girls were pressed into the corner, atop pillows and stuffed animals, as far from Krampus as they could get. Both were crying, clutching each other, trembling, their eyes full of terror.

Krampus took a step forward, and the girls let loose a shrill scream, kicking their legs as though something was biting them.

Jesse couldn't stand it, could only think of his own daughter. "Krampus," Jesse cried. "Stop, you can't—"

"Silence," Krampus snapped, holding up one finger. "Do not interfere, that is a command."

Jesse quieted; found he could do little more than watch, no matter how much he ached to pull Krampus from the room.

Krampus returned to the girls, knelt down upon one knee, and put his finger to his lips. "Hush," he whispered. "Hush, I am Krampus, the spirit of Yule. I come bearing gifts." His words were kindly, hypnotic. The girls stopped screaming, calmed a degree. "Would you like to see your gifts?"

Neither of the girls answered, only stared at Krampus with wide, terrified eyes.

Krampus set down the birch switches, slid the sack off his shoulder, closed his eyes, and stuck his hand inside the sack. He brought out two triangular gold coins, held them for the girls to see, and curiosity slowly replaced their fear.

"Gold coin from the realm of Hel. These can buy you many pretty things."

The coins mesmerized the girls.

"Would you like these?"

Both girls nodded.

Krampus held them out, but when the girls reached for them, Krampus pulled the coins back. "There is a condition. First you must speak my name. You can call me Krampus, the Yule Lord. Now, say my name."

"Krampus, the Yule Lord," the girls chorused.

Krampus smiled. "Good." He handed them the coins.

The girls admired their newfound treasures, and Jesse wondered what spell Krampus had set upon them.

"There is more, for the world is a hard place and nothing comes without a price. You should know that each year upon Yuletide I will fly overhead. I might, or I might not return. But should I honor you with a visit, I do expect tribute to be waiting. I expect to find tokens of your devotion. Traditionally, this is done by placing your shoes upon the step and leaving me a treat or trinket within them. Do you think you can do that?"

The girls nodded.

"Good, for if I find a treat, you might get another gold coin or something even better. But if I do not . . ." Krampus picked up the sack and the switches, stood to his full height, his voice dropping downlow and menacing. "If I do not find tribute then I will put you in my sack and beat you bloody." He smacked the sack once soundly with the switches.

The girls jumped back; Jesse thought they might start screaming again.

"Will I find shoes full of treats next winter?"

Both girls nodded adamantly.

"Good. And what is my name?"

"Krampus," they said together.

"Good." He patted them atop their heads. "Good night, my little sugar plums. Sleep tight." Krampus left the room.

Isabel sprinkled them with sleeping sand and tucked them in. They looked like sleeping angels. Jesse wondered how much they would remember come morning. He hoped not much, hoped they wouldn't wake up screaming every night.

THEY CAUGHT UP with Krampus at the sleigh; Chet, Vernon, and the Shawnee already aboard. Wipi held the turkey carcass in his lap, he and his brother, Nipi, were still eating, their fingers and faces smeared with dressing and grease.

"Onward to the next home," Krampus said and climbed into the sleigh; Isabel and Jesse followed suit.

"There's more?" Vernon asked dryly. "Oh, but will the fun never end?"

"Yes, more. Many, many more. Tanngnost and Tanngrisni shall take us from one neighborhood to the next, but it is not my goal to hit every dwelling. We need only visit the occasional home, as the children will do the rest. They shall spread the tale from there, will dazzle other children with their prizes and stories . . . will make them *believe*. And so long as they believe, so long as I have followers, Yule shall flourish, spread. My place will be affirmed and no god shall usurp my reign . . . not ever again."

He popped the reins and they took off, gliding down the middle of the street just above the car roofs, heading across town. They passed over a man sitting in his truck at a stop sign. The man watched them fly over, nodded at them, grinning the whole time, then drove on as though nothing had happened. A block later, a man and a woman leaned against a car. The man was trying to unlock the door but seemed too intoxicated to get the key in the lock. They looked up as the sleigh flew past, hollered something unintelligible, and both of them promptly fell over. Jesse wondered how many of these late-night boozers would blame what they'd seen on the drink come morning. Not much further along, a woman in a car slammed on her brakes as they barreled past. She stuck her head out the window, eyes wide in wonderment. It was apparent from her shocked expression that she wasn't drunk, but maybe she wished she were. About a mile later, they cruised by a dozen or so teenagers tailgating in the old water tower parking lot. "*Yule cheer to one and all!"* Krampus yelled, and waved. About half the kids managed a partial wave, mouths agape, the rest just stared, too stunned to do anything else. A flash went off and Jesse grinned, wondered if their picture would be pasted all over the Internet come morning.

They headed up Sipsey Ridge, along the edge of town, the houses were spread out, a bit more rural, small vegetable gardens and chicken pens popping up here and there. Krampus slowed down, peering up the long driveways.

"Hey," Chet said. "It's my place." He pointed to a small cottage with pink asbestos siding. A wood cutout of a woman in bloomers bending over stood in the flower bed, and a white wicker rocker sat on the porch.

"You live in a pink house?" Jesse laughed. "Explains a lot. Guess that's why you're so partial to that fancy coat you're wearing."

"Hey, fuck you. It's my aunt's house."

"You live with your aunt?" Jesse laughed harder.

"Kiss my ass," Chet said and jabbed Jesse.

Jesse raised his hands in surrender, did his best to stop laughing.

"It's temporary. She's just helping out until I get things worked out with Trish. So fuck off."

Jesse stopped laughing. "You and Trish split up?"

Chet nodded, couldn't hide the hurt on his face. Jesse knew that look too well. "Yeah," Jesse said. "I know a bit about how that goes."

Krampus drifted a few more houses up and slid to a stop in front of a flat-roofed, ranch-style home with water-stained cedar siding. An older-model Chevy Malibu with its tail end jacked up, missing its hubcaps, and badly in need of new paint, sat in the carport. The yard strewn with a few toys, a broken swing set, rusting auto parts, and a good number of PBR empties.

"Hey, man," Chet said. "That's Wallace Dotson's place. You sure as shit don't wanna go messing around there. He ain't right in the head, not since coming home from Iraq he ain't."

"How many children does your friend Wallace Dotson have?" Krampus asked.

"He ain't my friend. And that man don't know the meaning of the word 'birth control.' Got at least five or six brats running around, maybe more, and every one of 'em as mean and fucked in the head as their old man. Little shits will shoot you the bird just for looking at 'em."

Krampus hopped out and the Shawnee followed. Jesse, Isabel, Vernon, and Chet sat tight. A dog barked somewhere up the drive.

"Man," Chet said. "I'm telling you, you're picking the wrong house. Old Wallace, that man, he likes his guns, likes shooting them, too. Just pick another house why don't you?"

"Come," Krampus said. "All of you, now." They climbed out and followed Krampus up the drive.

Jesse nudged Isabel. "Look." He pointed to a hand-painted sign stuck in the front lawn. It read, NO SOLICITING. THIS MEANS YOU ASSHOLE!

Isabel shook her head.

All the windows were dark. Jesse hoped the family was away for the holidays. Krampus stepped onto the porch and a dog barked twice from the other side of the door. It sounded like a big dog. They could hear its claws clacking as it paced back and forth.

Krampus raised his fist to knock, stopped. "Maybe a little prudence is in order," he whispered. "A slightly different tack. Jesse, the key." Jesse handed him the key ring. Three of the skeleton keys were of the old-fashioned variety, but the rest were smaller, more modern in design. Krampus picked one of these, tried to insert it into the lock—it wouldn't fit. Jesse didn't understand how these six keys were supposed to open every key lock in the world, but after all he'd seen recently, he felt relatively optimistic. Krampus didn't disappoint; the second key slid in, he gave it a twist, and the bolt flopped over.

Jesse had no idea if the sleeping sand worked on dogs or not, but dug a pinch from his breast pocket and held it at the ready. Krampus twisted the knob and pushed the door inward. The dog jumped out at them and Jesse flicked the sand into its face. It was a basset hound—a really old basset hound. It looked at Jesse with big, sad eyes, wagged its tail, then collapsed.

Everyone gave Jesse a hard look.

"What?"

They stepped over the sleeping dog and entered the foyer. Voices and the cast of a flickering television came from the far end of the hall. Jesse smelled weed.

Krampus crept toward the light, avoiding the clumps of dirty clothes. They stopped in the doorway to the living room. A pudgy man with about a week's worth of beard lay sprawled across a sofa, fast asleep, an ashtray full of butts balanced on his chest, an empty bottle of whiskey on the floor, and a large gray tabby resting in his lap. The cat opened its eyes and stared at them.

The children, all six of them, were sitting on the floor in front of the television, their backs to them. They ranged in age from about ten all the way down to a toddler in diapers, two girls and the rest boys. An enormous, economy-size bag of Cheetos sat between them, orange crumbs littering the grungy carpet. *It's a Wonderful Life* was playing, and Jimmy Stewart was trying to convince the fine residents of Bedford Falls not to pull all their money from the Building and Loan, his disarming manner and warm sincere drawl holding the children spellbound.

There was no Christmas tree in this house, no Christmas lights, or any sort of decorations other than a lone group of pinecones hanging over the fireplace. Jesse found no new toys, or signs of any gifts. It appeared as though Christmas had pretty much passed these children by.

Isabel touched Krampus's arm, pointed to the man. Krampus nodded and she tiptoed over. The cat stretched, yawned, began to purr. Isabel dropped a few sprinkles of sleeping sand onto the man's face. His nose crinkled, but that was about it. Isabel shrugged. When she turned around, all the children were looking at her—six faces smeared with orange crumbs. Isabel raised her hand. "Hi."

They watched her step back over to the hall. "We should go try and find their ma," Isabel whispered.

"She ain't here," Chet said. "She run off about a year back."

"Oh," Isabel replied.

Krampus handed Isabel his switches. "I won't be needing these." He stepped into the room and every eye went to the towering Yule Lord, terror spreading across their faces.

"There is no need to fear," Krampus said in the same soft, lulling voice he'd used on the little girls at the previous house. "I am a friend."

Their terror appeared to lessen a degree, but one of the younger boys still began to cry. "Casey, you shush now," a girl said and stood up. The little boy did his best to stifle his tears. The girl appeared to be the oldest of the bunch, maybe nine or ten years old. She took a step forward, putting herself between Krampus and the rest. "What'd you want?" she said, trying to sound tough, but Jesse could hear the fear in her voice. "If you's looking to steal stuff, we ain't got nothing."

"We are not thieves," Krampus said, his voice calm and hypnotic. "I am the Yule Lord and I come bearing gifts for all of you."

Curiosity appeared on a few of the faces. They looked up at their big sister. She gave Krampus a hard, cynical look. "Folks never give you something, 'less they be wanting something. What'd you want?"

"You are wise beyond your years. What is your name, child?"

The girl hesitated. "Who's asking?"

The Yule Lord grinned. "I am Krampus."

"Well, Krampus, my name is Carolyn, and this here is Chris and Curtis, Casey, Clayton, and over there is Charlene."

Krampus nodded to each of them. The baby looked at Krampus, began to whimper. A boy, couldn't have been older than four, pulled the baby into his lap, found its pacifier, and patted it on the back, doing his best to reassure the child.

Krampus walked softly over to the children and unslung his sack.

The girl stood her ground. She looked terrified, but Jesse could see that she'd take a beating before she'd let anyone, even a horned demon, get their hands on any of these children.

Casey crawled behind his big sister and began to cry again. "Casey, I done told you to shush up, now. Y'know Pa don't stand for no tears."

"Please . . . do not be alarmed." Krampus knelt down on one knee. He placed the sack between them, slipped in his hand, closed his eyes, and pulled out a handful of the triangular gold coins.

Their eyes let up, all of them bedazzled by the ancient coins. He handed one to each and went on to tell them all about Yule, about the old traditions, about shoes on doorsteps and rewards for those who believe. They listened, captivated and hanging on his every word. Soon all trace of their fear was gone.

When Krampus finished, he stood, bid them Happy Yule, and headed out. The children followed them to the door.

"Hey," Jesse said to Carolyn. "Be sure not to let your daddy see them coins."

The girl nodded as though she was way ahead of him.

"Take them down to Dicker and Pawn. Ask for Finn, he's out to treat you better than most."

"Yeah," Chet put in. "You tell him Chet Boggs said he better treat you square. Got that?"

The girl nodded again.

Jesse and Chet caught up with the rest of the Belsnickels in the sleigh. Krampus popped the reins and the Yule goats leapt skyward. Jesse watched the children, their six small faces staring up at them in wonderment. Carolyn raised her arm and waved, all the children did. Jesse waved back.

CLOUDS OF BLACK smoke drifted across the gardens and through the topiary, shifting with the early-dawn wind. A few pockets of flame still crackled. The scorched beams and stones of the stable formed a stark skeleton against the morning sky.

Six women dug through the smoldering embers with pitchforks and rakes. Their dirty, soot-covered gowns clinging to the sweat of their bodies, ash smeared across their hands and tear-streaked faces.

"Here," the woman with the long white hair called. "He is here."

They all came, dropping rakes and forks in favor of their own hands, gently pulling the mutilated corpse from the ash. Some of the women turned away, could not bear to look upon the blackened, headless body.

"Help me," the woman said, and together they lifted the body and carried it across the courtyard, down a narrow path outside the wall, to a small, single-room chapel overlooking the sea. There they lay it upon a stone slab, beneath a window of golden stained glass in the shape of a cross. One of the girls fetched towels and a pail of seawater. Together they washed the body, wiping away the dirt and soot. The fire had burned away all of his clothing, but left his body untouched. It gleamed porcelain-white, perfect except for the great injuries inflicted by the spear. They washed his hands, scrubbed beneath his fingernails, toenails, his genitals, his wounds, and the grisly flap of torn flesh at his neck. They bathed him until no trace of soiled flesh remained, then wrapped him in white linen.

"Now," the woman said. "Stop your weeping. Grief is for the dead. Santa Claus can never die. For too many people believe in him. It is a time for prayers . . . time to call to the angels."

She reached out her hands and the girls linked together, forming a circle around the slab. She sat cross-legged upon the marble floor and the girls followed her lead.

"We serve him vigil. None shall eat, sleep, nor drink until the angels come. If they do not come then it is God's will that we perish at his side. Now close your eyes and call them down."

As they prayed, the morning sun cleared the horizon, blazing through the stained glass, bathing the room in golden light. "God is in the house," the white-haired woman said.

THE THIRD HOUSE that night sat near the river—stately new construction enclosed within a gate of red brick and elegant iron. Krampus dropped the sleigh down upon the wide circular driveway.

The Yule Lord found the front door unlocked and let himself in. The foyer led them into a dramatic living space open to the second floor. A wall of arched windows ran to the peak of the cathedral ceiling and faced out toward the river; at their center stood a towering Christmas tree dripping in ribbons and ornaments.

"Wow, that's pretty," Isabel said.

Krampus didn't appear to share her sentiment. He made a face as though force-fed a spoonful of cough syrup, but refrained from smashing any of the ornaments, instead heading up the grand staircase.

Krampus entered the first room they came to; he strolled right in as though invited. The room was spacious, a large flat-screen television hung from the wall, a movie playing, the sound down low. A man and a woman, in their forties, were sitting up in their king-size four-poster bed—the man pecking away at his laptop, the woman watching the TV while texting on her phone. The man looked up when his wife let out a loud gasp.

Krampus paid them no heed, staring into the big screen on the wall, his head cocked to one side.

The woman looked as though she were choking on something, and finally a scream escaped her throat. Jesse and Isabel both started over with the sleeping sand, but Krampus held up his hand. "Wait."

The woman screamed again, started to get up. The man yanked

the earbuds from his ears and threw an arm across the woman. "Stay calm, Nancy. Just *stay* calm." Nancy appeared about to hyperventilate, but somehow managed to sit tight, staring with absolute horror at the giant devil in her bedroom.

Krampus returned his attention to the screen, to the horses riding across a lush English landscape. He put his nose right in the screen, bumped his horns, grunted, and stepped back.

"It's a high-definition LCD," the man said, his voice shaky. "Sixty inches. It's yours if you want it. Please . . . just take it and go."

Krampus reached out, tapped the screen with his jagged fingernails, pressed his palm against it as though trying to push through it. There came a snap, the screen flickered, and a spiderweb of cracks spiraled out from beneath his hand. Krampus studied the fractured screen. "Hmm, it appears I have damaged it. I am sorry." He sounded sincere.

"That's okay," the man put in quickly. "That's fine. Not a problem. We have another one downstairs. You're welcome to it. The jewelry . . . is over there." He pointed to a mahogany box on top of the vanity. "I don't have much cash," his tone nervous, apologetic. "But you're welcome to what I have."

"We did not come to steal," Krampus said, and this bit of news served only to make the man and the woman more anxious. The woman tugged the sheet up to her throat, covering herself, spilling the laptop. Krampus stepped closer, peering at the glowing laptop screen curiously. The women let out a high-pitched squeal like a weasel in a snare.

"You want it?" the man asked. "It's yours." He held the laptop out to Krampus. Krampus looked it over, but didn't take it. "There's a new, fully loaded Mustang down in the garage. The keys are right over there." He pointed again to the vanity. No one looked. "I should make it clear," the man said, his tone becoming a bit more desperate, "that I'm involved with state government at the highest levels. And as someone with a lot of experience within the legal system, I must advise you against any acts of violence. If *anyone* in this house is harmed, or even threatened . . . the State of West Virginia will not be lenient."

"You a lawyer?" Chet asked. "You talk like a lawyer. I hate lawyers."

The man shook his head. "Not exactly . . . I consider myself more of a mediator."

"Well, I hate them, too."

"Chet," Jesse said. "You hate everybody. So why don't you just shut up and leave the man be."

Chet fastened his eyes on Jesse. "Don't remember anyone telling me I gotta take orders from you. So why don't you plug your whiney pie hole."

"Why don't you stop being retarded?" Jesse shot back. "Oh, I know, because you can't."

Chet's face knotted up. "You're a fucking dick." He shoved Jesse. Jesse came back with a full roundhouse, catching Chet against the side of the head, knocking him into the wall. Chet rebounded in a charge, drove into Jesse's waist with his shoulder. Both men flew onto the bed, rolled all the way across, and tumbled onto the floor on the far side, taking the lamp and nightstand over with them. The woman started screaming hysterically.

Krampus watched, obviously amused, and the Shawnee began laughing and hooting.

"*Krampus!*" Isabel yelled, and pushed him. "Krampus, make 'em stop before they kill each other."

Krampus shrugged and shouted, "*Enough!* Cease fighting. It is a command." And just like that, Jesse and Chet stopped, the two of them left sitting there on the carpet glaring at one another. "There is to be no more brawling between you."

Isabel evidently had had enough. She hopped over and dashed a pinch of sleeping sand on the screaming woman as though she were salting a potato. The woman swooned and passed out. "What did you do to her?" the man demanded, and promptly received a dose of his own, slumping over onto his wife.

"Well, now," Vernon said. "That was quite the show. Can't wait to see what you fine gentlemen come up with next."

Krampus laughed and headed out of the room.

Jesse passed two empty rooms and caught up with the Yule Lord peering into a dimly lit bedroom at the far end of the house. A teenage girl reclined in a beanbag chair, her face angled away from them. Like the man, she had a laptop, but she also had a flashy phone and was going back and forth between the two, madly tapping the keyboard and texting at the same time. She wore headphones, but Jesse could still hear her music all the way across the room and could only imagine the damage she must be doing to her ears.

Krampus watched her for at least five minutes, staring at the glowing screens, his brow furrowed, but she never looked up, lost in her own world, having no idea that a host of demons stood at her door. Krampus shook his head and kept going, following the hall round in a loop until they came to a closed door covered in video game-posters. Jesse heard muffled explosions and gunfire coming from within. Krampus opened the door and they found a boy, maybe eight or nine, sitting cross-legged on the end of his bed. The boy faced the big screen on the far wall, playing a video game, blasting away at an assortment of stumbling undead—explosions and body parts rocking the screen.

As with the girl, Krampus merely stood in the doorway and watched for several minutes. Other than his thumbs, the boy barely moved the whole time, staring glassy-eyed, his mouth half-open, looking like a lobotomy patient.

"He is bewitched." Krampus strolled purposely across the room, right up to the screen, and smashed it in with his fist.

The boy clutched the game controller to his chest and froze, his eyes threatening to burst from his head. Krampus leaned over to the boy. "You are free. The world is now yours. Go take it."

Krampus left the room, leaving the boy staring in perplexed horror. The Belsnickels looked from the boy to one another.

"Are we done then?" Vernon asked.

Isabel nodded and they followed Krampus from the house.

Stopping in the driveway, Krampus gave the home a deeply troubled look. "It seems there are other demons besides Santa's ghost to contend with."

Chapter Thirteen

TWEEKERS

Dillard sat in his recliner, a glass of whiskey in his hand, staring at his flat-screen television. The set was off, but he stared at it anyway—staring and staring at that big, dark screen. He rubbed the bridge of his nose, his head starting to hurt. He'd tried to sleep, but got tired of lying there in that big bed—*alone*. Linda slept in the room with Abigail. She'd locked the door.

He'd tried to talk to her again, but might as well have been talking to the wall. Finally, he'd had to leave the room, because if he hadn't, if he had to bear her grief-stricken face, listen to her sobbing over that fuckup for even one more second, he would've lost it again, would've done whatever it took to make her see it was Jesse, not him, that got Jesse killed.

He took another swig and wiped his mouth. *It's done between us . . . over. You know it. You can see it in her face. She's gonna leave you the first chance she gets.*

Things had been going so well. He'd come along at the right time, helped her out of a tight spot, and Linda seemed to really appreciate him. He liked that, liked the way it made him feel—like a knight in shining armor. It had been easy with her, easy to keep his temper, easy to be the good guy. But Jesse couldn't leave things alone.

Should have made that boy disappear when I had the chance, before this shit-storm, before everything got fucked to hell. If I had, if I had listened to my instincts, then Linda and me would be upstairs in that big warm bed together right this minute.

He thought of his wife, Ellen, Ellen's sweet, kindly face. Ellen had been a good woman, had done her best to please him. *Why had I been so hard on her? What is so wrong with me? "Ellen, baby,"* he whispered. *"God, how I miss you."*

His police radio squawked and Dillard started, almost spilling his whiskey.

"Chief, copy."

Dillard checked his watch; it was going on three A.M. "Fuck, what now?"

A youthful voice cut through the static. "Chief, copy." It was Noel Roberts, the new officer; just a kid, as far as Dillard was concerned, started back in October. Dillard still wasn't sure how he felt about him. Noel asked too many questions, wanted to do everything by the book, didn't understand that in small towns sometimes you had to bend the rules. Dillard hoped that changed soon, or things wouldn't be working out for Noel, not in Goodhope.

Dillard picked up the radio and hit the mic. "Go ahead, Noel. What now?"

"Code sixteen, possible code thirteen. Two locations, copy."

"Noel, how many times am I gonna have to remind you you're working for the fucking Goodhope Police Department, not the NYPD? Knock the academy bullshit off and just talk to me like a human being, all right? Now are you trying to tell me there's been two break-ins tonight?"

"Ten-four, chief."

Dillard rolled his eyes. "Mind giving me the whereabouts?"

"One on Second and Beech. Break-in occurred approximately oh-two-hundred hours. The other break-in occurred shortly thereafter at the residence at the end of Madison."

"End of Madison? Ain't that out where Doctor Ferrel lives?"

"Affirmative. Doctor Ferrel reports various acts of vandalism. Suspect smashed in his television."

Dillard smiled at that. In his book, Doctor Ferrel was a conceited asswipe—the man spoke to him as though he were addressing a ten-year-old, going on and on in that snooty upstate accent of his, telling him what he should and shouldn't be eating, drinking, and thinking, for that matter. And as far as Dillard was concerned, anyone that felt it proper to prattle on about the finer points of fly-fishing while giving a prostate exam deserved to have his television smashed in anyway. "Well, that's just a doggone shame," Dillard said. "Probably another meth freak. Did you get a description on the suspect?"

"Ten-four. Group of African-American males, wearing colorful costumes and disguises."

Dillard stood up fast. That sounded like Jesse's boys. "How many? What kind of weapons? Any injuries?"

"No report on weapons. Not sure how many. No one was injured. And chief . . . the odd thing is nothing was reported stolen. Just harassment and vandalism."

That don't make any sense, Dillard thought. *Why would they break in and not steal anything? What the hell were they after?*

"And also . . . the sheriff called."

Dillard stiffened. Sheriff Milton Wright was a straight shooter and had been known to come sniffing around Goodhope whenever he found an excuse. Dillard made a point of keeping both the man and his nose out of his town and out of his business. "Well, just what did our good friend Sheriff Wright want?"

"Informing us to keep an eye out. Apparently they've had at least a half-dozen similar calls. Breaking and entering, harassment. Descriptions match our suspects."

"Oh, shit," Dillard said without punching the mic. "What the fuck is going on?" He hit the mic. "Noel, I'll handle the home on Second." And, thinking how little he wished to talk to a man who'd had a finger up his ass, "Gonna let you take care of the good doctor. Copy."

"Ten-four, chief. En route."

Dillard went upstairs to get dressed, found his cell phone, gave the General a call—got no answer. Shouldn't have been a big deal, but Dillard couldn't help a growing sense of unease. He finished getting dressed, tugged on his belt, holstered his gun, and headed out the door. "Something's just not right," he said, shaking his head, "not by a long shot."

JESSE WATCHED THE lights of Goodhope disappear behind them, eclipsed by the dark mountainside. They headed east, deeper into hill country, leaving Krampus's gift of Yule cheer in over three dozen homes spread about as many neighborhoods all along eastern Boone County. Most of the visits went smoothly, as smoothly as one could hope for any home invasion carried out by a host of costume-clad devils. As the evening progressed into the a.m. hours, most occupants were already fast asleep, making the going much easier. Jesse, Vernon, and Isabel urged Krampus to use the keys, to slip in instead of knocking, and found this to be better for all involved. While Krampus was busy traumatizing the children, they'd mastered getting quickly to sleeping parents and making sure they stayed asleep with a quick dusting of the sand. And in one instance they found out that sleeping sand was equally effective on Shawnee, when an overzealous handful found its way into Nipi's face. Vernon claimed the incident to be an accident, but Jesse had his doubts. Nipi ended up sleeping it off in the sleigh for the next several stops.

"What is that?" Krampus asked, pointing below.

Jesse peered beneath them, but found only forest and great stretches of strip-mining.

Krampus drifted downward until they were flying along the rim of a vast land removal project. He stared at the devastated landscape, his face stricken, and Jesse realized that Krampus meant the miles of open earth and blasted mountaintops.

Krampus set the sleigh down upon a plateau overlooking the man-made crater. The faintest traces of dawn spread along the horizon, exposing the bald, angry scar upon the land. "Why, it goes on as far as one can see." The Yule Lord's brows tightened as though he was trying to make sense of what he was seeing. "Men did this?"

Jesse nodded. "Yeah, they did."

"They did this on purpose?"

Jesse nodded.

Krampus fell silent. "Why would they destroy the forest, the mountains . . . the very land?"

"For the coal. They blast the tops off the mountains to get to the coal."

Krampus shook his head, his face bewildered. "It is like cutting off one's own arm to feed one's self."

Jesse had never really figured it that way, but yes, he thought that was as good a way of looking at it as any.

The Yule Lord's shoulders slumped. "Soon there will be no place left for the spirits to dwell . . . the earth will become a soulless land . . . a place of ghosts, just like Asgard." He touched his cheeks, his fingers sliding downward, contorting his face into a mask of despair. "Does mankind truly hate itself?" His voice dropped, barely a whisper. "How can one surmount such irreverence?"

Krampus looked away, stared into the salmon-colored glow growing on the horizon. "I believe it is enough for one night. Let us return." He snapped the reins and up they went, heading down the valley, back toward Goodhope.

"LOOK!" ISABEL POINTED to a house coming up below them. "Is that a little girl?"

"Where?" Jesse asked.

"There. What's she doing out all by herself this time of the morning?"

Jesse saw her standing in the snow in the middle of a large field. A house and a single-wide mobile home sat together farther up the hillside; the only homes Jesse could see for miles around.

Krampus dropped down to tree level, and the girl looked up at them as they flew over. Jesse thought she couldn't be older than six or seven.

"Krampus," Isabel said, and clutched his arm. "Please land."

Vernon leaned forward. "If we're putting this to a vote, count me against."

Krampus didn't appear to want to, either; he'd been silent since discovering the strip-mining. But he grunted and put the sleigh down between the girl and the house.

The girl watched them land, watched them climb out and walk down the slope toward her. She didn't run, didn't look scared at all, not even particularly surprised to see them. She wore a ragged flannel jacket much too large for her, with the hem of her nightgown poking out below. Her legs were bare to the cold from the knees down and Jesse realized she had only socks on her feet. She looked far too thin, shivering, dark circles under her eyes, her hair greasy and matted to her skull. She held a shovel, the tool looking huge in her small hands. Jesse could see a patch in the snow where she'd been trying to dig up the frozen earth.

Isabel bent down, took her hand. "Why, you're freezing. When's the last time you had something to eat?"

The little girl wiped her nose across the back of her arm and looked up at Krampus. "Are you Satan?"

"No, I am not. I am Krampus, the Yule Lord. And who might you be?"

"Have you come to take my daddy to Hell?"

Krampus shook his head. "No, child. Why do you speak so?"

She didn't answer, just turned and headed up the hill, dragging that big shovel behind her. She left the shovel against the side of the house, climbed the steps onto the porch, and disappeared into the house.

"They're cooking," Chet said, pointing to a generator and several portable propane tanks sitting just outside of a basement window.

"Cooking?" Isabel said.

"Meth," Jesse said.

She still didn't appear to get it.

"Drugs," Jesse added. "Bad drugs." Jesse looked the place over, didn't like what he saw. The field appeared not to have been tended in years, fall's corn all dried up and still in the husks. Large sections of the vinyl siding had fallen off the house, lying in twisted heaps upon the ground, exposing the tar paper and weathered plywood beneath. Plastic sheets and tarps were duct-taped over the windows, and several had come loose and were flapping in the light wind. An overgrowth of dead weeds and blackberry vines from previous seasons pushed up against the house and tangled along the porch. The mobile home was set off from the house by about twenty yards. The blocks on one side had given way, and the trailer leaned to port like a listing ship, darkness peeking back at them through the broken windowpanes.

The place gave off a bad vibe, more than just neglect—something foul, and vile. Jesse couldn't remember ever feeling anything quite like it. He wondered if it had anything to do with his heightened senses, with Krampus's blood in his veins. Regardless, he didn't particularly wish to go up there. He glanced over at Krampus and could see the Yule Lord felt it, too.

"Looks like it's been a long spell since anyone gave much of a damn around here," Jesse said.

"Tweekers," Chet said, and spat. "Meth, crank, probably huffing, too. Y'know, whatever they can get their hands on. Bet my ass on it."

"Now there's a prize no one wants to win," Jesse said.

Chet's face soured. "Being a dickhead just comes naturally to you. Don't it?"

"Someone needs to go see about that little girl," Isabel said.

"We don't need to be going up there," Chet said. "Ain't nothing good waiting up there. Folks that's cooking is dangerous, folks that's using is dangerous, folks doing both are about as much fun to be around as nitroglycerin."

Isabel didn't wait around to hear more; she headed up the slope on her own. They watched her climb the porch and enter the house.

"I'm telling you," Chet said, "we got no business up there."

Krampus let out a sigh. "It appears my little lion feels otherwise." He started up after her. "Come."

A dog crawled out from under the porch as they approached, shaking and skittish; Jesse could count every rib. Krampus rubbed its head and it wagged its tail. They skirted around a scorched recliner and a pile of burned blankets, and mounted the steps. The front door stood half-open, the house dark. Krampus entered and they all followed. Jesse noticed he wasn't the only one on edge, both he and Vernon clutched the sleeping sand, and the Shawnee had slipped out their knives.

The dim morning glow filtered in through dingy shades, giving just enough light to see that the front room had caught fire at some point, leaving the paneling and most of the ceiling burned and blackened. The smell of damp, charred wood hung in the air. A man lay on a sofa against the far wall, half-covered in a blanket, his eyes heavy

BROM

and bleary. With twitching hands, he scratched absently at the sores dotting his face, didn't seem to even notice the pack of Yule demons staring at him.

Krampus stepped over, poked the man once in the ribs. The man looked up at the Yule Lord, seemed to focus on him for an instant. The man's face twisted into a mask of terror; he moaned, rolled over, and pressed his face into the sofa.

"This is a . . . tweeker?" Krampus asked. "He has the sickness?"

Chet nodded. "Yeah, he's got the sickness alright. Addicted to crystal meth. Craves it. Y'know, has to have it or goes all batshit crazy?"

"I understand addiction. It is like those who are enslaved to the opium."

"Yeah, like that, 'cept worse. These folks, they make this shit out of whatever chemicals they can get a hold of. They don't eat, don't sleep, and it slowly chews away at their brains."

"This plague, it is prevalent throughout the land?"

"Yeah," Jesse put in. "Thanks to douche bags like Chet here, it sure as shit is."

"What the fuck, Jesse?" Chet barked. "Your hands ain't exactly clean."

Krampus shook his head, left the man on the sofa, and continued into the kitchen. Jesse flipped the light switch, but the light didn't come on. In the dim morning glow they could see someone had removed all the doors from the cabinets, that there was nothing left on the shelves but a few packets of instant oatmeal and a box of Froot Loops. The place smelled of mildew, of meat gone rancid. Dozens of plastic garbage bags lined the far wall. Some toppled over, spilling out their contents, others had holes chewed into them where the rats had been at work. Stacks of unwashed dishes and pans cluttered the sink, counters, and stovetop.

"Fuck," Chet said, holding his nose. "How do people live in this filth?"

Jesse peered down the hall, searching for Isabel. The house was quiet, eerily quiet. He felt as though he were in a spook house, sure some horror was about to jump out at him from every shadow. A clang came from somewhere, possibly the basement, difficult to tell. "Oh, Good Lord," someone said, it sounded like Isabel. Jesse made his way down the dark corridor, trying not to trip over all the trash.

He found Isabel and the girl in a back bedroom. A man lay tangled in a sheet upon a bare mattress, staring up at the ceiling. His waxy skin and sunken eyes left no doubt that he was dead . . . long dead.

"Well, now that's a shame," Chet said over Jesse's shoulder. "Looks like Boone County's got one less dumbshit ice-head to hand food stamps out to."

Isabel spun around, set angry eyes on Chet. "Shut your fool mouth," she hissed. "That's her daddy you're talking about."

Chet flinched, looked at the little girl. "Didn't realize . . . hell, sorry."

"Her name's Lacy."

The little girl didn't turn around, didn't even seem to hear, just stood there staring at the dead man. Isabel bent down and pulled the sheet up over his head. Krampus and the others stood at the door. No one spoke.

"She says he's been dead a long while," Isabel said. "Maybe four or five days. That's what she was doing out there in the cold, trying to dig a grave for her daddy on account no one else would."

"This one," Krampus asked, pointing at the corpse. "The sickness? The meth?"

Chet nodded. "Yeah, body can only take so much, y'know. Probably enough chemicals in his veins that they won't have to even bother with the embalming juice."

Isabel took the little girl's hand. "We need to get her someplace warm. Get her something to eat."

"You planning on just taking someone's kid?" Chet asked. "You sure you wanna be doing that?"

She looked at Krampus. "I ain't leaving her here."

Krampus nodded absently, his face unreadable, staring at the body.

Isabel kneeled down next to the girl. "You wanna come along with me? Get something to eat?"

The girl wiped her nose and nodded.

"Well, that's all I need," Isabel said, and led Lacy through the Belsnickels and out into the hall. The Belsnickels stood unsure, watching Krampus, waiting for his next move.

A shrill cry cut the silence, *"Who the fuck are you?"*

Jesse pushed out of the room, saw a silhouette back toward the kitchen blocking Isabel's path. A woman, gaunt, with long, stringy hair, looking as close to death as a living person could, stood in front of the open basement door. She reeked of chemicals.

"What you doing here?" She spotted Lacy. "What you doing with my little girl? What the fuck are you doing? *You get away from her, you hear me!*"

Isabel let go of Lacy, grabbed the woman, and shoved her into the wall. Clutched her by the jaw, twisted her face, and forced her to look at her little girl. "Look at her. *Look!* Your little girl is starving to death. She's got no shoes on. She's so cold she can't stop shivering. What kind of mother are you? Tell me, huh?"

The woman blinked. Her eyes filled with pain and horror. It was as though she was seeing her daughter clearly for the first time in a long while, and Jesse guessed she probably was.

Isabel let her go and she slid down to her knees. "Oh, sweetie," the woman's voice broke, she began to sob. "I'm so sorry. Let's get you something to eat." She reached for the girl with a boney hand that looked more like a claw. "C'mon . . . mama's gonna fix you a grilled cheese. C'mon, shug."

The little girl backed away, tried to hide behind Isabel.

The woman's brow furrowed, her voice became taut. "Sweetie, come here . . . *now.*"

The little girl shook her head and stayed put.

The woman began to tremble, her face twisting into something miserable and grotesque. She saw Krampus, got a better look at the Belsnickels. Her eyes began to twitch, her lips to quiver. "Demons," she whispered. "Someone has let demons into my house." She stood, jabbed a finger at them, and shrieked, *"Devils! Oh, God, save us! C'mere, baby, don't let 'em touch you!"*

She leapt forward, catching Isabel by surprise, shoved her backward. Isabel stumbled and fell over a clump of trash. The little girl tried to run, but the woman caught a handful of her hair, yanked her around, started to drag her away. Jesse dashed forward, caught the woman by the arm. Vernon was ready; he rushed up and dashed a pinch of sleeping sand directly into her face. The woman let out a shout, wiped at her eyes, losing hold of the child. Isabel gained her feet, snatched Lacy up, and hustled her down the hall, disappearing into the kitchen.

The woman stopped struggling for a moment, looked confused,

sneezed, blinked, then caught sight of them again. *"Devils!"* she screamed and began slapping and clawing at Jesse. Vernon tossed more sand into her mouth and nose. She stumbled back, spitting and wiping at her face, sneezed again, and sat down hard on her ass. Even so, she still held on to consciousness, glaring at them as they passed.

"Damn," Vernon said. "Did you see that? A whole handful and she's still kicking."

"It's the crank," Chet said. "She's so jacked up, nothing's gonna knock her out."

They left the woman in the hall, passed through the kitchen and into the front room. The man, whoever he was, had not left the sofa. He had the blanket pulled up to his nose; his haunted eyes following them as they exited the house. They tromped down off the porch and rounded the house, caught up with Isabel in the yard. Isabel pulled the panda cap off her own head and tugged it down over Lacy's. The little girl sobbed, pressing her face into Isabel's shoulder.

Isabel turned as they approached, and all at once her eyes grew wide, she let out a cry, and Jesse caught sight of Lacy's mother. She came running up behind them, seemed to appear out of nowhere. She clutched a shotgun and her eyes meant business. Before anyone could move, do more than shout, she leveled the weapon at Krampus and pulled the trigger—the blast deafening at such close quarters, echoing up and down the valley. The buckshot caught Krampus across the back of his left shoulder, spinning the Yule Lord around and knocking him to the ground.

The kick hammered the woman back a step. She straightened up and slid the action, ejecting the spent shell and loading a fresh one. She brought the barrel to bear, aiming for Krampus's head. *"Devil!"* she shrieked. Makwa threw himself between the muzzle and Krampus. Another deafening boom and Makwa's chest opened in a spray of blood and flesh. The big Shawnee hit the ground hard, tumbled to Krampus's feet.

Krampus moved then, faster than Jesse thought possible. Before the woman could get another shell chambered, he was at her. He let loose a thunderous roar and swung; an upward thrust of his claws caught the woman in the lower bowels, ripping her wide open, and flipping her completely over. She slammed into the side of the house, spattering blood and gore across the vinyl siding. She landed in a heap, one leg twisted behind her back. She looked at the great wound running up her midsection, at the steam rising from her exposed entrails. She raised a hand and pointed at Krampus, tried to say something but couldn't. Her arm fell, her eyes frozen on the Yule Lord.

Isabel covered the little girl's eyes, picked her up, and walked quickly down the hill toward the sleigh.

Krampus stood, glaring at the dead woman, eyes aflame, chest heaving, great gusts of breath billowing from his nose and mouth in the winter air, his tail snapping back and forth. He stepped toward her, clenching and unclenching his clawed fingers as though about to tear her body to pieces, oblivious to the blood trickling down his back from the wounds peppering his shoulder. Makwa let out a weak moan and coughed, spat out a mouthful of blood. Krampus stopped, turned, his eyes found the big Shawnee and the fire left them, replaced by a profound sadness. "No," he whispered.

Krampus came to Makwa, dropped to both knees. He stared at the terrible wound across the man's chest, at the spreading pool of red melting into the snow. Makwa struggled to draw breath, taking in big gulps of air, a thin wheezing sound coming from his chest.

Krampus clasped the man's hand between both of his, looked him directly in the eye. "Makwa, my bravest warrior." His words were earnest and measured. "The great spirits call. It is time for you to go to them, to be honored for your loyalty and bravery. Mishe Moneto has gathered all your great fathers and they all await you with a magnificent feast. Go to them with your chin held high. Take your rightful place."

Makwa's eyes focused on something beyond Krampus. He nodded, and smiled. "I . . . see them, Lord Krampus." Tears streamed down his cheeks. "They . . . come. I see . . ." He said no more, his eyes frozen on the heavens. The big Shawnee's eyes slowly changed from orange to dark brown. The wind kicked up, a flurry of dry snow and corn husks spinning about them and then drifting away, across the field, disappearing into the forests.

Krampus smiled. "Makwa rides with his great fathers." He slipped his arm beneath the big man, lifted him as though he weighed nothing, climbed to his feet, and headed to the sleigh.

KRAMPUS

Isabel awaited, the girl in her lap, her face pressed into Isabel's shoulder, crying quietly. The Belsnickels took their places and Krampus handed the body off to Wipi and Nipi.

Krampus climbed aboard, gently popped the reins, and the goats tugged the sleigh into the air. It began to snow again, and no one spoke as they drifted silently over the hills and hollows back toward Goodhope.

Chapter Fourteen

DARK SPiRiTs

Dillard drove his cruiser up to the General's compound and stopped, sat there with his engine idling, staring at the open gate while his wipers shoved the slush back and forth across his windshield. He couldn't remember that gate ever being left open. There were no fresh tracks coming or going in the snow. "This ain't right," he said under his breath. He'd tried to call the General last night and most of the day, at least a dozen times now. It was getting near dark and still no answer. He'd even tried Chet—nothing. Dillard liked to run a tight ship, needed to know what was going on at all times, needed to be in control, and he sure as shit didn't feel in control right now. Not with all the insanity that'd been going on around Goodhope the last couple of days.

He pulled into the compound and up behind Jesse's truck. There were still plenty of vehicles, and again, judging by the snow, not a one of them had moved since last night. He didn't like it, not one bit, because unless they were having a slumber party, they shouldn't still be here. The bay doors were all down, but the side door hung open, been open, he could see a good dusting of snow piled up in the entranceway.

Dillard killed the engine. There'd be no calling in backup, not on this one, last thing he needed was Noel nosing about—raise too many questions. No, he was on his own. Dillard rubbed his eyes, his head still hurt. He hadn't made it to bed until six that morning, running from one call to the next. When he finally did get to bed, he'd hardly slept, worrying over why the General hadn't returned any of his calls. "Getting too old for this shit." He pulled the coffee cup out of the holder. The coffee was cold and stale, but he drank it anyway, then got out of the cruiser and sloshed his way up to the door.

He pushed through the entranceway and hit the hall light. Tracks, at least three sets of brownish footprints, led out of the bay. He knew it was blood, was working hard to convince himself it was Jesse's blood . . . that it had to be, because he didn't want to consider the alternative. He tugged out his pistol, pushed off the safety, and followed the tracks to the steel door leading into the bay. He set his hand on the knob and gave it a turn, pushed it inward. It was dim, the only light coming from the red Christmas bulbs, but it was enough to see that the men lying around in heaps were not sleeping. He snatched his flashlight from his belt, clicked it on, and braced it snug beneath his revolver, keeping the gun trained on the beam as he searched the room.

His heart drummed. "Fuck, fuck, fuck," he whispered, swallowed, forced himself to hold steady. He'd seen plenty of death in his thirty years on the force; it wasn't the blood that bothered him, it was the savagery of the carnage before him. These weren't typical gangland-style murders, these men had been ripped to pieces, arms, legs, and guts strewn everywhere. The smell of the gore overwhelmed him. He coughed, gagged, pressed his nose into the crook of his arm, all while trying to look everywhere at once.

He found no sign of a living soul, heard nothing, and as his eyes adjusted to the gloom, he began to relax a notch. He guessed by the congealed blood that this carnage had taken place many hours ago, convinced himself that whoever had done this must be long gone. He scanned each body, searching for the General, peering into faces, some so badly mangled he couldn't recognize them. He didn't find the General—nor Jesse, for that matter—but he did find the chair Jesse must have been taped to, saw the sheared duct tape. Someone had cut him loose, someone had got him out of here. "How'd you do it, Jesse? How the hell did you pull this off?" His hands were shaking. Things were getting out of his control. Hell, they *were* out of his control. Dillard forced himself to take several deep breaths.

A light still shone from the upper floor in the General's office. Dillard walked quickly across the bay and up the stairs. The door stood open. He peered in. *This is wrong, everything about this is wrong.* Nothing appeared touched, no rifled drawers, no damage to the safe, and he found no sign of the General, either. Dillard decided they'd probably taken the man with them—extortion perhaps, or maybe just for the pleasure of torturing him to death.

Tough titties for him, Dillard thought. *Got my own problems.* He glanced back down at the bodies. *Like how the hell I'm ever gonna cover up this clusterfuck?* Again, he felt his heart speed up, that pain in his chest. *Wait. I'm overthinking it. Maybe I don't need to cover anything up? Might just be the blessing I've been praying for.* He nodded. *Solve a lot of problems. Especially one big one by the name of Sampson Ulysses Boggs. Don't have to worry about his erratic behavior no more, about him blowing everything and taking me down with him. And . . . and since every dumbshit he had working for him is laying down there with their guts torn out, there ain't a soul left needing to be shut up. All I gotta do now is . . . shit . . . no.* He shook his head. "Jesse. There's that goddamn Jesse." *And Jesse will talk. Oh boy will Jesse talk. Tell them everything he knows about me and then some. Of course that's assuming they bring him in alive. What are the chances of that?* Dillard didn't know, but he didn't like loose ends. He liked things all tidied up, just like his color-coordinated Tupperware bowls—bowls on the shelf, lids in the lid drawer.

"I gotta find that boy. Gotta get to him before someone else does. Gotta shut him up for good." Dillard headed out, made it to the bottom of the stairs, and stopped, his face clouded. *There's two other complications, aren't there?* If they brought Jesse in alive and Linda and Abigail collaborated his story. Hell, even if they didn't bring Jesse in. Linda could hang him. With the General gone, she might just come forward on her own. If they called in them Internal Affairs boys, he'd sure have a lot of explaining to do. He just couldn't afford to have anyone raising suspicions, period. *Can't just make Linda and Abigail disappear, not that easy.* No, he'd managed to get rid of one wife without raising a stink, but having two women mysteriously disappear from his life wouldn't sit well with folks. Add a little girl to that and someone was bound to catch on.

Dillard's eyes raced back and forth across all the carnage. "Fuck." His chest began to tighten again. He found Ash staring at him, staring on and on without blinking, his mouth torn into something resembling a smile, not a mocking smile but the smile of someone who knows the answer to a riddle before you do. "What? What is—" Dillard's mouth clamped shut. He nodded slowly. He got it, and it was a doozy. All at once he found himself smiling back.

"So, Ash, correct me if I'm wrong, but the last I heard was that Jesse's running with a bunch of murderous maniacs. If, say, Linda and Abigail turned up dead, victims of a savage home invasion. People would have no problem believing that, would they? Whaddaya say, Ash? Makes perfect sense don't you think? An estranged husband full of jealous rage." Dillard nodded. "Then all I got to do is lead them to you and your dead pals here. Folks will make the connection real fast. Why, it'll all fit together like a pretty puzzle. No one would suspect my hand in any of it. Nope, they'd be too busy feeling sorry for me."

He slipped on his gloves and headed back down to the shop. He found a plastic bag and gathered a roll of duct tape, a knife, a few tools, and left, wiping down the doorknobs, careful to smear his boot tracks as he went, to clean the blood from his soles in the slush. He planned on coming back, to be the one to call it in. Because it would be best for him to be the one that discovered the crime scene, the easiest way to explain any evidence he might've left behind. But it never hurt to be too careful, to keep things tidy, just like his Tupperware.

He opened the door on Jesse's truck, popped the glove compartment, and added a few of Jesse's things to the sack, some evidence to leave behind for the forensic team. He climbed back into his cruiser, got the engine running, sat there until the window defrosted, then drove off, heading for home.

IT WAS APPROACHING dusk when Jesse awoke. He sat up fast, surprised that he'd slept so long, so soundly. He found Isabel and Lacy sitting at a makeshift table with a bag of oranges, a lump of cheese, a jug of milk, and a few king-size biscuits before them. Lacy peeped out from beneath the panda cap, wearing a milk mustache and munching away on a biscuit. Jesse guessed Krampus must've snatched the food from someone's kitchen using the sack, probably someone they'd visited. He wondered if by chance that someone had been lucky enough to witness Krampus's disembodied arm plucking food off their counter. Jesse looked for Krampus, but saw only Chet and Vernon curled up on the pews, and the lame wolf over by the potbellied stove.

"They went to bury him," Isabel said.

Jesse nodded and hoped that getting your chest blown wide-open wasn't the only way out of this madness. He tugged his boots back on, feeling the deep ache in his hands. He wiggled his fingers. They were almost back to normal. He sucked in a deep breath, felt a twinge in his chest and back from the knife wound, but was breathing fine now. He noticed that his skin had grown darker, that as the healing effects of Krampus's blood took hold, so, too, did the outward changes. He crawled to his feet and strolled over, noticing a pie pan full of bloody lead pellets sitting next to the stove. "They get 'em all out?"

"What?"

"The buckshot . . . from Krampus's shoulder?"

Isabel followed his eyes to the pan. "Think so."

A bright red bow sat atop Isabel's head. Jesse noticed two more stuck on the back of her jacket, one on the milk jug, and at least half a dozen all over Lacy. He spied a couple of bags of peel-and-stick bows, along with several rolls of old wrapping paper spilling out of one of the cardboard boxes. Jesse smirked.

The little girl regarded him timidly. She looked better, her eyes alert, some color to her face, but Jesse knew that such emotional scars ran deep, wondered if this girl would carry them the rest of her life, hoped she'd be lucky and her mind would suppress the worst of it. He sighed, knowing that was rarely the case, that more often than not the cycle of abuse and dependency just kept going round. Jesse slid a box over and took a seat next to her.

"Hey, kiddo, how you doing?"

The girl shrugged and scooted closer to Isabel. Isabel put an arm around her, gave her a squeeze. Jesse noted the way Isabel looked at the girl, wondered how well she would take it when it came time to give her up. Jesse tugged one of the furry panda ears, pulling the cap down over Lacy's eyes. "Like that cap, don't you?"

The girl pushed the cap up and nodded shyly.

Jesse plucked the red bow off the milk jug and stuck it on the tip of his nose. "You got any kin around?" he asked. "Y'know someone who might take you in?"

The girl glanced up at Isabel, her face troubled.

Isabel gave Jesse a warning look and rubbed the girl's back. "Don't you worry, doll. No one's gonna be taking you anyplace you don't wanna go."

Jesse shrugged. "All right then . . . that settles that." He plucked the bow from his nose, sat it atop his head. "Lacy, any chance you'd be willing to share one of them *gi-normous* biscuits with me?"

Lacy nodded and handed him one.

"Hey, Lace, watch what I can do." Jesse opened his mouth as wide as he could and crammed the biscuit in. He stared at her with his cheeks puffed and lips taut about the girth of the biscuit. She gave Isabel a quick, unsure glance, then Jesse began chewing, snorting, grunting, and making piggy noises.

"What the hell is wrong with you?" Isabel asked, her nose wrinkled in disgust. To which Jesse burst out laughing, blowing biscuit crumbs across the table and into Isabel's lap.

"Oh, yuck," Isabel cried, but Lacy's entire face lit up and she laughed and giggled the way a little girl was supposed to. A good laugh, Jesse thought, and felt there just might be hope for her after all. Isabel's scowl softened to a grin. "He's real funny, huh? A real Bozo the Clown."

Lacy grinned back, nodding her head back and forth and side to side, and the silly way she did it so reminded Jesse of his Abigail that he felt someone had socked him in the chest. He felt the sting of tears, suddenly missing his own little girl so badly it physically hurt. Jesse pulled the biscuit from his mouth, stood up, and walked over to the window, not wanting anyone to see him blinking away his tears. *Where was Abi now? Was she safe?* He propped his elbows atop the old piano and stared out across the winter landscape, at the approaching dusk. Had Dillard found out about the massacre at the General's? If so, what would he do about it? What lengths would he go to to cover his own involvement? Were Linda and Abigail in danger? *He won't kill them, won't go that far.* Jesse pushed his hand through his hair. *You're fooling yourself. You know exactly what that man's capable of. He's gonna want them out of the picture, and sooner than later.* "Fuck," Jesse whispered.

He felt a hand on his shoulder and turned.

"You're worrying on your little girl," Isabel said. "Aren't you?"

He nodded. "Yeah. Do anything just to give her a big hug right now."

"It's hard, I know. That feeling of someone needing you and you can't be there for them . . . can't do nothing about it. Tears you up inside."

Jesse looked at her, could see she needed to say something. He waited, giving her space.

"The other day . . . when I told you about trying to kill myself . . . there was more to it."

"Thought there might be."

"My boy . . . his name is Daniel."

Jesse couldn't hide his surprise, tried to understand how Isabel could possibly have a child.

"I miss him . . . every day." She waited for him to say something, but Jesse had no idea what, not to something like that. "It wasn't some cheap fling," she continued. "I ain't like that. I loved him. Loved him very much. Named his boy after him."

Jesse nodded.

She studied him a minute. "Can be hard sometimes for folks to understand. They tend to think the worst of you."

"I ain't in no position to be judging anyone. Wouldn't think no worse of you if I were."

"I know you wouldn't. Don't care much what folks might think about me, not anymore, not about that anyhow. But I do want you to know why things went the way they did: Why I would leave my own baby."

They watched Lacy take one of the biscuits over to Freki. She wasn't much bigger than the wolf's head. Freki sniffed the biscuit, then licked it right out of the little girl's hand. Lacy giggled.

"I didn't have a lot of friends," Isabel said. "Seeing how I was a Mullins and all. Folks tended to steer clear of us Mullinses on account that mental issues ran in the family. I know it's why my daddy ran off, because of Mama's fits. I'd known Daniel since I was six, he was the only

real friend I ever had. But that made no matter to Mama. She wouldn't
let us date. Said I was too young, and maybe I was. But that didn't stop
us. We took to sneaking around; dated in secret for near on a year. And
during that whole time we didn't do much more than kiss and hold
hands. I mean Daniel made a few halfhearted advances, but he was
just so shy about such things. He'd always been rather awkward, the
other kids liked to tease him about it, y'know. But that's what I liked
about him . . . he was such a goof. There was such a sweetness about
his way.

"Then he got drafted. Vietnam. Those bastards sent him his notice
just one week after his eighteenth birthday—one goddamn week. Off
he goes to Fort Bragg. And that two months he was gone to Basic, that
was the longest two months of my life. The Army gave him just four
days leave before he was to ship out to Vietnam and he spent most of
it on a bus coming home to see me. You wanna know what he'd done
while he was at Bragg?" Isabel looked at Jesse.

"Sure."

"He'd saved up all his pay and bought me something special." She
tugged a cord out from her jacket. A gold ring hung from the end of
it. "Had to hang it around my neck on account it won't fit my finger
no more. He couldn't afford a diamond, but it *is* solid gold. And it was
then, that night, after he gave me this ring, after he promised to marry
me, that's when we laid down together. We planned on getting hitched
just as soon as he got back. It was our secret. A thing only between us
and that made it all the more special. But things don't always go the
way folks want . . . or hope. Life ain't like that."

"He didn't make it back, did he?"

"He stepped on a mine. First month he was over there. One step took
him away from me forever."

"Isabel, I'm sorry."

"Me, too," she said, dabbing at her eyes. She sat down on the piano
bench. "So there I was, knocked up and without a man. Not the first
girl to ever find herself in that predicament, but you couldn't have told
me that, not then.

"About the time they shipped his body back I was starting to show. I
was so small and the baby rode high, so Mama found out soon enough
and when she did, she locked me in the closet, read me Scripture

through the door for two days. When she let me out she told me I was gonna have to get rid of it. I told her that was against the Bible. But Mama tended to only hear what she wanted to from the Good Book. Told me she was takin' me to see some woman she knew over in Madison . . . a fixing woman.

"That baby was all I had left of Daniel. There weren't no way I was gonna let 'em kill his flesh and blood. And I told her so. Made it clear she'd have to kill me first. And . . . well," Isabel cleared her throat. "She tried . . . that woman starved me, even tried to feed me poison once. She wouldn't let me leave the house, kept the shades down, such was her fear someone might find out.

"But somehow I had that baby, had him on the bathroom floor. And when I did, when I saw that baby boy, then I knew that Daniel's spirit was watching over us, because our baby was alive . . . alive and healthy. Had a strong set of lungs and let the world know he was here. I could see his daddy in his face, even that small, I swear I could. Gave him his daddy's name.

"I made it to my bedroom and passed out with him suckling at my breast. When I come to he was gone. Found them in the living room, Mama leaning over him, whispering, talking her God talk. At first I thought she was dressing him, thought maybe seeing his face had softened her heart. Then I saw, and what I saw turned my blood cold. She had a pillow over his face, over my baby's face. I could see his little hands clutching at that pillow. I snatched the crucifix up off the top of the TV and smashed it against the side of her head. Not once but several times, until she lay still on the floor. I think I killed her, but don't know, not even now. Because after I done that, I picked up my baby, wrapped him in a towel, and run off. And even though my insides felt like they'd been torn open, I walked the two miles over to Daniel's parents' house.

"Daniel's parents didn't know about the baby, not even about mine and Daniel's engagement. I showed them the ring and told them our story. I had no idea how they'd take it, but I didn't have no other place to go. Well, I never seen folks so happy to see a baby. It was all over their faces, it was as though I'd brought them their son back. I knew then that little Daniel would be safe with them. Told them I had to go get something out from the car. Of course I didn't have no car. I just walked down the driveway and kept going, didn't really know where I was headed, not then, just kept walking and walking, all that day and into the night until I found myself up in them hills.

"Well, y'know what happened after that." She shook her head. "Jesse, not a day goes by that I don't regret leaving my child. Not a day."

Jesse let out a long, heartfelt sigh. So he wasn't the only one hurting, no big surprise there. He wished he had something profound and uplifting to say, something to make her feel better, to make himself feel better. But sometimes there seemed to be so much bad in the world it was hard to see much of anything else. He set his hand on her shoulder, squeezed, and that was about the best he could do.

Lacy was now sticking bows all over Freki's fur. The giant wolf just lay there, looking at them as though pleading for help.

"Maybe Krampus will let us go soon," Jesse said with little conviction.

"Maybe." Isabel walked over to Lacy, picked her up, spun her around, and hugged her. Lacy giggled and hugged her back. Isabel beamed.

Jesse thought Isabel would make a wonderful mother, started to say so when he caught movement outside.

Three figures trudged through the light snow, followed by a lumbering wolf. Krampus and the two remaining Shawnee walked with their heads down as though from the weather, but Jesse knew better.

KRAMPUS AND THE Shawnee marched up the steps and into the church, tracking slush and mud across the floor. Krampus made his way to the wood stove and sat down heavily upon a cardboard box. Freki limped over and lay down next to him. Krampus began absently stroking the big wolf's mane.

Jesse hesitated. Krampus looked weary, beaten down . . . sad. Jesse knew it wasn't a good time to bring up Dillard. But when was it ever? Maybe he owed Krampus something, and maybe he didn't; regardless, he still had to find a way to take care of Dillard. And the longer he waited, the greater chance that Dillard might harm Linda or Abigail.

Jesse swallowed, walked over, and took a seat next to the Yule Lord. "I'm sorry about Makwa. Sorry for your loss."

KRAMPUS

Krampus didn't answer, didn't even look up, just stared at the fire.

Jesse's mouth felt dry, he wet his lips, cleared his throat. "I need to go and take care of Dillard."

"I know."

Jesse waited for more, but Krampus just kept watching the flame.

"I can take care of things on my own, y'know. Just need you to let me go. Won't interfere with your goings-on at all. I'll even swear to come back once I'm done."

Krampus clasped his hands together, let out a long sigh. "What do you believe in, Jesse?"

"Huh?"

Krampus looked at him, peered deep into his eyes. "What do you believe in?"

Jesse shrugged. "I dunno."

"There's nothing you believe in?"

"Whaddaya mean?"

"You have to believe in something. Your muse . . . your music perhaps?"

"No," Jesse said bitterly. "I've given up on that."

"God?"

"God? Well . . . hell, maybe. Sometimes I do, anyway. Y'know, when I'm scared or want something really bad."

"You are a religious man? A Christian?"

"I wouldn't go that far. I'm certainly a God-fearing man."

"There are other things besides gods in which to put one's faith. Earthly things."

"I suppose."

"Do you believe that the shadows are full of dark spirits waiting to prey on the unguarded?"

"What? No." Jesse laughed, then caught the sullen look on Krampus's face. "Well, okay . . . sometimes when I'm alone at night I can get pretty creeped out if that's what you mean."

Krampus didn't laugh, or smile; his gaze returned to the flame. "I am fearful most men of this age are like you. They have forgotten what it is to huddle in a hut with the beasts and demons howling outside their door. They no longer have want of a great and terrible spirit to protect them. They have lost their fear of the wild and with it their need

263

to believe. And I cannot blame them, for they now have the power to chase away the shadows with a mere flick of a switch. So I must ask myself, what role can I play in a world where men worship the moving-picture box, where they make and consume potions that eat away their own brains, where they ravage and pillage entire mountains, kill the very earth itself?

"Mankind has lost its connection to the land, to the earth, to the beasts and spirits. They gather their food not from the forest and fields, but from plastic bins and ice boxes. Their lives are no longer tied to the cycles of the seasons and the harvest, no longer do they need the Yule Lord to chase away the winter darkness and usher in the light of spring. Man has only himself to fear now . . . he has become his own worst devil."

Krampus picked up one of the branches that the Shawnee had gathered, snapped it into manageable lengths, and shoved them into the potbellied stove. "While sitting in that cave, I read the newspapers, read of such changes, but could not grasp their true meaning . . . their true effect. Not until I witnessed it with my own eyes.

"I fear Baldr might have spoken truth; that the world has indeed moved on, that there is no longer a place here for me. I now see how he sank so low. Baldr foresaw all this, tried to warn me. He gave them what they wanted, a pretty lie, and they believed, because a pretty lie is easier to believe than an ugly truth."

Krampus scratched at his shoulder, digging at the scabbing wounds with his long fingernails. He grimaced, pulled out a piece of buckshot, rolled the bloody pellet between his fingers. "How will I make a people who do not understand the power of belief believe? And without their belief Mother Earth will wither and Yuletide will fade . . . and so, too, will I . . . like all the spirits and gods before me."

NIGHT FELL UPON the little church, the spreading gloom matching the spirit in the room, and still Krampus sat staring into the flame, a bottle of mead in his hand, the sack at his feet. The Belsnickels kept their distance and even the wolves avoided him.

Jesse sat cross-legged upon the floor in front of a game of Chinese checkers. Lacy had discovered a box of old games and had managed to recruit Jesse and Vernon to play with her and Isabel.

"Go," Lacy said and prodded Jesse.

"What?"

"It's your turn . . . *still*," Vernon put in. "Perhaps if you kept your mind on the game, we wouldn't have to keep reminding you."

"Oh, sorry," Jesse said absently, and moved the first marble his hand came to.

"Ha!" Isabel said, a triumphant grin spreading across her face as she used Jesse's move to advance her marble all the way across the board.

"That was brilliant, Jesse," Vernon said. "I cannot even find the words."

Jesse nodded, hardly hearing him, maintaining his vigil over the Yule Lord, hoping Krampus would come around so they could finally get the show on the road. But over the last several hours, Krampus hadn't done much more than mutter to himself. And sitting there like that was certainly not getting Jesse any closer to Abigail. Jesse wanted to go over and shout at the beast, prod him, poke him, do something to get Krampus moving, anything besides sitting on the floor and playing checkers.

"Watched pot won't boil," Isabel said.

"This ain't working for me," Jesse growled, shaking his head. "Sure as shit it ain't."

"Get used to it," Vernon said. "He's in one of his black moods. Back in the cave he'd get that way and stay like that for weeks, months sometimes. Just curl up into a ball, not moving, hardly even breathing, as though he were dead. Only we were never so lucky as that."

"Weeks?"

"Yes, certainly. Or he'd work himself into a foul temper and there'd be no talking to him."

"Abigail doesn't have weeks," Jesse said and started to his feet. Isabel grabbed his shoulder. "Can't keep pushing him, Jesse. You're gonna go too far, and more likely than not just gonna make matters worse." Jesse pulled away, stood. "Worse for who? Not for Abigail?" He marched over to Krampus and stared at the Yule Lord. Krampus did nothing to acknowledge him.

Jesse bent, picked the sack up off the floor. He cleared his throat and held it out toward Krampus. "It's night. Can't be no Yuletide without the Yule Lord."

Jesse waited.

Krampus continued to stare at the stove.

"Are you giving up then? Is the Yule Lord turning his back on Yuletide?"

He saw Krampus stiffen, knew the beast heard him.

"I guess he won after all. Santa Claus . . . he beat you."

Krampus's troubled frown deepened and the end of his tail twitched.

Jesse sat the sack down on the box next to Krampus. "You might have your sack, your freedom . . . might have his head, but it appears he still won."

Krampus took a sip from the flask.

"You were asking earlier how to go about making people believe. Well, I say if you want them to believe . . . you have to give them something to believe in. You have to get out there and be great and terrible. You have to *make* them believe."

Krampus shifted his weight as though suddenly very uncomfortable.

"Well, shit sure ain't happening so long as you're moping around, so long as you're sucking on that bottle like it's your mama's tit."

Krampus took another swig, a long swig, leaned his head back, and closed his eyes as though the world didn't exist.

Jesse snatched the flask from Krampus's hand.

Krampus's eyes popped open; he stared at Jesse, utterly stunned.

"Ho, ho, ho!" Jesse cried and smashed the clay bottle to bits upon the floor. *"Merry fucking Christmas!"*

Krampus leapt up, gave Jesse a tremendous shove, knocking Jesse off his feet, sending him sliding backward across the floor and into Freki. The wolf yelped, hobbled to its feet, and limped away from the fray.

"I will tear your heart from your chest for that!" Krampus snarled and stomped after Jesse. Jesse sat up, met Krampus's burning eyes, grinned. *"There! That's it!"* Jesse cried. "Be terrible! Come on. That's what you do, be the Yule Lord, not some sulking brat!"

Krampus stopped, glared. "Who are *you* to lecture *me* about giving up?" He sneered. "You, a music-maker who is afraid to face his own muse. Who turns his back on the great gifts bestowed upon him, and denies the very core of his soul."

"Yeah . . . okay, great. You're a loser like me. Way to go."

"Bah," Krampus growled, throwing his hands up in disgust. He turned away, headed back to the stove, and snatched the sack up off the chair. He held it a minute, crushing the lush velvet in his hands, appeared to be carrying on a silent conversation with it, his head nodding slightly. He let out a grunt, picked up the birch switches. "Let's go." He tromped out the door and into the night.

The two Shawnee exchanged a troubled glance, but hopped up and rushed out after the Yule Lord.

Vernon slapped his marbles down on the checkerboard, glared at Jesse. "Thanks! Y'know, this was probably the first enjoyable evening I've had in . . . oh, I don't know . . . a hundred years. Now instead of playing games around a warm fire, I get to go creeping into people's houses out in the freezing cold. Gosh, somebody pinch me."

Jesse gave Chet a kick. "Wake up, fuckhead. Time to go."

Chet groaned, sat up, looked around as though trying to figure out where he was. Once he caught on, he let out a pitiful moan.

"Tall, Dark and Ugly is waiting for you outside," Jesse said.

Chet looked as though he wanted to curl up and cry, but managed to crawl to his feet and zombie-shuffle his way out the door.

Isabel grabbed Lacy's jacket, quickly bundled her up, wrapping a thick scarf around her neck and face and tying the panda cap earflaps securely under her chin. Lacy had to pull the scarf down and push the hat up in order to see. "Are we going for another ride in the sleigh?" she mumbled through the scarf.

"We sure are, dumpling."

"You can't bring her," Vernon said.

"Well, I ain't gonna be leaving her here."

"Isabel," Jesse said carefully. "You know we're gonna have to find someplace for her."

Isabel shot him a cutting look. "We'll just have to see."

Lacy clutched Isabel, clung tightly to her waist.

"Don't you worry, shug," Isabel said. "You can stay with me if that's what you want."

Lacy nodded that she did.

Jesse sighed. "Isabel, you know this won't work." And he saw by her face that she did, but he also saw how much Isabel needed this little girl right now.

"We better get going," Vernon said and headed out the door.

The wolves came out on the steps and watched them load up. Isabel and Lacy hopped up front, Vernon in the back, Jesse started to climb aboard, stopped. "It's gone."

"What's gone?" Isabel asked, following his hard stare over to the fallen downspout.

"Santa's head."

They all looked, but there was no trace of the trophy.

"Coyote must've got it," Chet said.

"No," Jesse said. "Not with them wolves around."

"Must've sprouted legs and wandered off on its own then," Chet said with a snort.

Jesse noticed something even more disturbing: footprints in the snow, human in size and shape, they led a few steps away, then ended. *As though the owner had just* flown *off.*

Krampus stared at the spot where Santa's head had been, stared for a long time, his face troubled. "It seems my time . . . it grows short," he said under his breath. Then he slapped the reins and once again the Yule goats leapt forward and pulled them into the sky.

Hoax or has the Christmas Demon come to town?

Chapter Fifteen

CHRISTMAS DEMON

Dillard pulled into his driveway and shut off the engine. He tugged the plastic bag open, peered in at the gloves, the duct tape, the knife, and the ball-peen hammer he'd taken from the General's shop, at the hat and screwdriver from Jesse's truck, and the wad of hair he'd plucked from the brush he'd found in the glove compartment—enough evidence to place Jesse at both crime scenes. Dillard knew investigators wouldn't dig much further once they had all the pieces, and he planned on making it real easy to find all the pieces.

Dillard took a moment to gaze at the white Christmas lights illuminating his front porch, sparkling across the snow and ice, at the pretty evergreen wreath perched on his red front door—a picture-perfect Christmas scene. *They're in there, waiting, got no idea what's heading their way.*

He'd killed plenty of people over the years; some died easy, some died bad, but regardless, once the act was done, he'd never felt much of anything. Things were different with Ellen: not a single day passed that he didn't think of her. Would it be the same with Linda? He didn't think so. He loved Linda, but he could never love anyone like Ellen. He felt that, with time, Linda's ghost would fade and he'd move on. He hoped so, because this wouldn't be a clean, execution-style death: their deaths

BROM

would have to match those at the General's compound, would have to look like the work of an enraged, jealous spouse. That sort of thing just might haunt a man.

He closed his eyes, took a deep breath, tried to turn his feelings off. Linda would no longer be the woman he'd made love to, nor Abigail the little girl he'd made smile and giggle. Once he walked in that door, they were meat, to be bled and cut up.

He exhaled, opened his eyes, plucked the plastic bag off the seat, and got out of the car. "Try not to feel," he told himself as he strolled up the stone path. "Try not to feel."

He eased the front door open and stepped quietly inside. He found three grocery sacks stacked along the wall, Linda's and Abigail's clothes folded neatly within, and two plastic garbage bags with the dolls Jesse had given Abigail along with the rest of the things they'd brought over. The fact that she was gathering their things to leave bothered him less than the fact that she was paying no heed to his warnings. Her disregard only confirmed to him that she couldn't be trusted, that he was doing the right thing. Doing what he had to do.

The sound of the television drifted out from the living room and he caught Linda's voice talking to Abigail. *Good,* he thought, *they're together.* He threw the bolt behind him and slid the bags in front of the door. He knew it wouldn't keep anyone in, he just wanted something to slow a person down, say if they were in a real hurry to leave, for some reason.

He walked down the short hall, past the bathroom on his left, and then into the living room. The living room contained a small dining room area separated from the kitchen by a bar-style counter. Abigail sat in one of the stools, her back to him, playing with two of her dolls. Linda stood in the kitchen, fixing something on the stove. She caught sight of him and started, her eyes turned cold, and she looked away.

"See you got your things packed," Dillard said.

Abigail stopped playing, looked over at him, no trace of her usual joyful smile. She glanced anxiously at her mother.

"I would like my keys back, please," Linda said, she sounded tired and drained.

"Okay," he said, and walked across the living room to the dining room. He unclipped his police radio, turned it up, and sat it on the table, wanting to be sure he didn't miss any calls on Jesse. He sat the plastic bag down next to it and dug her keys out of his pocket, dropping them on the table.

Linda went about fixing Abigail a grilled cheese, keeping her back to him, going out of her way not to look at him. Dillard leaned over and slipped the locking pin into the sliding glass door—another precaution, should things get out of hand. He glanced out upon his backyard; a hint of sunset still outlined the hilltops. He owned close to five acres backing up to the river; his nearest neighbor was Tomsey through the woods to the south. Between the forest and old Tomsey being near deaf, he wasn't too worried anyone would hear any screaming.

Dillard knew he should get this show on the road, that every minute he spent was one more minute someone could come along and discover the slaughterhouse over at the General's, or that Jesse might show up somewhere in town. But he found the next step much harder than he expected. He watched Linda flip the cheese sandwich over in the skillet, stared at the back of her head, at her beautiful hair, and imagined the look on her face when the first blow landed, the pain, the confusion, the horror. He would have to live with that for the rest of his life.

He clenched his jaw. *Now's not the time to get weak.*

He picked up the plastic bag and headed back to the hall and into the bathroom. He emptied his bladder, then stripped down to only his socks. Footprints in the blood could be used the same as fingerprints; it would be easier to just burn the socks later. He didn't worry about his DNA evidence, it was his house, they'd be expecting that, but blood, blood was a different matter. If he planned on matching the brutality of the murders at the General's place, then there'd be plenty of blood and he had to make sure none of it got on his clothes. He stacked the clothes, his watch, and his shoes on the floor next to the sink. After he was done killing the girls and planting Jesse's evidence, he would shower and then come back down and dress.

He opened the sack, pulled out the gloves, slipped them on, then took out the ball-peen hammer. Figured that'd be the right tool to start with. He'd hit Linda hard, but not too hard, just enough to knock her down, maybe a kneecap next, something to keep her from running while he took care of Abigail. Then he would get the knife and do the job right.

He opened the door and stepped out of the bathroom, the cool air tingling against his nakedness. *"Meat,"* he whispered. *"They're just meat."*

NOTHING.

Blackness.

Light.

Adrift, the current tugging him down, down, down.

Drowning. Choking. Weight. The pain of flesh. Santa Claus felt cold stone beneath his back, opened his eyes. All was bathed in golden light. Blurry shapes shifted about him.

His wife's face slowly came into focus, hovering over him, not Nanna, but Perchta, his earthborn wife. She clutched his hand, worry etched into her ageless eyes.

"He lives," she whispered, then, loudly, "Santa Claus has returned to us!" A great clamor echoed about the chamber. Santa blinked; he lay in the chapel, encircled by his lesser wives. All of them weeping and wailing with joy. The sounds stabbing into his head like knives.

So that was death. No thoughts. No memories. No regrets. Nothing. So very sweet.

Two beings—neither male nor female—in golden robes stood at his feet, their white wings almost too bright to look upon. One of them spoke. "It seems God does not wish you dead."

"Why?" he coughed, clearing his throat. "How do I matter to God?"

The two angels exchanged a surprised smile. "Why? Because you amuse her."

"Amuse?" Santa sat up. The world spun about him. He clutched the slab to steady himself. "Amuse? Do I serve no higher purpose than to entertain?"

"You bring a smile to God's lips. Is that not enough?"

Santa swung his feet off the slab, tried to stand. His knees buckled and Perchta caught him, kept him from falling. "I am not but a plaything."

"You are upset?"

"I am done *amusing* the gods. Done with this song and dance."

"You wish to be done?" The angel's brow furrowed. "But there is no greater calling than to serve the Lord. Is it not an honor?"

Bells, far away, growing louder, voices, it was that song, that silly, silly song: "Here Comes Santa Claus." Santa glanced around at the women, none of them seemed to hear. "I am done, I said. Done with all of it. Tell God to leave me be!"

"You would give it all up?" The angel shrugged. "If it is your wish to let it go, to become mortal, it can be made so." The song, the bells, they began to wane. "Your name, like your song, will fade, and eventually the name Santa Claus will be forgotten."

The song ceased; his breath the only sound. The silence chilled his heart.

"What name shall you be called henceforth?" the angel asked. "I would guess not Baldr. Bob? Mike? Tom? Who will you be now?"

"Stop it. Why do you torment me?"

The angel laughed. "You only torment yourself. Do you truly believe you are an equal to the likes of Jesus, or any of the great prophets? You are a curio, a man in a red suit handing out gifts."

Santa ground his teeth.

"We will honor your wish. But remember, it was you that turned your back on God." The angels withdrew, left the chapel, headed up the path.

"No," Santa said.

They kept walking.

"No," he called. "No . . . do not leave!" He took a step after them, clutching the slab to keep upright. *I take it back!* he cried. *I take it back!* His voice broke into a sob. "I take it back."

They stopped, studied him, their eyes full of pity. They returned. "Who are you?"

He glared at them. "I am Santa Claus."

They smiled. "Take heart, Santa Claus. You spread hope and cheer in a world of darkness. You please God in a universe where so many do not. Be happy with that."

The bells returned, they warmed him, reached to his core, touched his very soul. A great weight lifted from his chest. He inhaled deeply and once again felt whole.

"Now, enough of this silliness," the angel said. "The world needs Santa Claus and God wishes to know if there is anything she can do for you."

Santa started to shake his head, stopped, met the angel's eyes. "Yes, most certainly. There is a devil in need of killing."

"THERE, THAT'S AS good a place as any." Jesse pointed to the steeple below. "Lights are on. Appears to be plenty of folks around."

Isabel bit her lip. She'd already vetoed the previous two churches they'd flown over. She shook her head and hugged Lacy.

"What? Why not?"

"I don't know that church."

"They're Methodists, Isabel."

She wrinkled her nose.

"What, you don't like Methodists now? First Pentecostal, now Methodist. Whoever heard of anyone having a problem with Methodists? Isabel, I think you're just looking for an excuse. Now you got to think about Lacy."

Isabel frowned. "Okay," she said, in little more than a whisper.

"What?" Jesse asked. "Did you say okay? Okay, for the church?"

She nodded, her lips tight and drawn.

"Okay," Jesse said to Krampus. "We can take her there."

Krampus landed them in a small field behind the church. A line of hedges afforded a reasonable amount of cover from the homes just across the street. Krampus didn't seem to care much one way or another, not having spoken a single word since leaving. He stared at the church as though it were a blight upon the land.

Jesse helped Lacy down while keeping his eye on Isabel, who continued to scrutinize the church. He knew she was looking for the slightest reason to call the whole thing off.

Isabel took Lacy's hand. After a good minute went by without anyone saying a word, without Isabel taking a single step forward, Jesse sat his hand on Isabel's shoulder and whispered, "You're doing the right thing."

Isabel nodded, "I know. I know." Yet, still, she stood there.

"I'd be glad to come with you."

"No. Don't want anyone to see us . . . any of us. Would only make things harder on Lacy." She looked down at the little girl. "Okay, Lace, let's go find a really nice person for you to stay with awhile." Isabel made an obvious effort to sound upbeat, but Jesse could hear the strain in her voice. "Okay?"

Lacy looked scared and unsure, but when Isabel pulled her along she came readily enough, and the two of them headed up the walkway, sticking to the shadows as they made their way toward the front of the church.

Jesse could see people through the windows; they appeared to be decorating the chapel in preparations for New Year's Eve. A tall Christmas tree stood in front of one of the windows, its lights blinking. Krampus stared at it, a thunderous scowl upon his face.

Vernon slipped through the hedges, over to a row of mailboxes. Plastic newspaper bins with the *Boone Standard* logo hung beneath the boxes. One still held a paper and Vernon helped himself, opened it, scanning the pages as he walked back over.

"Oh, my," Vernon said. "Krampus, you just might wish to read this."

Krampus ignored him, just kept staring at that Christmas tree.

Vernon cleared his throat, began to read. "Santa's Henchmen Dance Across Boone County. Strange reports have come in from all across Boone County of a string of bizarre incidents of home invasions and flying sleighs. The incidents are connected by descriptions of oddly dressed individuals that appear to have horns and glowing eyes. Some claim they're Christmas demons, others blame the trouble on a crime spree perpetrated by a gang disguised in bizarre costumes. Sheriff Wright would only say that they are investigating. Sources close to the sheriff confirm that gang activity is at the forefront of the ongoing investigation. Several victims have come forward and given their harrowing accounts of assault, vandalism, and intimidation." Vernon skipped down a few lines. "But no one has yet been able to explain the dozens of reports coming in of a flying sleigh pulled by goats, which reportedly is carrying this host of most curious criminals."

Chet chuckled and shook his head.

"Wait," Vernon continued, "there's also this. *Standard*'s own Bill

Harris received a very different accounting from Carolyn, age ten, of Goodhope, and her five brothers and sisters. Carolyn recounts a tale of a tall, horned beast that claims the title Krampus, Lord of Yule, and leaves behind coins to those who honor him with a tribute (in the form of a treat or trinket left in their shoes upon the front step). Further, she added those who don't offer tribute risk the Krampus demon putting them in his sack and whipping them. Upon follow-up with children of other victims in the area, all collaborated this same very strange tale. Further credibility is given due to the fact that each of these children had in their possession these same triangular gold coins. When asked if they intended to put treats and trinkets in their shoes and leave them on their steps next holiday season, they all adamantly stated they certainly would."

Vernon showed them the pictures: one, a clear snapshot of Carolyn and her siblings, each holding a triangular coin; another, this one a bit blurry, of Krampus and the Belsnickels flying down a street in the sleigh; and a final one, a cartoon of a gleeful, black-faced devil with horns, hooves, and a twisting tail, wielding a handful of switches. Vernon read the caption. "Hoax? Or has the Christmas Demon come to town?"

Vernon put on his own devilish smile and showed the picture to Krampus. "Why, old boy, they've certainly captured your likeness spot-on. Wouldn't you say?"

Krampus tore the paper from Vernon's hand, crumpled it, slapped it on the ground, and stomped it, practically did a dance upon it. "Christmas Demon!" Krampus growled. "Santa's henchman! *No! No!*" He glared up at the church. "They see devils everywhere when the only devils left are themselves. Why must they twist Yule tradition into something wicked? Why must they pervert all that is mine. Like that tree. That is a Yule tree, not a Christmas tree. Bringing evergreens into the home to celebrate the Goddess that never dies, the return of the sun's warmth, is a tradition dating back before even the ancient druids—and long, long, long before the Christ child was spewed forth in that filthy little manger. Who are they to plunder my traditions, to desecrate and profane? It is time I showed them the Yule Lord will not stand for such mockery." Krampus spat loudly on the newspaper and stomped away toward the church.

Jesse and Vernon exchanged a panicked look.

"Wait," Jesse said, catching up and grabbing Krampus's arm. "Isabel asked us to stay back."

Krampus shrugged him off and continued up the path, heading for the front steps. The Shawnee fell in step behind him.

"Way to go," Jesse said to Vernon and gave him a shove.

Vernon threw up his hands. "What?"

Chet laughed and fell in. "Never much cared for the Methodists nohow."

MARGRET DOTSON STOOD in her kitchen and watched the man in the funny getup steal her paper. She'd made a point of not reading the *Standard*, not since it came out in favor of Clinton back in '92 anyway, but it still didn't sit well with her for some degenerate to help himself to what was rightfully hers. She was just about to head outside to give him a piece of her mind, when she caught sight of his cohorts loitering in the glow of the church windows. What stopped her was the way their eyes caught the streetlight, an orange glint like bike reflectors. That just wasn't right, that was weird. She had no idea who they were, or what they were, except for the tall one, the one with horns, that one she recognized right away . . . that one was Satan.

Margret picked up her phone and dialed the Goodhope police station. She was pleased to hear the new hire, that young officer, Noel, instead of that rude, bossy Dillard, who'd once reprimanded her for picking the flowers growing in front of the post office.

"Goodhope Police Department. Officer Roberts speaking."

"This is Margret Dotson, on twenty-one Hill Street, over by the Methodist church."

"Yes, ma'am, what seems to be the trouble?"

"Well, *something* just stole my newspaper."

"I . . . see."

"Yes, I was hoping you could come over here and get my property back."

"Hmm, yes, well . . . we're a bit busy at the moment. Maybe—"

"Maybe nothing. It's standing right across the street. Why don't you get on over here and arrest it before it runs off?"

"Mrs. Dotson, I'll be sure to drive by just as soon as I can. Here, why don't you give me a description of the suspect."

"Well, there's six of them. They're wearing strange outfits, dark faces, horns, and glowing eyes. One of—"

"What? Oh, gosh! Oh, jeez!" the young officer's voice rose. "Did you say you were across from the Methodist church? The one near First?"

"Why yes, that's exactly what I said. There ain't but that one."

"Ma'am, stay inside. We're on our way."

Margret hung up the phone, a smug look on her face. She had no intention of staying inside. She made herself a gin and tonic, walked out on her porch, and watched the group of devils head up toward the front of the church. She took a seat in her porch swing, looking forward to the show.

LINDA SCOOPED THE grilled cheese out of the skillet and onto Abigail's plate. Dillard entered the kitchen through the den entrance, coming up behind her, not running, just strolling in clutching the ball-peen hammer, in nothing but his black socks and gloves.

Abigail screamed, a shrill, piercing sound, and Linda spun around. Dillard swung for her head. Linda darted back, crashing into the stove. Dillard hadn't counted on her moving so fast, and the hammer smashed against the counter, the momentum causing him to stumble. A second later, he found an iron skillet coming at him and tried to duck. Linda connected the flat of the pan against the side of his head—a flare went off, all bright light. Sizzling grease splattered across the side of his face, the searing heat causing him to scream and stumble back. He clasped his cheek, dropping the hammer. Through the blinding pain he saw her rear back for another swing. She clutched the panhandle in both hands, her face contorted with disgust and venom, a savage snarl escaped her throat as she brought the skillet round. Dillard threw up his arm, catching the blow with his elbow. The skillet flew from her hand, bounced off his shoulder, and clanged across the floor.

Linda dashed out of the kitchen over to where Abigail sat staring on in shock and horror, grabbed her, pulling her over to the sliding glass door. Linda gave the door a yank; it clacked in its track but didn't slide open. In her panic, Linda yanked it twice more before realizing it was pinned.

Dillard snatched up the hammer and came after them, tromping into the dining room before she could pull the locking pin loose. Linda grabbed Abigail and fled in the only direction left—the living room. There was no way out of the living room except past Dillard; the only other choice was down into the basement. But this didn't concern Dillard, because there was no way out of his basement. He had them trapped, only the couch and coffee table standing between them.

Dillard took a moment to catch his breath, to pull himself together. He plucked a clump of cheese from his hair, wiped as much grease from his face as he could. His skin felt as though it were still burning, his headache was back, back with a vengeance.

He threw a leg over the back of the sofa, started to climb over. Linda snatched up the bowl of decorative wooden apples off the coffee table, and threw one at him. Dillard put his arm up, the apple striking his elbow, the same elbow she'd clobbered with the pan, and a fresh jolt of pain shot up his arm. *"Stupid fucking bitch!"* he screamed.

She threw another, and another, then the bowl, forcing him to duck, and when he did she leapt over and yanked the basement door open. She darted inside, tugging Abigail after her, and slamming the door behind them. He heard their feet drumming down the basement steps.

He hesitated, unsure what she was thinking. It was a ground basement, a cellar. She knew there was no way out other than by the windows, and those were small, set high on the walls, and sealed shut with old paint. There was no way you could pry them open without tools.

Dillard walked to the basement door, pulled it open, and peered down the stairs. He heard something fall over, a creak then a loud clang, and instantly knew where they were. "Shit." He rushed down the stairs, around the stairwell, to the metal door built into the wall.

What Dillard liked to brag about as his wine cellar was, in fact, a bomb shelter left over from the previous owner, a relic of the Cold War era. It had a very substantial metal door and, like most of these shelters, it latched from the inside. Dillard had removed the decades-old drums of K-rations when he'd moved in, and renovated it along with the rest of the basement, putting in racks, amassing a pretty good collection of wines. He grabbed the latch and gave it a hard yank. It didn't budge. "Shit!"

He stood there, staring stupidly at the door. *This is not fucking happening.* He raised the hammer, brought it down hard upon the latch. A hollow *bong* filled the basement, the sound driving into his head like a spike. "Fuck!" He closed his eyes, pressed his temples until the throbbing lessened. He examined the latch. The hammer had hardly made a ding. He steadied himself against the wall and tried to think through his headache. There was no way he could bust that latch with a ball-peen hammer. He needed something more substantial, needed the sledgehammer out of the shed. "And some earmuffs," he said under his breath. "Don't you dare forget the goddamn earmuffs."

He made it halfway back up the stairs when he heard his police radio squawk, heard Noel's high, excited voice. "Dillard," he cried, "Dillard. Heck, Dillard come in!"

Now what? Dillard wondered, but had a pretty good idea and hustled up the last few steps and over to the dining-room table. He snatched up the radio.

"Yeah, this is Dillard."

"Dillard, it's them! That gang! They're right here in Goodhope! What'd we do?" The boy talked a mile a minute, stumbling over his words, any trace of procedure gone right out the window. Under other circumstances, Dillard would've smiled at the boy's befuddlement.

"Whoa, now. Slow down. Where in Goodhope?"

The boy managed to calm down enough that Dillard could understand him. "We got a report of five or six of them. They're at the Methodist church."

Up on the north side of town, Dillard thought. "Meet me in the parking lot. No sirens or lights. And don't do anything except keep them in your sight until I get there. Got it? On my way."

Only he wasn't on his way. He had two girls badly needing taking care of. He was in what his grandfather called one fine pickle. He closed his eyes, rubbing his forehead, trying to think. Decided he had to do something about his headache. He stumbled into the bathroom, yanked open the medicine cabinet, knocked over several bottles of medications until he found a prescription bottle labeled Imitrex—took double his normal dose. He caught sight of himself in the mirror, realized he was still naked. "Oh, for fuck sake." He grabbed his pants and slid them on, then his shoes. "Okay, priorities. What's the priority? Sort it out. It's Jesse . . . that little shitfuck Jesse. Because there might not be another chance to kill that son'bitch. And the girls? Well . . . they ain't going nowhere are they? No. I can see to that."

He finished dressing as fast as he could and rushed back down into the basement, shoved the freezer over, blocking the storm shelter door, came back upstairs, throwing the basement door deadbolt as an added precaution. He snatched up his radio, did a last quick look around. Tried to convince himself things were under control here, at least for now, at least until he could get back. A couple minutes later he was in his cruiser heading north toward the Methodist church, one thing on his mind: killing Jesse Walker.

ISABEL PULLED LACY into the shadows next to the front steps of the Methodist church. She knelt down, looked Lacy directly in the eyes. "Okay, Lacy. It's time. Like we talked about. You ready?"

The little girl's face clouded. "I don't want you to go, Isabel."

"I know. I don't wanna go neither. But I got to. So, I need you to be strong . . . strong for the both of us. Because if you start crying, you're gonna make me cry. Then they might catch me. I might get in bad trouble."

Lacy set her face and nodded. "I won't cry none, Isabel. Promise." Isabel saw then just how much mettle this little girl had, understood that she had to be strong to have survived what she'd been through.

Two women, both looking to be in their late thirties, both overweight, with faces that appeared to have seen plenty of hardship, came up the walkway, mounted the steps, and entered the church. They looked like good, God-fearing folk to Isabel, hill folk, the kind of women she felt she could trust.

"Lacy, I want you to go inside and introduce yourself to those two ladies. You remember what I told you to say?"

"That my mamma and daddy are dead. That a lady I don't know dropped me off. That she told me to find someone to help me."

"That's right. Now give me a hug and run on in there after them."

The girl hugged her, hugged her as tight as a six-year-old could. Isabel had to blink back the tears, knowing the last thing Lacy needed right now was to see her crying. Isabel pulled away, pointed Lacy in the direction of the steps, and gave her a light push. Lacy headed up the steps, reached the big doors, hesitated, giving Isabel an unsure look.

Isabel nodded and blew her a kiss.

Lacy tugged on one of the heavy double doors. It budged a little, but she couldn't get it open. She tried twice more, then looked at Isabel and shrugged.

"Heck," Isabel said, dashing out of the shadows and up the stairs. She pulled the big door open, ushered Lacy in, and took a quick peek inside. A foyer with double doors led into the chapel; through the stained-glass windows, she could hear music and see people moving. A flight of steps headed down on the right and left side of the foyer. She caught sight of a handwritten sign that read: DIVORCE RECOVERY. An arrow pointed down the stairs on the left, and Isabel understood where the women must've been heading.

"That way," she called to Lacy in a hushed tone, pointing toward the stairs.

"Huh?" Lacy said, looking confused.

"The women went down—" Isabel heard voices coming up behind her, and a quick glance over her shoulder revealed four women heading up the walkway. Having no other route, she ducked into the foyer, snatched Lacy by the hand, and hustled her down the short flight of stairs. They pushed through a set of swinging doors at the bottom of the steps and came out into a long, dim corridor. There were two doors ahead, the closest one was shut, the one at the end of the hall stood open, a bright light pouring out into the hall, revealing another handwritten sign.

Laughter, the drumming of feet, people were coming down the stairs behind them. Isabel ran up to the first door, gave the knob a twist. It was locked. There was nowhere else to go. She put her shoulder into it, gave it a hard slam, the door held. She tried again, harder, heard the doorjamb crack.

"Excuse me. Can we help you?"

Isabel spun about to find four women staring at her from the bottom of the stairs. She tried to keep her head down, her eyes averted.

"Do we know you?" a stout woman, wearing a woodland-green hunting jacket, asked loudly. She was the smaller of the four, but her manner let you know right away that she didn't put up with any nonsense. "Girl, look here at me." She took a step closer, got a better look at Isabel, and stopped in her tracks. "What in the hell?"

"What's going on?" another voice called from the opposite end of the hall. A woman, slight of build and wearing a simple knee-length dress, stood in the glow of the room light. "Gail, is that you. What's the matter?" Three more women came out of the room behind her.

Isabel realized she was trapped. She gauged the women in front of the stairs, figured she would have to rush them, barrel her way through, and hope for the best. Only she wasn't so sure she could, not if they put up a fight. These were big, hard-looking women, wearing flannel shirts and boots, the wives and daughters of miners, solid women who'd raised plenty of kids and been around more than their fair share of mean. And just when Isabel thought things couldn't get much worse, five more women came down the stairs, peeking curiously over the others, trying to get a better look at her and Lacy.

"It's one of *them*!" one of the newcomers shouted. She pointed at Isabel. "Look. One of the ones from the paper. One of the crazies that's been causing all the trouble."

"Lady, whatcha doing with that little girl, there?" the woman in the hunting jacket asked, and Isabel heard everything she needed in that tone, knew what she was being accused of, knew her trouble had just ratcheted up a notch.

"Cindy," the woman called. "Go call the police. Tell Mark and the boys to get down here. Quick now, run!"

One of the girls in the back of the pack scampered back up the stairs. Isabel understood that she had to do something quick. She took a step away from Lacy.

"Don't even think about it," the woman said. The women pushed the double doors shut behind them, flipped the latch, and tightened ranks. "You ain't going nowhere."

REVEREND OWEN STOOD halfway up the ladder, clutching a mirrored disco globe the size of a basketball to his chest.

"Hold it steady, Scott," he said with more than a hint of frustration.

"I got it already, Granddaddy. Here, you want me to hang it?"

"No," Reverend Owen snapped. "I don't want *you* to hang it. I want *you* to hold the dadgum ladder steady." The reverend wasn't the least bit happy about turning his church into a disco hall, but he wasn't blind, either, at least not yet. He could see that his congregation was aging and if he didn't step up his efforts with the younger generations, soon he'd have no church at all. Still, at times, he felt he was spending more time catering to social club activities than preaching the Good Word.

The reverend missed the old days, back when his wife and him went door-to-door, a Bible tucked beneath their arms, spreading the gospel, giving people who had nothing something to believe in. He recalled being chased off by dogs, being shot at, being cursed and ridiculed. But that had only fired him up, because he was a soldier of the Lord, casting out Satan wherever he found him, and filling the hard-living folks of Boone County up with the Holy Spirit. It'd been a long time now since the reverend had last felt the Holy Spirit pumping in his own veins, long time since he'd felt much other than the fatigue of managing his ever-mounting administrative duties and the frustration of sorting out the petty squabbles of his congregation.

Reverend Owen was about to take another step up the ladder when he heard shouting coming from the basement. He looked down at his grandson and rolled his eyes. "Had a bad feeling about that divorce counseling shindig from the outset. Get together a bunch of bitter women and there's always bound to be trouble."

Cindy burst through the chapel doors and collided with Mrs. Powell, knocking the tray of candles she was carrying from her arms and onto the floor.

"Scott, get over there quick! Get them candles put out!" Each year the reverend tried to talk them out of using all those candles, and each year Mrs. Powell and her Seniors Decorating Committee insisted on lining the windowsills with them, claiming it was tradition, just like the popcorn streamers. And the old-timers clung on to their conventions like ticks to a dog's ear.

Cindy slapped out the candles on the floor and jumped to her feet, looking as though she might hyperventilate at any moment. The reverend tensed; Cindy was prone to hysterics, and he braced himself for her latest round of drama. *"There's one of them devil people in the basement!"* Cindy cried. *"And it's got hold of a little girl. I ain't fucking shitting you! Call the police! Someone call the goddamn police!"*

Reverend Owen thought about calling the police on Cindy's foul mouth. He took a step down, doing his best not to drop the disco ball, doing his best not to fall off the ladder, got one foot onto the floor, and that's when the devil walked into his church.

It pushed right through the double doors, stomping past Cindy and Mrs. Powell, and headed up the center aisle. Satan was a lot larger than the reverend had imagined, standing seven feet tall, with wild, stringy black hair, pitch-black skin, a tail, glowing red eyes, and massive horns twisting up from his forehead.

All commotion ceased, the chapel fell quiet, even Cindy was speechless. They stared: the kids, the adults, all of them. Their faces shocked and fearful, backing away, giving this devil all the room it wanted, but not the reverend, not Owen Augustus Elkins. No, sir. Satan had just picked the wrong church, the wrong preacher to tread on. If the devil wished to scrap, to pit its black dogma against the reverend's faith, then it was in for a brawl, for the reverend was a soldier of the Lord. And for the first time in nearly twenty years Reverend Owen felt the Holy Spirit pumping again in his veins. The reverend stepped forward, blocking the devil's path.

The devil glared at the Christmas tree, tried to sidestep the reverend, but the reverend held his ground, struggling not to be cowed by the very size and vileness of the beast before him, calling on the Lord to give him strength. The devil locked eyes on him. "I have come for my tree," he pronounced in a deep, gravelly voice. "Now out of my way you wretched little man."

The reverend wasn't sure he'd heard right. *Tree? Satan wanted . . . the tree?* The reverend had no idea why Satan wanted his Christmas tree, but he sure as heck wasn't about to let him have it. The reverend shook his head and stood his ground.

"It is a Yule tree," the devil said. "It does not belong in this house. Why do you, a man of the cloth, feel it is acceptable to make a mockery of Yule? To trample upon the beliefs of others?"

The reverend hesitated. *A Yule tree? What's he talking about? Be careful,* he cautioned himself, *trickery is his language. He's trying to throw you off balance, that's all.* And he heard his own words come to him: *One mustn't allow the devil to get the upper hand.* "You dare challenge the Lord's authority in His very house? God will not stand for such. In the name of the Lord Almighty I cast ye out! Now be gone, Satan! Be gone!"

"Satan? I am not Satan!" the beast growled. "I am Krampus, the Lord of Yule. Now if you do not get out of my way I will tear out your heart and eat it!"

The reverend held up the disco ball, meaning to throw it at the unholy beast before him if need be. "Back, devil! Return thee to Hell!"

The beast rolled its eyes. "I am not a devil, fool. Do you ever wonder why you seek the Devil with such vigor? I shall tell you. Because you cannot face your own wickedness. The truth is there is no Devil making you torture, rape, murder, and sodomize one another, or making you destroy the very land that feeds you. There is only you. So look at yourself, for you are the only devil in this room."

"You trick no one with your flimflam," the reverend shot back. "I see you, for Jesus lends me His eyes. The Good Lord sees you and will smite you with His sword of righteousness. He will cast thee back into the eternal flame to burn and burn!"

"Burn? Smite? Punish? Why is your god so intolerant? So jealous? Why must there be only one god? Why is there not room for many?"

"What?"

"One god, why can you honor only one god?"

"Why . . . every child in Bible school knows the answer to that. It is the first commandment: 'You shall have no other gods before me.'"

"You have not answered my question. Wherein lies the harm? Since earliest time men have sought the shelter of many gods, harmony with all the wild spirits. It would seem the more gods one had standing watch over one's self the better. Would it not?"

"I will not denounce the Lord if that's what you're asking. Jesus is my Savior and I shall not stray from His flock."

The devil's shoulders sagged a bit at that and Reverend Owen knew he was winning, that the Holy Spirit was wearing Satan down.

"Silly man, no one is asking you to denounce anyone. Only to open your heart. To invite them all into your house."

"I believe only in Jesus and the Good Lord above."

The devil perked up at that. "And Santa Claus? Do you believe in Santa Claus?"

Santa Claus? What did Santa Claus have to do with anything? "Of course not. Santa Claus is a fantasy."

The devil grinned, let out a small laugh. "There. That, at least, is something we can agree on." He patted Reverend Owen lightly on top of the head, then shoved him aside, continuing up the aisle toward the tree.

The reverend stood there for another minute, unsure of what had just transpired. He certainly didn't feel as though he'd passed any great test of his faith, that he'd put Satan rightly in his place. As a matter of fact, the only way he really felt at the moment was highly annoyed, and now the gangly beast was shaking his Christmas tree, shaking it so hard that the ornaments were flying off in all directions, smashing and crashing into the walls and floors. *What is it with that tree? "Hey!"* the reverend cried out. *"Stop that! I'm telling you to stop that!"*

The devil ignored him, giving the tree a tremendous shove and toppling it over onto the pulpit, ornaments bouncing and shattering all over the place.

"NO! NO! NO!" Reverend Owen screamed and threw the disco ball. The mirrored globe hit the creature on the back of the head, shattering upon its horns. The devil stumbled forward, but didn't fall. It shook its head, shaking the bits of broken glass from its mane, turned, locked its eyes on the reverend, eyes that had become two burning slits of venom. A low, dangerous growl escaped its throat. It snarled, showed them its sharp teeth. The reverend saw no reasoning being here, no soul to banter and debate. He saw a primal beast, something wild, something bloodthirsty and savage. The reverend fell back a step, another, turned to flee, and collided with the ladder, knocking the top rung off its perch against the chapel's ceiling. The tall ladder teetered a mo-

ment, then started downward, gaining momentum, crashing through all the streamers—the very ones he'd spent the last two hours putting up—and smashing down atop the pews.

Reverend Owen watched aghast as the paper streamers landed in the candles perched along the windowsills, amazed at how quickly they caught fire. Whatever materials the Sunday school teachers had used lit up like a fuse. The flaming streamers hit the curtains, the original curtains put up when they'd first moved into the place back in '68, which, guessing by the way they were starting to blaze, predated any fire codes. In no time they had fires going on both sides of the church.

"FIRE!" Cindy screamed at the top of her very capable lungs. *"FIRE! FIRE! FIRE!"* People found their senses and began a panicked rush for the exits.

Reverend Owen didn't move. He stood there, watching the rapidly growing flames, and did something he'd never done before. Within his own church, Reverend Owen took the Lord's name in vain, not once but over and over again.

OFFICER ROBERTS HEARD the shouts and screams from almost a block away. He sped up, taking the last corner hard, shooting into the parking lot of the church. He'd driven over without using his siren and lights, as the chief had instructed, to keep the element of surprise, but watching the people streaming out from the front doors of the church, he didn't believe it even mattered.

He snatched up his rifle, jumped out of the cruiser, using the car for cover, bracing his rifle across the hood just like they'd taught him at the academy. He was only about thirty yards from the front steps, but it was still hard to tell who was who as he watched figures running to and fro—mere silhouettes in front of the growing flames.

Noel glanced up the street, hoping to see the chief's cruiser heading his way. Dillard had ordered him to stay back, but folks needed help, things were getting out of hand fast. He hit the mic. "Chief, I'm at the scene. We have an emergency. Please advise." He waited a few seconds that felt like forever and hit the mic again. "Chief. Copy." Nothing.

KRAMPUS

Where was he? What was taking him so long? Noel changed frequencies, put a call in to the dispatch. "Dispatch, we got a ten . . . a ten . . ." His mind drew a blank, all the codes went out the window. "We got a fire, Methodist church in Goodhope . . . possible dangerous suspects." He heard his voice rising, racing, forced himself to slow down. "Hell, we got all kinds of trouble! Send fire and rescue . . . let the sheriff know right away!" He got a confirmation that help was en route, then the radio clicked again and Dillard's calm voice cut through the static. "Just hold on. Cutting across First now. Almost there."

Noel started to reply, but forgot what he was trying to say, because a towering figure with horns came out of the burning church, towing a Christmas tree behind him and carrying a man over his shoulder. The suspect matched the description, no doubt about that whatsoever. He dropped the man down from his shoulder into the snow. Officer Roberts recognized the man, it was Reverend Owen, he looked confused but okay.

The deputy locked the sight of his rifle on the suspect—the man, or beast, or whatever it was—tried to hold his aim steady. "Oh, good gracious alive! Dillard you better get your ass here and quick!"

A LOUD THUD reverberated through the ceiling. Isabel and all the women looked up.

"What the hell's going on up there?" the woman in the hunting jacket asked.

A moment later they heard screams, cries, and the sound of feet drumming overhead. Isabel had a pretty good guess. *Aw, shit, Krampus. What've you done now?*

Someone up the stairs screamed *"FIRE!"*—and at that moment smoke began to pour out of the ceiling vents.

"OUT!" The woman in the hunting jacket yelled. *"The place is on fire! Everyone get out!"*

The group of women standing in front of the double doors all turned and rushed for the exit, pushing those closest to it into the doors. And since the doors only opened inward, toward the hallway, this jammed them shut.

"Stop! Wait!" someone yelled. *"You're gonna all have to back up."* It was the woman behind Isabel, the one in the simple dress. She started down the hall toward the wedge of women. *"Stay calm. You must stay calm."*

A few women were trying to pull themselves out of the tangle, but the others, in their panic, only pushed harder. Isabel started forward, intent on pulling the women off one another, when she heard screams coming from behind her.

At least a dozen women had come out of the room at the far end of the hall and were stampeding toward her. Lacy stood right in their path. Isabel scrambled to get to her, but she had no chance. The woman, the one in the dress, grabbed Lacy, shoved her into the shallow door well, the one in front of the locked door. The women drove past. Isabel didn't see what happened, the next thing she knew she was knocked back down the hall, slammed to the floor, and caught up in the press of grappling bodies.

The air grew dense, the smoke making everyone cough, spurring on the panic. Isabel found herself pinned, struggling to get air in her lungs. She heard her name, a deep, booming call that resonated above the din of screaming, crying women. There came a terrific snapping and splintering of wood, and all at once light appeared at the top of the double doors. There came another snap, more splintering, and a large chunk of the door ripped outward. She saw him then, his glowing eyes and unmistakable silhouette. Krampus wrapped his large hands on the door, let out a roar, and gave a mighty tug. The door frame popped and snapped, one of the double doors broke free, crashing down onto the steps.

And there stood the Yule Lord, tall and terrible, the Belsnickels just behind him. Krampus pulled the women out of the tangle, pushed them up the stairs; the Belsnickels, in turn, lead them out of the death trap.

"Isabel!" Krampus yelled, his voice frantic. *"Where are you?"*

"Krampus!" She managed to get a hand free and wave. Krampus shoved women left and right, plowing his way to Isabel, grabbed her, and pulled her to her feet.

"Hurry!" he cried, pushing her toward the stairs.

"Wait," Isabel shouted. She looked down the dim, smoky hall searching for Lacy. And there she was—in that woman's arms, the one in the

dress. The woman coughed, her eyes streaming with tears, but she held tight to Lacy. Isabel leapt to them, put an arm around both of them, and steered them to the stairs. The last couple of women were stumbling up the steps with the help of Jesse and Chet. Isabel led Lacy and the woman up and out, followed lastly by Krampus.

They came out into the night air. Isabel drew in a deep breath; never had air tasted so sweet. Ash and glowing cinders fell upon the snow, smoke billowed around them. Isabel saw Krampus's tall, horned figure before the hellish landscape, surrounded by his Belsnickels, and could not help but think of Satan and his host of demons.

"Come," Krampus called. "Let us find the Yule goats before they stray." He headed back around the side of the church, followed by the Belsnickels, all of them disappearing into the smoke.

People were gathering in the parking lot. Isabel started to lead the woman and Lacy that way, spotted a police cruiser barreling into the lot, nearly hitting two bystanders. It skidded to a stop beside another cruiser. Isabel halted, dropped to one knee, gave Lacy a quick kiss on the cheek, and hugged her tight. "I gotta go, Lacy. You be good. Okay?"

"You be good, too," Lacy said and hugged her back.

Isabel stood, clutched the woman's arm. "Her name is Lacy. Please look after her." The woman gave her a confused look, but nodded earnestly, picking Lacy up and heading away from the flames. Isabel wanted to watch them go, but tears blurred her vision and she turned back, darting away into the smoke after Krampus.

CHIEF DILLARD DEATON leapt from his car, almost forgot his shotgun, reached back in, yanked it across the seat.

"Aw, jeez!" Noel cried, running over. "Chief, man, am I ever glad to see—" He stared at Dillard's face. "Heck, chief, what happened to you?"

"Where are they?" Dillard asked, walking briskly toward the fire.

Officer Roberts jogged to keep up. "Um . . . well . . . hard to say with all the smoke, y'know. They were heading around the side of the building last I saw."

"I told you not to let them out of your sight."

"I know, but the sheriff told me to sit tight until backup arrived."

"What?" Dillard spun on his heels. "The sheriff? You called this in?"

"Well, yeah. Had to. We're outside the town limit. Outside our jurisdiction."

"Do I look like I need a lecture on whose jurisdiction we're in?"

"But the fire. I thought it was procedure to—"

"Shut up. Just shut up!" Dillard almost punched the boy, almost laid him out flat, and wouldn't that have added an interesting layer to his growing list of troubles. He stepped forward, got right into Noel's face. "I don't wanna hear another word about procedure. You go back to the vehicles and wait for the goddamn sheriff to show up. Got that? Don't you move unless I say so. Got it? Got it?"

Noel nodded and headed back, looking every bit the whipped pup. The truth was Dillard planned on going down there and shooting Jesse dead on sight and he sure as hell didn't want Officer Boy Scout anywhere near him when he did—didn't want any witnesses at all.

Dillard heard a distant siren racing their way. *Dammit. Just what I don't need. Fuck! Gotta find that boy quick-like.* He chambered a round, pushing through the smoke. He spotted footprints in the snow, at least five or six sets, followed them around the back of the building, where they ended in a cluster around a wadded-up newspaper. He found deep ruts and fresh droppings—deer or goat maybe, he wasn't sure which, only sure that nothing quite made sense. If he'd happened to look up at that moment, he might've caught sight of a sleigh pulled by two large goats heading east, toward the hills, but just then flashing lights caught his attention. It was the sheriff, pulling into the parking lot.

Dillard rubbed the bridge of his nose, tried to stifle the growing pain behind his eyes. He suddenly felt very tired, very old. "Gonna be a long night. Gonna be a long fucking night."

Chapter Sixteen

HORTON'S

Jesse watched Krampus stare at the plastic play gym and the handful of toys scattered about the yard of a small ranch home some-where just south of Whitesville. Krampus had been staring—without a word, without so much as a grunt—at the toys for going on twenty minutes. So long that Jesse began to wonder if he'd planned to get out of the sleigh at all.

The whole crew was quiet, lost in their own thoughts, perhaps con-templating the craziness at the church—or, like him, how they'd ever ended up with this strange, moody creature in the first place. Jesse was quickly losing whatever hope he might've held that there'd be a resolu-tion to any of this . . . some path that might lead to a way out.

They'd already visited two homes, both without much incident, but also without much enthusiasm. Krampus had actually walked past a blow-mold Santa without smashing it. Jesse got the impression the Yule Lord was just going through the motions, even his speech to these children had lacked any real passion. Jesse felt he was on a sinking ship with no way to jump overboard. He exchanged a glance with Isa-bel, raised his eyebrows, and shrugged. Isabel shrugged back. After another long moment, she cleared her throat. "Krampus," she said in a soft tone. "Maybe we should head on back. Take the night off."

"Why, what a splendid idea," Vernon added. "Certainly has my vote."

Isabel cut him a sharp look.

"What?" Vernon said in a defensive tone. "If Krampus is in one of his intolerable moods, I see no reason why we should all have to suffer along."

"He is right," Krampus muttered. "There is no more need. It has all been in vain, I fear. The world does not want to remember, and now it appears . . . I am out of time."

"Out of time?" Isabel asked. "What do you mean?"

Krampus only shook his head.

"Krampus? What's going on?"

Krampus looked up the driveway, sighed, grabbed the switches and the sack, and stepped out of the sleigh. "You can join me if you wish. Matters not." He started up the drive. The two Shawnee jumped out and followed.

Isabel elbowed Vernon. "Could you not be such a jerk?"

"You know," Vernon said, sounding uncharacteristically terse. "Sometimes you forget that I'm not along for the joy of it. I'm his prisoner . . . his slave. Frankly, I really don't give a damn what happens to the old goat."

Chet nodded. "Amen, brother."

"Well, some of us do," Isabel said, slipping out, chasing Krampus and the Shawnee up the drive. Jesse looked at Vernon and Chet, shrugged, and followed after Isabel, catching up with them as they gained the porch.

Krampus reached for the door handle and froze. He let out a gasp. Jesse followed his eyes to the steps, saw nothing more than two pairs of shoes, started to ask what the matter was, then looked again.

The shoes were propped up as though on display in a shoe store; arranged within each shoe sat an array of candies. A card stood pinched between the shoes.

Krampus dropped the sack and the birch branches, reached for the card, held it open so they could all see. Krampus's hand actually trembled. The card read: HAPPY YULETIDE, KRAMPUS. WE ARE VERY GOOD KIDS. LOVE, MARY AND TODD.

"Well, I'll be," Isabel said.

"Bet they read about Krampus in the paper," Jesse said.

"Maybe," Isabel said, "or maybe we visited one of their pals or some of their kin last night."

Krampus dropped to one knee. He plucked up the candies, held them in his palms. *"Thank you,"* he whispered. *"Thank you for your tribute."* The Yule Lord wiped at his eyes and Jesse realized the great beast was actually crying. "Their reward," Krampus said. "They need their reward. Jesse, retrieve some coins."

Jesse picked up the sack, held it out.

"You gather them. My hands are full," Krampus said without taking his eyes from the treats; he held them as one would most precious stones.

Jesse pulled open the sack, hesitated. Hadn't Krampus spoken of these coins being in some sort of hell? Jesse wasn't sure he wanted to go putting his hand in hell . . . any hell. Everyone waited on him. He sighed, thought of the triangular coins, and inserted his hand. He felt coldness, closer to the feeling of fear than an actual temperature. The chill penetrated right to his bones, to the very marrow. It tingled, almost painful, made his teeth hurt. Jesse tried to concentrate on the coins, wanting to get things over with as quick as possible. His hand bumped something crusty and brittle—rotting things came to mind. Then something touched him, more of a caress, like someone pulling gauze across his skin. He let out a small squeal, yanked his hand out. "Fuck, Krampus. There's something in there!"

Krampus let out a snort. "Of course. The dead. Do not fear, they cannot hurt you. They are only ghosts . . . lost souls, the ones that could not find their way home."

Jesse peered into the smoking darkness, thought he heard something—wailing. Sounded faint and far away, but there was no mistake, he heard them. He shuddered as a chill slid down his back.

Krampus put on a mischievous grin. "You just want to be careful not to fall in. You would wander about those endless catacombs until your body wasted away, the dead following your every step . . . waiting to claim you as their own."

Jesse swallowed loudly, did his best to focus on the coins, and stuck his hand back in. This time his fingers found what he was searching for. He pulled out a handful of the triangular coins and held them out to Krampus.

"Good, place them in the shoes."

Jesse did. Six coins total. "Those are gonna be some happy kids," Jesse said. "Probably buy themselves a right decent car with that."

Krampus handed each of the Belsnickels a piece of candy and held one back for himself, a red lollipop. He stared at it a moment, the way someone would upon a long-lost photo from their youth, then pulled off the wrapper and slipped it into his mouth. "Our work here is done," he said, and headed down the drive to the sleigh. Jesse noticed a light spring to Krampus's step. The Yule Lord hopped aboard, glanced back at the house, and nodded, the moonlight glistening off his broad smile.

"The Yule Lord has returned at long last."

KRAMPUS PRACTICALLY SKIPPED up the drives of the next several houses, his tail swishing playfully back and forth, almost wagging. He did not sneak or creep about, not anymore, he entered boldly with a loud cry and cheer of Yuletide greetings. The Belsnickels scrambled to subdue alarmed parents while Krampus thrilled and terrified the children with his tales and gifts. At one home, a man actually unloaded both barrels of his shotgun and would've most likely killed Vernon had Chet not managed to wrestle the gun away. They flew from house to house, skimming the treetops, Krampus shouting out Yule cheer to any and all he saw below, and soon Jesse lost count of the homes they hit.

Sometime well past midnight, they heard music as they were flying fast above a lonely stretch of highway well out in hill country. They flew around a bend and saw a building set off the highway. A handful of cars, motorcycles, and trucks were parked in the glow of the neon beer signs. Krampus circled over the place, watched a cluster of people carrying on and laughing as they stumbled their way into the joint.

Jesse caught the name, Horton's, and realized he knew the place, that he'd actually played there once, a while back. He recalled it had a rough crowd, one of those joints where they put chicken wire up in front of the stage to keep the players from getting hit with beer bottles.

"Is it a feast hall?" Krampus asked. "Or a tavern, perhaps?"

"It's a bar," Chet said. "Another crappy little honky-tonk."

"What are they celebrating?"

Chet shrugged. "Another day on this shitty planet be my guess."

Krampus nodded. "It is indeed a good day to celebrate." He dropped down, landing the sleigh behind the bar. He grabbed the sack and hopped out.

Jesse recognized the tune; a sloppy version of that old Oak Ridge Boys' tune, "Elvira." Jesse had always hated that song. *But it's loud,* Jesse thought, and *sometimes that's all that matters.*

"Come," Krampus said and started away.

"Don't suppose I might sit this one out?" Vernon asked.

"No. It is time to celebrate the return of Yuletide. Time for all of us to celebrate."

"Yes, well, I was afraid of that."

They climbed out and followed the Yule Lord around to the front.

Chet began chuckling to himself. "If this goes even half as well as that church, then we're in for one hell of a fine time."

"Might be more his crowd," Jesse added.

"No," Vernon moaned. "He doesn't have a crowd. This will be another disaster."

"Can't wait," said Chet.

HORTON WHITE STOOD behind the bar. A picture of Neil Diamond autographed to him hung on the wall above the rows of liquor, right beside the one of Hasil Atkins. Everyone around Boone County had a soft spot for old Hasil, but Horton couldn't say the same about Neil. Folks just didn't care much for the old crooner and weren't the least bit shy about letting him know it. Horton kept the picture up nonetheless, because he liked Neil Diamond, a lot, and because this was his bar and he'd put up anybody's picture he damn well felt like. Of course if folks didn't start buying some drinks soon, this wouldn't be his bar for much longer, be just another run-down shack along the highway.

The first of the month was almost on him and Horton had no idea how he was going to make rent. He knew he couldn't afford to be late again, not with the General threatening to bust up the place if he was. He usually pulled in a pretty good crowd between Christmas and New Year's, counted on it to catch up financially, but not this year, especially not tonight. Maybe thirty folks had shown up, tops, about half his usual crowd, and the worst of it, no one was buying. He'd had to let his cook go last month, which left him managing the bar while trying to take short orders. Not that anyone was exactly lining up for his burned French fries and microwaved hot dogs.

He scanned the sullen faces. Folks were out of sorts, appeared beaten down, tired, even the band couldn't keep the beat—kept screwing up their sets. Nothing too unusual about that, what *was* unusual was the fact that no one seemed to give a hoot. No boos, or catcalls, certainly no one throwing bottles. Only two people were on the dance floor, Martha and Lynn, dancing with each other as usual on account that none of the men wanted to dance with them.

Other than a handful of bikers, it was mostly regulars: Rusty, Jim, Thornton, and the rest of that bunch from the mill. Tom Mullins and his four brothers had shown up, making Horton a bit nervous at first, as trouble followed that family around like a hungry puppy. But even Tom was mellow tonight, sipping—not drinking—his beer, just playing pool with that butchy gal Kate from down Goodhope way. The bikers were mostly keeping to themselves over in one corner. Horton smelled weed, wanted to ask them to take their smokes outside, not because it bothered him none, only because maybe then they'd drink a bit more. But he didn't know these boys, didn't want to stir anything up, but he sure wished someone or something would stir things up—something to get the evening going.

"Shit," Horton said, speaking to the handful of dour faces before him at the bar. "Someone die I don't know about? Or maybe the post office just forgot to deliver everybody's welfare checks?" No one gave him so much as a snicker.

The door opened; Horton didn't bother to look over, at least not until he caught the look on Lucy Duff's face. A man, a very tall man, entered the bar along with a cold gust of night air. The lights were dim, but not so dim that Horton couldn't see that the man had horns twisting right out of his forehead.

"Well bend me over and fuck me silly," Lucy said, her words slurred. She elbowed her friend Nelly. "Hey, Nell, check that one out."

Six more figures came in behind the tall devil man, dressed in old-time costumes, their faces streaked black. Some of them wore furs, and masks with horns. But it was their eyes that made Horton uneasy, the way they caught the light and gleamed orange in the shadows.

Is this a joke? Horton wondered. *Someone's gotta be playing a prank on me, because last I checked we weren't running any costume contests.* He spied a large sack; the tall one handed it off to one of his gang, a lean-looking man, spoke something in his ear and pointed to the bar. *Oh, fuck.* Horton understood the disguises, realized that they were actually about to try and rob his place. Horton stepped quickly over to the icebox, set his hand on the sawed-off under the counter. *Are they nuts? Do they have any clue the kind of folks they're dealing with?* Horton guessed half his patrons were packing right this minute, and the rest carried a knife or some other means of defense. Hard men and hard women, the kind of folks that didn't back down from a fight. Horton had no doubt that if these fools drew weapons, someone was gonna end up full of holes.

"It's *them*," Lucy said. "Y'know. The ones from the paper."

"What ones from the paper?" Nelly asked.

"Dan," Horton said sharply. "Hey, Dan. Back me up."

Dan sat next to Lucy. Horton had spent half a tour in Nam with Dan, knew Dan didn't go anywhere without his piece, knew he was a good man to have at your back. Dan saw that Horton had his hand under the counter, looked to the door, and sobered up quick. He shifted round, dropped his hand into his jacket pocket.

The lean man with the sack approached the end of the bar. The man was even creepier up close. The makeup and that odd glow to his eyes looked so very real. Horton had no idea how he got his eyes to do that. Some new type of contacts?

"Mister," the slim man said. "Beg your pardon. Got a question for you."

Horton stared at the man from where he stood, not about to take his hand off his shotgun. "Yeah, what can I do you for?"

"Like to open the bar for the evening."

Of all the things Horton had expected the man to say, that wasn't on the list. He cut a glance over at Dan, but Dan's eyes stayed locked on the man.

"I bet you would, son," Horton said. "Bet everyone in here would."

"Don't worry . . . we'll be paying up front," the man said and shoved his hand into his sack.

Oh, shit! Horton felt his heart leap into his throat. *He's going for his piece.* Horton yanked the shotgun out from beneath the counter, leveled it at the man. Dan tugged out his .38.

"Whoa!" the lean man said. "Hold on a sec, now. It ain't what you're thinking."

"How about you take your hand out of there nice and slow," Dan said. "Then we'll figure on what we're thinking."

The man nodded, then did something funny. He shut his eyes as though concentrating real hard. Horton wondered if maybe the guy was jacked up on something. Horton stole a quick glance over at the rest of the gang, knowing this would be when they'd make their play. Only they hadn't moved, weren't even looking his way. Just standing there watching the band like nothing in the world was going on.

"Okay," the man said. "I'm gonna pull my hand out nice and slow. I'd appreciate it if you two don't shoot me when I do."

"Well, now that all depends on what's in your hand," Dan said. "Don't it?"

The lean man slowly withdrew his hand and instead of a gun he held a clump of tarnished triangular coins. He laid them on the counter. "These are gold. Should be enough to cover it."

"This some sort of joke?" Horton asked.

The man shook his head. He didn't look like he was joking.

"He wants to pay with play money," Dan said and chuckled.

Horton started to join in when a glint of gold caught his eye. He stepped forward for a closer look. Horton had done a spot of panning in his day with his grandfather in the hills. He knew what real gold looked like, felt like, tasted like. He picked up one of the coins, weighed it in his hand, bit it. His breath left him. "Well, I'll be damn, Dan. This is real." He counted seven coins in front of him, more than enough to buy all the beer and liquor in the joint.

"If you let me stick my hand back in this sack, I can add a bit to that."

"What?" Horton said, still mesmerized by the amount of gold sitting on his bar. "Why, yeah, son. Go right ahead. Knock yourself out."

The lean man pulled out five more coins. "That oughta do it. Don't you think?"

Horton didn't answer, couldn't find the words.

"What'd you say? We got a deal?"

Horton nodded. "We sure do. We sure as hell do." He set the shotgun back in its hitch and quickly slid the coins into his bar towel, wrapping them up, getting them out of sight. He was amazed at how heavy they were. *Hell,* he thought. *Got rent covered for a year or so. Maybe even a vacation or two.* He hid them up under the ice chest, out of reach of any sticky-fingered barflies.

Nelly, who'd been nursing the same beer all night, gave Horton a sheepish smile. "Why, I'll take a shot of bourbon, Bob, straight up. And, hey, make it the good stuff, will ya?"

"Yeah, me too," Lucy said. "Make mine a double." She looked the lean man up and down. "Hey, just who the fuck are you guys?"

The man smiled. "You'll see. Just keep your eye on the tall ugly one over there."

JESSE NODDED TO Krampus and gave him the thumbs-up. Krampus nodded back and proceeded across the dance floor, headed toward the stage. The two dancing women stopped and stared at him. Jesse pulled up a stool, having no idea what Krampus was up to, not sure he wanted to find out.

Chet, Vernon, and Isabel wandered over, pulled up stools next to Jesse. The two Shawnee stayed in the shadows, keeping a close eye on the Yule Lord, looking uncomfortable and out of place in the bar.

Krampus stopped in front of the chicken wire, turned, and surveyed the crowd. Now, with the stage light on him, people were starting to notice that there was a seven-foot-tall devil in their midst. But they didn't react the way Jesse would've expected, especially after what had happened at the church. No hysterical shouting and screaming; instead, plenty of confused double takes, pointing, and drunken laughter, but mostly curiosity, folks trying to make sense of what they were seeing.

Krampus said something to the band, a three-piece, and they stopped playing. Instead of angry protest, a few folks actually clapped.

The stage—or platform, rather, as it wasn't more than a foot high—was draped in Christmas lights, two slow-spinning spotlights of yellow, red, and green, shown from either side, adding a festive, dramatic touch to Krampus's presence.

"Hey, asshole," someone shouted. "This ain't Halloween."

Jesse realized that no one understood that a true monster stood among them. They obviously thought Krampus was in costume. Jesse hoped it stayed that way so they could soon be on their way without anyone getting stabbed or shot.

Krampus raised a hand. "Please, hear me . . . for I would speak." It was his tone that captured their attention, powerful and resonating—the voice of a god. Krampus waited as the snickers died down and the hall slowly fell quiet.

"Well, get on with it then," a stout woman called from the bar. "Ain't got all night."

Krampus grinned, and there was something beguiling in that grin, like an invitation to play, and, to Jesse's surprise, he found plenty around the bar smiling back.

A brash young man over by the pool table took a couple of steps forward and shouted, "Hey, just who the fuck are you supposed to be?"

Krampus set eyes on him, intense, piercing eyes, eyes that made it clear they'd hold one accountable for what was said. "I am Krampus, the Yule Lord," he boomed. "I come to celebrate the splendors of life and seek worthy souls to join me. People who wish to make merry . . . to shout, dance, love, brawl, and sing. Souls willing to turn their backs on the angels and share in a little debauchery. To be alive *now* . . . this very night. To shake their fist in the face of death, knowing whatever ills tomorrow may harbor nothing can steal this moment if you live it with all your vigor. What say you? Will you drink with me this night and chase the Draugr from the shadows? Will you sing with me to Mother Earth, to all the ghosts of Asgard? Will you herald in Yuletide with me?"

People were nodding, were eating it up. Jesse saw the same fervor on their faces as those of the Shawnee. There was no denying that there was something infectious about the Yule Lord's spirit; Jesse could feel it in the air.

An old man, bent and rail-thin, wearing a sweat-stained cap atop long, silver hair, squinted at Krampus and called out, "Who's buying?"

The crowd laughed and the Yule Lord laughed with them. "I am," Krampus exclaimed, his eyes gleaming. "Tonight is a night of excess. All the mead one can hold and all on me."

Almost every head swiveled to the barman, hopeful faces searching for confirmation. The barman nodded. "Open bar all night!" he called. With that, a great cheer rang out and most everyone in the tavern headed for the bar.

The band started back up, a spirited rendition of Willie Nelson's "Whiskey River." Krampus waded into the crowd. One of the bikers handed him a beer and cried, *To Krampus!* Mugs were raised all around, accompanied by shouts of *Krampus! Krampus!* The Yule Lord drank down the beer, took another, then another.

"Well," Chet said. "I ain't gonna sit here and let them drink this place dry on their own." He grabbed a pitcher of beer, rounded up a few glasses, and filled them up, handing one to Isabel, Jesse, and to Vernon. Isabel dragged Wipi and Nipi over, shoved a beer into each of their hands. "Come on, time to enjoy yourselves a little."

The Yule Lord grabbed two women from the bar, hooked his arms into theirs, and began to dance. Both of the women squealed, and a loud hoot went up from the crowd and soon more women joined in. Krampus swung from arm to arm, a sort of square-dance jig. The tavern erupted in howls. The band broke into "Muleskinner Blues," kicking up the tempo and really belting it out. More and more folks joined in until the entire dance floor was full of men and women hooting, hollering, clogging, and acting like fools.

Drinks were spilled, tables and chairs knocked over, but Krampus's spirited laughter could be heard above all the ruckus, a booming sound that warmed the heart. Jesse had never seen this side of the Yule Lord, and it occurred to him that he was seeing the real Krampus, the Krampus of ancient times, the great and wild Yule spirit that galvanized mankind to brave the darkest primeval nights, kindled their will to survive the trials of the harshest winters. He could almost see the horned beast dancing this very jig within the communal houses of primitive man. Jesse saw the way the people fed on Krampus's spirit, and how, in turn, Krampus fed on theirs. And understood now just why those shoes, with their small tribute of candies, meant so much to the Yule Lord. That what Krampus needed more than anything was a flock to shepherd, to protect and inspire. Jesse found he was tapping his toes and smiling, that he couldn't help himself, couldn't help but get caught up in the fervor.

"Well, I'll be damn," Chet grumbled. "Everyone's sure in a good god-damn mood. I was hoping to see the old goat take a few in the stomach, not prance around like a mountain troll."

"I commiserate with you wholeheartedly, chum," Vernon said. "Who would've guessed a bit of candy was all it would take to turn Old Tall and Ugly around."

"That was a whole hell of a lot more than a piece of candy to Kram-pus," Isabel said. "I think that was his validation, proof that his spirit has truly returned to this here world."

"Hey look." Vernon pointed and let out a laugh. Wipi and Nipi were out on the dance floor, stomping their feet with the best of them.

"Sure look to be having a blast," Isabel said.

Vernon stood, extended his arm to Isabel. "Shall we?"

Isabel lit up with a big smile. "Heck yeah!" She hooked her arm in his and the two sauntered out onto the floor.

Jesse glanced at Chet. "You see that?"

"See what?"

"Over there. That guy, the one with the red bandanna." Jesse nod-ded to a bearded biker with an impressive paunch, kicking up his heels on the floor. "He's had his eye on you since you walked in."

"What? So?"

"So? So? Are you blind? I believe he wants to dance with you."

"Fuck you, Jesse. Why'd you always gotta be such a dickhole?"

Jesse laughed, and it felt good to laugh. He leaned back against the bar and watched Isabel dance. She danced really nice, a lot like Linda used to. Jesse thought of all the nights Linda and him had danced to-gether and slowly his smile faded. He ached to hear her laugh again like in the old days, to feel her close to him as they slow-danced, and there, surrounded in a sea of smiles, laughter, and cheer, Jesse felt completely alone.

"I miss Trish," Chet said, looking fairly miserable. "Sure wish she were here to dance with." Hearing Chet voice his same sentiment startled Jesse, then he noticed the way Chet watched the couples, the longing in his eye—wasn't too hard to understand.

"Fuck," Chet said. "Swear to God, if I ever get out of this mess, gonna do right by her. Sure as hell I am."

Jesse nodded, took a long swig, and lost himself in thoughts of what he'd do if he ever got free.

Krampus appeared in front of him, holding a guitar. Jesse blinked as though awakened from a snooze. Krampus held the guitar out to him. "Come, music man. Play me a song."

Jesse stared at the guitar as though it might bite him. "No, that ain't happening."

Krampus took a seat next to him. "I would like to hear you sing."

"No, I told you I was done with that."

"Jesse, what do you believe in?"

"Krampus, we've already been over this. I told you I don't believe in nothing."

"No, that wasn't what you said. You said you didn't know."

Jesse shrugged.

"Well, I do know," Krampus said. "You believe in music. It is at the heart of you."

"No, I'm done with music."

"You can never be done with music. No more than you can be done with breathing. The day you quit is the day you die."

"Krampus, I appreciate what you're trying to do, but you don't seem to understand . . . I got other things on my mind and—"

"I know, the Dillard. We will go and take care of him."

"You done said that before."

"Jesse, if you will get up there and play me a couple of songs, then I give you my solemn word that we will leave this place and go kill that bad man."

Jesse stared at Krampus. "Is that the drink talking or do you mean it?"

He met Jesse's eyes, held them. "You have my oath as Yule Lord."

Jesse scrutinized his face a moment longer, saw that the creature indeed meant it, at least at this moment he did, and Jesse decided that was the best he was going to get. Jesse stood and took the guitar. He skirted the dance floor and waited on the side of the stage for the band to finish up their song. When they did, he asked if they'd like to take a break and get a beer, then stepped up onto the stage.

All eyes fell on him and he felt sure they could see right through him, could see that he just didn't add up. Jesse slipped the guitar strap over his shoulder, strummed the strings, twisting the keys, pretending to tune the guitar while trying to get a handle on his nerves. He adjusted the mic and looked out over the crowd, unable to shake the feeling he had no business on stage. He swallowed, started to say something, then forgot what it was.

"You gonna sing or just gawk at us like a chicken?" a woman shouted and everyone laughed.

"Like to . . . share a little number . . . with you," he stammered. "Something I came up with a while back. It's called . . . 'Night Train.'"

He hit the strings, caught a few sour notes. Stopped.

"*Next!*" someone cried, followed by a few boos.

"Sorry about that . . . been a little while."

People began turning away, laughing and cutting up, drifting back toward the bar for more drinks.

Jesse's chest tightened. *Who am I fooling?* He made himself start up again, hit a few more sour notes, but this time kept going. His fingers were still a bit stiff, but he knew that wasn't the problem. He began to sing, his voice stale, he could hear it, could see it on their faces.

People shook their heads, a few put their hands over their ears, laughing, laughing at his singing. Jesse caught Krampus watching him from the bar, the Yule Lord's eyes steady and intense. Krampus spoke, and even though there was no way Jesse could've heard him across the crowd, he did, actually feeling it more than hearing it, deep down inside of him. "Free your spirit."

It was silly nonsense, but Jesse closed his eyes, tried to forget the crowd, concentrated on his music. Slowly the din of the crowd faded and it was just him and his guitar, alone, just like in his room. The tension melted away, the stiffness left his hands, his fingers found the right chords, and he began to sing, to really sing.

It was an up tempo number, a song about a man running away from his mean, mean woman. About a minute into the song the music came

310

alive, the melody and notes became so clear he could almost see them. The music flowed through him, felt more like he was weaving a spell than performing a song, and he strummed the guitar hard and fast as though meaning to tear loose the strings. He finished the first song and went right into the next, and then another. And it was as though someone had pulled cotton from his ears and he was hearing his own music, his own voice, for the first time. He wasn't sure if it had something to do with the spell Krampus had woven about the tavern or his heightened senses as a Belsnickel, or maybe a little of both, but what mattered was that he liked what he was hearing just fine. Decided his songs weren't half bad after all, were quite good, actually.

Jesse opened his eyes and found the crowd thought so as well, folks no longer cutting up but watching him, marking the beat, and moving to the rhythm. He'd never felt such a connection with an audience, it was as though he was touching their souls. He saw Krampus grinning at him and knew then that the Yule Lord was right, he could no more quit music than breathing, and while he needed air to live, he needed music to truly be alive. He stamped his boot with the beat, shouted and yowled with the best of them, sang on and on, his voice clear and strong, the music lifting him higher and higher.

Krampus moved among them, bopping and clapping in time. A deep hum arose from the crowd, a warm sound, almost a purr. The music took on a life of its own, the melody of his song fading as he strummed the guitar to some distant, primitive beat. Krampus began to chant and the crowd joined in. Jesse found himself chanting along, his song forgotten, babbling without meaning, only feelings. At some point the band had joined in and the pounding of drums and deep pluck of the standup bass swelled, setting the pulse. Every person in the hall moved out onto the floor romping, dancing, and stomping to the beat. They nodded and swayed, eyes half closed as though in a trance.

The primal rhythm grew, filled Jesse from head to toe, to his very core. The crowd pushed together, forming a wide circle, hands on the hips of the person in front of them. Krampus headed the parade, circling round and round the hall, the two women from the bar holding on to his tail, laughing and stumbling after him. The beat continued to rise as though a hundred drums had joined them. Jesse felt cocooned in the warm cacophony of sound. The hall grew murky and the lights flickered like flame, sending a host of shadows dancing across the wall and ceiling, the shapes of men and woman hopping and prancing. Jesse blinked, saw some with horns and tails, then beasts, stags, bears, and wolves all swirling together across the walls like ancient cave paintings come to life.

At some point Jesse must have joined in, because he found himself adrift in that sea of bodies, feeling as though floating in a dream. The drums were accompanied by hoots and howls, not just those of the men and women, but bleating, braying, growls and howls. He heard his heartbeat, then the heartbeat of all those around him, they fell in sync to the rhythm, and he understood it was not drums he was hearing but the pulse of life itself, of Mother Earth. It pumped through him, a sensation of purest joy, and he saw how he was part of this pulse. How he truly belonged. An overwhelming affection for those near him, for life, for all life swelled in his chest.

The heartbeat hammered on, the dancers broke from the circle and began writhing and grinding together, it seemed there were more and more people in the room, many wearing bones, half-dressed or nude, some wearing masks and covered in ash and paint. At one point Jesse found himself in the clutches of a woman, his hands on her bare sweaty hips, her tongue in his mouth. She smelled of honeysuckle, had pointy ears, and—he blinked—there were small antlers growing from the top of her head. She spun away from him and a moment later he held the fore-hooves of a goat, the beast swirled him around, laughing, its yellow eyes full of mirth. Jesse laughed right along with it.

Outside the revelers, within the deepest shadows, Jesse perceived other shapes, shapes of things he'd never seen before, yet some deep part of him recognized. He shivered. They, too, seemed drawn to the heartbeat, but, Jesse sensed, for a different purpose. The shapes watched them reproachfully, but none entered the circle of light, ducking away as though in pain each time Krampus laughed or bellowed.

Krampus began to chant again, and they all joined in, laughing, drinking, whistling, shouting, and swirling into one another, all of them drunk on his spirit. Jesse had no idea how long this went on, only that at some point he collapsed and either fell asleep or lost consciousness.

KRAMPUS

SOMEONE SHOOK JESSE awake. He opened his eyes and found Krampus grinning down at him. Jesse looked about at the sleeping, snoring bodies. They lay everywhere, some curled up together right on the dance floor, others draped across the bar, tables, and benches. He searched for the woman with the antlers, found no sign of her, or the wild, painted people either, or any of the other strange beasts.

"It is time to go put things right with the Dillard. Are you ready?"

Jesse sat up quick, nodded. "Oh, yeah. I'm ready."

Krampus's grin widened, a dangerous, toothy smile. "Then let us go and be terrible."

They headed outside, the chill helping to wake Jesse up. He stumbled after Krampus, feeling light-headed. The rest of the Belsnickels sat waiting in the sleigh, looking exhausted but happy and content, even Vernon.

A ghost of a dawn showed along the ridge line. Jesse stopped in his tracks.

A bear sat in the snow beside the sleigh. A very big bear.

Jesse started to point this out when he noticed the three deer standing next to the bear. He glanced around, saw more deer, another bear, raccoons, a fox, rabbits, animals of all sorts. They were gathered around the tavern. He also noticed that much of the snow and ice around the tavern had melted away, leaving a broad swath of exposed earth. Here and there new grass sprouted, leaves and fresh buds bloomed from the nearby trees, even a few fresh flowers peppered the landscape.

Jesse glanced at Krampus.

Krampus shrugged. "We sang to Mother Earth last night. She heard us." He plucked a flower from the snow, sniffed it. "And this with the spirit of just a handful of drunks. Imagine . . . imagine what we might do with a thousand voices, a hundred thousand, a million."

Chapter Seventeen

GOD'S WRATH

Krampus brought the sleigh down behind the old church. Geri and Freki sat waiting for them on the back porch. The Belsnickels crawled out and stumbled in, leaning heavily upon one another. Krampus strolled up onto the porch, dropped the sack on the steps, and took a moment to rough up the wolves' thick pelts.

Isabel stoked and fed the potbelly while Vernon, Chet, and the two brothers found their beds and collapsed. Not Jesse: he hustled over to the cardboard box holding the weapons and cash, passing up on the machine pistol, going instead for a Colt revolver, wanting a gun he could depend on. He pocketed one of the stout hunting knives and a box of ammo. He snatched up the keys to Chet's truck, feeling it would be best to take the pickup. It'd be dawn soon and a flying sleigh wouldn't be the most inconspicuous means of getting around.

"Where you going?" Isabel asked.

"Taking Krampus on a snipe hunt."

She scrutinized him for a moment, then shook her head. "Nu-huh?"

"Going to take care of things."

Her face tightened. "You watch yourself."

"Try to," he said and headed out.

Jesse found Krampus sitting on the porch between the two wolves, rubbing their fur and looking up at the fading stars.

"Ready?" Jesse asked.

"Please, here, sit." Krampus moved the sack over, made a spot. "There are a few words I would share."

Jesse tried not to show his frustration; he wanted to be off—to get this thing done. He felt a growing sense of dread that he couldn't explain, and the last thing he wanted to do right now was to be drawn into another one of Krampus's lengthy conversations.

"I shall keep it brief."

Jesse sat on the step next to Krampus.

Krampus inhaled deeply. "It was a glorious night. Was it not?"

"It was."

"Jesse, your songs, they touched my heart . . . and not just me. Did you see them, see their faces? You touched them all. Your muse is full of magic."

Jesse smiled, nodded. *Magic.* He liked that. It was the only way to describe how his songs had made him feel last night. "Was that your hand at play?"

"Oh, yes indeed, but the music . . . that was your muse. I only helped you to truly see her, to free yourself from your own fears, to let go. But I promise you, it was your spark that captivated."

Jesse nodded. He'd never put himself out there like that before, never truly bared his soul. He still felt the rush; still felt one with the melody. And more, he felt no trace of his former misgivings, actually couldn't wait to play in front of an audience again.

"And my eyes, too, have been opened," Krampus said. "For I clearly see that mankind has not yet forgotten who they are. That deep down their wild spirit still burns. That they need only a little nudge to be set free." Krampus grinned, beamed. "And I will always be there to give them that nudge . . . in some shape or form, no matter what games the gods may play."

Jesse nodded; he hoped so. He'd never felt more alive, more connected with the world around him, and he fully understood that it was Krampus's Yule magic that had awakened these feelings. He inhaled deeply, savored the feeling, found he still felt the rhythm, that strange primitive beat from last night, it faintly pulsed through his entire being.

"Jesse, when the sun rises it will be a new day . . . the start of a new age of Yule. Yule will spread, my flock will grow, of this I am sure, and I wish only to have those who desire to serve near. Thus, I intend to release the Belsnickels from bondage . . . to return those that wish it back into their human flesh."

Jesse sat up straight, looked at Krampus in wide-eyed astonishment. "You can do that then? Change them back? Change *us* back?"

Krampus smiled. "Of course. It is my blood. I can call it back at any time."

Jesse could hardly believe his ears. He'd resigned himself to dying a Belsnickel. "Wow, no fucking kidding?"

"I intend to offer each of the Belsnickels a choice. I am starting with you. You have paid your debt to me. If you intend to kill this bad man, I believe you would prefer to do that as a free man . . . for him to see the true eyes of his slayer."

For Jesse, there was nothing to consider. To return to his own flesh, to have another chance with Linda—why, he'd do whatever was asked. He nodded wholeheartedly.

Krampus held out his hand. "Your knife."

Jesse fumbled in his pocket, plucked out the hunting knife, handed it to Krampus. Krampus pulled the knife from its sheath, tested the tip. "Give me your hand."

Jesse put his hand out, palm upward, and winced.

Krampus laughed. "Do not fret. It is but a mere drop that I need call home." Krampus pricked Jesse's fingertip. Touched the mark with his own finger, and closed his eyes. Jesse's body tingled from head to toe. Krampus opened his eyes, removed his finger, and there, on the tip, sat a smear of shimmering blood. Krampus licked it clean.

Jesse inspected his own finger. "That's it?"

"That is all."

Jesse didn't feel different. He examined his hands. His flesh was still a blotchy gray.

"It will take a little while," Krampus said. "For now we should . . ." His voice trailed off. He leaned forward, peering intently upward. His brow furrowed and slowly a look of alarm and confusion spread across his face.

Jesse followed his eyes; saw a star falling earthward.

"What's that?"

"No," Krampus said, and stood up fast. Geri and Freki both raised their heads, a low, menacing growl coming from deep in their throats. The shooting star headed their way, growing in size as it approached. Krampus stepped out into the yard, peering up at the pulsing light. "This cannot be so. Not now. Not so soon."

A voice fell upon them, little more than a whisper. "Krampus," it called. Jesse felt it more than heard it.

Krampus's face hardened. "No, this is not fair. Why could they not wait? Why could I not have but a bit longer?"

The two Yule goats snorted and began to stomp about in the snow. Krampus walked to them, snatched the mistletoe spear from its post on the sleigh. Stood a moment, absently stroking their necks, staring at the spear, his face tense, his eyes distant. Finally, he let out a great sigh, nodding as though coming to some profound decision, and walked quickly over to Jesse. "Here." He picked up the velvet sack, pushing it into Jesse's arms. "The keys? You still have my skeleton keys?"

Jesse patted his pocket. "Yeah . . . why? What's—"

"Jesse, it appears that I have misjudged, that my time here is to be far shorter than I had hoped. You must take the sack, get in your carriage, and go far away." He clutched Jesse's shoulder. "You are free now, so I must beg this of you. Please, do what you must to keep this sack out of his hands. Go deep into the mountains and bury it somewhere. Burn it if you have to. Just do not let him have it. Please."

"What? No! Why?"

"Baldr comes now, and with powerful allies."

"Baldr? But—"

"The game is rigged. A cruel joke. I will *not* run . . . not this time. There is no escape for me anyway. It should be interesting to see where this will all end." Krampus smiled. "Do you not agree?"

Jesse tried to say more, but Krampus shook his head. "Jesse, make haste. Go now or the chance will be lost." Krampus led him down the stairs, pushed him toward the side of the building. "Go!" Krampus called. *"Hurry!"*

Jesse stumbled around the corner, stopped, and looked back, found himself transfixed by the golden orb-shaped glow. Krampus faced the light, his tall shadow stretching out long behind him. He raised the spear, pointing it at the orb. "I am Krampus," he stated solemnly. "The Yule Lord. I will hide in caves no longer." The two wolves slunk over, stiff-legged, fur bristling, and stood on either side of Krampus.

There came a sound, soft and low, yet it blocked out all others, a chorus of a thousand voices joined together in a hymn. Krampus held his ground, pulled himself up to his full height, shoulders back, eyes clear and resolute.

The orb alighted upon the snow between two apple trees, the golden glow fading away, revealing three figures. Santa Claus stood in the center, dressed in heavy white robes trimmed in thick fur. His long beard and hair loose of braid fluttered in the light morning breeze. He was framed on either side by two winged men, or maybe women, impossible for Jesse to tell, as they shared features of both, their faces stern, beautiful, and terrible at the same time. A slight golden aura surrounding each of them, thin, wispy robes fluttered loosely about their lithe, elegant frames and white wings spread out from their backs. Long swords hung in gold scabbards strapped across their chest. Jesse wondered if they were angels, wondered what else they could possibly be.

One of them set eyes on Jesse, cold, penetrating eyes that weighed his very soul, that promised his due. Jesse's fingers bit into the velvet sack as a chill shot to his core, his throat constricted as though icy hands were about his neck. He stumbled away, struggling for breath, back around the church, out of sight of the terrible angels. The chill faded. He gasped, trying to regain his breath. *What the fuck was that?*

Go! Go! He heard Krampus's voice in his head. He didn't need to be told again, sure that things were going to end badly and there was nothing he could do other than get himself killed.

Jesse sprinted for Chet's truck, yanking the door open and throwing the sack into the passenger's seat. He hopped in, fumbled for the truck keys, jammed them into the ignition, and fired up the engine. Jesse shoved it into gear and stomped it. The big wheels spun in the icy mud, caught, and the pickup lurched forward, fishtailing back and forth, spraying mud as it plowed up the small drive.

He could still feel the chill on his neck, still hear that hymn, a thousand voices pursuing him. Jesse focused on keeping the vehicle out of the ditch as he careened onto the gravel road. He floored it and raced away, shooting down the road as fast as he dared, trying to push the voices from his head, wanting only to escape those terrible angels.

CHIEF DILLARD NOTICED the sun peeking at the horizon and glanced at his watch; it was just after seven A.M. *Shit, never gonna get out of here.* The fire crew was still hosing down parts of the church, which was just a waste of time, in Dillard's book, at least at this point, as the structure appeared a total loss. He would've left several hours ago, if not for the pileup. Seems Billy Tucker had tail-ended some teenage girl's jeep and then Johnny Elkins came along and plowed into the both of them. None of which would've happened if the three of them had been watching the road instead of the fire. Noel had been rushed off to the emergency room after sustaining burns along his arm while trying to keep Mrs. Powell from going back in the church after some precious hymn book. This left Dillard to take care of the mess, all while trying to keep the scene secure.

The sheriff had been no help, leaving a couple of hours earlier, him and his deputies out scouring the area for Jesse and that gang. *Fuck, that son of a bitch's probably snooping around the General's compound this very minute.* And on top of that Dillard still had Linda and Abigail to deal with. *Least they ain't going nowhere . . . least I hope not.* He felt his chest tightening. *Calm down . . . no way they could've gotten out of there. Shit, just too many loose ends . . . too many loose ends.* Dillard knew he didn't do well when things got out of his control and he couldn't remember things ever being more out of his control. He took off his hat, rubbed the side of his head. Wished he'd brought along a few of those pills.

The fire chief, John Adkins, came walking over. "You seem out of sorts, Dillard. Something bothering you?"

"Yeah . . . got a darn headache that just won't let up."

John looked at the burn mark on Dillard's face. "You ought to get that looked at."

"I will."

"Looks like all the bystanders are gone home," John said. "Don't see much reason for you to be standing out here in the cold. Why don't you head on home and get some sleep. A bit of shut-eye is the best thing I've found for a headache."

Shut-eye, Dillard thought. *Won't be getting any of that for a while. Not until I'm done with Linda and Abigail, anyway.* "Well, all right, if you think everything's under control."

"Looks that way to me."

Dillard bid the fire chief a good one, got in his patrol car, started up the engine, and got the defrost going, warming his hands up in the heater. He dropped it into gear and started home. *Gonna have to make it quick, just get in there and get this mess over and done with.*

SANTA CLAUS STEPPED forward. "Krampus, I gave you fair warning. Told you there would be no place to hide. You did not listen." His voice calm, almost melancholy, contrite even, no hint of anger or malice.

"The dead should not speak, for their words smell of rot," Krampus replied.

Santa shrugged. "It seems the gods do not wish me dead. It appears my destiny is bound to their whims and I am eternally condemned to play my role."

"Do not dare blame the gods for your own misdeeds. You have sold your soul. Sold it cheap."

"Cheap?" Santa replied, his voice somber. "The cost has been more than one can bear."

Krampus leveled the spear tip at Santa Claus. "How many times is your god willing to resurrect his little dancing dog? Come closer, my spear would like to find out."

"No, my friend, I will not be the one who dies, not this day. God will not allow it. Maybe one day my servitude will be finished, but until that time my sacrifices are for her glory."

"Stop playing the martyr, it does not suit you. You, Baldr, you are the villain in this fable. You have committed foul deeds, have stolen that which does not belong to you . . . betrayed all who have aided you. Fate will punish you."

"Fate? God? What is the difference? Either way, I am afraid it has already doled out plenty of woe. Once, I was as you. I thought I could build my own kingdom. Build it right under the noses of the gods. Instead all I have built is a prison. One from which there is no escape . . . not even through death."

Krampus snorted. "Should I shed a tear?"

"Death has taught me many things. But here is the truth, the only one that matters. God takes on many faces . . . many guises. But no matter which guise, she is *always* . . . *always* before, *always* after." Santa laughed harshly. "And that is the joke . . . on me, on you, on all of mankind. There is only the One God, has always been only the One God. All the gods that have been and that are, they are the same, all part of the One God. We are but pawns in her great game. We all serve her . . . even *you*. Beyond that, there are no answers . . . for that is the only one that matters."

Krampus mulled this over, then shook his head and spat loudly. "What absolute, utter dung. Losing your head has not been good for you. Go on, concoct tales to try and placate your own guilt, but do not try and sell me your fantasies. The truth, the only one that matters, is that you are a buffoon, a nitwit, a puppet, a tick upon God's wrinkled scrotum." Krampus laughed. "How can you even hold your head up? Where is your shame?"

Santa let out a long sigh. "Krampus, my dear old friend, there is no reasoning with you. There never has been. Your arrogance, your single-minded stubbornness makes you blind. All my efforts to save you were wasted, because you cannot leave the past behind, and thus have condemned yourself to extinction. And even now, in the face of all your failings, you are still too bullheaded to know when to call it a day."

"I am not your friend. And I do not seek an excuse to prostrate myself such as you. I am a lord, I kneel for no one. You, you are but a pathetic ass, and shall always be a pathetic ass, one who suckles upon the end of your god's cock like a gutter whore. I will kill you as many times as need be to be shed of your stench. Now, come hither. I hunger to taste your blood."

Santa shook his head, a contemptuous sneer upon his face. "Sadly, you still do not see what is right in front of you." He nodded to the two angels. They drew their swords, shimmering blades of silver light, and came for Krampus. The wolves shot forward, snarling, leapt for the angels. The angels' movements were quick, precise, their swords but blurs of silver. The blades passed through the wolves; there came no blood, no wounds, only a loud yelp, and a second later both wolves lay dead upon the ground.

"More death, more murder!" Krampus cried. "How much blood does it take to placate your god?"

"Krampus?" Isabel called. She stood on the porch, clutching the door frame, her eyes wide and terrified. Vernon and Chet leaned out the door behind her. There came a wild cry, and Wipi and Nipi pushed through them, running for the angels, spears raised.

The angels faced the Belsnickels.

"Wait!" Krampus shouted, raising his hand to Wipi and Nipi. "Stay back." The Shawnee halted, poised, glaring at the angels. "There is nothing here for you but death."

The Yule Lord pointed his spear at Santa. "So, the son of the great Odin shows his true face at last, hides behind the skirts of angels. Come, coward. *Face me!*" Krampus came for Santa Claus, tried to dart around the angels. The angels intercepted him, brought their swords up and down in a great arc. Krampus made to block the silver blades, but the swords passed through his spear, through his arm, and down his torso. Searing, biting cold followed their path, yet they clove nothing, not spear, arm, nor torso. Still, the pain was beyond his experience. He grit his teeth, glared at the angels, determined to keep his feet.

The angels exchanged troubled looks.

"I still stand!" Krampus taunted, letting loose a mad laugh. "Seems your great god is not so great!"

They struck him again.

Krampus roared, his voice thundering across the icy landscape, shaking limbs and knocking snow from the church eaves. The sound blocked out the song of the angels. They flinched as though struck. Krampus rushed them, driving into the foremost angel, knocking one into the other, knocking them to the ground.

He headed for Santa, his breath bellowing out in blasts of steam and spittle. "You will never be shed of me," Krampus snarled. "Not so long as a single man still lives . . . for I am the wild spirit that dwells within their breast. And there is nothing, nothing you nor your god can ever do to change that!" He stumbled onward, spear leveled at Santa's chest.

Santa Claus backed away, his contemptuous sneer replaced by dread. He stumbled, fell, but before Krampus could close the distance, the angels were upon him. They struck the Yule Lord again, and again, their swords carving paths of numbing cold through his body. The world began to fade, to lose its color and density, sounds muffled as though coming from behind a wall. Still he pushed onward, one step, another—each step harder than the last as they continued to strike and stab.

The Yule Lord dropped to one knee, then to his hands, panting, the world now ghostly shades of gray. Yet he persisted, crawling, one hand after the next, determined to put the spear through Santa's heart.

Krampus collapsed. The angels did not relent.

"Wait," Santa called, climbing to his feet and stepping forward.

The angels stopped and Santa Claus knelt, prying the spear from Krampus's fingers. He stood, slid a boot beneath the Yule Lord, and flipped him onto his back. Krampus glared up at him.

"You are a most mulish beast," Santa spat. "But your time is done."

With supreme effort, Krampus managed to laugh—a wild, mocking laugh.

Santa raised the spear high and drove it into Krampus's heart.

All the pain disappeared. Krampus found himself light as the air. He began to drift. The world now so faint he could barely see the outlines of the figures around him, their voices came as from far down a tunnel.

Wipi let out a wild, mournful howl and attacked. *"Stop!"* Krampus shouted, but his voice was small, only an echo. No one heard him.

The angels cut Wipi down, came for Nipi.

Krampus didn't see what happened after that, the gray shapes, the voices, all of it faded away, leaving nothing.

JESSE HIT THE highway and raced north toward Goodhope. Until that very moment, his focus had solely been on getting away, but now he realized he wasn't getting away, he was going somewhere and that somewhere was Dillard's house.

He had no idea how much time he had. Was he on Santa's death list? Had God condemned him for his role? How did one escape the wrath of God? He had no answers, he only knew he was still alive, and so long as he was breathing, he might still have a chance to do something about Dillard.

With the General gone, it was only between them now. *Am I gonna shoot him?*

Jesse thought back to when Dillard challenged him to do that very thing. How many times had he wished for that chance again? If he did get the chance, what would he do? *One thing's for certain, gonna see to it he never hurts Linda or Abi again.* Abigail's scream echoed in his mind, the terror in her eyes. *I'll at least blow his knees out . . . take him down a notch or two. Hard to beat a woman from a wheelchair. Hell yes, it is.*

Jesse drove fast, but not recklessly. It was early Sunday morning, so other than the occasional big rig, the road belonged to him. He made good time, hitting the edge of town just as dawn's glow began to spread across the eastern sky. This time he slid up the river road that ran behind Dillard's house, hiding the vehicle in the trees.

He killed the engine, started to get out, stopped. *Slow down. Don't fuck this up again.* Jesse slipped out the Colt, double-checked that it was fully loaded, and shoved it into his pocket. His eyes fell upon the velvet sack; he stared at it for a long moment. *What am I supposed to do with that? Fuck, for all I know it might lead Santa and his monsters right to me.* He shook his head. *Have to figure it out later.*

He quietly pushed the door shut, moved quickly from tree to tree, toward the back of Dillard's house, stopping every dozen yards or so to look and listen. He held the gun out, finger on the trigger—steady and ready. Jesse wasn't counting on God or luck this time; he was counting on himself.

The kitchen and dining room lights were on. His heart sped up—someone was home. He followed the hedges around the shed then up to the garage. He peeked around the front of the house. No sign of the cruiser or the Suburban. Linda's sad little Ford Escort still sat in the drive and, judging by the clumps of snow around it, hadn't been moved in a long while.

Jesse returned round the house, deciding the back garage door would make the best entrance. The door was locked. He tugged out the skeleton keys. The first key let him in. He hit the light and found Dillard's Suburban inside. The hood was cold. Jesse took a deep breath, aware that Dillard may be home after all.

Everything in the garage was neat and tidy, all the tools in their outlined spots on the peg board, the boxes labeled and stacked evenly along the shelves. His eye fell on a sewing box with red roses, and he froze. Chet had at least been telling the truth about the sewing box. Jesse wondered if it were all true. *Keep going.* He started away, and stopped. *I gotta know the truth of it.*

Jesse leapt over to the box and popped the lid up. Within sat a jewelry box, a bouquet of dried flowers, folded lace, and a few articles of women's clothing. The wedding portrait of Ellen Deaton, framed in simple black wood, lay atop the lace. Ellen had indeed been a striking beauty in her day, smiling brightly, the joyful smile of a woman with her entire life ahead of her.

Jesse flipped the frame, twisted the pins, and popped out the back. A Polaroid fell onto the lace. Jesse sucked in a quick breath. "Shit." It was Ellen, but the woman in the Polaroid lay upon a gold-slate floor in a pool of blood. She stared up with wide blank eyes, her neck slit open. Her top had been torn away and the angry slashes and puncture wounds had turned her breasts into something unrecognizable.

Jesse spun away, leaving Dillard's morbid shrine behind. *"Linda,"* he whispered, his heart racing. He'd known Linda was in trouble, but until that very moment he had not believed, had not allowed himself to truly believe that Dillard was capable of such savagery. Jesse tried to push the image from his mind.

He darted to the door leading into the house; it was unlocked and he slipped in. The kitchen light was on. Again he froze, his heart hammering in his chest. A skillet lay on the floor, a glass of milk spilled across the counter. He spotted the overturned chairs in the dining room, darted through the living room, down the hall, gun out and ready. The bedroom doors were open. He eased up, peering into one, then the next, searched every room and every closet, found no one.

He returned to the hall, spotted Linda's clothes and Abigail's toys, pushed up in front of the door. The flooring drew his eye and he realized why at once: The tiles were gold slate, just like in the Polaroid. El-len had died right here, right where he was standing. *That picture will hang Dillard. Send him away for a long time. Don't you dare leave here without it.*

Jesse gave the bathroom a fleeting glance, blinked, and looked again. He flipped on the light. Duct tape and a knife sat on the vanity. He gasped, grasping their meaning right away, but he also saw his own hat, his hairbrush, and the screwdriver from his truck. It took him a moment to understand that Dillard planned not only to kill Linda and Abigail, but to pin it on him. It was as though someone had punched him in the gut. *Am I too late?* He tried to push the thought from his mind, but his eyes kept returning to the duct tape and knife. "No! Oh, fuck no!" He stumbled out of the bathroom and into the living room. *Where are they?* He spied the door to the basement and his heart went cold. "Oh, God." He leapt over to the door, threw the bolt, rushed down the steps, thinking of the picture of Ellen the whole way down, of the bloody ribbons of flesh across her chest. *No. No. No.*

He saw the freezer shoved up against the storm door and had his first shot of hope. He banged on the door. "Linda! Linda! Abigail!"

"Jesse?" He heard her then, it was Linda. "Jesse?"

He shoved the freezer out of the way, yanked the door handle. It was locked. He banged on the metal door. "Linda, it's me! It's Jesse!"

The latch turned, the door opened a crack, and Linda's terrified face peeked out. He yanked the door open and threw his arms around her. She hugged him back, hard and tight. She began to sob.

Jesse saw Abigail, pressed back in the corner, her big eyes scared and unsure. Jesse let go of Linda. "Abi. Abi, honey. It's all okay. All okay now." Abigail burst into tears. Jesse scooped her up, held her tight, pressed his face into her hair, and closed his eyes, inhaling her scent. And for that moment, for that second, it was all he needed in the whole world.

DILLARD PULLED INTO his driveway, cut the lights, and killed the engine. He sat there a moment longer, rubbing the bridge of his nose.

All he wanted to do was take another dose of Imitrex and curl up in bed
for twelve hours, only way he'd found to get rid of a migraine. But that
wasn't gonna happen. Not with the sheriff nosing around Goodhope.
He needed to take care of Linda and get back over to the General's as
soon as he could.

Dillard headed inside, stepping softly to avoid any jarring movements as he mounted the front porch and entered the house. He closed
the door gently behind him, careful not to make any loud noise that
would set off the flare between his eyes. He found his way into the
bathroom, pulled the bottle of Imitrex out of the cabinet, and took two.
He caught sight of the dark circles under his eyes, at the angry red
grease burn along his temple, and doubled the recommended dosage.

He stared at the duct tape and knife. "Fuck, got a lot to do." Now
that he'd had a bit of time to think, Dillard realized he didn't need
a sledgehammer to get the girls out, just a few tools to unscrew the
hinges and the steel door should pop right off. He left the bathroom,
heading for the garage, made it two steps and stopped cold. He heard
voices. Dillard peered into the living room and the air left him—the
door to the basement stood wide-open. Footsteps, someone was coming up the stairs. His hand dropped to his pistol. He clicked his radio
off and slipped back into the shadow of the hall.

Linda came up first, followed by Jesse carrying Abigail in one arm,
a revolver held loosely in his right hand. Abigail clung tightly to Jesse's
neck, the top of her head pressed against his cheek.

Dillard let them walk past, then slipped up behind them, shoving
his pistol into Jesse's back. "Drop it, Jesse! Drop it *right* now!"

Linda let out a cry.

Jesse tensed and there came a second when Dillard thought sure the
fool would try something. He didn't, just froze and dropped his gun. It
hit the carpet with a solid thud.

"All of you, over to the table. Keep your hands out."

They did as ordered. Dillard tugged his gloves out of his jacket,
slipped them on, stooped, and picked up Jesse's gun, shoving it into his
pocket.

Abigail began to cry.

"Dillard," Linda said. "Oh, God, Dillard. Please think about—"

"Shut the fuck up, Linda."

Dillard couldn't believe his luck. He had all three of them, and even through his migraine, the perfectness hit him. He would shoot Jesse first, then use Jesse's gun to kill the two girls. All he had to tell investigators was he'd come home and found Jesse standing over their dead bodies, then, when Jesse tried to shoot him, he fired first. He couldn't have arranged it better if he'd planned the whole thing out. Every person who was connected to the General would be dead, there'd be no witnesses, no one left to tie him to the General in any way. Dillard smiled, couldn't help it. Just needed a clean shot on Jesse; didn't want to risk screwing everything up by accidentally hitting Abigail with a bullet from his gun, or splattering Jesse's blood all over her. That would never get past forensics.

"Put her down," Dillard said calmly.

"Dillard . . . dammit," Jesse said, his voice tense and tight. "You don't have to do this."

"Put . . . her . . . down."

Keeping his right hand up, Jesse let Abigail slide to the ground. "Go to Mommy," Jesse whispered. Abigail ran to Linda. Linda pulled her around, shielding her.

"Keep those hands *up*," Dillard snapped. Linda brought her hands back up, they were shaking.

"Jesse, turn around . . . nice and slow." He intended to shoot Jesse from the front, to be sure it looked like self-defense. "Keep them hands up."

Jesse turned, looked Dillard straight in the eye. "The moment you pull that trigger you're a dead man."

"And how's that?"

"They're out back, Dillard. The whole group, all heavily armed."

Dillard felt his blood go cold; the mutilated bodies at the General's compound flashed in his head. He was certain Jesse was lying, yet couldn't help a quick glance out the patio window.

"There are three men out back," Jesse said. "The rest are down on River Road. You pull that trigger and they'll be all over you. They've been looking for you, Dillard. They know it was you that killed their friends."

Dillard started to pull the trigger. Hesitated. Fought to clear his head. *He's fucking with me.*

"We're all in this shit together, Dillard. Ain't nobody gonna be singing about any of it. If I was to turn you in I might as well turn myself in. Just let us go."

Dillard felt flushed, his eyes watery. He blinked rapidly to clear his vision, noticed a tremor in his hand, couldn't tell if it was on account of the migraine, lack of sleep, or just plain nerves. All of the above, he guessed.

"If you head out the front door right now," Jesse continued, "before they catch on, you just might get out of here alive. But you better make it quick, they could come walking in any second."

"Bullshit."

"The General didn't believe me either . . . he's dead now. Dillard, you don't want to fuck with these guys."

He's lying, you know it, Dillard thought. Yet Jesse sounded so damn sure of himself. There was steel in his eyes, he seemed deathly calm, his voice steady as though he were the one holding the gun. Dillard became very aware that this wasn't the same Jesse he'd kicked around for all these years.

"I'll give you Ellen's picture back," Jesse said.

"What? What did you say?"

"I was gonna use it to blackmail you."

"What picture?"

"You know what picture. The one of your wife. The one where you cut her throat wide-open. The one you kept behind the wedding photo."

Dillard felt the room reeling, wanted to sit down. *He can't be making this up. Got to be on the inside somehow. A double-cross? Who? They were all dead—Chet? Don't recall seeing Chet's body. Had Chet sold them out? The guns, the photo . . . fuck, who else? Chet hated the General. Had he teamed up with those Charleston boys? Was Chet out there right now?*

"It's in my breast pocket." Jesse nodded with his chin. "You want to get it or you want me to?"

Dillard blinked rapidly, tried to keep his eyes focused, glared at Jesse. "Give it to me," Dillard hissed. "Give it to me *now!*"

Jesse lowered his hand slowly to his pocket, slid in a few fingers, a few perfectly sound fingers. *What?* Dillard did a double take, glanced rapidly back and forth between Jesse's hands. All of Jesse's fingers were fine, just fine. *How . . . no? That's not possible. Why, I broke them—felt them snap.* Nothing made sense. Blood thundered in Dillard's ears, he felt sure his head was about to split open.

Jesse pulled out his hand. His fingers were covered in sparkling sand. "Sorry, it's in my other pocket."

This is all wrong. Shoot him, just shoot him!

Jesse flicked his fingers, fingers that should have been twisted and broken. Dillard felt a few grains of sand hit his face, his vision blurred, the room began to spin. Jesse moved, and Dillard fired, pulled the trigger two times, then he was falling, falling into darkness.

PAIN—DEEP, SHARP PAIN—PULLED Dillard out of the darkness. He cried out, opened his eyes, found himself on his belly in his living room. He tried to sit up, realized his legs were bound, his hands cuffed behind his back. His finger throbbed, felt on fire, felt like someone had just broken it.

"That was for Abigail."

Dillard blinked; Jesse came into focus.

Jesse sat on one of the dining-room chairs, staring at him with hard, steely eyes. A large black velvet sack rested against his leg and the plastic bag from the bathroom lay at his feet—the duct tape, knife, and hammer spilling out onto the carpet. Jesse held a gun pointed at Dillard's face.

Dillard had, at one time, given Jesse a gun and dared him to shoot him; he'd never have given the man before him now a gun. *Never.*

The barrel of the gun came down on top of Dillard's skull. Blinding bright pain racked his head. He pressed his eyes shut, squeezing tears down his cheek, the pain drumming in his ears.

"That's for Linda."

"Ah . . . *fuck!*" Dillard cried, tasting his own blood. "*Fuck!*"

Jesse stood, picked up the black sack, dropped it at Dillard's feet. Dillard stared dully at the sack, trying to make sense of its purpose.

"Put your legs into the sack," Jesse ordered, his voice completely devoid of emotion, like that of a hangman with a job to do.

Dillard squinted at Jesse. "What . . . in the sack? I don't get it."

"You're going to hell, Dillard. Gonna go hang out with the dead."

"Jesse, slow down. Let's just—"

"I'm gonna repeat myself this one time . . . this one time only. *Put your legs in the sack.*"

"Jesse, I don't know what you have in mind, but—"

Jesse drove his boot into Dillard's ribs.

Dillard screamed. *"Fuck!* Okay, okay. Whatever the hell you want!" Dillard tried his best to hook his feet into the opening. Jesse grabbed the lip of the sack, keeping the gun trained on Dillard as he lassoed it over Dillard's feet, tugging it up his legs, all the way up to his waist.

Dillard stopped, froze. Something was wrong, something was very wrong. He felt a chill, not like the air, but like liquid seeping into his flesh. It made his teeth hurt. "Hey, what's that? What's going on?" And at that moment he decided he wasn't going into the sack, that he'd take a bullet before he'd go into that sack. He twisted, kicked out wildly, but found nothing to kick against; it was as though he were floating. Jesse dropped his gun, grabbed hold of Dillard's collar, and yanked the sack up over Dillard's arms. Dillard tried to twist free, to throw his weight against Jesse, discovered he had no leverage. Jesse easily shoved him deeper into the sack, up to his neck and then . . . and then, just held him there. The only thing in the world keeping him from sinking all the way down was Jesse's hold on his collar.

Dillard heard voices, whispers like the sound of insects scuttling across the floor, and wailing, it came from deep within the sack. "What's that? What's that sound? What the fuck is it?"

"That's the dead . . . they're waiting for you."

Dillard's eyes threatened to leave their sockets. "Jesse, don't let go of me," he blubbered. "Please, for Christ's sake. Don't do this. I'm begging you, Jesse. *Please!*"

"People can live twenty-eight days without food before they starve to death. But you're a tough fellow. My money says you can make it at least thirty. That's thirty days in hell, thirty days with the dead singing you their song. Then . . . why then I guess you'll get to join their choir." Jesse let go of Dillard's collar, gave him a hard shove, pushing him deep into the sack.

There came a moment of darkness, of falling, then Dillard's feet struck something substantial, there came the chink and clink of metal on metal and he found himself tumbling and sliding. He crashed into something hard, knocking dust and brittle shards onto his chest and face.

He spat, tried to shake the debris from his face, blinked open his eyes, and found a skull, its cranium busted open, lying on his chest and staring sadly back at him. He inhaled sharply, filling his nostrils with the pungent odor of sulfur and dry rot. He glanced wildly about and was greeted by a hundred more toothy grins, skulls and bones of every sort, most black, as though burnt, all covered in gray ashy dust. The very walls and ceilings appeared to be composed of nothing but bones and they went on as far as he could see up and down the gloomy caverns and corridors.

The handcuffs bit into his wrist as he struggled to sit up, his fingers struck cold metal and he glanced down, found he sat atop a mound of coins, not any coins, these were gold and triangular. The pile continued upward, building into a tall pyramid, disappearing into the smoky gloom just above him. It was the way out, he was sure of it. He struggled to get his feet under him, tried to kick and worm his way up the pyramid, but the coins shifted beneath his feet, causing him to slide farther and farther down the cavern. Finally he gave up and just lay there panting, trying to stifle his sobs, trying to get some control of himself.

He felt them. He couldn't see them but he knew they were there, moving around him. Not much more than a breeze at first, the dust stirring upon the bones. He heard them, the whispers, calling his name. As the sound grew, so did the wind. It began to take substance and as it did, he saw them . . . the *dead*. He saw their tortured smiles, their woeful eyes. And all those dead eyes were on him, all so very glad to see him.

Dillard screamed, and screamed, and screamed, and the dead . . . the dead screamed along with him.

JESSE STARED INTO the sack, could only see the smoldering darkness, but thought he heard screaming, far away—it sounded a lot like Dillard. He wanted to smile, but found he was too sickened by all of it.

Jesse left the living room, and peeked out the front, making sure Linda hadn't returned. He'd sent her and Abigail off to Linda's mother's in her little Ford while he took care of things. She'd started to protest, but when Abigail began to cry, she'd left.

Jesse went out into the garage, picked up the Polaroid of Ellen, and brought it inside, leaving it on the floor next to the tape and knife. He wanted to be sure the police found it, that they knew just what kind of person Dillard really was. He snatched a hand towel from the kitchen and wiped his prints off the Polaroid, the tape, and the knife, then walked through the house, wiping down any surface he remembered touching. He felt he was being overly cautious, because without a body there was no crime. Unless, that was, some very clever detectives figured out how to search the bowels of hell.

Jesse had taken Dillard's police radio, gathered it up along with the things Dillard had taken from his truck, grabbed Krampus's sack, and brought them all with him as he headed out through the garage.

Jesse stepped out into the morning, the sun peeking over the nearby hills, lighting up the river fog. He started for the woods, for the truck, when he heard a snort and froze. There, just across the lawn, stood Santa Claus in front of the Yule goats and sleigh. The two angels, those terrible angels, stood on either side of him.

Jesse glanced to the woods, wondered how far he could get before they caught up with him.

"There is no place to run," Santa said. "There is no hiding from God."

Jesse let out a great sigh; at least he'd taken care of Dillard, at least he could die now knowing he'd done that much for Linda and Abigail.

"I waited," Santa said. "Until you were finished. I did not have to do that."

Jesse looked at him, puzzled.

"I could have intervened, but your deed needed to be done. Now, there is a little less evil in this world. Despite what Krampus may have told you, I have only love for mankind . . . my charity comes from deep within my heart."

Santa extended his hand. "The sack."

Jesse looked at the two angels, their piercing eyes, and swords of light, and knew he had no choices left. He brought the sack to Santa.

"And my keys?"

Jesse tugged the skeleton keys from his jacket, handed those over as well. Santa gave him a nod and climbed aboard the sleigh.

"Is Krampus dead?"

Santa looked Jesse in the eye. "Yes. He is gone from this world."

"You didn't have to kill him."

"You did not have to send that man to Hel."

Jesse was quiet for a moment. "Yes, I did. That had to be done."

"You should understand then . . . that there are things that have to be done, no matter how horrible." Santa gave him a judicious smile and seated himself, popped the reins, and the two goats tromped forward and climbed into the morning sky, leaving Jesse alone with the two terrible angels.

The angels watched him with their ominous, condemning eyes. Jesse knew they were about to take his life, maybe more. But they only lifted their heads heavenward and drifted upward, disappearing into the blinding rays of the morning sun.

Chapter Eighteen

GOD'S WILL

Jesse sprinted through the woods. He'd asked Linda to give him about an hour then call the sheriff, to send him over to Dillard's. Told her to tell the police the truth, everything exactly as it had happened, except for that last bit with Dillard, to instead say she'd got out of the basement on her own and driven home, and let him worry about filling in the blanks.

Jesse reached Chet's truck and climbed in. Cranked it up and headed over to the General's compound. The plan was to trade out Chet's truck for his own. He knew this could be the tricky part. He had no way of knowing if his truck was even still there or if anyone else might be around.

His truck *was* still there and he saw not a soul. Jesse wiped his prints off Chet's keys and steering wheel, grabbed Dillard's police radio, and got out. He walked quickly up to the side door of the motor bay. Jesse used his sleeve to open the door and headed up the short hall. He hesitated there, knowing what awaited him inside. He swallowed and pushed the door inward.

Jesse tried not to look at them, the mangled bodies, but did. Surprised to find he actually felt bad for many of them, men he'd known most of his life. They'd not all been rotten, at least not so rotten as to deserve what came.

He wiped his prints off Dillard's radio and dropped it just inside the door. Jesse figured the police would find plenty of evidence connecting Dillard to the General once they started looking, but a little insurance wouldn't hurt.

Jesse left the building, hopped into his truck. The keys were still in the ignition. He gave them a twist and was rewarded with a grinding noise. "Not good," he said, knowing the old F-150 had been sitting too long. He held his breath and gave it another go, nursing the gas. It turned over once and quit. "C'mon, you can do it." It started on the third try and Jesse dropped it into reverse and got out of there.

TWENTY MINUTES LATER, Jesse turned down the narrow drive to the old church. He pulled around the building and hit the brake. Krampus lay upon his back in the snow, the frost sparkling off his great mane. Wipi lay facedown next to the Yule Lord, stiff and unmoving. Nipi knelt at their side.

Jesse cut the engine, got out, walked slowly up, searching for Isabel. Seeing Nipi still alive gave him hope, but he found no sign of her or any of the others. He stepped round the wolves and over to Nipi. The brothers were human now, their flesh once again butternut-brown. There were no wounds on Wipi, or the wolves, but a great gash glistened across Krampus's chest and a circle of crimson snow spread round his body.

Jesse knelt next to Nipi. "Sorry about your brother."

Nipi seemed not to hear.

Jesse studied the Yule Lord's face, noticed that even in death Krampus kept that half-smile of his, as though he had one trick left up his sleeve yet. But his eyes were pale, all the fire gone. "It's a shame," Jesse spat. "A real goddamn shame. Hell if it ain't."

Jesse sat a hand on Nipi's shoulder. "Where's Isabel?"

Nipi glanced around as though unsure where he was, shrugged.

Heavy clouds drifted in and the sun slowly faded from Krampus's face. Jesse knew it would start snowing again soon. He stood, headed up the steps and into the church. He blinked as his eyes adjusted to the gloom and found her sitting in front of the potbelly, her hands clutched together between her knees, staring at the stove. No fire burned, and she was shivering. Almost all traces of being a Belsnickel were gone, and the first thing that struck him was just how young she looked, a bit boyish, with a sprinkle of freckles across her nose, but pretty in her own way.

Jesse sat down next to her. Isabel didn't look up, but when he put his arm around her, she clutched his hand and leaned against his shoulder.

They sat in silence for a long while; finally, Isabel spoke. "They murdered him. Murdered all of them. How can murder be God's will?"

Jesse didn't have an answer, all he knew to do was to clutch her tighter. Isabel pressed her face into his shoulder and began to sob.

After a bit, Jesse noticed that the cardboard box where they'd stashed the guns and cash still sat next to the piano. "Be right back," he said and walked over to the box. All the money appeared to still be there.

"Isabel . . . where's Chet and Vernon?"

"Not sure." Isabel talked without looking up. "As soon as Krampus fell . . . well, the both of them, they lit on out of here . . . just run off. Guess I should've run off, too, but I didn't. Just waited for those horrible angels to come kill me. But they didn't seem much concerned with me. Santa took the sleigh and left . . . and them angels . . . they went along with him."

Jesse pulled out the guns, wiped off his prints, and left them on the piano. He folded the top on the box down over the cash and tucked it beneath his arm. He walked over to Isabel. "We have to go."

She looked up at him and he was struck by how green her eyes were.

"It'll be trouble if we're found here," he said.

She nodded and stood up.

They headed out the door, down the steps. Isabel walked over to Krampus's body, knelt next to Nipi, put her arm around him. Jesse headed over to the truck, tossed the box into the cab, then came back over and stood with them. "Isabel . . . Nipi . . . c'mon now. We gotta go."

"Can't just leave them here like that," Isabel said. "Wouldn't be right."

Jesse let out a sigh. "No, guess not. Guess we should find a better place than this for Wipi and Old Tall and Ugly. Nipi, how about it? Sound like a plan?"

Nipi nodded.

THEY LOADED WIPI and Krampus into the back of the truck. It surprised Jesse that the Yule Lord didn't weigh more. He wasn't exactly light, but still, he seemed lessened, as though the body were a mere husk without the weight of the Yule Lord's great spirit.

They drove the bodies up into the hills, the same hills where Krampus had been chained for all those years. It took most of the morning and two trips for the three of them to carry the two bodies up to the cave. Nipi led them to a pile of stones in the rear of the cavern. Makwa's spear and bear hide lay atop the stones. They placed the bodies next to Makwa's, with Krampus in the middle, and also covered them with stones. They laid Wipi's cloak atop his stones, but the Yule Lord's stones remained bare.

They stood staring silently at the three mounds.

Jesse broke the silence. "Don't guess he would want a prayer?"

Isabel shook her head and a small smile touched her lips. "No, but I know what he would like."

Together they gathered up an armload of mistletoe, then Nipi cut a handful of birch branches. Isabel tied them into a bundle. She arranged the mistletoe around Krampus's mound and sat the switches on top. By the time she finished it was beginning to snow.

"We need to get on back before we get stuck up here," Jesse said.

Isabel nodded and they headed out of the cave. Nipi stayed behind.

"Nipi," Isabel called. "C'mon, we need to go."

Nipi shook his head.

"You can't stay here," Isabel said.

"Yes, it is where I belong."

"You don't belong in some smelly old cave. You're human again, in case you haven't noticed, and you're gonna catch your death of cold."

"I have lived many lifetimes. Have been honored to serve the mighty Yule Spirit. If the Great Fathers call me home . . . I am ready."

He tapped the bag. "There's around twenty thousand dollars cash there. Won't go far these days, but should help you get on your feet. Oh . . . and here." He handed her a wadded-up piece of paper. "This here's Linda's mother's phone number. Her phone might not be working just yet, but if you get in a fix, run out of money, if anything, I mean anything, comes up you don't hesitate to give—"

She put her fingers up to his mouth. "Jesse. It's okay. I'm gonna be all right."

Jesse let out a long sigh.

"Jesse . . ."

"Yeah?"

"Thank you. Thank you for looking out for me."

He grinned. "Of course."

Isabel leaned forward, surprised Jesse with a kiss on his cheek. Before he could respond, she opened the door and hopped out.

"Wait," he called. "Jeez, you forgot your bag." He held it up.

She came back, trying not to meet his eyes, but he could see her tears.

"Hey," he said. "Don't be forgetting that snipe hunt I promised you."

She shook her head and grinned, took the bag, and headed away toward the church. Jesse watched her mount the short flight of steps, pausing on each step. She sat her hand on the door, stood that way for a long moment before finally pushing the door inward and walking inside.

Jesse caught a glimpse of soft, warm light, of people holding hymn books, the organ and the sound of their song drifted across the parking lot. The church door swung slowly shut and he was left alone with the falling snow.

Jesse waited close to an hour. When she didn't come back out, he figured she just might be okay.

VERNON FOLLOWED THE railroad tracks north along the Coal River, doing his best to avoid the icy patches as he trudged through the hard-packed snow. He'd forgotten the true bite of winter, but now, returned to human flesh, he clutched himself, trying to stifle his shivering. Dusk approached, and with it falling temperatures. Vernon wondered bitterly if, after all his trials, his final fate would be to freeze here alone, along this desolate river.

He'd been trapped up in those hills for close to a hundred years and realized anyone he'd ever known would now be dead, the world he once knew gone. He had no money, no real idea of where he was headed, other than as far away from Krampus and those terrible angels as he could get. Yet, he couldn't help but smile. *I am free!* He inhaled deeply, filling himself up with the feeling. *I can go anywhere. Do whatever I like.* He laughed. *At least until I starve or freeze to death.*

A freight train headed down the tracks toward him. Vernon climbed the embankment and watched it clang past. He smelled grease in the air, his stomach rumbled. He glanced up the highway, spotted a familiar structure, and started toward it.

Horton's didn't appear to be open yet, but a light shone from inside and a vehicle sat out front. Vernon hoped it belonged to Horton, because the two of them had hit it off pretty good the night before, well enough that he felt sure the man would let him come inside and warm up, perhaps even give him a bite to eat.

Vernon noticed that the fresh buds, new grass, and flowers about the place had all withered, as though in mourning for the Yule Lord. Vernon hated to admit it, but a part of him actually felt bad that the old goat had come to such an ill demise. He sighed, stepped up onto the porch, and noticed a COOK WANTED sign propped in the window. He plucked the sign off the sill and carried it inside with him.

"THEY'RE NOT REAL happy with you, Jesse," Elly said.

Jesse leaned back in the steel office chair, peered through the glass partition into the lobby of the sheriff's office. He could see Sheriff Wright talking with the state investigators; the conversation didn't appear to be going very well.

"Can't please everyone, I guess."

She smirked at him. Elly had gone to school with Jesse, he liked the way she played guitar, and at one point they'd even collaborated on a song or two. These days she worked for the sheriff. "Every news agency in the country is covering it," she said. "They got the governor breathing down their necks to come up with some answers. Why, you should've heard 'em on CNN this morning, going on and on about all them mutilated bodies and speculating on rampant gang warfare in rural West Virginia." She snorted. "Talking about Boone County like we're some kinda Third World country."

Jesse just shook his head.

"Oh, here, one last thing." She pulled a blue form out from the stack in front of her and handed it to him with a pen. "Need your John Hancock right there if you want your stuff back."

Jesse signed the form and she handed him a manila envelope.

"So that's it?" he asked. "I'm free to go?"

"Looks like it." She smiled. "Sheriff ain't none too happy about it though. He's just sure you know more than you're telling."

"Hey," Jesse asked in a casual tone. "Thought I overheard someone say Chet Boggs might've had something to do with all this mess?"

"All I know is they had me issue a statewide APB on him. But no one seems to have found him yet."

Jesse thought they were wasting time looking for Chet in West Virginia; thought they'd do better to look down Mexico way, or even Peru. Jesse opened the envelope, pulled out his wallet and keys.

"Chet's not the one I've been wondering about," Elly said. "I wanna know what happened to Chief Dillard Deaton. Last I heard they still hadn't found a clue of his whereabouts."

Jesse shrugged. "My bet's he's sitting in Hell right this minute wishing he'd been a nicer person."

She shook her head. "Still don't surprise me none that he was wound up in this mess. There was something offputting about that man." Elly leaned forward and whispered, "Don't tell no one I told you, but turns out they got some hard evidence linking him to his wife's death."

"You don't say."

"They found this photo of her . . . *dead* . . . I seen it." She wrinkled up her nose. "Gruesome. I sure hope you're right, I sure hope he *is* rotting in Hell right now."

"We're done then?" Jesse asked.

"Yeah, we are."

Jesse stood and she escorted him to the door and let him out into the lobby. The sheriff and investigators stopped talking when he came out. The sheriff gave him a hard look. "You remember what I said, Jesse. Things will go a whole lot easier on you if you just come clean with what you know."

"I'll be sure to keep that in mind, sheriff," Jesse said as he pushed out the door. "Now you have yourself a real fine day, you hear."

Jesse pulled into Linda's mother's driveway. He drove a Ford Ranger with the extended cab, not new, but newer, paid for in full. He parked, walked up onto the porch, and knocked on the door; a minute later, footsteps shuffled his way. "Just a sec," someone shouted. Polly Collins opened the door. "You got a haircut."

Jesse nodded. "I did at that."

"Looks sorta funny."

Jesse frowned.

"Bet you're not here to talk to me," she said.

"You'd make money on that bet."

"Well, I got something to say to you anyhow. I don't know what part you played in all that mess, but . . ." She bit at her lip, seemed to be searching for the right words. "Well . . . it's just . . . well, the way Linda tells it, sounds like she got herself in a bad spot . . . a really bad spot. I don't know exactly what it was you done about Dillard . . . don't ever need to know, but Jesse . . ." Jesse realized the old woman was choking up. She touched his hand. "I want you to know . . . I appreciate it." She smiled at him then, the first time she'd ever smiled at him. "Let me fetch Linda."

"Mrs. Collins, could you maybe do me a favor? Could you take Abigail out back for a bit, just need some time alone with Linda."

She nodded. "I can do that."

Jesse waited maybe a minute, felt more like ten. He noticed he was wringing his hands and made himself quit, shoving them deep into his pants pockets. This was the first time he'd seen Linda since that morning at Dillard's and he had no idea where he stood.

Linda pushed the screen door open and stepped out onto the porch. The two of them stood apart, neither speaking, neither seeming to know what to say.

Linda looked at his feet. "See you got yourself some new boots."

"Uh-huh."

"They're real nice."

"Yeah . . . Linda?"

"Yes."

"I'm heading to Memphis."

Her lips tightened. "Your music? You gonna go play your songs?"

He nodded. "Gonna go give it all I got and then some. No more honky-tonks. Gonna follow up with that DJ, see if he can get me some leads. If I can't land something in Memphis, I'm headed for Nashville."

"Jesse, that's wonderful. And it's about damn time. You're gonna do just—"

"Linda, you once asked me how you were supposed to believe in me if I didn't believe in myself. Well, I met this . . . this . . . uh . . . real tall fella just recently, and let's just say he opened my eyes to a whole lot of things. The long and short of what I am trying to say is I *do* believe in myself, my music . . . but I also believe in us . . . more than ever. And I was hoping that maybe you and Abigail might just wanna come along with me."

Her eyes brightened.

"I ain't saying it'll be easy, but I can assure you that I'm a different person now. I got a bit of cash tucked away, but more importantly . . . I got a plan. Whaddaya say? Think we're worth another try?"

She looked long and deep into his eyes, seemed to be searching for something. Jesse guessed she must've found it, because she nodded. "I'd like that, Jesse . . . like to give us another go."

He smiled and she hugged him, hugged him tight, and after a minute he felt her crying. "I'm sorry, Jess. I'm so sorry about . . . about all of it. I just didn't know—"

He put a finger on her lips. "Hush. None of that. If we go to Memphis, we start over. We leave all that behind. Deal?"

"Deal," she said.

Chapter Nineteen

YULETIDE

BOONE COUNTY, WEST VIRGINIA
One year later
The night before Christmas

Excerpt from the Boone Standard, *December 24*
by Contributing Editor Bill Harris

Nashville up-and-comer Jesse Walker played to a packed
house Saturday night, headlining the first-ever annual
Krampus Festival held at Horton's out on Route 3, near
Orgas. Horton White, the proprietor of Horton's and festival
organizer, says that the festival is a celebration of Winter
Solstice and ancient Yuletide traditions. Participants engaged
in folk dancing, body-painting, chanting and drum circles,
with the highlight of the evening being the massive Yule Log
bonfire. Prizes were awarded for best costumes. Activities
continued on well into the morning hours.

The festival was not without controversy, as the sheriff's
office received several complaints claiming a group of
intoxicated revelers dressed in furs, wearing chains, bells,
and horned masks, arrived in town and chased bystanders
with switches. Sheriff Wright confirmed reports of public
intoxication and nudity, but stated rumors of deputies
joining in on the festivities are greatly exaggerated. Reverend
Owen condemned the event, calling the festival a sinful and

shameful display of pagan heathenism and a pathway to eternal damnation. He warned that all God-fearing Christians should stay away.

The Krampus Festival is just the latest in the growing local fascination with the little before known mythical spirit of Krampus. Ever since the notorious and as-yet-unexplained incidents of last Christmas season, interest has spread statewide. But Boone County has all but claimed Krampus as their own, with souvenirs of the devilish character to be found in most local gift shops, including switches, cheap knock-offs of those infamous triangular gold coins, and T-shirts and mugs sporting cartoons of the fiendish Krampus, bearing such notable taglines as "I Believe in Krampus" and "Krampus Is Coming to Town."

Heavy clouds rolled across the hills as twilight turned to night. A string of Christmas lights came to life, blinking along the gutters of a small ranch home on the edge of town. A boy of about ten and his little sister, no more than eight, came out onto their porch. Their mother came along with them. The children each held a pair of old shoes and carried a sack of candies. They set the shoes on the step and carefully arranged the candy.

When they were done, the boy looked up at his mom. "You think Krampus will really come?"

"Might," she replied. "Might not. That's what they say. Right?"

The children nodded.

"Josh," the boy said. "He said that Krampus came to his house last year, said he actually saw him."

"Yep," the little girl added. "So did Charles. Susie said she saw him, too, but I don't believe her. She's a big fibber. But I believe Charles, because he had one of them funny gold coins."

"Yeah," the boy said excitedly. "So did Josh! He brought his to school and I actually got to hold it." He looked up at his mother again. "Mom, do you believe Krampus is real?"

"Well, it don't hurt none to believe. Now does it?"

"Nope, but it might not to. Josh said if you don't put out candy, Krampus will put you in his sack and give you a beating."

"Yeah," the girl said. "All the kids at my school said they were putting out candy, y'know . . . just in case."

Their mother grinned. "Well, it's a good thing you're putting out candy then. Wouldn't want either one of my children to get put in a sack and beat silly."

"I think he's real," the boy said.

"Me, too," the girl agreed.

"Well," the mom said. "If enough folks believe in a thing, I guess it becomes real enough. Don't it?"

THE SNOW FELL the whole night long that Christmas Eve, fell all across Boone County, across Goodhope and the surrounding hills. The snow blew about the entrance of a small cave cut into the rugged mountainside, swirled inside, and a few flakes even drifted far back to a mound of rocks surrounded by dried mistletoe.

From beneath the rocks came the sound of laughter, at first as light as a whisper, but as it grew in volume a small patch of snow about the entrance of the cave began to melt. A single flower poked its head up through the winter snow. The flower bloomed, fluttering to some unheard pulse, and the laughter swelled, deep and booming, echoing out from the cave. The wind and snow carried the sound down the valley and there were those the next morning who swore they heard it, swore it was Krampus, the Yule Lord. And they told their children they better be good, because Krampus . . . Krampus is coming to town.

AFTERWORD

In Search of Krampus

Several years ago my wife, Laurie (who is infinitely hipper than I), turned me on to a devil that prances about at Christmas, whipping naughty children with a birch branch. I was immediately smitten with the character. "Stuffs them into a sack and beats them bloody, you say? Tosses the really bad ones into the river? Takes some home to devour? *Please* . . . tell me more!"

My endearment for the horned beast only deepened as I discovered the abundance of vintage greeting cards portraying him cheerfully carrying bawling children to Hell in a barrel and spanking the bottoms of buxom women with fiendish delight. What was not to love?

I soon discovered that this holiday gem had a long and colorful history, that there are winter festivals called *Krampusnacht* in many Alpine villages, where participants don wonderfully wicked, handcrafted Krampus costumes then roam the streets, rattling chains and bells and chasing random victims with sticks and switches. These runs, called *Krampuslaufen,* are fueled (not surprisingly) by alcohol; schnapps being the customary offering to Krampus. I noted Krampus was often portrayed in the company of Saint Nicholas, the tall, thin saint adorned in his bishop vestments, carrying his ornate ceremonial staff and looking stern.

There was a lot that seemed not right here, at least by my North American perceptions of Christmas and Santa Claus traditions. I had a litany of questions, but foremost in my mind was . . . hey, what does Santa Claus think of this guy? What exactly is their relationship? Call me crazy, but to me it seems a bit disingenuous for Santa to have an evil imp brutalizing and kidnapping children while he's handing out gifts and shouting "Ho, ho, ho!" Who came first? Whose idea was it to work together? Were they doing the good cop/bad cop thing, like God and the Devil? Was Krampus Santa's slave? Were they pals or mortal enemies? Which leads to the question most every schoolboy would ask: Who would win in a fight? And it was these questions, especially the last, which inevitably led to the writing of this novel.

Thus began my search for the origins of these two seemingly diametrically opposed holiday figures. Working backward from modern perceptions through the vast variations of Santa and Krampus, I traced Yule traditions to their earliest pagan roots in the winter solstice. And for those who enjoy such things, I would like to share my findings, but with the disclaimer that, as with most ancient folklore, there are many versions, varying from country to country and even region to region. Here I have gathered together the most common threads from which I wove the mythos of this fable.

Who came first? Santa Claus or Krampus? It could be argued that they both sprouted from the same origins, but variations of Krampus far preceded any of the more humanized, charitable versions of Santa Claus.

Winter solstice and its associated celebrations date back long before the birth of Christ. Yule sprang from pagan winter festivals in Germanic regions, celebrating the rebirth of the land with feast and sacrifice, and tied into Odin's Wild Hunt and other Norse myths and legends. One of the more prominent symbols of Yuletide is the Yule Goat, which is one of the first manifestations of the Krampus that we so dearly know and love today.

From the beginning, Krampus represented the change of seasons, a nature and fertility god who chased away wicked spirits and assured a bountiful growing season in return for tribute. Later, he was assimilated into the evolving lore and legends of Germany and Austria. This lore spread into Croatia, Czech (Slovakia), Slovenia, Switzerland, and northern Italy. The original Yule Goat was said to be an ugly creature that frightened children while making certain that Yuletide traditions were carried out properly. Later, the Yule Goat, or Krampus, was also attributed with handing out Yule gifts.

In some legends, Krampus has been associated with or said to be a version of the Norse god Loki, who is at times portrayed as a horned, devilish trickster figure. These legends also suggest that Krampus carted children away to Hell, or Hel, Loki's daughter. These early manifestations had no association with Saint Nicholas.

Once Christianity came along, Krampus was cast, along with many other horned nature spirits, into the role of a demon or devil. Despite several attempts over the centuries by the church and some European governments to stamp out Krampus celebrations, Krampus and Yuletide have endured and, as with most pagan traditions, have been adopted (or as Krampus would argue, *stolen*) by and into their Christian counterparts, such as the bringing of evergreen trees and wreaths inside the home, and the leaving of gifts in socks or boots.

Santa Claus's origins can be traced back to early Norse mythology, and I seized upon historians' associations of Santa Claus with the white-bearded Odin. But after digging deeper, I felt Odin's son Baldr made a closer comparison. It is written that Baldr was loving, gentle-natured, gracious, and fair to behold, and that he spread charity and goodwill among the downtrodden—a Christ-like figure in many ways, including his death and rebirth. His legend fit perfectly into my tale, from his tragic death by a mistletoe spear at the hands of his blind brother Hoor (guided by Loki) to his subsequent imprisonment in Hel and eventual rebirth after Ragnarok and the fall of Valhalla.

As much of Europe transformed from paganism to Christianity, a few of their gods and spirits made the transition with them, in one form or another, but most were left behind and forgotten. This adaptation to a changing religious landscape also fit perfectly into what I was trying to depict.

Saint Nicholas as a Christmas figure is probably the first recognizable incarnation of our modern Santa Claus. Though the real Saint Nicholas died in 342, he was not recognized as a saint until the 800s, around the same time that Christmas was established as a holiday. He gained widespread popularity in the 1200s as pagan practices began to wane, and Christmas hit its stride in the late 1300s and 1400s. It was during this period that Krampus first became known as a Christmas devil and Saint Nicholas's slave.

In the 1500s, the gift-giving figure of Father Christmas rose in popularity, followed in the 1700s by the first mention of Santa Claus as "St. A. Claus." In 1809, the novelist Washington Irving wrote *A History of New York*, inventing the modern version of Santa Claus, followed shortly thereafter by Dr. Clement Moore's famous poem, "A Visit from St. Nicholas." The 1930s Coca-Cola ads by Haddon Sundblom established the current well-known, cheerful, chubby-faced Santa Claus in his bright (and conveniently Coca-Cola red) suit.

So it was this rich tapestry of legends and mythology that inspired my story. I discovered many other wonderful elements along the way and here are a few of them:

Angels: In Belgium, Germany, Poland, Ukraine, and Austria, angels often accompanied St. Nick on his Christmas runs. In the Czech and Slovak tradition, the angel is a protector of children against the devil.

Belsnickels: Another of the many variations on Krampus, the Belsnickel tradition was brought over to America by early German immigrants. Some of the Belsnickels were known to wear masks and dress in shaggy bearskin coats or skunk-skin caps. They often carried whips, sticks, or sometimes even shotguns, handing out treats and doling out punishment to children as they found befitting.

Boone County, West Virginia: Though the township of Goodhope is fictional, many of the other locations in this book are based on actual places in and about Boone County. Boone County captured my attention due to its long history of colorful characters, bandits, and musicians, such as the dancing outlaw Jesco White and his notorious family; singer-songwriter Billy Edd Wheeler; and the local, legendary one-man-band Hasil Adkins (see more below).

Geri and Freki: Odin's wolves.

Hel: Both the name of the Norse netherworld and its queen, Hel (Loki's daughter).

AFTERWORD

Huginn and Muninn: Odin's ravens.

Perchta: Female witch/spirit that roamed the midwinter countryside of Bavaria and Austria. Punished or rewarded children depending on their behavior during the year.

Spain: The Dutch tale goes that Saint Nicholas lives somewhere in Spain and arrives in Amsterdam each December by ship, to hand out presents to good girls and boys. I can certainly understand why Santa would rather live in Spain than the North Pole.

Tanngrisnir and Tanngnost: The goats that pulled Thor's chariot through the sky.

Hasil Adkins (1936–2005): Is famous for such songs as "No More Hotdogs," which includes the poetic line: "I'm gonna cut your head off, and you can eat no more hot dogs," and such timeless lyrics from the song "She Said" as:

> I wen' out last nigh' and I got messed up
> When I woke up this mornin', shoulda seen what I had
>   inna bed wi' me
> She comes up at me outta the bed, pull her hair down
>   the eye
> Looks to me like a dyin' can of that commodity meat . . .

In 2005, Hasil was deliberately run over in his front yard by a teenager on an ATV and he later died from his injuries.

Areas in Boone County, like so many other rural communities, are suffering from the tragic effects of the growing meth epidemic. Strip-mining is also taking a devastating toll on both the community and the land.

It has been a delight spending time with Krampus. I now feel a much closer kinship with him than his jolly counterpart. It is my hope that Krampus will continue to catch on around the globe and reclaim his rightful place as Yule Lord. If you share this sentiment, then be sure to leave out a few treats in your shoes this coming Yuletide and, who knows, you just might find a gold coin or two in return. If you don't . . . well, you've been warned—Krampus is coming to town.

Brom
Yuletide 2011

357

ACKNOWLEDGMENTS

To Diana Gill, for her downright supernatural instincts for story and character, as well as all of her hard work shepherding my musings along. I would be lost without her guidance. Thanks, Diana, for your editing voodoo.

To the phenomenal Julie Kane-Ritsch, for her continued friendship, enthusiasm, diligence, and a multitude of other superpowers. Thank you, Julie.

A lot of wonderful people worked very hard to help bring this tale to life. I would like to express my deep appreciation to the following people for all of their efforts and contributions: Jie Yang, Dale Rohrbaugh, Paula Szafranski, Rich Aquan, Pam Spengler-Jaffee, Shawn Nicholls, Jessie Edwards, and Will Hinton.